D1037497

DESTINY'S DANCE

Rosemary Gard

Copyright © 2014 Rosemary Gard

ISBN 978-1-63263-325-5

All rights reserved. No part of this publication may be reproduced, stored in a retrieval system, or transmitted in any form or by any means, electronic, mechanical, recording or otherwise, without the prior written permission of the author.

Published by BookLocker.com, Inc., Bradenton, Florida.

The characters and events in this book are fictitious. Any similarity to real persons, living or dead is coincidental and not intended by the author.

Printed in the United States of America on acid-free paper.

Booklocker.com, Inc.
2014

First Edition

Dedicated to the memory of Jack Mortimer,
beloved friend and avid reader

and

to all the immigrants who bravely
left their homes to find a new life in America.

Destiny does not lead us in a straight line. As if to some silent music, people and events come into our lives. We are led this way or that and sometimes in a circle. Unknowingly, we all move to life's silent tune. This is Destiny's Dance.

Rosemary Gard

PROLOGUE

Destiny is unpredictable. For some, Destiny lays out a smooth life journey while for others, the path is one of hardship and confusion. Such a rocky path was laid out for Katya Balich. At birth she was taken from a convent and delivered to a Croatian village far from where she belonged. She believed, as did everyone in the village, that she had been born there.

When the beautiful red-haired Katya was 15, she was sold to a Turk. Her adventurous escape brought her to a Gypsy camp, where she was given an ancient bracelet which had the power to protect her and twice saved her life.

Katya was the happiest she had ever been when she was 17 years old. She discovered who her birth mother was. Also she found she had a respected grandmother in Trieste who owned an import company. On a visit to her family in Vladezemla, she realized she was in love with the Gypsy Zolton.

The bracelet saved Katya when Zolton's fiancé, Roha, tried to stab Katya. The knife grazed the protective bracelet instead of fatally finding its mark. It was Ivan Balaban, a man in love with Katya, who pushed aside the jealous Gypsy girl, giving Roha a killing blow to her head when she fell on a rock.

Cruel Destiny! The Gypsies wanted revenge. Ivan and Katya escaped to Trieste, but an attempt on Ivan's life meant they needed to go somewhere…somewhere far where the Gypsies could not find them.

CHAPTER 1

Fall of 1909 – German Ship S.S. Prinzess Irene

Katya, alone and feeling terrible, lay on a not so comfortable bed in the stuffy steerage section of a German ship steaming for America. Tears silently slipped from her green eyes rolling down her pale cheeks. She and Ivan were sharing a cabin with four other people.

Being on this ship was not the plan. The plan, after the attack on Ivan by the Gypsies, was to go to America on the sailing ship *Vincenti*, the cargo ship belonging to the import company her family owned.

Katya loved Zolton. Because of her, Ivan's life was in danger. She married Ivan so they could travel as husband and wife to America.

It all happened so quickly. She was responsible for the attempt on Ivan's life. Katya had once loved the handsome Ivan. That was back when she first arrived at Vladezemla with her Godfather, Milan, after her escape from the Turk. Milan had brought her to his cousin, Ivan's father, for safety. It was an instant attraction for young Ivan. He couldn't take his eyes off the beautiful red-haired Katya, and she admired Ivan's warm smile, his gold-flecked eyes and curly, light brown hair.

In time, the couple fell in love and hoped for a future together. However, Ivan's jealous mother, Vera, overheard the young couple's talk of leaving. The scheming mother convinced Katya that Ivan believed the girl had used witchcraft to make him fall in love with her. Believing Ivan's mother, the broken-hearted Katya left for Trieste.

Now, on this German ship, her family in Italy and Croatia, she lay on the bunk feeling so very ill. Sea sick, Mal de Mer, she heard someone say.

The S.S.Prinzess Irene had first and second class accommodations, but Ivan and Katya were in the steerage section. More than 1500 people were in the lower section and many of them as ill as Katya. This section was crowded, smelled of vomit, perspiration, and damp clothes.

Ivan appeared in the state room using his cane to steady his step over the raised partition in the doorway. He was never without his cane. His leg never properly healed from his attack years ago by the Turk searching for Katya.

Concerned he asked, "How are you feeling?"

She couldn't hide her annoyance at being on this ship and in steerage. "Why are we down here? Couldn't you get us above this level? Couldn't you find a better ship?"

Ivan was taken aback by Katya's mood. His handsome face showed the hurt he felt from her tone. He said, "You know the captain of the *Vincenti* docked at Naples when he decided she could not make the trip over the Atlantic. He said we had to take the first ship sailing for America." Ivan's tone was apologetic, "The captain made the arrangements. I wasn't sure what to do."

Katya felt a wave of nausea, but didn't throw up. "Couldn't you find us a cabin to ourselves? I don't enjoy being stared at by strangers."

"There are no private cabins in this section." explained Ivan, sitting down on an empty bunk. He added, "I don't think we should spend the extra money for second class. We don't know how much we will need in America."

Ivan looked quite handsome in the brown tweed suit, part of a wardrobe put together for him by Katya's mother and grandmother. He was not aware of what other clothes were in the wooden, leather-strapped trunk provided by the family. A small wicker suitcase holding necessities and towels was on the floor under Katya's bunk.

Katya stared at Ivan saying nothing.

Ivan saw her stare and felt her disappointment. He said, "I am your husband now. I must think about our future and how I will take care of you."

Katya kept her eyes fixed on him. *Had it been necessary to marry him? Couldn't he have gone to America alone?* Everything had happened so quickly that afternoon on her grandmother's terrace in

Trieste. The priest had been summoned, a ring was slipped on her finger and wine was poured with everyone toasting, "Amerika."

Katya and Ivan sat silent for a long while. A women with space assigned in the cabin entered. She smiled nervously at Katya and Ivan, and then went to her own bunk, sitting down.

Katya turned her face to the wall. She didn't want the stranger to see her crying.

"I am going out on deck." said, Ivan. When Katya did not reply, he rose, steadying himself with his cane, and then left the cramped cabin.

The S.S. Prinzess Irene had two funnels, two masts, two propellers, and eight quadruple engines, giving it a speed of 15 knots. At that speed the crossing would take 15 days. This was their third day out with only 12 more to go. The cost of travel from Naples to New York was ten U.S. dollars.

Out on the deck, Ivan deeply inhaled the evening sea air, enjoying the feel of the misty wind against his face. He enjoyed walking the deck or leaning on the rail while looking at the sea. He had never been on the water before and found it exciting. He was sorry Katya was so seasick. He was especially disappointed she could not see the leaping dolphins, the white curling waves, and especially the moonlight glistening off the water at night. He wanted to share with her the view of the stars at night; so many, so bright and clear, while overhead the half moon glowed as if it were lit from within with a lantern.

Ivan had made some friends out on the deck. There were some Croatians on board who advised him what to expect in America. He and Katya had no relatives to stay with, so that meant they had to find lodgings and food. All this would take money. He felt for the leather money belt under his clothes. The soft leather hugged his waist snugly. He was warned to watch for thieves and to be careful that no one saw him remove his hidden money. His excitement of going to America was tinged with worry. Where would they live? Could he find work, and most of all, would he be able to make Katya happy?

He had to make her happy. Ivan knew that Katya married him out of sense of duty or guilt, perhaps both. Somehow he would make it up to her. He loved her so very much. He had never stopped loving her. He would have followed her to Trieste back when his mother lied to Katya, but his damaged leg did not heal and prevented him from walking for extended periods of time.

Two weeks before leaving for America, his heart nearly broke when he saw Katya and Zolton making love in the grass. Roha also saw Katya and Zolton together, so the young Gypsy set out to kill Katya. Instead, Roha was accidentally killed.

Destiny once again brought Ivan and Katya together. He was determined to make their marriage work. In time, he was sure Katya would love him again. Of that he was certain.

"Dobar Vecer, Ivan." Hearing the greeting, Ivan recognized Slavko Mravich, another passenger traveling to New York. Slavko was a big man, broad-shouldered, with a barrel chest. He came from Karlovac, in the Lika region of Croatia. The shave marks over his ears and to the back of his head indicated a recent haircut. His warm smile was nearly hidden by his black mustache and beard. Under his dark bushy eyebrows were twinkling dark brown eyes. His size and appearance were in great contrast to his gentle personality.

"Dobar Vecer," replied Ivan, pleased to have Slavko's company. Slavko knew so much about America from his brother, Nikola, who had already been in the U.S. for two years. Nikola had sent the money for his passage to America. In time, Slavko would earn money so that their younger brother, Joso, could join them.

"How is the Gospa today?" asked Slavko, using the polite form when referring to Ivan's wife. He hadn't seen Katya, but knew that Ivan had married.

"Not so well." explained Ivan. "She hates it in the cabin."

Slavko pointed to the various clusters of people huddled on deck, preparing to spend the night sleeping out in the night air. "Would she be more comfortable out here?" he asked.

Ivan looked around, seeing some already wrapped in their coats, in anticipation of the night's cool air. "It certainly smells better out here." he said, giving the suggestion some thought. "I don't think she could make it up the stairway and I can't help her very much." He touched his leg with his cane, indicating the problem.

"I will go with you." said, Slavko. I can carry Gospa for you. If she doesn't like it out here, I can take her back."

Ivan hesitated before replying. Katya had been annoyed when he left her. Perhaps she wouldn't like a stranger seeing her so ill.

"She was in a bad mood when I left her." said Ivan, looking into Slavko's eyes for some reaction.

"Of course she is in a bad mood. It is not so nice down there." Slavko waved his hand at the deck, slowly filling with more people. "See all the people coming to escape? I have a mother and two sisters." He explained, "You think I don't know about women's moods?"

Ivan had to laugh. "All right," he said, "who knows, she may like the idea."

Below in the cabin, two more occupants arrived while Ivan was on deck. They stared at Katya speaking a language she could not understand.

Much to Ivan's surprise, Katya quickly agreed to being carried out to the boat's deck.

As she was carried up the stairs, Katya held her arm around the big man's neck. He had not seen her before tonight and her beauty took his breath away. He could not understand why Ivan, dressed as a man of means, in a continental suit and his beautiful wife in a green silk blouse and skirt, were traveling steerage. He thought they surely belonged in the upper class accommodations.

Once on deck, Ivan placed the wicker suitcase, taken from under Katya's bunk, on the deck. Out of the suitcase he took some towels and spread them for Katya to sit on. Gently, Slavko placed Katya on the towels. He watched as she took deep breaths of the fresh, clean air. From the few lanterns giving light on the deck, Slavko saw the pale color of Katya's face.

Slavko had this overpowering desire to take care of her; to be her protector. This was an insane thought and he knew it. She was married and belonged to Ivan.

Katya smiled. "This is lovely. The night is so beautiful." She looked at Ivan, "I am glad you thought to bring me out here."

"I didn't," said Ivan, "It was Slavko's idea."

Katya offered her hand to Slavko. "Thank you for carrying me. I wasn't sure I wanted to come."

Embarrassed, Slavko took her hand and marveled at how small and soft it was. All the girls he knew worked in the fields or the barns and had strong, rough hands. He didn't know what to say to her, so all he could think to say was, "I will be near. Let me know when you want to go back to your cabin." He started to walk away.

"Don't leave, Slavko," said Ivan, "stay and keep us company."

"Yes," said Katya, "stay."

Katya looked at the assortment of people around her. There were languages spoken she didn't understand. Some words sounded musical while others sounded rough or guttural. She was fascinated watching all these people, different in their dress, but yet alike in their desire to go to America. Almost all the women had their heads covered with a scarf. All wore long skirts. The different woven aprons and designs on their blouses and vests denoted what village or country they were from. Katya couldn't identify most of their nationalities.

Slavko and Ivan, seated on wooden boxes alongside Katya, smoked Turkish cigarettes. The smoke didn't bother her now, but in the cabin the smell made her sick. She was aware that most of the passengers suffering seasickness appeared to throw up almost continuously. Katya only threw up in the mornings.

"Those are Greeks." said Slavko. "I can tell by the hats they wear. There on the left are some Serbian women. Notice the heavy wool aprons and the curled toes on their shoes."

"How can you tell?" asked Katya.

"Because of the designs and colors in the weave of the apron. Our people have designs of flowers on their clothes." Slavko looked at Katya's green skirt and blouse. "You and Ivan dress more continental."

Neither Ivan nor Katya wanted it known that their family owned large parcels of land and an import company. To change the subject, Katya said, "I hear music."

Slavko said, "That is the Bosnian shepherd. He plays his flute so softly it is like a lullaby." He paused, "Listen. There is someone with a tambura joining him."

The soft and gentle music cradled the listeners. The cool evening breeze along with the movement of the ship relaxed Katya.

Before Katya slipped off to sleep, she heard Slavko say, "During the day, several musicians play together and we have lively dancing on deck. There is some polka stomping and kolo dancing.

Somewhere in the distance, a baby cried.

CHAPTER 2

Spring, 1910 - Lakawanna, New York, U.S.A.

The Buffalo Creek Reservation, once inhabited by the Seneca Indians, was now the center of the Lakawanna Steel Company. Strong and eager to work, newly arrived immigrants easily found employment in the steel mill.

Slavko Mravich's married brother, Nikola, had a room with one bed prepared for his brother which Slavko shared with another steel worker. Nikola and his wife, Ivanka, were hard workers offering room and board to those willing to pay for it.

At Slavko's urging, Katya and Ivan were living in Nikola's house. He worried about this couple who were so different from most of the people coming from the Old Country. To Slavko, both Ivan and Katya seemed more educated. They could read and write while most of the immigrants could not. Also Katya could speak Italian. There were many Italian immigrants settling in Lakawanna.

Because of Ivan's bad leg and his use of a cane, he was not able to find work in the mill. It was fortunate that Anton Vladislav, Ivan's birth father, taught Ivan to read English as a young boy. This, along with his ability to do accounting, got Ivan a position as a teller in a small, privately-owned bank. Ivan could help the Serbians, Croatians, Macedonians, and even the Poles and Russians fill out the necessary paperwork to send money to their families back home. If he could get the mill workers to come to the bank to cash their checks, instead of cashing them at the local taverns, there was a chance they would deposit some money in a savings account. Once the checks were cashed in a saloon, the money was soon gone, spent on liquor or women.

Nikola's wife, Ivanka, was not fond of Katya, who was still ill.

Nearly twenty years of age, Katya, was pregnant and wished with every fiber of her being that she could be back in Trieste with her mother, Sofie, and grandmother, Lucia.

"She doesn't do anything to help." complained Ivanka, adding some water to the pot of sarma, the stuffed cabbage leaves cooking on the stove. "She stays in her room writing letters, always writing letters."

Ivanka was a plain woman. Her face colorless, long, and thin with matching thin lips. Just as in Europe, her hair was always covered with a scarf tied in back at the nape of her neck. Her arms were boney, but strong. She got paid for doing the wash for the mill men and she cooked for everyone who rented rooms in the house. For this evening's meal she planned cabbage rolls, boiled potatoes, and the bread she had baked early that morning. Besides herself and Nikola, six others lived in the house.

Nikola was seated at the kitchen table. He was built like his brother, Slavko. With a beard, he could be Slavko's twin.

"They pay their money." said Nikola, tired of his wife's constant complaints about Katya. "She doesn't have to work." Like his brother, Nikola was an admirer of Katya. "Besides," he said, "I think you are jealous because she can read and write." He didn't add, 'and because she is so beautiful'. Like most men, he was fascinated by those emerald green eyes and the flaming red hair, often worn loose around her shoulders. The hair did not go unnoticed by other women. After all, she was married...her hair should be discreetly tucked under and covered with a scarf.

"There is something wrong with them." said Ivanka, lowering her voice, so that they would not be overheard, should someone be near. "Their clothes are too fine. And... they never talk about their families or where they came from. And...I don't think she lets him do anything in bed."

Disgusted, Nikola growled at her, "For God's sake! She is ready to have a baby." He went to the sink and used a hand pump to draw water into a glass. "You have been obsessed with her ever since they arrived."

Ivanka removed her head scarf and scratched her warm scalp. She said, "Haven't you noticed how your brother worries about her? How he takes care of her?" After a pause she added, "Don't you find that odd?"

9

"For God's sake," he exclaimed again, "Ivanka, stop with this nonsense!"

"Don't yell at me," said Ivanka, hotly. "We can't have a crying baby in this house. The men need their sleep. I have always kept this house quiet and orderly."

Ivanka and Nikola did not see Katya standing in the doorway, her face pale, dark circles under her eyes.

Having heard what Ivanka said, Katya stared through the woman who appeared uncomfortable, but not embarrassed. To Nikola, Katya said, "Could you find someone to help me? I think it is time." She turned back towards the room she and Ivan shared, then her knees buckled and she slowly sank to the floor.

Nikola ran to her side, lifting her up in his arms and carrying her to her bed.

"She is going to ruin the mattress and the sheets." Ivanka called after them.

When Nikola came back to the kitchen, Ivanka saw the look in his eyes and for a moment, thought he was going to hit her.

"Go get the midwife." he demanded. "And hurry!"

Wrapping the scarf once again around her hair, Ivanka ran past Nikola to the old woman two houses down who was an experienced midwife. She ran quickly, seeing the look on Nikola's face. It was a look she had seen before, the look just before he struck her.

Slavko was coming up the walk as Ivanka ran past him, saying nothing. He had finished his 6 to 5 shift. Nikola worked the midnight shift from 10 to 9, which gave him time to do repairs around the house during the day. These were pre-union days and the men worked long, hard hours, grateful for the pay.

Slavko saw Nikola at the sink, wetting a towel for Katya. "She is ready to have the baby." His brother said.

"Is Ivan home yet?" asked Slavko.

"Not yet." said Nikola. "I sent Ivanka for Baba Mara."

Setting his metal lunch bucket on the table, Slavko said, "We have to find somewhere else for Ivan, Katya, and the baby to live. I know Ivanka doesn't like Katya, and it will be worse when the baby comes."

The door burst open and the short, thin midwife, Baba Mara, along with a plump younger woman scurried past the two men towards the direction Nikola indicated. Ivanka stood near the doorway, assessing Nikola's mood. He no longer had the angry look that had frightened her. She took a glass and poured some warm coffee into it. Sitting at the wooden kitchen table, she sipped the coffee plain, not bothering with the sugar cube she usually had in her mouth when she drank coffee. Ivanka was not looking forward to washing the birthing sheets and possibly replacing the mattress.

Coming home from his day at the bank, Ivan pulled open the screen door and entered. He saw the concerned looks on their faces and asked, "What is wrong? What has happened?"

Slavko offered Ivan a chair. "Sit down. The women are with Katya. She is having the baby."

Nikola placed three small glasses on the table, he said, "Let's have some wine." He poured the small, juice-type glasses only half full. The men raised their glasses in a toast saying, "Na Zdravlje…to health."

Ivan took a sip of the wine. He looked past his friends to the hall leading to the room where Katya and the women were.

Ivan thought, so *the baby is coming…Zolton's baby*. When Ivan discovered Katya was pregnant, he thought his heart would break. Katya's seasickness was in fact, morning sickness. Just like her mother, Sofie, Katya was ill throughout the pregnancy. *How was he going to help raise this child, this Gypsy baby? Zolton's baby!* He would love it, he told himself, sipping more wine, not hearing the conversation between Slavko and Nikola. He was sure he could love this baby because it was a part of Katya.

The slender young woman who came to assist Baba Mara, quietly slipped into the kitchen, not looking at the men. She went directly to the seated Ivanka and whispered into her ear. Without a word, Ivanka quickly rose and followed the woman to Katya's bedside.

The three men looked at one another in bewilderment. Ivan started to rise, but Slavko put a hand on Ivan's shoulder, to keep him there.

He knew the women would let Ivan know when he could come see the baby.

It was quiet...too quiet. There was no running back and forth for towels and water, no one shouting out orders, and no sound of a baby crying. Why wasn't there the sound of a baby crying? Why was it so quiet? The three men sensed something was wrong. Was Katya alright? An uncomfortable feeling surrounded the three men.

Ivanka entered the kitchen trying very hard to hide the smug look playing on her face.

Her husband was the first to speak. "What happened? Is anything wrong?"

Ivan did not wait for an answer. He leapt from the chair and ran to Katya's side.

In Ivan and Katya's room, standing at the foot of the bed, Baba Mara looked at Ivan and said, "Mertvo." Dead.

The dead baby was wrapped in a small blanket and placed next to Katya, who was exhausted, her face damp with perspiration. The two attending women did not bother to wipe her face or clean her body, which they normally did after a birth.

Ivan went to Katya's side. "Katya, Katya," he repeated, "are you alright?" As he said this, he looked at the tiny dead body in the blanket. It had shiny black hair and dark, wrinkled skin. There was no mistaking it as a Gypsy baby. It had none of Katya's features. It looked like Zolton.

At first Ivan was shocked to see the dark baby. Realizing it was dead, he let a momentary look of relief show on his face. Katya saw that look and it pained her greatly.

Baba Mara and her assistant walked through the kitchen, not stopping for the usual after birth visit. As a rule, there would be some coffee, a bite of strudel, perhaps a little wine, or chatter about the delivery and what a cute baby they had just delivered.

This time the two women went straight for the door, past the smug Ivanka and the bewildered Slavko and Nikola.

As Baba Mara passed through the door, she was heard to say, "Kurva." Whore.

Two weeks later, Slavko and Ivan were sitting in the back yard of the house. Slavko was using a wooden crate for a seat, while Ivan sat on a crudely made bench, painted brown. All around them were vegetables not yet ready to be picked. A newly planted apple tree and a pear tree, in need of watering, stood behind the seated men.

The men were smoking cigarettes that Slavko had hand-rolled. Slavko could roll a nice cigarette, while Ivan's attempts were always failures, with the tobacco spilling out of the poorly-shaped cylinder. In frustration, there were times Ivan would twist the end paper of the cigarette to keep the tobacco in place.

Ivan looked at his friend, his only friend in America. Ivan inhaled the loosely packed cigarette, then, while exhaling said, "Katya and I owe you much. You have been a good friend." He paused, seeing the puzzled look on Slavko's face. "I want to tell you about myself and Katya, before we leave this place. I want you to know what an unusual life she has had."

And so Ivan spoke and Slavko listened, enraptured by the tale Ivan told him. Slavko said nothing as Ivan revealed what he knew of Katya before she came to Vladezemla, or of the diary left by the local priest Father Lahdra naming Sofie as Katya's birth mother.

Slavko's eyes grew large when he heard of the Turk buying Katya, of her escape, and how the cruel villagers branded her as a witch. The burly man sat in stunned silence as Ivan told of the Turk finding Katya, of the Turk's death, and how Katya healed Ivan's wounds with herbs and potions.

When Ivan finished his narration, he was silent for a while. Slavko said nothing, digesting all he had heard, realizing that Katya was even more special than he had imagined.

"I blame myself for much of Katya's unhappiness." Ivan's voice brought Slavko out of his deep thoughts about Katya. "I was a coward." said Ivan. "She loved me once. I should have let her know how I still felt about her when she returned last summer to Vladezmla with Teta Sofie." Ivan looked up, past the yard to the sound of a barking dog in the distance. "Perhaps if she knew I loved her," he said, "she would not have turned to Zolton and the Gypsy women would not have thrown stones at her."

CHAPTER 3

1911 - The Magic City - Gary, Indiana

The Standard Oil Company built its refinery in 1889 in Whiting, IN. It was 1906 when the United States Steel Corporation chose the land east of Whiting and East Chicago for its plant. The boosters of this new city called it "The Satellite City" because of its nearness to Chicago. Others described the city as "Miracle City," "Magic City," or "City of the Century."

Katya and Ivan rode the NY Central & Hudson River Railroad train from New York to Chicago. With the train traveling at 20 miles per hour, the trip took about 24 hours. Always concerned about money, Ivan chose neither to pay for a compartment, nor for sleeping arrangements.

Whether depressed or still weak from having the baby, Katya was very quiet on the trip. She watched the passing landscape with only a small amount of interest. Her mind and heart were full of sorrow for being away from her family and for the loss of the baby.

Ivan made friends with a fellow train passenger, who was also going to Gary. Mato Gerbich was small and thin. His dark hair was combed straight back and covered with a flat cap. His pants were a faded grey and the suit jacket he wore was of a darker and heavier fabric. His face was thin with dark eyes, which seemed to be watching everyone and everything. He glanced often at Katya, who either gazed out the window or napped. Mato, with an understanding nod, accepted Katya's lack of conversation when Ivan explained about the death of the baby.

With great interest, Ivan listened to Mato Gerbich, who appeared to be very informed about Gary. His brother Milan was the owner of a bar and had sent the money for Mato to come to America. As Ivan listened to his new friend speak of his brother's success and Mato's own dreams of making a lot of money, Ivan was hopeful. Perhaps he could own his own business and have a nice house for Katya. He wanted so badly to make a good life for Katya.

After changing trains in Chicago, they arrived at last in Gary. Mato helped Ivan place the trunk and wicker suitcase, along with some paper bags filled with their possessions, on the streetcar. The starting point of the street car was located at the most northern part of Gary. Behind them were the great steel mills responsible for building this city.

As the streetcar rattled on, Katya looked with wonder at the buildings and storefronts. The Gary Express & Storage Company was in the Phillips Building at 5th & Broadway. The Gary Heat, Light and Water Co, had an office also at 5th & Broadway. The impressive Gary Hotel was on 6th & Broadway. Farther down the block The Elwood Tailoring Co. was at building number 680. The sign in the window offered 'Suits cleaned along with tailoring done for Gents and Ladies'. The First National Bank Building was at 632-4 Broadway.

Established in 1906, the Knotts & McRoberts Insurance Co. was at 7th Ave and Broadway. Their phone number was…1. The Post Office was also at 7th Ave & Broadway. None of these names meant anything to Katya.

With a city growing so rapidly there were many realtors, such as Robert Orosz, Edward Gastin Smith, and Harry King & Co,

On 908-910 Broadway was Stephen J. Kertesz, Steam Ship Agent, who advertised tickets to and from all parts of Europe. It was here that Mato's brother purchased the ticket for him to come to America.

Katya and Ivan looked with wonder at this wonderful city, so shiny, so new, looking so grand.

U. S. Steel didn't know enough about town planning, so Katya and Ivan's first look at Gary was the North side growth, there were beautiful homes for those who could afford to live there. Those homeowners were the corporate people of U.S. Steel.

It was obvious that the mill put all their efforts into producing steel and building stockholder profits, and none in the welfare of the workers.

After many stops, where passengers boarded or exited, the streetcar stopped at 21st and Broadway. Here, along with many mill workers, whose skin was grimy from working their shifts, was where Ivan and Katya disembarked. Mato again helped with the trunk and bags. Katya looked with dismay at the contrast of the north side to this south side.

Ivan was as stunned as Katya. Taking her hand in his, he looked into her eyes. There was no more anger, no hurt, just a silent communication of...*What will we do? Where will we live?*

The voices around them were familiar and comforting. They heard snippets of conversations in Croatian, Serbian, and Macedonian along with languages they did not understand.

Mato approached some of the men who got off of the streetcar and asked for directions to his brother Milan's tavern. His smile was huge as he told Katya and Ivan that his brother's bar was not so far away. With their arms loaded with suitcases, the three walked in the pointed direction.

Most of the houses they passed on their walk were small. Some settlers lived in tents or tar paper shacks. It was not uncommon for landlords to charge inflated rents or to sell property under illegal liens, and then terminate a contract if one payment was missed.

Katya did not like the smell of this place. The land was marshy, there were many unpaved roads and alleyways, and the air was strong with the odor of outhouses.

Katya saw some black children playing in a small yard. A little black girl looked at Katya and said in fluent Croatian, "Dobar dan, Gospa...Good day, madam", much to Katya's surprise. In 1910, the Negro population was approximately 400. Many of them lived in the Patch, which was the name for the south side of Gary. It wasn't unusual for some of the black children to speak Croatian. The black children taught the foreigners English and in turn, learned Croatian or Serbian.

Along their walk to the tavern, Katya and Ivan were stared at by the people of the Patch. Katya, as always, made people look twice, as they wondered who this red-haired beauty, dressed in a blue, long sleeved blouse and full skirt, could be. Her hair flowed loose to her shoulders, which according to the women of the Patch, should have been coiled about her head and covered. Men looked at her with admiration or lust, perhaps a combination of both. Some people nodded a greeting, while others just stared, some open-mouthed.

To the people of the Patch, Ivan, in his European suit and Katya, in her Italian- made outfit, appeared to be people of wealth. They did not look as if they belonged with the immigrants. The stares made Katya uncomfortable.

Ivan took Katya's hand. He nodded and gave smiles to those who openly stared at them. There were a few men who removed their hats as an act of respect, not sure who these newcomers were.

"There it is!" shouted Mato, seeing the sign on a long wood frame building. The blue letters over a white wooden background spelled "Milan's." "It is my brother's place." He ran ahead, leaving Katya and Ivan to quickly follow.

As Mato burst through the door, he shouted, "Milan, Milan…I am here." He looked around for his brother.

From behind the bar came a shout, "Bratso…brother!" Milan was taller and heavier than Mato, a big man having the same dark hair and dark eyes. The brothers ran to hug one another with Milan, planting kisses on each of Mato's cheeks.

The tavern patrons all clapped and shouted, some slapping their hands on the bar in approval. The clapping and shouting lessened and then stopped when the patrons of the tavern noticed the handsome, well-dressed couple behind Mato.

Mato let go of his brother and happily introduced Katya and Ivan, pulling Ivan by the arm. Milan was more than mildly surprised to see that his brother had such an elegant couple as his friends. Milan wiped his palm on the soiled bar apron around his thick middle before shaking hands with Ivan. He took in Katya's beauty as he gave her a low bow.

With a broad smile he said, "Molim…please, come sit at this table." He motioned for the two men already sitting at the table to get up. As soon as the men moved to the bar, Milan wiped the table with the edge of his apron. "What can I get for you, slivovica, vino or maybe some pivo?"

Katya gave Milan a warm smile, "Vino, please." She was starting to feel a bit more comfortable. She noticed some of the men, lifting their glass as a toast to her. In return, she smiled and nodded. When Ivan's beer came he reached for some money, but Milan was offended. "No. I cannot take pay from my brother's good friends. Can I bring you some food?" He asked this looking at Katya.

Before Ivan could reply, Katya said, "Not right now. I am almost too tired to eat." She looked around at all the faces staring at them, making her feel a bit uncomfortable. "I just want some quiet."

Milan understood and took his brother by the arm, away from the table, to the bar. "Let them be alone." he said, "She looks tired." To the men at the bar, their eyes on Ivan and Katya, he hissed in a low voice, "What are you looking at? Stop staring."

The tavern was a long, rectangular room with walls and floor made of wooden planks. There were several odd and mismatched tables and chairs along the wall. A Croatian flag was pinned on the wall above the bar, next to it, a crucifix. The pictures tacked on the walls were from magazines or newspapers, pictures of Europe, and some of pretty women.

At one table, some men were playing cards and in a far corner, at another table, sat two men with tamburas. Seeing Ivan and Katya settled, the men started to play their string instruments and somewhere, a man started to sing. It was a sad melody about their domovina, their home. A couple of men left the bar to join the musicians, singing the words they all seemed to know.

The atmosphere was friendly. Though the men were all strangers to her, the familiar smells of sweat, garlic, and beer were comforting to Katya.

Standing quietly behind the bar was a plump, blond woman wearing the clothes of the old country. Her skirt was white, homespun cloth with only a small amount of embroidery along the hem. Her blouse, covering an ample bosom, had embroidered flowers trailing down her sleeves from her shoulder to her wrists. The apron she wore was large enough to cover almost all her clothing.

She sliced some freshly baked bread while glancing at the lovely red-haired woman. The bread was warm and smelled wonderful. She had heard Katya say she was too tired to eat. Never the less, Roza, Milan's wife, prepared a plate of the bread, along with some cheese and tomato slices.

Going to the table, she smiled at Katya and Ivan. "Zdravo, hello, I have brought a little something for you." Her brown eyes were warm and friendly. "I am called Roza. Milan is my muz, husband."

There was something so comforting in Roza's voice and manner. Most women, upon meeting Katya seemed resentful or jealous, perhaps both. Roza's warm manner made Katya relax.

Before Ivan could say anything, the brothers, Mato and Milan, took him by the arms and led him to the bar, where he was greeted with laughter and raised glasses as if he were an old friend.

Roza put the plate on the table and without asking sat down across from Katya, pushing the plate towards her saying "Eat a little something. It will make you feel better."

Katya smiled at the friendly woman, taking a bit of cheese and a slice of the still warm bread. "I suppose I am hungry." she said, biting into the cheese, while taking in all the activity around her.

Roza watched Katya eat the cheese saying, "I made the bread and the cheese." She went on to explain, "I have two goats out back and use the milk for the cheese. I do it the way we did back home. I wrap the curd in cloth and hang it outdoors to ripen."

Katya liked this woman who had friendly brown eyes. It was as if she were talking to someone from home. Katya never felt this warmth from any of the women she had met in Lakawanna. She felt herself relaxing, absorbing the friendly mood in this room. The sounds of laughter, the tamburitza music, the singing, the smell of the bread, all surrounded her with the nostalgia she had not felt since arriving in America. She just might like it here in Gary, Indiana, she thought.

"Have you been married long?" asked Roza, wiping a wet ring from the table with her apron.

"Almost a year." said Katya, taking a bite of the delicious bread, "And you? How long have you and Milan been married?"

"Two years. My fiancé sent me the money to come and join him."

Katya looked a little puzzled when she heard fiancé. Roza continued, "My fiancé was from my village. We liked each other ever since we were children. He was here for a year and sent a paid ticket for me to join him." For a moment she stopped talking, as if composing herself, she said, "When I got here, Mishka wasn't here."

Before Katya could ask where he had gone, Roza said, "Mishka was killed in an accident in the mill. All I know is that he fell in a pit." She wiped a stray tear from the corner of her eye with her apron.

Katya reached a hand across the table and laid it over Roza's rough hand. Roza gave Katya a grateful smile. She said, "Milan was holding Mishka's money and gave it to me when he knew who I was. Milan gave me a place to sleep and was good to me." Her gaze went to Milan at the bar. "He kept the men away from me. It is hard for an unmarried woman here, too many men," she explained, "and not enough women."

Roza straightened herself in the chair, as if to work out a kink in her back. She went on, "Some of the men knew I had a little money and that made me a good catch." She let out a long sigh, "Others just…just…wanted me. Not to marry, but to be with."

Katya said nothing, but the look of understanding in her eyes encouraged Roza to go on. "Milan never asked anything of me. He treated me with respect and even hit a man who said something crude to me." She smiled at this memory. "That was when I asked him if he wanted to marry me."

She laughed remembering this. "He said yes, and admitted he had been afraid to ask me for fear I would say no and leave."

Katya saw Ivan at the bar laughing at something someone said. He seemed so at home here. She asked Roza, "Is Milan a good husband?"

"Oh, yes!" she said emphatically. "And I know how lucky I am. I see the bruises some of the women have from the beatings they get from their husbands." She went on to explain, "Not all of them are mean, but they come home tired, working 12 hours every day, and they worry about enough money for the rent and food. Sometimes, they don't want to talk, they just want to have some quiet." She said nothing for a few moments, looking out into the room. "It isn't as wonderful as we all had expected. There is no money to pick up off the streets. The men are paid 13 cents an hour." Her voice was low, "Often sick men go to work though they should stay home…they need the money."

Two men nearly stumbled into the tavern. One leaned across the bar sobbing, "Sveti Issus...diy me rakia. Holy Jesus...give me whiskey."

CHAPTER 4

Roza jumped to her feet, knocking over her chair, her face contorted as if she were ready to cry.

"Sveta Mayka…Holy Mother," she kept repeating.

There was silence. The music and singing stopped; no laughter and no talking. Everyone waited for the news, the terrible news. All eyes were on the two men, who held their whiskeys with shaking hands. Their clothes were soiled from working in the mill, their faces blackened and streaked with sweat and tears.

Katya rose and stood mesmerized by the sight of the two, as curious as all the others in the bar. Neither Ivan, standing at the bar, nor Katya, her hands flat on the table in front of her, had any idea what was happening or what was about to happen. But, it was obvious the patrons of this bar had an idea and were waiting to hear.

Ivan could feel the tension in the room and in the men around him. He felt he didn't belong among them. Ivan turned away from the bar, his cane clicking as he walked to where Katya stood at the table. Taking her hand he said, "Let's sit." He pulled his chair nearer to hers and did not let go of her hand when he sat down.

To the larger of the two men, Milan said in a soft voice, "Govori…talk." He poured two more whiskeys for the men. The taller man, Faba, tossed his drink down. His voice cracked as he said, "Klarich is dead."

Roza clutched her hand to her breast, thinking of Klarich's wife and newborn baby.

Most of the men made the sign of the cross. The words, "Sveti Bog…Holy God, or Mayka Boza…Mother of God," were murmured. Someone slapped his fist on the bar in anger or frustration. They all knew it could have been any one of them or that, God forbid, next time it might be.

"How did it happen?" someone asked.

Faba tapped his whiskey glass on the bar for another one. He needed it to tell them how Klarich died. He wanted to tell them without crying.

He began, "The pot of molten steel tipped and spilled on the wet sand." He swallowed hard and continued, "The damn sand exploded! It threw the melted steel out and...and ...it hit Klarich." Now his hands were shaking and so was his entire body. "We saw him cooked to death!" Faba covered his face with his hands and sobbed, as did some of the men in the bar.

"Anyone else?" asked Milan in a low voice, his hand on Faba's shoulder.

"They took Crnkovich to the mill hospital" said the short, thin man who had came in with Faba, His pants were too large, tied with rope and he wore a kerchief around his neck, as did several of the other men.

"He was burned. I don't know how badly."

Ivan, still holding Katya's hand, could feel her trembling. All the color was gone from her face. She looked as if she would faint. Ivan shouted, "Milan!"

Seeing Katya, Milan, in an instant, was at her side with a small glass of slivovica, the plum brandy. Ivan took the glass and lifting it to Katya's lips. "Take a sip," he said softly. "Here, take another sip."

Katya looked at her trembling hands and thought, *Why am I shaking this way?*

She didn't remember shaking like this when she escaped from the Turk and she certainly didn't tremble when the Gypsy women threw stones at her.

Seeing Katya so pale, Roza ran to the table, she held Katya by the arm and lifted her from the chair with Ivan's help. Milan stepped in, seeing Ivan had trouble trying to hold onto Katya with one hand and his cane with the other.

Roza said, "Come with me. You need to lie down. We live in back. There is a bed there."

In the morning when the sun shone through the window Katya heard, "Wake up, Katya." Ivan gently nudged her shoulder. "Roza and Milan have breakfast for us."

Katya looked about in confusion. It took her a moment to remember where she was. "Is it morning? Did I sleep all night?"

"Yes, you did." He smiled at her. "You were more tired than you realized."

She nodded towards the door leading to the bar. She asked, "Who is out there?"

"Just Mato, Milan and Roza, the bar is closed until later." He pointed to a wash bowl filled with water and threw a towel to her, "Hurry, breakfast is ready."

Katya wore the same blue dress as yesterday because she had slept in her clothes. Before going out to the bar, she did coil her hair back into a bun, which showed off the lines of her lovely face even more than when her hair was loose and wild.

Two square wooden tables had been pushed together to accommodate everyone. There was a white table cloth embroidered with colorful flowers and on it was a glass bottle filled with white Queen Ann's Lace, a flower Katya did not recognize.

Mato and Milan rose from their chairs as Katya entered. She smiled at everyone. A couple of windows were opened in the hopes of catching some cool morning breezes, but along with the breeze came the smell of the Patch.

Milan asked, "Did you sleep well?" To him, she looked even lovelier now that she was rested.

"Yes, very well." Katya, noticing some blankets and pillows folded on a nearby table, said, "I took your bed. I am so sorry. We could have gone to a hotel or somewhere." She nodded towards the blankets, "You are too kind to us." She looked at Ivan, "We must pay for all they have done for us."

Roza, carrying one plate of cheese filled palachinke and another plate filled with homemade cherry jam palachinke, set the crepes on the table and in a voice filled with authority said, "You will not pay us. Milan and I did not have a family before Mato arrived." She put her hand affectionately on her brother-in-law's shoulder, "And, we have you." With hands on her hips, she said to Katya, "In the short while we spoke, I knew you were to be my friend...my good friend." She looked at Milan with a big smile, "Just as I knew he was going to be a good husband, I know you will be like a sister to me."

Mato clapping his hands said to Milan, "You have to find me a woman like Roza. She is wonderful."

Not wanting to ruin the mood of the cheerful breakfast, no one mentioned the sad events of the previous evening, but it was in all their minds.

Coffee was served just as it was back in the old country, equal portions of hot milk and coffee, poured simultaneously.

Roza made the meal as perfect as she could, with flowers on the table and cloth napkins. She was sorry that the napkins were only plain cloth, but she had not found the time to embroider any designs on them.

His meal finished, Mato pushed his plate away with a satisfied smile. "That was so good, Roza." Turning to his brother he said, "How do I get work in the mills? Should I go with someone?"

While the men talked about finding work, Katya helped Roza clear the table. They carried the dishes into rooms behind the bar, where Milan and Roza lived.

"Leave them." said Roza, meaning the rest of the dishes. "Sit down. I want to tell you how it is here."

Katya was puzzled by the serious tone of Roza's voice.

"Sit, sit." said Roza again. "You will have to be careful here. You are too pretty. Men will go after you."

Sitting across from Roza on a wooden stool, Katya didn't know what to say. She didn't know what had brought on this conversation. She opened her mouth to speak, but Roza interrupted. "I told you last night that there are many more men than women. When they are drunk, they may go after you."

Katya's eyes widened as Roza said, "The men here don't know what kind of woman you are. Here some of the women take in boarders. They are paid for providing a place to sleep, meals, getting their clothes washed...and some offer companionship for a little extra money."

"Oh, my, will I have to be such a woman?" Katya's voice sounded thoughtful. "Will I have to take in boarders and do their wash?"

Roza burst into laughter. "No! Of course not! I was just telling you how things are here. You see," she poured the last of the coffee equally in both their cups, "a woman alone here has it hard. They marry as soon as they can. When they lose a husband, sometimes they are married within a month." She didn't mention Klarich's widow by name, but that was who she meant. "A widow cannot make it alone."

"You must stay away from the wire fence." Roza warned. "You haven't seen all the bars or the fights, here in the Patch. We are not in the middle of the fence area. The fence is three more streets away. Here, Milan is able to keep the men from getting crazy, but in the other bars, it isn't nice."

"What do you mean by the wire fence?" asked Katya.

"Don't go near there…" warned Roza. "That area is all fenced off. It is where the men get crazy drunk and often get into bloody fights. They spend the money they should send home on gambling and the women who walk the street.

The kurvas…whores, manage to take or steal the money meant to bring the wives left behind in the Old Country."

Katya put her hands together as in prayer, touching her lips with her finger tips. Through her fingers she said, "Why are we here?" meaning herself and Ivan. "Oh, Roza how can we live is such a place."

"Listen to me, Katya. There are good people here. With you and Ivan as our friends, we can all try and make a better place for ourselves." Roza reached out and touched Katya's arm. "We have no choice. Don't you see? We have to make it better." She said again, "There are good people here. It is just so hard on the men. They were used to working the fields, tending sheep and herding cows. Now they have to work in a mill where they don't understand the language. Here are all these men from different countries working together and not understanding one another. So much anger and fighting. It is no wonder they come home and hit their wives."

Ever since Katya had left Trieste, she wore long sleeves with a button at the wrist. This way, the bracelet Queen Valina had given her was not seen. She made a point of hiding it when she went into labor, so that no one would know about it.

Now…and she didn't know why, she unbuttoned her sleeve and pulled it up, revealing her bracelet.

"What is that?" Roza said, her eyes growing wide. The sparkling jewels, the ankh, the odd swirls and circles were something she had never seen and did not understand.

Katya stretched out her arm so Roza could get a better look. "It was given to me by a Gypsy Queen as protection." she said. "It saved my life twice, once when the Turk came to kidnap me and another time when a jealous woman tried to stab me."

Roza's mouth was open in wonder. Her voice was a whisper when she said, "Katya, who are you? How is it you know Turks and Tzigany…Gypsies?"

"It is a long and not so happy story." said Katya, dropping her sleeve to once again cover the bracelet. "If we are to be such good friends, I wanted to show it to you. Some other time, I can tell you more about Ivan and myself and the Gypsies."

Before Katya could say more, Mato was at the door, "Come," he said, "Milan has something he wants to tell you."

CHAPTER 5

As early as the 1820s, Dalmatian seamen began arriving in New Orleans. It wasn't until 1891 that the handsome widower Stevo Markovich arrived in New Orleans on the Falkenhayn, an Austro-Hungarian merchant ship. With him was his ten-year-old son, also named Stevo. No one knows how the senior Stevo was able to bring his son on board the ship. Perhaps he bribed someone, or hid the boy as a stowaway.

Stevo stayed on in New Orleans when the Falkenhayn sailed for South America, working as a longshoreman and later, as an oysterman. He was a blue-eyed man with sandy-colored hair and strong, muscular arms from laboring as a seaman.

Father and son lived in one of the boarding houses in New Orleans. The owner of the house was a woman, born in America of an Italian mother and a French father. She was petite, very pretty with dark eyes. She wore her hair in two braids, pinned so that the braids wound around her head.

Theresa inherited the boarding house from her father, who was found dead in the street of a knife wound. No one was ever arrested for the crime. Her mother had died many years earlier in childbirth. Theresa was not only a hard worker, but clever.

It wasn't long before Theresa and Stevo were attracted to one another. Stevo needed a mother for his son and Theresa was pleased to have a responsible man in the house. A pretty and young woman didn't have much protection without a husband or brothers.

Stevo was 24 years old when his father was buried in an above-ground vault, so common in New Orleans because of the high water level under the city.

There was an impressive attendance at Stevo Markovich's funeral Mass held in St. Ann's, a Catholic church built in 1852. Croatians from other Louisiana parishes, some wearing the colorful clothes from their villages back home, came to honor one of their own. The procession from the church was accompanied with the beloved tamburitza music.

As was the custom among immigrants, an envelope with money was given to the widow by friends and mourners.

With his father gone, young Stevo was heartsick. Theresa, his stepmother, appeared to handle the accidental death of her husband without a great show of grief. Stevo, on the other hand, was devastated. His father had been helping repair a friend's roof when he fell to his death.

The guilt Stevo felt nearly crushed him. His father had asked him to come and help, but Stevo claimed he had an important errand that afternoon. Perhaps, had he gone to help nail down some tar paper, it may have saved his father's life.

Dressed in rumpled grey trousers and an equally rumpled green shirt, his heart full of grief, Stevo sat on the tiny wrought iron balcony outside the home he shared with Theresa, and two nine-year-old half brothers.

Stevo was handsome and was aware that women stared at him when he passed them on the street. His hair was light brown, almost blond in the sunlight. Deep blue eyes looked out of a face that made women turn and men envy. His nose was straight and his strong chin had a hint of a cleft, his skin was without blemishes.

On the street below, Stevo could hear women under wide straw hats selling baskets of flowers, fruit, or baked goods, calling "Nice oranges for sale." or "Fresh sweet cakes." The sing-song voices of the women were mingled with the clip clop sounds of horse hooves and the shouts of children chasing one another down the street.

A fresh breeze from the Gulf of Mexico drifted through the city.

Stevo stamped out the cigarette he had been smoking, tossing it to the street below. His father had been buried three days ago and Stevo could not bring himself to leave the house. He was numb. He had loved his father so very much. He remembered how his father would not leave him behind with relatives when young Stevo's mother had died. Somehow he got the young boy on the ship to America. They had worked together as fishermen, as handy men, and even at harvesting oysters. Father and son were as one, almost always together.

As Stevo got older, his father used to ask, "Why you no get married? You are good looking boy. Time you had a home of your own."

Stevo had thought about that often. It wasn't for lack of opportunity or beautiful women. In New Orleans one could choose from many nationalities: German, Croatian, Italian, or Creole. He just wasn't sure what he wanted to do with his life. He was fairly certain that he didn't want to be a fisherman or a longshoreman. He didn't want to smell of fish and sweat for the rest of his life. Often, while walking through the streets, he admired the colorful shops and wondered if he could ever have a business of his own. What kind of a store would he have? He knew nothing about business, but he was good with figures. He spoke English fluently, and could read and write.

From the balcony, Stevo noticed movement in the adjoining room. Through the closed glass door covered with filmy white curtains, he saw his stepmother seated at a small, kidney-shaped French desk. She wore the customary black clothing of someone in mourning. Stacked on the desk were the many envelopes received at the funeral.

Stevo watched as she placed a wooden Old Cheroots cigar box on the desk. With a knife, she sliced open each envelope, and looked at the money inside. She would smile when the money seemed generous, but smirk when she felt it wasn't enough.

When done separating the money from the envelopes, she put the cash in the Cheroots box. Stevo never knew about this box, so he watched with fascination as she went to the wall, moved a large picture slightly, just enough to reveal a hole in the plaster behind the picture. Theresa placed the box in the opening, positioning the picture as it had been, hiding the hole.

She looked around the room gathering up the empty envelopes. Smiling, she left the room.

Stevo stared for a long time at the picture on the wall. Had his father known about this hiding place? His father brought home the money when he was paid and gave it to Theresa, assuming she would pay the bills and put what was left in the New Orleans National Bank.

Stevo never felt any motherly warmth or love from Theresa, but she was never unkind. When the twins, Franko and Petro were born, it was as if Stevo did not exist. He assumed her devotion to the boys was because they were so young and he was then, almost an adult. His mind floated back to his own childhood and he wondered if she had ever loved or cared for his father. Bewilderment gave way to a growing mistrust and then, into anger.

Theresa was in the kitchen sitting at the table. Before her was a pot of water ready for the potatoes she was peeling. She looked up at Stevo and wondered about the look on his face, which she couldn't quite read.

She hesitated a moment and then tried to say casually, "So, now that your father is gone, what are your plans?"

The unexpected question made him pause. He stared at her, "What do you mean my plans?"

She kept her eyes on the potato in her hand. "When are you leaving?" She still did not look up at him.

"Leaving? Why should I leave? This has been my home for fourteen years." His voice betrayed his confusion, his anger building. "My father and I have given you our earnings as long as we have been here. This house is as much mine as yours."

Wiping her hands on her apron, she stood up looking directly at Stevo. "This house was left to me by my father. It is in my name. Nowhere does your father's name appear, or yours."

"What about the bank account? His name is there."

With the smallest of smiles playing on her thin lips, she said, "Your father never had any bank accounts."

Stevo's mind was in a whirl. Had his father been so in love with this woman or just naive? It was becoming obvious to Stevo that Theresa was extremely clever and had taken advantage of his father, and of himself.

He asked, "What did my father leave me?"

Her burst of laughter startled him. She said, "He didn't leave you anything. And, don't ask me for money, I don't have anything to give you."

She turned to the sound of sizzling coffee boiling over on the iron stove. Grabbing a towel she removed the pot from the heat. Turning back she saw the anger in Stevo's eyes. Backing away from him, she stood so that the table was between them. She let out a startled scream when he angrily grabbed the table cloth and pulled it roughly sending the potatoes, pot of water, and cutlery crashing to the floor.

Stevo rested his palms of the empty table top. He leaned forward, glaring at the woman who had been his stepmother for fourteen years...now she was a stranger to him.

"I could kill you." His voice shook with dark anger. "But...I won't because you have my half brothers to care for."

Theresa's eyes were wide with fear. "You can stay!" She nearly shouted the words. She tried to smile, but her fear made the effort a contortion of her lips. Words came pouring out of her. She had always been able to control men, but she was terrified of Stevo.

"You are right." her voice disclosed her fear. "This is your home. Forgive me for asking you to leave." Again she repeated, "This is your home. Forgive me."

Theresa stared at his face seeing the blue eyes dark with disgust. She watched him leave the kitchen walking in the direction of his room. With weak knees, she lowered herself on the wooden kitchen chair. She crossed her arms on the table, dropping her head, sobbing with relief.

In his room, Stevo stood at the open window overlooking a gated courtyard where a tulip poplar tree showed off its blooms and the air was sweet with the scents of magnolia, oleander, and jasmine. He inhaled deeply. He needed to calm down...to make plans. His hands trembled slightly as he lit a cigarette. A bookcase stood next to his bed, where a half full bottle of anise-flavored absinthe rested. Not bothering to look for a glass, he pulled out the stopper and took a swig.

He looked around his room, the room where for fourteen years he had lived. The bed was the same wooden, four-poster from his childhood. Against the wall was a cabinet for his clothes and a plain table he used for writing and reading. No comfortable lounging chair was in the room, just a wooden, straight back chair at the table. A small oval mirror, along with some pictures of far away places decorated the walls.

Looking at these meager surroundings, he wondered why he should stay. Somewhere there had to be something better for him. He pulled up the pillow to cushion his back as he sat on the bed, leaning against the headboard, the absinthe bottle still in his hand. He had to think. The words, *'there is something better'* kept running through his mind.

Sometime later, there was a knock at his door. His young brother Pietro said, "Stevo, Mama has supper on the table. She wants you to come down."

When Stevo didn't answer the boy knocked again. This time Stevo called out, "Tell her I don't want any supper." He added, "Tell her I am not hungry."

So, was stepmama trying to make a truce? He wondered.

Pietro did not reply, but Stevo heard the sound of the boy's footsteps as he walked away.

Later in the night, when the clock chimed eleven times, the house was silent except for the ticking of the clock. Outside a dog barked, a horse whinnied, and the sound of carriage wheels rolling on the pavement could be heard.

Stevo, with the agility of a cat burglar, slipped into the room where earlier, Theresa had counted the funeral money. The floor creaked and Stevo wished he had taken off his shoes. The moonlight through the balcony doors shone brightly enough so that Stevo could see the picture on the wall, the picture covering the hole behind it. Cautiously, he crept to the wall and gently moved the picture, ever so slightly, just enough to find the hole. He reached in and felt the box. Holding his breath he slid it out, careful not to drop it or spill its contents.

Now was not the time to count what was in it…it didn't matter. What mattered was that he had money, money with which to get away…hopefully far away, up the Mississippi River.

The box containing his clothes, tied with rope, sat outside the kitchen door. As he opened it, Stevo noticed freshly-ironed pillowcases stacked on a chair. He grabbed one of the pillowcases and dropped the cigar box in it.

CHAPTER 6

Milan called Katya and Roza to come from the living area to the tavern where he and Ivan sat. Come join us, he said to the women, "We just heard some news that might interest you."

Katya and Roza sat in the straight-backed chairs, while brother Mato stood at the bar. Milan continued, "We just heard that Anka Klarich is moving to Whiting to live with her sister." Anka was the widow of the man who died at the steel mill the day before.

"So soon?" said Roza.

Milan said, "As soon as her sister heard of the accident, she and her husband came with a wagon and they spent the night packing." He let out a deep sigh, "She and the baby are leaving this morning. They are going to bury Klarich in Whiting so Anka can be near his grave. Anka doesn't want to leave him here…alone."

Ivan and Katya looked from Milan to Roza, not understanding what this news had to do with them.

Seeing the confusion on their faces, Milan said, "This means that Anka wants to sell her house." He opened his hands, palms showing, "We thought you might want to see the house and buy it, before someone else does."

Roza knew that Anka Klarich had come to the tavern the night before, but she had no idea of Anka's plan to move to Whiting.

Roza said, "It isn't very big, but for the two of you it could be very nice. It would be better than renting." She went on, "There is a shed in back and the area is fenced in."

Katya and Ivan looked at one another confused, *a house…here in the Patch?*

"We don't have much money. What does a house cost here?" Ivan looked to his new friends for advice. "I have no work." His face showed concern. "How soon does this have to be done?"

"I spoke with Anka," said Milan, "She is leaving sometime this morning with her family and a few belongings. I have the key to the house and have promised to sell it for her and send her the money."

It wasn't unusual to have slivovica, the plum brandy, early in the day, so he poured four small glasses. He raised his glass to Ivan and Katya, "Nazdrovlje...to your health." He swallowed the brandy and continued, "I won't show the house or tell anyone about it until you have seen it and decided if you want it."

Roza said to Katya, "I can help you with the house and show you where to buy what you need."

At the sound of the tavern door opening, they all looked up. A smiling Stevo Markovich strolled in. He looked splendid in a three-piece dark gray wool serge suit, made in the skeleton style of the time, single breasted with five buttons, for which he paid five dollars.

Instead of the high-top button style of shoe, he wore the modern black patent leather Goodyear welt oxfords which used laces instead buttons.

Under his open suit coat, he sported a gold watch chain which held his 18-jeweled Waltham gold-filled hunting case watch, ordered from the Sears catalogue for eleven dollars and seventy-five cents.

Gone was the son of a fisherman. Very handsome, Stevo now had about him the air of a successful business man and one of sophistication. The money in the Cheroots Cigar box was enough to buy him a new life.

His furniture store was successful. He spoke fluent Croatian, Serbian and had a working knowledge of some of the other Slavic languages. He would have no reason to speak the Cajun French of New Orleans in Gary. His English was without an accent, however sometimes when he spoke the softness of the South could be heard.

To Milan, he said, "Is it too early to come and meet the new comers I have heard so much about?"

"Dobro jutro...good morning." said Milan shaking his friend Stevo's hand. They had been good friends for four years.

Bowing towards Katya and Ivan, Milan said, "Please meet my friends, Katya and Ivan Balaban."

Ivan started to rise, but when Stevo saw the cane, he motioned for him to remain seated. Stevo shook hands with Ivan and felt his heart skip a beat when he looked at Katya. Smiling politely, she offered her hand. Stevo took her small, soft hand. As he had seen done in the better places of New Orleans, he lifted her hand to his lips, to the quiet surprise of Milan and Roza.

Ivan said, "Please sit, we just had slivovica. Would you like some or perhaps some coffee?"

Stevo forced himself to take his eyes from Katya, saying to Roza, "Coffee would be very nice."

He had expected to see Ivan and Katya in the regional clothing of their part of Croatia, so he was more than pleasantly surprised to see Ivan in a nice suit and Katya in a high-collared continental dress of blue lace.

Stevo said, "I have just sent my driver with a casket to Whiting. You know Anka Klarich, don't you?"

"Has she left already, this early?" asked Milan.

"Yes, I just came from there. They have a wagon with her belongings in it. She didn't have much in the way of furniture." Stevo tried to only glance at Katya, not stare. "The casket is in my wagon and it shouldn't take too long to get to Whiting." He didn't mention that he had placed Klarich in the casket.

Milan pulled up a chair and joined the trio. Before Ivan or Stevo could make polite conversation, Milan said, "We need to find work for Ivan."

Stevo would have preferred a little conversation. He wanted to know more about Ivan and Katya. Yet, this could be Destiny at work. Who knows?

Seeing the interest in his friend's eyes, Milan was encouraged to add, "Ivan worked in a bank in Lackawanna and speaks some English. He also can read and write."

Stevo's mind was a jumble of thoughts, all of them mixed with thoughts of the beautiful Mrs. Balaban.

He put his hands together forming a steeple with his fingers. He tapped his lips, his way of thinking.

Roza bustled in with a tray of cups, coffee, and slices of nut roll. She placed the cups and napkins before each of them. The silence at the table made her pause...she sensed she was interrupting something. All were silent as she poured the coffee and milk into the cups. All eyes were on Stevo. Roza sat down and looked around the table, wondering why everyone was silent.

Everyone could see that Stevo was thinking, and waited for him to speak. He placed his hands in his lap and looked briefly at Katya, and then rested his eyes on Ivan.

"I would like you and Gospa Balaban to come to my store, to see what it is like. Perhaps I can find some work for you there." He looked from Ivan to Katya, as if he thought she too, might work for him.

Ivan said, "No need to be formal, referring to Stevo's use of Gospa when addressing Katya. Call us Ivan and Katya."

Slapping Stevo on the back, an excited Milan said, "That would be wonderful." He reached for a slice of nut roll with one hand and lifted his cup with the other. "That would be wonderful." he repeated.

Ivan smiled, not sure about the offer. He asked, "What kind of store do you have?"

While everyone was sipping coffee and helping themselves to the nut roll, Stevo said with pride, "I have a very nice furniture store, the best quality."

"Yes." agreed Roza. "Everything is so beautiful. Someday I will buy the lamp with the painted roses."

"You want that lamp?" Stevo saluted her with his coffee cup, "You come and get the lamp. You can pay me a little each week." Saying this, Stevo was hoping to impress Katya. The look on her face was pleasant, but showed no indication that she was impressed.

Ivan however, was impressed and very interested. "What sort of work could I do?" he asked.

"Well," thought Stevo, "I need a good bookkeeper. Also, someone needs to be at the store when I am away."

Before Stevo could say more, Milan urged, "Go, Ivan. Go see the store. Maybe you will want to work there."

All those around the table wore satisfied smiles, except Katya. The look on her face remained a pleasant one, but she reflected none of the excitement of the others. Things were moving too quickly for her liking.

Outside Milan's tavern was an Acme Royal Buggy to which was hitched a handsome black horse. The top of the buggy was leather with full back and side curtains, which could be dropped when needed, to protect from the weather.

Milan and Roza, as pleased as if they were Ivan and Katya's parents, waved goodbye as the three rode away with Katya seated in between Stevo and Ivan.

Ivan and Stevo chatted, while Katya was deep in thought. It was as though she was no longer in control of her life. There was a house her new friends wanted them to buy, and now there was a place where her friends thought Ivan should work. These were things that Ivan and Katya needed to discuss…to take time to think about.

It was a short ride to 18th and Washington, the first street west of Broadway. Stevo's property took up almost half of the block. The wooden front of his store had three large glass windows. The center window had painted in gold letters, MARKOVICH FURNITURE. The same wording, but in larger blue letters, was painted above the windows on the wooden part. The gold paint was to signify the wealth he hoped to have and the blue was in honor of the sea, which brought him to America as a boy. He had not left behind all the superstitions of New Orleans.

To the side of the store was a tall fence made up of two large wooden gates. On the floor of the buggy, under the seat, was stored a handheld bell. Stevo reached for the bell, gave it a couple good shakes, the sound ringing loudly. In a matter of seconds, the gates were pulled open from the inside by a tall, slender black man.

Katya and Ivan saw what appeared to be a shed for the horse. When they heard a distant whinny, they realized there were more horses.

The buggy they rode in was not the only vehicle Stevo owned. There was a large, rectangular grocery wagon with the Markovich Furniture name painted on each side. Katya surmised it was for delivering the furniture. What did make her wonder was the extended surrey. Instead of just one seat, there was a second seat behind it, so that four or six persons could ride in it. *Why would he need such a vehicle?*

At the back of the building was a door which led to living quarters, and a vegetable and flower garden flourished nearby.

Stevo did not introduce the black man to them, who was now leading the horse and buggy to a shed.

Walking in front of the store, Katya looked at the windows and saw the dark oak and mahogany furniture on display. Across the street she saw what appeared to be a tavern or restaurant with the sign reading, Strincich Liquor House.

Stevo unlocked the door, holding it open for Katya and Ivan to enter. He then took a straight-backed chair from inside the doorway and set it outside. This was a signal used by many shopkeepers to let passers-by know that the establishment was open for business.

Katya looked at the rectangular-shaped room with all the furniture. Stevo was very proud of his store, but Katya only half-listened as he described some of the pieces while leading Ivan around, mentioning certain items of particular interest. Stevo noticed that Katya was not following them. Instead, she wandered about on her own. He thought better of calling to her. He concentrated on impressing Ivan, hoping to have him as an employee.

Seeing the quarter-sawed golden oak table with its enormous twisted pillar legs and the solid oak, round top tables in the Eastlake style made her long for the beauty of the inlaid Italian marquetry furniture in her Nona's home in Trieste. She was overwhelmed by the dark furniture. What she saw made her miss Trieste and its beauty more than ever. All around her were big, heavy wooden tables and chairs. She saw no beautiful brass tables from India, or the Belgian tapestries and certainly nothing like the Nubian figures at the foot of the staircase in her grandmother Lucia's home.

Everything she looked at appeared strong and sturdy. Katya longed to see something of artistic beauty, something to remind her of home. This store depressed her and brought about more feelings of homesickness.

The bell on the door rang. A man with his arms full of small furniture struggled to get through the doorway. Seeing the salesman, Stevo hurried to him saying, "Hello, Adams." Nodding towards Ivan, he said, "I have some important people here. Can you give me a few minutes? Come back a little later?" Stevo pointed to a table, "Just leave your samples here."

Seeing Katya's interest in the small furniture, Stevo said, "The furniture companies send out their salesmen with small samples for us to see. We can decide on what to order from these pieces. Sometimes I buy the samples so customers can special order what they like, such as this chest." He pointed to a small dresser, something the size of a child's toy.

Stevo touched Katya's elbow saying "I want to show you what else we do." He motioned for Ivan to follow and led them both to the back of the store, where a 10-foot wide velvet curtain hung from a large brass rod. He pulled a cord and the curtain parted, revealing a room...a room where various coffins were on display.

Ivan and Katya stared. They were sure they knew these variously-designed containers to be coffins. In the villages of Croatia, coffins were built by the family or a friend. There, the caskets were simple wooden boxes, usually with some nice fabric laid in them.

Stevo was proud of his casket selection. He led Katya into the room, which had four large caskets and a small one for a baby, which Katya had yet to notice.

"Why do you have these?" asked a confused Ivan. "You sell furniture."

Stevo explained, "Many furniture stores have caskets for sale. It is not unusual." He took Ivan's arm, "Here, look at this one." He pointed to the glass window in the top of the closed casket. "It is lined with metal so we are able to pack the body with ice and the mourners can view the deceased."

Now Katya understood why he was with Anka Klarich that morning.

He offered Ivan a chair and another for Katya. Stevo used a low wooden foot stool as a seat and said to Ivan, "You see, I need someone like you, someone who can speak both Croatian and English." He paused, waiting for Ivan to say something. When Ivan didn't reply, he said, "When we deliver a coffin to a house and set it up, placing the body in it, I have to close the store. If you are here, I can keep the store open."

He turned to Katya, "It would be helpful if you could come to the homes when I deliver the caskets. A woman is always more comforting than a man, especially when a baby dies."

Now Katya understood the large, boxlike wagon. It could haul not only furniture, but caskets. What she didn't know was that during funerals, the store name was covered with an appropriate black fabric with gold tassels. And the surrey which had two seats was no doubt for transporting the mourning family to the cemetery.

Pulling the small coffin out, Stevo said, "It is always better to have a woman help with the burial of a baby."

Upon seeing the tiny, brown wooden box, Katya stood. The pain of losing her own baby overcame her. "I will be outside, Ivan." She struggled with the words. "You and Stevo can decide what you want. I can't stay here." She paused for only a second, looking at Stevo, "I can't work here."

She almost ran out the door. She couldn't get out in the sunlight and the fresh air soon enough, out where the sight of the heavy furniture and coffins would no longer smother her.

To a startled and confused Stevo, Ivan explained, "She recently lost her baby in childbirth."

From a windowed curtain looking out into the shop, back in the living quarters of the store, a blond woman frowned as she had watched Stevo appear to hover over Katya.

The plain-looking short, slender, Ema Harper was not pleased at what she observed. Ema had no feminine curves. Her blond hair was straight and worn pulled back into a bun. The only color in her skin was what little she got when she worked in the garden, or walked to the Greek grocery store.

Two years earlier, Stevo hired her as his housekeeper and cook, as well as to keep the furniture dusted in the store. In the far corner of the kitchen she had a small bed. There was no privacy curtain around the bed, because only Stevo and Ema were ever in the living quarters. On occasion, Ema was called to Stevo's bed.

CHAPTER 7

Neither Milan nor Roza could understand the mood of Katya upon her return to the tavern.

Bobo Johnson, the black man who worked for Stevo, brought them back to the tavern in the buggy, while Stevo stayed behind to work with the furniture salesman from Grand Rapids, Michigan.

Bobo and Ivan exchanged a few words during the ride. Bobo's Croatian was not fluent, but he knew enough to get along, as did some of the other blacks living in the Patch.

Katya would have preferred to walk back to the tavern, but the walk would have been long and after a while, it would have been difficult for Ivan.

The tavern was already full of customers. Many of them called out greetings upon seeing Ivan and Katya. Ivan returned the greetings, but Katya walked directly behind the bar and into Milan and Roza's living quarters. From there she walked outdoors to the garden area, away from everyone.

Giving Milan an apologetic look, Ivan followed Katya. He didn't pause to tell Milan whether Stevo had offered him a job or not.

Seeing the coffins and reliving the pain of losing her baby reminded her of her love for Zolton, and brought renewed sadness to Katya. She needed to lash out at someone or something. So, it would be Ivan who would feel the full brunt of her unhappiness.

Ivan was becoming frustrated with Katya. Married, but living like brother and sister, was wearing on him. He had hoped that Katya would grow to care more for him. Instead, it appeared she cared for him less. She married him out of a sense of duty because it had to do with her loving the Gypsy Zolton.

Katya stood with her back to him, watching Roza's white and brown goats eating grass.

Ivan sat on a tree stump behind her. "All right Katya. What is wrong?"

43

When she didn't reply, he said, "I know the coffins upset you. I could see it."

Still she didn't reply.

"Damn it!" he exclaimed, "I can't live this way. I need to know what you want...what you are thinking."

Still with her back to him, she said, "I wish I were back in Trieste, back with Lucia and Sofie. I want to be back where the air is clean and fresh with smell of the sea, away from the stink of this place."

He rose and stood behind her, leaning on his cane. "Oh, Katya," he said wearily, "we can't turn back time." He paused a moment, then continued, "I wish you were the young girl with wild, loose hair again, the girl who came to my brother's wedding. I wish I could have followed you to Trieste and let you know how much I loved you, when I had my fall. I wish Roha hadn't died when I pushed her...I wish you could forgive me for whatever is in your head. After all, I have forgiven you for having Zolton's baby."

When Katya turned to look at Ivan, she saw the tears in his eyes. She wished she could love him, to be a wife to him. When the baby was stillborn, something inside of Katya had died.

"Sit down." she said. "I know your leg hurts."

He kept standing. She shook her head slowly. Katya knew when Ivan was being stubborn. In a low voice she said, "I don't know if I can love again." She looked away into the distance. "I just...am, with no purpose. I am living each day, not thinking of the next. It is as if my tomorrows no longer matter." She returned her gaze to Ivan, "I am here with you because I have to be. It is because of me the Gypsies back home want to harm you...and me."

She didn't think Ivan could look more saddened than before, but he did.

"Oh, Ivan!" she touched his cheek, "What a cruel trick Destiny has played on us both."

Having no sense of guilt or embarrassment, Roza had followed Ivan and Katya as far as her kitchen. There, she pushed the slightly-opened door wider, so that she could hear their conversation. And...hear them she did. She knew she did not dare tell Milan what she overheard. He would be angry that she could betray their new friends by sneaking to hear their private conversation, and worse, he would be angry and disappointed if she repeated what she heard.

Gossip was a way of life for most of the people in the Patch, just as it had been in the villages of their homelands. She planned never to repeat what she had heard. Not only had she heard their words, but she had felt the pain and anguish their words caused. No, she would never tell anyone. She would pray to the Virgin Mary to protect and help her new friends.

Sad, and now a little ashamed, Roza went back into the tavern and did not wait to hear the rest of Ivan and Katya's conversation.

With more urging from Katya, Ivan did sit down on the stump. Katya turned over an empty wooden half barrel and used it for a seat.

Katya was the first to speak. "So, what are we going to do? Are you going to work for Markovich?"

The anger gone out of him, he stared at the ground. He tapped his cane trying to form his thoughts into words. A breeze slightly lifted his light brown hair. He patted his mussed hair into place. Finally he said, "I would like to work in the store." He looked up at Katya, "But, how can I get to and from the store each day? If we find a place to live here, near Milan and Roza, I couldn't walk that far. Perhaps we can find a boarding house close to the store."

"I suppose we could find lodgings." said Katya. Then she added, "But, I don't want to live with anyone." She was thinking of Lakawanna and the horrible Ivanka, their landlady. "I want to be alone. Can you understand that?" She looked into his eyes.

"Where do we start? Ivan asked, "Do you want to see the Klarich house?"

There was a pause… Katya said, "Let's take it!"

A very surprised Ivan said, "What do you mean, let's take it? We don't know where it is and if we will like it."

"I don't care!" She was definite in her decision. "I don't care…I want us to be on our own. We need to make a life of our own. We can't think and plan with people around us. I can't go on feeling this empty, I need something…something. I just don't know what."

"Katya…the people we have met here are good people. They care about us and want to help us."

Katya stood up, taking Ivan's arm to help him stand. "Come, let's talk with Milan. If we don't have the money, we will do like Markovich told Roza about the lamp. We will pay a little each week."

A very pleased Milan left a very quiet Roza and Mato to the bartending duties.

He drove Katya and Ivan in his wagon, to the available Klarich house at 15th and Adams Street.

Milan was so very excited for his friends. Ivan had a job with his good friend, Stevo Markovich, and the Klarich house was less than two blocks away from the store. The Klarich house was three houses into the block on the east side of Adams Street. All the houses were similar wooden structures with only three steps leading up to the entrance door.

Seeing the house, Katya thought the front of the structure looked like a face. The door being the mouth and the windows on each side of the door were like eyes. It wasn't a pretty house. From the street it appeared to be long and narrow. Tar shingles were on the pitched roof, while peeling brown paint covered the wooden edifice.

Ivan and Milan went up the three stairs to unlock the door, but Katya followed a gravel walkway along the side of the house to the back. There was a storage shed of some sort at the far end of the yard. The outhouse was halfway between the house and the shed. A not-so-pretty wire fence separated the properties on each side of the house. There were metal buckets and some items that suggested chickens and animals may have lived in this yard.

The back door opened. "Come inside, Katya." called Milan, "Tell us what you think."

Just as in the front of the house, there were three steps at the back which Katya climbed. She stepped into a small storage room the width of the house, more like an enclosed porch with windows.

Through another doorway was the kitchen. The first thing she saw was an iron wood-burning cook stove with its large pipe reaching upward, and then into an outer wall. The sink was enameled metal with a twenty-four-inch oak drain board and a hand pump for water.

Through another door was the sitting room, or as some called it, the front room. In the corner, to heat the room and probably the entire house, was a small, round nickel-plated urn sitting on four metal legs. The plaque on the side read: Acme Magic Todd Heater, with a warning that it only burned wood.

Ivan leaned against the wall watching for a reaction from Katya. Milan thought he could feel the disappointment coming, but said nothing. Neither man said a word as Katya made one more tour of the house. The bedroom was off the kitchen. It was as if the bedroom had been built later, as it stuck out the side of the house, but was flush with the back porch.

"Alright," she said firmly, "we have a problem. There is a small table in the kitchen and two wooden chairs. I see some chipped plates and cups and only one pot to cook in." She walked into the bedroom. "We have no bed, no chair, but there is a crucifix on the wall." In the front room she said, "We have a heating stove, which we won't need for another few months, and one worn, green cloth chair."

Apologetically, Milan said, "Katya, if you don't want it, I can understand. I didn't know Anka had left it this bare." He added, "They probably didn't have much."

With her hands on her hips, she turned in slow circles, thinking. "Leave me here," she said. "You both go to Markovich. See if he can leave the store. We need to talk furniture." Then she added, "It isn't the kind of furniture I like, but we have no choice."

With the men gone, Katya went outside to inspect the space under house and decided it could be used as a root cellar. It wasn't deep enough for any other use. As she walked through the yard, the lace on her skirt caught on a nail sticking out of a step as she started back into the house. She realized that she would need suitable clothing for living in the Patch.

In a short time, a very pleased Stevo arrived with the men at the house. He was almost ecstatic when he jumped off of Milan's wagon.

He didn't wait for the men to join him. He flew up the stairs and into the front room where Katya was studying the soot-covered walls.

"Gospa Balaban...Katya," he stammered. "Tell me what you want, what you need."

"Look." She swept her hand in a circle. "We have nothing. No bed, no furniture. Look!" she repeated.

"Da, Da...yes, yes, alright," He was mentally making a list. "Come to the store with me and pick out what you want. I have a good idea what you need. It is already late afternoon and I will be closing the store soon."

At the store, a very annoyed Ema Harper, once again watched from the back of the shop as Stevo led Katya throughout the store, telling her what she needed and asking her what she preferred. He pointed out beds, tables, bookcases, chairs, kerosene lamps, and even a five-piece parlor set, made up of a dark blue velour sofa and four velour chairs trimmed with tassels.

To his disappointment, Stevo watched Katya choose the least decorative pieces, while he preferred she take the heavily-carved and ornate items.

Seeing Stevo with Katya, Ema went beyond annoyed, to a simmering anger when she overheard Stevo say to Katya, "I would like to make a housewarming gift of this cabinet." He had to explain what the term 'housewarming' meant. The cabinet he chose was a combination bookcase and writing desk. Having noticed that Katya did not care for the ornately-carved furniture, he presented her with a rather plain, highly-polished oak piece with a beveled mirror above the hinged drop desk.

Ema hated the dazzling smile of gratitude Katya gave Stevo.

Katya said, half thinking out loud, "Too bad you don't sell dishes and bedding. I need sheets and towels and," she laughed, "I don't even own an apron."

"Molim...excuse me." he said. "I will be right back."

From the back, Ema slowly moved her way through the store closer to Katya. With her arms crossed over her small bosom, she glared at the beautiful foreigner. When Katya noticed Ema, she smiled at the woman. Her smile was not returned.

Bobo and Milan moved furniture to the street onto Milan's wagon, and some pieces on Stevo's moving wagon. Ivan tried to help by carrying small things like drawers and sofa cushions.

Stevo returned in a matter of minutes. "Here," he said, handing Katya several sheets of his business stationary with writing on it. "Ema," he pointed to the sulking woman, "will go with you to the market just down the street for food and things. You don't need money. Give the owner one of these letters and keep the receipt he will give you." When he saw the confused look on Katya's face, he said, "Don't worry, Ivan and I will be keeping a record of your expenses and we will work it out." He took her hand, "Katya, I am so happy you are letting me help you and Ivan."

Had Ema been a firecracker, there would have been an explosion when she saw Stevo give Katya letters of credit and holding her hand a bit longer than needed. Furthermore, Ema was insulted that he expected her to take Katya to the stores for food and other supplies.

Sensing Ema's foul mood, Katya insisted that Ivan join them in their shopping. Ivan was more useful to Katya than he was at moving furniture. It was a good thing that Ivan came with Katya, as he could speak some English and Ema was of no assistance, clearly showing her displeasure. After the grocery market, Ema did direct them to a dry goods store where they purchased things for the bedroom.

Ivan had no way to carry all their purchases to the house. So the items were stacked into a box on wheels, which was tied to the back of a bicycle and delivered by a young boy.

During the shopping, Ema never said a word to Ivan or Katya. Even though Katya was a married woman, Ema felt threatened. Never in the two years of working for Stevo, had he showered Ema with gifts, or for that matter, with anything. He paid her one dollar a week for housekeeping and cooking. And that he considered generous because he supplied her with a roof over her head and meals.

Arriving at the house, both Ivan and Katya could barely believe their eyes when they saw what was inside. The three men, Stevo, Milan and Bobo beamed with pride at their accomplishment.

Stevo looked a bit rumpled from all the moving of furniture. Even with his light brown hair mussed and a streak of dirt on one cheek, he was, as always, quite handsome.

He said, "You can re-arrange the furniture however you prefer. This is how the three of us thought you might like it."

The two friends, Stevo and Milan, were filled with pleasure and pride as Katya walked through the house, touching and admiring the furniture which she had originally thought ugly. Now in her home, the pieces appeared more attractive. She noticed pieces she had not picked out, but liked them, such as the kerosene lamp with hanging crystal prisms. In the kitchen was an oak ice box, something she had not thought of.

Milan explained, "There will be a card that you place in your front window when you need ice. The driver will see it and bring you a block of ice through the back door."

Katya was so moved that she sat in one of the new oak kitchen chairs and sobbed, alarming the men.

"What is wrong?" Milan put his hands, big as paws, around her shoulders. "I thought you liked what we did."

To all their surprise and Stevo's envy, Katya turned and wrapped her arms around the big standing man. "Oh, Milan, I may not hate America so much now."

Milan, the big tough guy that he was, wiped away a tear of his own.

After a few moments, Milan announced, "Come, we must go to the tavern and celebrate. I have cold pivo for all of us, you too, Bobo."

Bobo said, "Hvala...thank you, but he wouldn't go. He was black and knew his appearance might cause some trouble."

Ivan shook Stevo's hand. "I never thought we would find such wonderful friends and I thank you. Tomorrow we can go over the accounts and work something out." He turned to Milan, "The same with the house. Tomorrow we will talk business."

Katya stepped up to Milan and kissed him on the cheek. She did the same to Stevo, who was sure he blushed and lastly, she kissed the wonderful Bobo, who thought he might faint when the white woman's lips touched his cheek.

A bewildered Roza watched as the happy and laughing Ivan and Katya, whom she had earlier heard arguing, came into the tavern with an equally jubilant Milan and Stevo Markovich.

Roza had spent the entire afternoon worrying about Katya and Ivan, sending prayers to Heaven for them. She had expected Katya and Ivan to be on non-speaking terms. The conversation she had overheard was full of pain and suffering...and now there was all this gaiety!

Before Katya could sit down, Roza had her by the arm, almost dragging her to the back living quarters. Once away from the tavern patrons, Roza slapped at Katya's arm.

A surprised Katya cried out, "What is that for?" She rubbed the hurt arm.

An angry Roza said, "I have been sick with worry all afternoon for you and Ivan. You don't love him...you can't love him? I heard you say it! He killed someone? You had another man's baby? What's the matter with you people?" She hit Katya's other arm.

"Oh, Roza, my wonderful Roza," laughed Katya, wrapping her arms around the plump woman. "You are so wonderful to care about us." She let go of Roza, who was now confused. "Ivan and I will always be together. It is our Destiny to take care of one another."

"Are you crazy?" said Roza, angrily.

Katya smiled with great affection at Roza, who still looked confused. "Someday, Roza, when we have the time and you are not so angry, I will tell you how I was sent away because the villagers thought I was a witch."

Hearing this, Roza's eyes grew wide. She was about to speak. Before she could say anything, handsome Stevo Markovich was in her kitchen. "Come you two. Tonight is a time to celebrate." He had each woman by an arm and led them out to the room filled with cigarette smoke, to enjoy the laughter and music.

51

Still full of questions, a suspicious Roza looked at the happy, laughing Katya. She watched as Stevo led Katya to the table where the smiling Ivan waited.

CHAPTER 8

Ivan left for his new position as bookkeeper and assistant at the Markovich furniture store. He took care with his grooming and wore a brown suit, one of only two suits he owned, given to him by Katya's family.

Katya was dressed in a loose, white-laced morning dress as she bid Ivan goodbye. Watching him descend the stairs to the walk, Katya felt content for the first time since coming to America. She and Ivan had a wonderful evening at Milan's Tavern.

It was true, thought Katya. America was wonderful! Only two days in Gary and already Ivan had a job. And they had a house filled with new furniture.

Katya turned and admired the front room. She still felt the furniture was a bit heavy and bulky for her taste, but had to admit it looked good. It was far superior to the furniture that was in the house she and Ivan stayed at while in Lakawanna. She looked at the bare walls and thought of the Belgian tapestries on her Nona's walls in Trieste. Those gorgeous weavings would be so out of place in this small room.

In the kitchen were the items purchased at the market and the dry goods store, all needing to be put away. The night before she had only taken out the bedding items and a couple of towels, leaving the rest still boxed.

She was looking forward to the evening when Ivan would come home. She was anxious to hear how his day at the store went, hoping he would like it there. Then, he and Katya would look over the amount owed to Stevo and think about how to pay for it.

A loud knock sounded at the door, startling her. She thought Ivan must have forgotten something.

Katya opened the door to see a stern-faced Roza standing before her.

With a smile, she said, "Roza, how nice, you are my first guest. Dobro jutro...good morning, come let me show you the house."

What she saw in the front room made Roza pause with more than a little envy. "Oh, Dragi Bog...Dear God, this is worse than I thought."

A disappointed Katya said, "You don't like it? It is too big and heavy, isn't it?" She took Roza's arm, "Let me show you the rest."

Silently Roza followed Katya to each room, finally settling in the kitchen, where each had a cup of coffee with milk.

Katya said, "All right, Roza. What is on your mind? I can see you don't like the house and the furniture."

"It is not the house. It is the furniture...people will talk. No one buys a full house of furniture at one time." With some annoyance Roza said, "Here we buy a piece at a time. When it is paid for, we choose another table or chair. In one day you have a house and such grand furniture." Roza felt more than envy for what Katya and Ivan had immediately upon arriving to Gary.

Katya sipped her coffee. She looked at Roza and with a heavy heart said, "Oh Roza, do you begrudge me this furniture? Can't you be pleased for Ivan and me?"

Roza stared at Katya. She wondered, was Katya that naïve or was she very clever? "People are already talking about you." she said.

Katya laughed, "It seems people have always talked about me. Many thought I was a witch. Remember, I told you that."

Roza said, "It certainly appears you have bewitched Stevo. What is going on with you and Stevo Markovich?"

Katya's eye widened. "Stevo? What are you talking about?"

"I saw it last night...everyone saw it," said Roza "This thing between you and Stevo."

Katya confused, jumped to her feet shouting, "Thing! What thing?"

"He is crazy about you and everyone can see it," said Roza. "It looks as if you have set your sights on the most successful man in our community."

Katya sank into her chair. She felt sick. She looked at Roza a long time, before saying, "Is that what you think?"

Roza broke the silence, "People will turn against you. Already they think you and Stevo will be lovers. Everyone at the tavern saw you and Stevo stomping to the polka, while Ivan sat there watching. Everyone knows now why you have all this furniture."

Katya looked at Roza, asking, "And who told them about the furniture?"

Roza dropped her eyes, no longer looking at Katya.

In a weak voice Katya said, "Of course Ivan sat watching. He can't dance because of his crippled leg." Katya pushed the coffee cup to the center of the table. "Is this what you think of me...that I would make a fool of Ivan by having an affair, so that all his new friends would laugh at him?" As an after thought Katya added, "Are you jealous of me?"

Ignoring the question, Roza said, "What can I think? I heard Ivan say he forgave you for having Zolton's baby. How many lovers have you had?"

As soon as these words were out of Roza's mouth, she regretted having said them seeing the anger on Katya's face.

Her voice shaking with emotion, Katya said, "I was going to tell you about Ivan and me." Her throat tightened and she paused for a moment. "I was going to tell you about our families and why we had to marry." Katya stood, supporting herself with palms flat on the table.

"Go away, Roza." she said softly, "I don't need friends who think such things of me. You can go back and tell your friends they may think whatever they want. I don't need you or them."

Roza stood and reached out to Katya, aware she had said too much and said it in a wrong way. She thought she was helping...instead she had made a grave mistake.

Katya stepped away from Roza's out stretched hand, "I won't be coming to the tavern anymore. You and your friends will have to find someone else to gossip about."

Katya turned her back on her first friend in Gary, then walked without a word to the bedroom and closed the door.

A sorry and bewildered Roza stood looking at the closed door. *What had she done?*

Had she been wrong? Was she being envious of the beautiful Katya? Could it be she was jealous of her beauty and of all this lovely furniture?

She went to the closed door and knocked gently. "Katya..." She heard no reply. "Katya...I am sorry. Don't you see how it looks...Markovich giving you all this furniture?"

Still no reply from the other side of the door... "Good by, Katya. Zbogom...go with God. Please come to the tavern and we can talk some more."

Silence...

A heavy-hearted Roza looked around, as if forgetting something. She slowly walked to the entrance of the house. Once more she looked back, hoping to see Katya come out of the room. When she realized Katya was not coming, Roza left the house.

On the walk back to the tavern, she wondered what Milan would think of what she had done. Perhaps she wouldn't tell him about her visit to Katya. Roza was sure Milan would be angry.

Lost in her thoughts and worrying about the consequences of what she had said to Katya, Roza forgot that she meant to go to Markovich's for the banquet lamp painted with roses. The cost of the lamp was $1.85. She had saved thirty cents to use as her down payment.

In their new home, a very troubled Katya cried. Her tears were a combination of hurt and anger. This matter about Stevo Markovich brought back the pain of being called a witch in Vladezemla. She was angry and hurt back when she escaped to Trieste. Well, there was nowhere to escape to here in America. She was with Ivan. Destiny put her in this city and she would have to make the best of it.

She longed for the comfort of Anton Vladeslav's private chapel, the chapel where she often prayed and was comforted by the large crucifix over the altar.

She needed a church. She needed a haven.

CHAPTER 9

Some of the men at Milan's looked up when Roza came from her visit with Katya. From the guilty worried look on Roza's face, Milan sensed something was wrong.

She was overheard, even though she thought she was whispering. "I went to see Katya. I told her people knew she was headed for trouble with Stevo."

A worried Roza had never seen her gentle giant of a husband look so angry.

"Sveti Issus...Holy Jesus! What gave you the right to interfere?" He didn't try to hide his anger. "Watch the bar." he said to Mato, as he gripped Roza's arm roughly and dragged her into the back and out the door to the back yard, startling the goats.

"What the hell do you mean you told her about trouble? What do you think you know?" He still had a grip on her arm as he spoke.

Roza tried to squirm away, but couldn't. "Milan, I was worried what people were saying about her."

"Just what were people saying?" he demanded. "I didn't hear anything."

Still trying to wriggle free of his grip she said, "About her and Stevo. Anyone could see that something was going on between them."

When Milan let go of Roza, he flung her away from him with such force that she slammed into the trunk of a young cherry tree.

"I spent the day with all of them and I saw nothing." said Milan, "I saw a genuine friendship from Katya. If you think Stevo wanted more, well you saw what she looks like. Most men admire her...want her."

Roza knew better than to ask, "Do you want her?" So, she remained silent.

"Just what did you say to her?" he demanded.

"I told her that it was odd that she got an entire house of furniture and that maybe she was already having an affair."

Milan shook his head in disgust.

"You stupid, jealous woman." he said. If my friend, Stevo, hears what you are thinking…saying, what will he say? And what about Ivan, how could you insult him this way? You have no proof."

He took her again by the arm, but not as roughly as before. "Tell me," he said, "name one person who said there was something between Stevo and Katya."

When she did not answer he said, "I thought not. I am so ashamed of you."

He turned away from Roza and went back to his work in the tavern, ignoring the questioning looks on the faces of the men, aware that there was a family quarrel.

Ivan was very pleased with his first day at work. His desk was at the back of the store, just left of the velvet curtain, which closed off the room of coffins. In the desk drawers were some gray cloth-covered ledgers. One ledger was for accounts paid out for merchandise, the care of the horses, and salaries. Another was for time payments made by customers, and yet another was for personal loans made by Stevo to several Croatian business owners.

Stevo and Bobo were gone most of the day, delivering and setting up a casket in a home. As always, they placed the coffin in the front room of the house, and then helped place the body, already clothed and prepared by the family, into the coffin. They never hurried when called for a funeral, wanting to give the family all the attention desired.

Upon leaving, Stevo promised to make arrangements to have Bobo return with a black mourning wreath for the front door of the house. He would add this to the necessary charges.

His first day at Markovich's, Ivan didn't need to do any selling, but he did take a payment from a customer, gave a receipt and entered it on the proper page, crediting the payment.

He went through invoices and entered them in the books where necessary. Ivan liked this work. He enjoyed working with numbers and keeping accounts in order.

He started to set up a page for himself showing what he owed the store: Parlor set, $18; Ice Box $14; Iron Bed $5.90; Wire Bed Springs $5.25; Mattress $3.95.

Tomorrow he would complete the list of charges.

At the end of the day, arriving home he found Katya waiting at the back door. Her eyes were swollen from crying. Seeing her, Ivan dropped his cane and wrapped his arms around her. "My God, Katya. What is it? What has happened?"

Katya looked at Ivan, his hazel eyes so full of concern. She picked up his cane and said, "Come into the kitchen."

Over the table was a plain white table cloth, set with a plate of cheese, salami, bread and olives, making up the evening meal.

Seated across from one another, Ivan asked again, "What has happened?"

"After you left this morning, Roza came." she said.

Not touching any of the food, Ivan waited for her to continue. When she didn't say anything, he said, "And? Roza came and...and...?"

"She accused me of having an affair with Stevo. She said if we haven't already, it is obvious we will."

With wonder in his voice he said, "Why would she say such a thing?"

"Because of the furniture." said Katya, a trace of disgust in her voice. "Roza thinks the furniture was some sort of a gift. I never had the time to tell her you would eventually pay for it."

"She really said that?" Ivan was bewildered.

"Yes. She claims everyone at Milan's was talking about us and seeing that something going on between us. She especially didn't like that we danced together."

Ivan stood. "I am going there and have a talk with them."

Katya said, "Eat something first. You haven't eaten since breakfast, have you? Please eat something. I need to tell you more."

Ivan sat, sighed deeply, and reached for a slice of salami and some cheese, while Katya poured a small glass of wine for them both.

Katya sipped the wine and said, "When we were in Roza's yard talking, she was listening to our conversation."

Ivan's eyebrows rose as his eyes widened in surprise.

Katya went on, "She heard you say that you forgave me for having Zolton's baby. She asked me how many lovers I have had."

Ivan pushed his plate away. No one could ever understand the bond that held Ivan and Katya together, regardless of their odd relationship. Destiny pulled them apart once and then pushed them together again. They needed one another and would always take care of each other.

He stood, "I am going to the tavern. Are you coming with me?"

"No," she said, "I will never go there again. I am done with Roza." Concerned she said, "Ivan, you can't go. It is too far to walk."

"I will see if Bobo will take me there in the buggy."

When Ivan walked into Milan's he was hailed with the usual "Kako si...How are you from most of the men at the bar. There was the usual greeting with shaking of hands and slaps on the back.

Milan with a somber look on his face, suspected the reason for this visit. He nodded to Ivan.

Ivan said, "Where can we talk, alone. What I have to say is for you only." When Ivan said "For you only," he gave Roza who was standing behind the bar, a hard stare.

Seeing the look Ivan gave to Roza, Milan said to his brother, who was pouring drinks, "Don't let her leave here." The slender, Mato nodded, somewhat confused.

Once more in the yard with the trees and the goats, Ivan sat on the tree stump, while Milan squatted.

Ivan said, "Milan, what I am about to tell you, I have only told one other person here in America. That was my friend in Lakawanna. I want your word, as my friend, that you will not repeat what I am about to tell you...especially not to Roza."

"I promise." said Milan, solemnly.

Ivan proceeded to tell him how Katya had been sold to a Turk and the story of her escape. He told Milan about their love and his fall the night the Turk tried to kidnap Katya, and later about the lies his mother told Katya. He pretty much told him the same things he told Slavko Mravich in Lakawanna.

Ivan told him about the priest's diary which told of Katya's birth, and who her real family was; about Lucia Kurecka, her grandmother in Trieste, and the trading company and the ship, the *Vincenti*.

He told Milan everything, everything about the death of Roha and why they had to marry and come to America.

When Ivan was done, he asked again, "Will you keep your word and tell no one what I have just told you?"

Milan stood, his knees stiff from squatting the whole time Ivan spoke. "I give you my word." He pulled a pack of cigarettes from his pocket and offered one to Ivan before taking one himself. He lit Ivan's cigarette and then his own. Exhaling from his long first drag, Milan said, "You and Katya have had a hard life. It sounds as though you came from a family of means, so it must be hard for you to live here in Gary. Have Katya come here and I will make things right again."

Ivan, also a bit stiff from sitting so long, stood. "Milan, I understand the attraction men have for Katya. As for Zolton, she was in love with him and probably still is." He tapped the head of his cane on the tree stump, "She will never come here again. Katya does not forgive. She never forgave my mother for lying, saying I believed her to be a witch. That lie ruined the love we had. But, we are still devoted to one another, and I still love her."

As they walked back into the building, Milan said, "Let's have a drink."

"No, hvala…thank you." replied Ivan, "Bobo is waiting to take me back."

Walking with Ivan to the buggy, Milan passed the bar and gave his wife a hard-eyed look, which made her shiver. He had never been as disgusted with her as he was today.

CHAPTER 10

During the first week of moving into their house, Katya soon found that she was uncomfortable wandering the city alone. Gary was a wide open town with few women and plenty of men staring and making lewd comments. This was a world she and Ivan never expected.

It was evident that Milan's Tavern and Steve Markovich's furniture store were not the true indicators of what it was like in the Patch. Once Katya saw the real south side of Gary, she couldn't believe this was to be her home.

In the Patch, there was so much fighting that at times the streets were blood stained and gun shots could be heard in the night. Men drank, brawled, and some of them died. Gambling was commonplace in the saloons, but Milan didn't have slot machines in his establishment, though on occasion, a fight would break out. Milan was big enough that he could stop the altercation or throw the fighters out.

He did everything he could to help the men who came into his bar to focus on sending money to the Old Country for their families, just as he had done for his brother.

Men working in the mills 60 hours a week could receive a weekly pay of $9.60.

Katya and Ivan soon became aware that they were trapped in Gary. Ivan had signed notes to Milan for the house and to Stevo for the furniture. His salary of $2.50 a week would not get them out of debt quickly. Once out of debt, they might leave, but had no idea where they would go.

Ivan suspected that Stevo Markovich's ledger with loans to some businessmen in the Patch, were really his portion of the profits from the slot machines he co-owned. Ivan noticed that about once a week, it was only the tavern owners who made payments on what were listed as loans in that certain ledger. He overheard one of the men saying that the fifty-cent machines were getting more plays than the quarter machines. It wasn't long before Ivan realized that more money was coming in from the slot machines than from the sale of furniture. He minded his own business, not wanting to lose his position as bookkeeper.

Katya and Ivan's neighbors on Adams Street would nod or speak when they met, and it wasn't long before Katya recognized most of them. The visiting and interaction of the neighbors was done outside and not by invitation into their homes. Privacy was very important to the people of the many nationalities. Assimilating with other cultures was difficult for most of them.

Language was the greatest barrier. On one occasion, a foreman kept repeating "Go on...go on..." which sounded like the Serbian word *govan,* meaning body waste. This led to a fight. The immigrants not understanding the orders of the mill foremen led to many tragic accidents, some resulting in deaths.

It was not uncommon for even the young men to leave the mills after their shift with shaky legs, too tired to eat, then to fall asleep almost the moment they sat down.

Sleeping two and three in a bed was commonplace. Beds were constantly in use. Those working at night used the beds during the day and those working the day shift had the beds at night.

Some of the mill workers wanting to return to their homes in Europe would work, sleep, and save. They returned to their homeland with the money earned in America, suggesting wealth. It perpetuated the myth that one could pick up money off the streets of America.

It wasn't long before the frustration of their situation actually drew Ivan and Katya closer, instead of apart. They had only one another and realized if they were to have any sort of a life in this city, they would have to plan and work together for their future. They put aside their wishes or thoughts of the Old Country, now their plans were all about paying off the house and the furniture.

Katya heard of an immigrant doctor with a small office only a block away from their home. She was excited and hurried to see him. She thought she would be valuable to the doctor because of her knowledge of healing.

Doctor Alberto Costa was an Italian immigrant who regularly patched up knife wounds, broken bones, and some industrial accidents. He was a small man who was always busy. His black hair was graying, but his youthful face betrayed his 45 years. Dr. Costa looked sternly at Katya under bushy eyebrows.

"What's wrong with you? Are you hurt? Pregnant?" he fired off the questions.

Katya smiled, thinking he was a funny little man. She said, "There is nothing wrong with me. I thought I would like to work with you."

He was pleased she spoke Italian. "What qualifications do you have? What schools did you attend?" Again he spoke rapidly, his back to her as he washed his hands.

Katya hesitated before answering, "I have not been to school, but I know much about natural healing."

Costa put his hands on his hips and snorted. "Hah, I need a nurse." His tone was sarcastic. "You come tomorrow morning, early, and you can work here."

Katya was pleased, smiling she asked, "What do you pay?"

"Pay? What pay?" he was almost shouting. "You will be here to learn. I shall teach you. There is no pay!"

Katya said nothing, just turned and walked out the wooden door, past a table where some waiting patients were playing cards. She would not be back.

Smiling to herself as she walked, she was glad that she was not going to work for Dr. Costa. He was probably very hard to please and it appeared he had a gruff manner.

Turning onto Adams St., on the opposite end of the block from where she and Ivan lived, she saw a small boy in front of one of the houses crying. Katya recognized him as part of the Armenian family.

Seeing her, he came running and grabbing her hand, pulling her desperately towards the house he lived in. He was sobbing, speaking words she didn't understand. She let herself be pulled into the house, aware that something was wrong.

Once inside the house, Katya was led into a room where she saw a woman moaning not on a bed, but on a mattress on the floor. Kneeling by the mattress, Katya saw a young woman, her face wet with perspiration, grabbing at the mattress while crying out in pain.

The woman was having a baby. Katya gently pushed the little crying boy out of the room, motioning for him to stay there before she closed the door.

Back at the woman's side, Katya could see her water broke and the baby was on its way. With a soothing voice in words the woman could not understand, Katya tried to comfort her. The cries and screams through the closed door frightened the little boy who cried even louder when hearing his mother's cries of pain.

The baby came with soft mewling sounds, soon breaking into a healthy cry.

Katya wrapped the baby in a cloth and placed it next to its mother, while she proceeded to clean the afterbirth and place some clean cloths under the exhausted woman.

She went into the next room and saw an indoor hand pump. Grabbing a bowl from the sink, she filled the bowl. Returning to the woman who kept saying words Katya could not understand, Katya bathed the woman's face.

Finished with the mother, Katya took the baby, unwrapping it from the cloth, to wash it. Katya's hands stopped moving. What she saw shocked and puzzled her. It was something she had never seen before.

Was the baby a boy or a girl...or, "Oh, Holy Mary..." was it both?

Katya calmed herself and washed the beautiful baby. Katya knew the mother did not understand Katya as she said, "It is a beautiful baby, such a beautiful baby."

With the baby in her arms, the very young mother lifted the cloth to see if she had a boy or a girl. Her look of shock turned into one of heartbreak. She sobbed as she put the baby to her breast for milk.

Katya brought the little boy in to see that his mother was alright. He saw the baby and heard the sobbing, but seemed less distressed than he had been. She led the boy into another room, stayed with him, washing his hands and face, all the while speaking words to him he did not understand. She found an apple in the kitchen, cutting thin slices for him, which he took and ate.

The boy heard his father at the door and ran to him calling "Baba...Baba...Father."

The father only recognized Katya as someone who lived down the street. Immediately the man thought of his pregnant wife. He ran into the bedroom with his little son following him.

When Katya heard the father wail, she knew he had seen the baby.

He came out to face Katya. They could not communicate. He didn't speak Croatian and she didn't know any Armenian. His face was pale and troubled.

Katya reached out and touched his hand, which he pulled back as if she had burned him. He watched as Katya touched her breast over her heart with her right hand, next, she put both hands over her lips, indicating silence, and lastly made the sign of the cross.

The father was a small man, with a dark beard and sad, dark eyes. He looked at Katya for several moments thinking about what she had done with her hands. Then, hoping that he understood her as promising not to tell about the hermaphrodite birth, he reached out and shook her hand.

Katya smiled at the father, touched the boy's head, and walked out the door. She never told anyone about the baby, not even Ivan. It would be up to the parents if the baby would be raised as a boy or a girl.

CHAPTER 11

Another lonely week passed for Katya. She tried to clear the backyard in the hopes of having a kitchen garden similar to the one Klara had at Vladezemla.

That evening when Ivan came home, he announced, "I would like you to go with me to Milan's tonight." Before Katya could protest he continued, "There is going to be a meeting there in the hopes of building a church for our people…a Croatian church."

With a tilt of her head, she looked at him, "You know I don't want to see Roza."

"I am not asking you to be friends again. I just want to be seen with you." In a softer voice he said, "I don't enjoy going there alone. People ask about you and I am sure they wonder where you are and why you no longer come to Milan's. "Besides," he added with a smile, "the men like to look at you."

Ivan followed Katya into the kitchen, which smelled of beans and cabbage. The evening meal was already on the table. Katya let out a long sigh as she sat down. Ivan sat across from her. "Is this so very important to you?" she asked.

He smiled aware that she was considering going with him. "Yes," he said, "Stevo will be here with his carriage to take us there."

Seeing the frown on her face he reached across the table, touching her hand saying, "You can't keep avoiding him. I know he admires you. Men have always admired you. Zolton is the only one that bothers me."

Katya looked into Ivan's gold-flecked eyes, the same eyes she had noticed the first time she met him at his brother's wedding, back in Vladezemla. Noticing the few grey hairs glistening among his light brown hair made her see they weren't so very young anymore. Katya realized she had hurt him so very much in the past, although she never meant to.

She said, "Eat, while I change clothes."

Katya's European clothes were folded in a drawer of the oak chest of drawers. She had hand sewn for herself, not the regional flower-embroidered dress of Croatia, but a white, gathered skirt and simple scoop neck blouse, similar to the ones she wore in Italy. The fabric cost five cents a yard.

From the black junk man who traveled the unpaved streets in a horse-drawn wooden wagon, she bought a piece of red cloth for a penny. From that red fabric she cut out small flowers and appliquéd them along the hem of her skirt.

Happy shouts greeted the trio as they walked into Milan's. The familiar smells of cigarettes and beer assaulted them. Some patrons raised glasses saluting them and several men came forward to shake hands.

Milan's eyes danced under his thick eyebrows. He was especially happy to see the three of them. He said to Roza, standing next to him behind the bar, "Don't go to Katya. If she wants to be friends, she will come to you." He gave his wife a stern look, "Understand?" Roza nodded and looked away.

Stevo wandered about the room, greeting people and making conversation, while Katya and Ivan sat with Milan's brother Mato at a nearby table.

Seeing that Mato was very pale and unusually quiet, Ivan said, "What is wrong. Why aren't you working the bar...are you alright?"

Mato, sick with pain pointed to the back of his neck. Katya rose to see what he was pointing to.

"Mayka Boza...Holy Mary! I have never seen a boil this large." she exclaimed, staring at a large purple and red mound, its center an ugly yellow.

To Mato, Ivan said, "Katya can fix it." He was recalling the boil on Vanjo's chest, a musician at his brother's wedding on the day he met Katya. Katya had mixed something in his mother's kitchen and applied it to the boil, which caused the boil to burst the next morning without being lanced.

Some people nearby, hearing the conversation moved closer.

Mato raised his hand as if to stop Katya, "Don't touch it. Please don't touch it." he pleaded. "I know you want to cut it with a knife, but don't do it." He was near hysterics.

Seeing the crowd gathered around the table, Milan went to see what was going on.

"What's wrong?" he asked. "Why are you all standing here?"

Ivan said, "Katya can heal that boil, but Mato doesn't want her to."

"She wants to cut it?" asked Milan. "I could cut it if he would let me."

Ivan smiled. "I told you she was a healer. She can mix a potion to make it drain without cutting."

There was murmuring among those around the table, "Healer, a healer from the Old Country," was passed from person to person.

Milan said to his brother, "I can't have you moaning here. Let Katya do what she has to, so you can work again."

"Aeee…" cried Mato, fearing what Katya would do to him.

Milan asked Katya, "What do you need?"

"I need to go to your kitchen." she said. "I think I can find what I need there."

Seeing the crowd of people, Stevo joined Ivan and the moaning Mato, "What is going on? Is something wrong?"

With the same pride Ivan had those many years ago in his father's yard when Katya spread the healing mixture on Vanjo's boil, he said, "My wife can do magic with her healing." This was a poor choice of words for uneducated superstitious immigrants to hear.

Roza, curious, stayed at the far end of the bar watching as Katya went into the kitchen.

A rough looking mill worker left the table and came to the bar for another pivo, beer.

"What's going on?" asked Roza, nodding towards the crowd at the table.

Taking a long drink of the cold beer, the man said, "Maybe we have a witch here. She is going to mix something up to put on Mato's boil."

In a matter of minutes, Katya returned carrying a small bowl with a thick mixture of melted lye soap, salt and vinegar.

Mato was on the verge of crying, fearing he was in for more pain. Now everyone in the bar watched as Katya unbuttoned Mato's shirt, removing it, leaving him only in a loose and not so fresh tank top undershirt.

"Bend your head down on the table." instructed Katya.

When Mato hesitated, looking suspiciously at Katya, his brother ordered, "Bend your head down!"

From a spoon, Katya dripped small amounts of the mixture, waiting for it to slightly thicken, before adding more.

The room was quiet. Even the musicians stopped playing and came to watch.

Mato kept waiting for more terrible pain. Instead, ever so slightly it felt better. The pain didn't go away, but the lye mixture had a trace numbing effect.

With his head still bent over, Katya loosely wrapped a piece of cloth she tore from a clean towel in the kitchen around his neck.

"That's it." she said. "I don't know how soon it will drain, but that is all I can do."

Men gathered around her asking, "What did you do? What did you use?"

Milan dispersed the curious men saying, "Leave the lady alone. Go back to the bar." The men left, some of them turning back to look at the beautiful red-haired woman, wondering what else she knew about healing.

Stevo sipped his wine, admiring Katya. Her uncovered hair added to her mystery. Her hair was supposed to be covered, after all she was married. It made some men who didn't know better, think she was single.

Seeing Stevo's stare, Katya looked back at him with those bewitching, emerald eyes. Stevo said to Ivan, "I think you are married to the most beautiful woman in Gary."

"I think so," agreed Ivan, smiling. "She is not only beautiful, but very special."

Katya turned to Ivan, "You have never said anything so lovely to me before." She felt her cheeks redden.

Seeing Ivan and Katya look at one another with such great affection, Stevo realized Katya was not the kind of woman to go after.

He found that he admired her for that and he was more than a little envious of his bookkeeper.

CHAPTER 12

Sitting at the table with their breakfast coffee, Ivan and Katya heard a knock at the back door. It was the custom to enter at the back and not the front.

Opening the door, Katya was pleasantly surprised to see Milan and Mato, their arms full of packages. Instead of "Good morning", she asked, "Is something wrong?"

From the kitchen Ivan called, "Come in. Have some coffee."

Katya stepped aside to let the men pass. As Mato passed Katya, he gave her a huge grin.

"What are all the packages?" asked Ivan still seated.

Milan and Mato placed the packages on the table. "Look," said Milan pulling his brother by the arm, "look at his neck."

Ivan rose and with Katya, saw the still slightly red, but drained boil.

"That was fast." Said Katya, "I never know how long it takes for the mixture to work."

Ivan motioned for the men to sit while Katya got more glasses for the coffee.

A pleased and excited Mato said, "I was trying to sleep on my stomach and side. The morning light was just starting when I felt my pillow and neck were wet." He made a face saying, "It smelled awful."

Katya looked at the drained boil. "Maybe you can dab a little whiskey on it." She was thinking out loud, "It will probably sting, but I think it will heal faster."

Milan removed a loaf of still warm bread and some of Roza's goat cheese from the newspaper he used as wrapping.

"This is to pay the doctor." he said, pleased.

"This is for the doctor, also." said Mato as he produced a bottle of wine.

"Thank you, both." said Katya, affectionately placing a hand on each of their shoulders.

Ivan asked, "What are you doing out so early?"

"Oh, we'd better go." said Milan, realizing they were running out of time. Milan drank his coffee down in one swallow. "We have to meet the train to get our barrels of beer."

As the two men were leaving by the same door they had entered, Milan paused saying "Come again to the tavern, Katya. It was so nice seeing you."

With Mato and Milan gone, Ivan prepared to leave for the furniture store. He said, "That was a nice surprise." Smiling at Katya, he said, "Watching you last night...it reminded me of the first time I saw you. Remember how you put the mixture on Vanjo?"

She laughed at the memory of the skinny musician. "That Vanjo was such a baby." She said, "I thought he was going to cry."

With Ivan gone, Katya sat at the kitchen table for a long while remembering the first time they met at his brother's wedding. Feelings she thought buried were surfacing once more. She remembered how much she enjoyed Ivan's company. How much she wanted to be near him...how handsome he was.

Her thoughts of last night, helping Mato, made her long for the collection of dried herbs she left behind when she escaped Selna. She wished she had them hanging once more where she could reach them, where she could smell them.

Katya went to the long, narrow back porch. She looked at the ceiling envisioning her herb bundles hanging from a strung wire. Where could she find those herbs, would she recognize them, she wondered? More importantly would she still remember what they were used for?

Katya cleared the table and rinsed the dishes before dressing.

A very surprised Ivan, working at his desk, looked up to see Katya walking towards him. It had been three weeks since furniture had been delivered to the house and this was Katya's first visit to the store. Smiling he walked towards her.

"Katya, what a pleasant surprise." he quickly added, "Is something wrong?"

Stevo, from the curtained window in the living quarters, was equally pleased to see her. He smiled as he hurried to his room to change his shirt, which didn't need changing.

Ema Harper, dish towel in hand, did not smile when she looked through the curtain. *So that was why Stevo had a smile and was changing his shirt*...she thought.

Emerging from his room, and just about to go out into the store, Ema said using the derogatory term for Slavic immigrants, "I see the hunkie whore is here."

She never saw the slap coming. For that matter, Stevo was as surprised as Ema, for the slap had been a reflex at the insult to Katya. For a brief moment, he almost apologized. Instead, he only gave her an apologetic look before going out to greet Katya.

Ema, rubbing her stinging cheek, watched Stevo approach Katya and Ivan. For two years she held onto the hope that someday Stevo would marry her. She knew he found other women for entertainment, but Ema thought of herself as the one he always came home to. The jealous hate she felt for Katya consumed her.

"Katya, good morning." said Stevo, "How nice to see you."

"Good morning," she replied, "I hope it is alright that I came to ask Ivan some advice."

"Of course," replied Stevo, starting to move away to give Katya and Ivan privacy.

"Don't go," she said, "perhaps you can help."

Turning back to Ivan, Katya asked, "Remember the night of the Turk, when they brought you to the house after your fall down the hill?" When Ivan nodded, Katya continued, "Remember all the herbs and plants we put on your body to heal the cuts and scratches?"

Ivan laughed at the memory. "I was covered in green slime and you had me drying out in the sun for the whole village to see."

Stevo found this conversation fascinating.

Katya said, "I want to go out and see if I can find some of the herbs and plants here. There must be some wooded places where I can search."

Stevo interrupted, "You can't go into the woods or marshes alone. It might be dangerous."

Ivan added, "It is too difficult for me to walk through woods or uneven ground." He saw the disappointment in her face saying, "This is important to you, isn't it?"

"I want to go search for the healing plants I remember. It is all I have thought about ever since Milan and Mato left this morning."

Seeing Stevo's questioning look, Ivan said, "They came to show us Mato's neck. The boil drained this morning."

"Really?" said Stevo, "That mixture was successful?"

Ignoring Stevo's question, Ivan waived his hand at Katya, saying proudly, "She saved my life. With spider webs she stopped the bleeding." He reached for Katya's hand and said softly, "For that the villagers called her a witch."

Stevo studied Katya. There was so much more to this woman than just her beauty.

Stevo suggested, "Would you go with Bobo in the buggy? With him you would be safe, unless being seen with a black man would make you uncomfortable."

Katya was taken aback by Stevo's comment, "There were many black men on the docks in Trieste and occasionally my Nona had black sailors on her ship."

Seeing the bewildered look on Stevo's face, Ivan said, "Ah yes, our Katya is far more than a peasant girl. Sometime I must tell you how she escaped from a Turk who bought her."

"You're joking." said Stevo, dubious.

"I wish I were." said Ivan grimly, "I got this bad leg the night the Turk found her."

Katya, becoming embarrassed by the turn in the conversation, said, "When can Bobo and I go searching?"

"If you want, you can go now." said Stevo. "Bobo can clean the stalls another day. And he speaks enough Croatian to get by."

Bobo Johnson was a slender and tall black man with a pleasant face and nice dark eyes. He wore his hair short. He was pleased for the change in his daily routine. He liked Katya and searching for herbs and plants was not new to him. His grandmother knew the folk remedies of the South, and as a boy Bobo would go in the woods and help her gather.

From Washington Street, Bobo drove the buggy east across Broadway and Massachusetts Streets to Connecticut Street, where he turned north towards the lake. There were fewer dwellings on the east side of Broadway than on the west side.

More than once, upon seeing wild vegetation, Katya wanted to stop and look, but Bobo always said, "Wait."

Bobo crossed 4th Avenue to where the land, green with plants, all natural and wild, had sprung up from sandy soil. He handed Katya one of the feed sacks he had thought to bring along.

Katya walked through the overgrowth of plants and bushes, not seeing any familiar plants.

"Look here, Mrs.," Bobo pointed to some May apples. "These are powerful. You want these." He walked a bit farther and said, "Here we have some wild ginger and over there, see the red flower? You want that. Indian paintbrush is another powerful medicine."

It wasn't long before both feed sacks were full with joe-pye weed, witch hazel, and some black elderberry.

On the ride back, Bobo described the uses of the plants to Katya.

"Now, that wild ginger is good for an upset stomach, it keeps you from throwing up. And," he held up the pretty Indian paintbrush, "this here is as good as garlic."

At Ivan and Katya's house, Bobo carried the two sacks to the back putting them in the back room. He said, "I know where we can get some chokeberries and dandelions." He smiled, pleased with her company and how excited she was with his knowledge of plants. Just before he left he said, "There's lots of food out there in them woods. I can show you what my granny fed us."

Alone in the storage room, which some called an enclosed back porch, a very pleased Katya set up the old rickety kitchen table left behind by Anka Klarich. On the table she emptied one bag of plants. She picked each one up, studying it and smelling it. She hoped she remembered all that Bobo had told her.

She went out in the unkempt yard, looking for wire or anything to string up as a drying place for her herbs.

CHAPTER 13

Katya heard loud cursing and yelling coming from the street. She saw a boy running towards her, a cloth sack in his hand. Seeing her, he stopped, quickly scanned the area and then scrambled under the three steps at the back of the house to hide.

In those brief seconds, it was as if she could feel his fear. Seeing the boy hiding under the stairs brought back the memory of the fear she felt when she escaped from the Turk in Selna, and hid under a bush on the hillside.

Katya jumped at the sound of a whip crack. She saw a short, stocky man coming along the side of the house. Instead of shoes, he wore boots. His pants were wrinkled, made of brown, heavy cloth as was his shirt. Over the shirt, he wore a black vest and on his head, a wide-brimmed brown hat. As he walked, he coiled the whip and draped it over one shoulder.

His face was fleshy, with mean eyes under bushy brows.

"Ver is he?" roared the red-faced man, glaring at Katya. "He come here...I see him run here."

Katya's use of the English language was limited, but she knew what he said. She feigned a blank look, hunched her shoulders, and spread her hands in an 'I don't understand' gesture.

"Boy...I want boy." He shouted as he pointed to the street where Katya saw a large, wooden farm wagon pulled by two grey horses. In the wagon were three young boys, looking to be fourteen or fifteen years old. "See..." he demanded, "Look...I want boy."

Katya hoped the look on her face was convincingly bewildered. He started to push her aside, immediately thinking better of it. There could be a man or men in the house. He couldn't risk a fight, which could occur if someone came out to defend her.

"Dumme frau" he muttered in German, under his breath...dumb woman! He stood looking around, wanting to search, but not daring to. "Dumme hunkie...dumb hunkie!"

Katya followed him at a distance as he went to his wagon. The boys huddled in the wagon wore the uncertain looks of greenhorns…new to America.

One of the boys, slender and brown haired, smiled at Katya, "Zdravo Gospa. Hello Madam." She waived as the wagon pulled away. Katya was sure the man's yelling was swearing, though she did not understand the words.

Surprised at the Croatian greeting, Katya wondered if the boy under her steps was Croatian.

She waited a while, until she no longer heard the rolling of the wagon wheels. Once sure the man was gone, she went to the steps and said in Croatian, "You can come out now." When the boy didn't move, she said, "He is gone. I can't see the wagon anymore."

Slowly, with a feeling of uncertainty, the young boy, his face and clothes covered in dirt from his hiding place, slipped out from under the stairs. He eyed Katya with suspicion, not sure what the pretty woman was going to do with him.

Katya looked him over. He might be fifteen or sixteen years old and he looked Slavic. His straight, brown hair fell across his forehead over one of his brown eyes. His face was a nice face, a bit thin. His nose was straight and when he smiled shyly, he appeared to have good teeth. Over his homespun white shirt, he wore a jacket too large for his slender build. His brown pants were held in place by a too-large black belt, tied instead of buckled.

"What is your name?" Katya asked.

Standing in front of the stairs, not sure if he should run or stay, he said, "Tomo Mandich."

Katya wondered what was going to happen to the boy. Why did he run away while the other boys didn't?

"Well," she said, "take off your jacket and shake off the dirt. Try to brush off the dirt from your pants. Then we can go inside and you can wash your face and hands."

Ivan's work day had finished, and upon entering the kitchen to his surprise, he saw a young boy at the sink pumping water into a bowl.

Seeing Ivan, Katya, with a fresh towel in her hand, said to him, "Meet our guest, Tomo Mandich."

The boy bowed a greeting, unable to leave the sink to shake Ivan's hand, as his were wet with soap.

Ivan had noticed the bags of plants on the floor and those scattered on the table in the porch. Leaning on his cane, he said, "I see you brought home more than plants."

It took Katya only a second to realize he was referring to Tomo. She smiled at Ivan's remark. Pulling out a chair she said, "Come sit down. I have been gone all day, so I didn't cook anything. We can have bread and cheese and tomatoes. There should be some salami to slice up."

Tomo dried his hands and face and turned from the sink to face Ivan and Katya. He wasn't sure what he was supposed to do next.

Seated at the table, Ivan looked at Katya, his eyebrows raised and his opened palm extended towards Tomo, waiting for an explanation.

Katya pulled out the chair opposite Ivan's. She said to Tomo, "Sit. We can talk while we eat."

Nervous and feeling very uncomfortable under Ivan's gaze, Tomo timidly sat down. He folded his hands in his lap looking around the room so as to avoid Ivan's eyes.

Katya placed the bread and knife in front of Ivan, who with his eyes on Tomo, proceeded to slice the bread. As curious as Ivan was about the boy, he couldn't help but stifle a smile watching Katya trying to be so casual about the stranger. She was behaving like a child who brought home a puppy, and wasn't sure if she could keep it.

Ivan said, "Katya…sit down. Let's talk."

Putting the last of the food on the table, Katya sat.

No one touched the food. Looking at the boy, Ivan said, "Alright. I know your name it Tomo Mandich. That's all I know." First glancing at Katya with the look a father would give a naughty daughter, then looking at the boy, he asked, "Who are you and how is it you are here?"

Katya said quickly, "He was being chased by a big man and hid under our stairs."

Ivan put up his hand to silence her. Turning to Tomo, he said. "Before we eat, tell us where you came from and why someone was chasing you."

"Oh, Ivan!" said an exasperated Katya, putting some bread and cheese on the boy's plate.

Not touching the food Katya gave him, Tomo, his hands still in his lap said, "I come from Selo Sibich outside of Zagreb."

Katya's eyes grew wide. Sibich was not far from where she grew up in Selna. She started to speak, but Ivan put his hand on hers, a signal not to interrupt.

Tomo raised his eyes to meet Ivan's. "A man came and told us we could go to America and it would cost us nothing. He said America needed young strong workers and all I had to do was sign the paper." Here Tomo dropped his eyes, "I don't know how to write my name, so the man told me to put an "X".

To Katya, Ivan said, "Let's open the vino Mato brought. We can all have a glass with our meal. Tomo can tell us more, as we eat."

As Katya went to get the wine, she affectionately ran her hand across Ivan's shoulder. She poured three small juice size glasses with wine and set a glass before each plate.

Tomo was feeling shy. He didn't know these people or what would happen to him. Ivan said, "Eat some of the cheese. Our friend makes it from goat's milk, just like in the Old Country."

The boy was hungry, he hadn't eaten all day and he was a little embarrassed to eat in front of these strangers, in such a nice house. Ivan passed Tomo a slice of the homemade bread from Marko and said, "Put the cheese on it and take some salami."

Tomo did as he was told, trying not to devour the food, eating slowly.

The trio ate with no conversation.

At last, Katya broke the silence, "There were three boys in the wagon. Where is he taking them?"

Tomo swallowed his food, took a sip of wine, and said, "To a place called Crown Point. I couldn't understand him, but one of the other boys told us that the man, Gunder Schmidt, has a farm where we were supposed to work."

"You don't like farm work?" asked Ivan. "Isn't that what you did in the Old Country?"

"When we came to America, we didn't know we were supposed to work for him for two years. When I asked about pay, the boy told us that we got no pay. The pay was our ticket to America and a place to sleep with meals."

Ivan looked to Katya, and then to Tomo. Ivan asked, "Do you know how much your ticket to America cost?"

With a mouthful of salami, Tomo could only shake his head.

To Katya, Ivan said, "The boat passage and the train could not have been more than twenty dollars." Ivan was almost angry when he said, "That man wanted Tomo to work two years for only twenty dollars!"

Both Katya and Ivan looked at Tomo with expressions of compassion.

"I can see why you ran away." said Ivan. "Didn't the man who had you sign the paper tell you where you would be living once you got to America?"

"No, he just said that when we got to America someone would help us find work."

Tomo, finished with his bread and salami, looked at the plate of cheese, reluctant to help himself. Sure that the boy was still hungry, Ivan pushed the plate towards Tomo.

Ivan was rewarded with a grateful smile as the boy reached for another slice.

Katya asked, "Do you know anyone here in America...any relatives?"

"I have no family. Back in Sibich, I was living with an aunt. My mother and father are both dead. That is why I wanted to come to America. I knew my aunt didn't need another mouth to feed. I tried to work, but the farm was poor and we didn't have any cows."

Ivan touched his glass, indicating to Katya for more wine. He looked at Tomo, who shook his head, not wanting any more.

When all the bread and salami were gone and only a few slices of tomato and cheese remained, Katya scooted her chair closer to Ivan.

She took his hand, which to him was a pleasant surprise. She asked, "Where will Tomo stay tonight?"

Ivan gave this some thought and said, "I've been wondering the same. We don't have another bed and the parlor sofa isn't made so that anyone can lay on it."

"I can sleep in a chair," suggested Katya, "and Tomo can sleep with you."

The look Ivan gave Katya totally dismissed that suggestion. Responding to Ivan's dismissive look, she asked, "Where then?"

Tomo was embarrassed and uncomfortable, watching these two people who had taken him in and fed him. Uncertain what to do, he said, "I think I should leave. I can find somewhere to sleep."

Katya demanded, "Where...under some stairs?" She turned to Ivan. "Think of something!"

Ivan took a sip of wine, his eyes on Tomo. He drummed his fingers on the table while deciding what to say. What were only seconds, to Tomo and Katya seemed like minutes. When Ivan spoke he said, "We don't know you...Tell me, can we trust you, a stranger here in our home?"

A little bewildered, Tomo looked first an Ivan and then at Katya. "I don't steal. Even when I was hungry on the boat, I didn't steal food."

Ivan said, "Tonight all we can offer you is the floor. We will make other plans tomorrow, that is, if you think you want to stay awhile."

Katya took Ivan's hand in hers while they waited for Tomo's answer. The boy felt his eyes filling with tears and turned away, so as not to be seen. After all, he was almost a man. Men aren't supposed to cry.

Katya didn't wait for an answer. She stood and started clearing the table, saying, "You can sleep here in the kitchen. For tonight you can use some towels and the table cloth as a pillow."

Realizing the decision had been made, Tomo said, "I have my sack under the steps with some clothes in it. I can use that as a pillow."

CHAPTER 14

Ivan was at the store a little earlier than usual. To his surprise, he found having the boy not at all unpleasant. There was a time he thought he could never share Katya's attention, but now he wasn't so sure. Thinking how he and Katya were so very comfortable with Tomo last night and again, this morning at breakfast, gave Ivan a warm feeling. Could it be contentment he was feeling for the first time since they were married? In fact, it was the first time they both agreed on something so completely.

Ivan walked to a far part of the store and looked at some sleeping cots. He considered a 6-foot canvas one with a hardwood maple frame for $1.75, but another with fabric of woven wire looked sturdier and was only ten cents more.

He decided on the sturdier cot and went back to his work station. He pulled out the book with his and Katya's accounts and listed the bed in the debt column.

Ema, from the living quarters, was spending more time watching Ivan and what went on in the store, than usual. She was hoping she could observe Ivan doing something which would cause Stevo to dismiss him. She hoped that with Ivan gone, Stevo would have no reason to be so friendly with Katya. She frowned when she saw Katya come into the store, accompanied by a rather nice-looking young man.

Ema hoped Katya would be gone before Stevo returned. Earlier, Stevo had taken the Broadway Streetcar to 5th Avenue to make a deposit at the Gary State Bank.

She watched as Ivan led Katya and Tomo to the far wall where the cots were located. He saw them nodding, seemingly agreeing to something. Back at his station, Ivan pulled on a cord located behind his desk which made a bell ring in the yard to summon Bobo.

Bobo smiled broadly when he saw Katya. He had a slightly puzzled look when he saw Tomo. "Hello, Mrs." he said. "Are we going picking again?"

"Not today," said Katya, in Croatian. "Meet our new friend, Tomo."

Tomo took Bobo's extended hand, while staring openly at the black skin.

Ivan led Bobo to the sleeping cot. With Tomo's help, Bobo carried it out to the furniture carriage.

Ema couldn't hear what Katya and Ivan were saying. She saw Katya touch Ivan's cheek and leave.

Ema could see the cot being loaded by Bobo and the boy. *So that was it,* she thought. *When Stevo is away, they help themselves to furniture.*

The housekeeper paced in her small kitchen. She was anxious for Stevo to return so she could tell him about his hunkie whore and his thieving bookkeeper. Jealousy was changing Ema's personality from fairly pleasing to dark and ugly.

Bobo had returned from the cot delivery and was back at work when Stevo came into the yard. Ema saw Bobo and Stevo have a brief conversation.

As Stevo walked in the room, Ema, with her hands on her hips, said smugly, "Well, while you were away your bookkeeper helped himself to some merchandise."

With a questioning look, saying nothing, Stevo entered the door that led from the kitchen into the store.

"Good morning, Ivan." He greeted. "Bobo tells me you bought a cot. Wouldn't a bed be better?"

"We have a young man...well, really a boy, not quite a man, staying with us. The cot will be fine." said Ivan, handing the ledger with the page showing his and Katya's accounts on it. The last entry in the debt column was $1.85, the cost of the cot.

Stevo was lost in thought over the accusation made by Ema. He tapped his finger on the page, thinking. He said abruptly, "I forgot something."

Back in the kitchen he saw Ema sitting at the table drinking a cup of tea. She had a pleased look on her face. She was sure that Stevo no longer thought Ivan such a wonderful employee. Her pleased look changed when she noticed Stevo's dark look.

"What's the matter?" Her voice was thin. "Why are you looking at me like that?"

Standing over her, he said in a low, controlled voice so that Ivan could not hear, "What the hell is wrong with you woman? I have a business to run. You are trying to make trouble for me with the best employee I have ever had."

She only stared at him, not knowing what to say.

He went on, "The cost of the cot is entered into the ledger. You want me to think Ivan is a thief? How dare you?" Now his voice was shaking with anger, "I took you in when your husband was killed in the mills. I gave you work and a place to live and you repay me with lies."

Stevo stalked out the back door, going out into the yard. He had to get away from her. He wanted to hit her.

Alone in the kitchen, her hands trembling, Ema was afraid. Stevo wasn't a mean man. She was sure he wouldn't beat her, but worse, he could send her away. The thought never occurred to her before, but now…it could happen. She buried her face in her hands. She had to think. First, she would beg his forgiveness…make some excuse. She would tell him it looked as if Ivan was stealing. Yes…yes…then she would promise never to say another word about Katya.

Ema was determined to make everything right again with Stevo. She would start by changing the sheets on his bed. He liked fresh sheets. Then, she would straighten his room. He didn't like her going into his room when he wasn't in there, but she wouldn't be there long, just enough time to change the sheets and pillowcases and dust a little.

From a linen closet at the far end of the kitchen, Ema pulled out the necessary bedding. With a firm resolve that she could make everything alright again, she walked straight into his neat, uncluttered room. It was part sleeping quarters and part office space. Before reaching the bed, her foot felt something uneven on the floor. Placing the sheets on the bed, she looked at the rug where she had felt something unusual. Bending down, running her hand over the colorful Oriental rug, she felt the bump. Raising the carpet edge, Ema saw a loose floor board. She had never noticed that bump before. Meaning to push the board level once more, she first needed to lift it. She pulled up the board...that was when she saw it...a Cheroots Cigar Box.

It was a fun evening for everyone at Milan's that night. Again the reason for the gathering was to plan the new Croatian Catholic Church.

Ivan was in very high spirits. He had been chosen as the bookkeeper, which so far did not include any money, just the listing of pledges made in a ledger.

Once again, Stevo drove them in his buggy. This time Tomo sat in the middle and to Ivan's great pleasure, Katya, dressed in the white dress with flower appliqués, sat on his lap.

Stevo liked Tomo. He liked the boy a lot. Perhaps it was that Tomo reminded him of himself at that age, when Stevo was in New Orleans. But, Stevo had his father, while Tomo had no one. Well, he thought, perhaps Tomo had Katya and Ivan and possibly himself. He heard the story of how Tomo was given free passage to America with a signed contract making him an indentured servant. Stevo wondered how many boys and men were tricked into such a scheme.

At Milan's it seemed that everyone wanted to meet Tomo. Where did he come from? Maybe he knew someone they knew back home. Who came with him? Was he alone? On and on the questions came, making him the center of attention.

To Tomo's dismay, Katya kept sending back all the beers and glasses of slivovica bought for him by the older men, remembering how much they enjoyed getting drunk when his age.

Because of the success curing Mato's painful boil, several men stopped to ask Katya if she had any cures for rashes and other ailments.

The smoke filled room smelled of beer and sweat. Roza kept her distance from Katya when she moved about wiping tables or mopping spilt beer from the floor. As usual, there were musicians in the back playing their prims and braches.

Tomo found himself watching with great interest the tamburitzans and listening to their music. He excused himself and moved closer to the back of the bar to better hear it. Tapping his foot, he heard a familiar song, CHUJES MALA…Listen Little Girl. He started to sing the familiar words softly. The men playing the instruments looked at him pleased…at last someone with a good singing voice.

One of the men said, "Sing louder." Embarrassed, Tomo stopped singing. "Come on, Dechko, Boy…Sing!"

They continued with the song and Tomo timidly started singing. There were encouraging shouts and even some applause. When the song was finished, the room burst into shouts and more applause. Without a pause the next song was RAZBILA SE CHASHA, The Glass Is Broken, and Tomo never skipped a beat, singing this drinking song to the pleasure of the boisterous crowd.

The fun-filled evening at an end, and after dropping off Ivan, Katya and Tomo, Stevo entered his living quarters, humming Razbila Se Chasha. He was in an excellent mood. What a great night, he thought, so much good company with singing and even some kolo dancing when the tables were pushed aside.

There was no light over the kitchen table. Usually when Stevo was out for the evening, Ema would leave on a low light for him. With the moonlight shining through the kitchen window, Stevo felt for the light switch.

He glanced at Ema's cot in the far corner of the kitchen. It was empty. This was the first time he came home to see the cot empty.

"Ema…" No response. He called again, "Ema, where are you?"

He looked around. The unusual stillness was unnerving.

In his room, he had to use the hanging pull chain to turn on the overhead light.

The surprise of seeing the rug pulled aside and the board lifted up was as if he had been struck a blow. He fell to his knees and looked into the empty hiding place. IT WAS GONE! The Cheroots box with money was gone!

CHAPTER 15

Ema had accused Ivan of stealing a $1.85 cot, and then took the box with Stevo's fortune.

Where could she go? Where could she hide from him? How much of a head start did she have? Thoughts crowded one another in his head.

He called aloud, Bobo's name, as he ran towards the barn where the man slept. Inside, he shook the sleeping man, "When did Ema leave?"

Bobo sat up, not fully awake. "Who? What you talking about?"

"Ema! When did Ema leave?" Stevo was shaking the man to waken him fully.

Bobo sat up, rubbing the sleep from his eyes. Now awake, he said, "I didn't see her leave. But the light was on till about 9 o'clock. I was surprised to see the house dark."

It was now eleven. Stevo decided she must have gone two hours ago.

To Bobo he said, "Get the buggy. We are going into town…now. Hurry and let me know when you are ready."

Stevo ran back to the kitchen. He pulled open a cabinet door and reached for the brandy. He uncorked the bottle and took a swig. Putting the bottle down, he pressed his hands to his face trying to calm himself. He had to think…think like a woman running away. She wouldn't stay in Gary, he was sure of that. He would find her sooner or later.

Going into his dark store from the kitchen, he found the phone which was on a shelf cut into the wall. The first call he made was to the Chicago, Lake Shore & Eastern Railroad located on 2nd Avenue and Broadway.

"When is the next train to Chicago?" He asked, aware that his voice sounded hoarse.

"Not till tomorrow morning," the voice on the other end replied, "six in the morning."

Stevo thought about this. She had to stay in a hotel until morning. He went through the city guide, reading the names of the hotels on Broadway. Gary Hotel, 6th Ave; West Hotel, 7th Ave; New World Hotel, 11th Ave; Marine Hotel, 9th Ave.

He started with the one closest to the train station. When the night clerk answered the phone at the Gary Hotel, Stevo said, "This is Steve Markovich." He was known as Stevo only in the Patch. "I am going to describe a woman and I would be most appreciative if you could tell me if she checked in there, probably after nine tonight."

John, the night manager, knew who Steve Markovich was and told him, "Yes, a woman of that description checked in, and is here on the 4th floor."

"Thank you, John." said Stevo, "I am on my way. Please be available to go to her room with me."

John, the night clerk, medium build, neatly dressed in a blue suit, blue tie, smiled when he saw Stevo enter the hotel lobby. John was young, smooth-skinned, blond, and blue-eyed, probably of Scandinavian descent.

As Stevo shook the clerk's hand, he slipped John some paper money. Smiling, John said, "Here is the key. She is in room 402."

Stevo said, "Come with me. I want you to remain outside the room."

John nodded. He secretly hoped this encounter would not end up in such a manner that the reputation of the hotel would suffer.

Once at the door of room 402, Stevo, with a nod of his head, indicated that John knock on the door.

"Who's there?" Ema's voice sounded wary.

"Miss, it is the night clerk, John. May I come in?"

"What do you want?"

"I need you to sign the registration card. I know you signed the book, but I also need you to sign the card for our files." he lied.

When she opened the door, Stevo whispered his earlier instructions to John, "Wait out here. Do not leave."

Ema's face went white. She never thought he would find her, or for that matter, that he would look for her. She should have known better. There was a lot of money in the Cheroots box.

In the clean room were a bed, a chair, and a small, mirrored chest for clothes. A kerosene lamp converted to electric, glowed on the dresser.

Stevo pushed her into the chair. She was dressed in a long, yellow crepe dress. She was so frightened that her weak knees let her collapse into the chair.

"What are you going to do to me?" her voice broke. "I promise I will never run away again." Her eyes full of fear, she pointed to her cloth travel bag. "The cigar box is in there."

When Stevo said nothing and made no move to get the cigar box, she said, "I'm sorry. I thought you were going to turn me out." With some optimism she said, "You are here for me. You want me back."

Stevo sat on the bed across from the frightened woman. He studied her for a long time before speaking. "What made you think you could speak to me about Katya the way you did? And…why did you want to lie about Ivan?"

Tears welled in her eyes. "Because I thought we belonged to one another, you and me."

Seeing the surprised look on Stevo's face, she said, "We were as good as married. I kept waiting for you to marry me."

Stevo's jaw dropped. He said, "Why would you think we would marry. You were my housekeeper, nothing more."

When Ema heard those words, the tears rolled down her cheeks. She said in between sobs, "I was a wife to you. I did everything for you. I went nowhere. We made love when you wanted."

Her last sentence hit Stevo like a stone. *Did she think those nighttime visits meant love?*

"Ema…," Stevo wasn't sure how to express his thoughts. "When a man sleeps with a woman, it doesn't always mean love." He cleared his throat. "I'm sorry if you thought we had anything more than an employer/employee relationship, but that is all that it was."

She was crying, "I love you. Isn't it enough that I love you?" Her face was red and tear stained.

Stevo stood, reaching for her cloth travel bag. He took out the Cheroots cigar box, opening it. "How much did you take out of here?" he asked.

She pointed to her purse, "I don't know." She wiped her eyes with her sleeve, "I just took a handful." Quickly she said, "Some of the money is what I saved from my salary."

Stevo dumped her purse out on the bed. He riffled through the contents. Left what he thought was her money and put the rest back in the Cheroots box.

Ema stood, thinking she was going back with Stevo. He studied her for a long moment. He opened the cigar box and took out several paper bills. He dropped them on the bed.

"Goodbye, Ema." He said, walking out the door and out of her life, leaving the bewildered woman standing alone.

There was no conversation on the buggy ride back to the store. Bobo didn't ask about Ema, but he was very curious. From time to time, he glanced at Stevo, who stared straight ahead. The look on Stevo's face disturbed Bobo. He liked Stevo. He worked for him from the time Stevo came to Gary. Now, for the first time, he worried about his boss.

Bobo got out of the buggy and opened the gate. Before he could climb into the rig to drive the buggy in, Stevo had already done so.

Stevo climbed down without a word, glanced up at the moonlit sky, and turned to go into the kitchen.

"Goodnight." said Bobo, watching his boss slowly walk away.

Stevo, his back to Bobo, said, "I need a new housekeeper." Then he added, "Find me one that doesn't live in. Just to cook and do some cleaning."

Bobo asked, "Does she have to be white?"

"No." said Stevo, going into his dark kitchen.

CHAPTER 16

At breakfast, Ivan and Katya were having their usual bread sprinkled with sugar and coffee, half with hot milk.

They were feeling contented. Last night was such a pleasant evening at Milan's and Tomo was such a joy to be with. It turned out that Tomo was the star of the evening with his singing and dancing the kolo.

Ivan asked, "Where is the boy? Still sleeping?"

Katya laughed pleasantly, "He is in the yard, digging up a space for a garden."

Ivan went to the back door. "Look at him." he said. "The boy is really strong. Come, Katya, come and see how much of the yard he has already cleared."

At Ivan's side she said, "I like him. I hope he stays."

Ivan turned to face her. "Why do you want him to stay?" His tone was thoughtful.

She thought a moment and said, "Because I want to be needed and I want to love someone."

The words stabbed at Ivan's heart. He looked into her green eyes. "Oh, Katya," he said broken hearted, "Can't you love me? Can't you see how much I need you?" He emphasized the word 'I'.

Later, with Ivan gone to work, and Tomo digging in the yard, Katya sat at the kitchen table deep in thought. Ivan's words kept running through her mind. 'Can't you love me?' She did love him. Yes, she decided, she did love Ivan. She no longer felt any anger at the past events of her life. Awakened in her was the realization that she could no longer blame Ivan as the reason they were in America. It no longer mattered that the Gypsies had wanted to harm him. Destiny meant for them to be in America. Most of all…when was the last time she thought of Zolton?

What Katya and Ivan had was a comfortable, trusting relationship. In their history was the passion of their youth…perhaps some of that was still somewhere deep within them both.

A knock at the back door brought her out of her reverie. She was surprised to see Dr. Costa standing on her steps. She opened the door, "Come in," she said in Italian.

From the yard, seeing the stranger, Tomo stopped digging and came to the foot of the steps to see what was going on.

Dr. Costa stepped inside the doorway onto the porch, but did not go any further.

"What can I do for you?" asked Katya.

"For one thing," he said in the gruff manner she remembered, "You can stop playing doctor."

Seeing the perplexed look on Katya's face, he said, "I have patients wanting your witches' brew to cure boils."

Katya burst out laughing. "Is that what this is all about? I thought you wanted me to work for you."

Ignoring her remark, he continued in his fast and gruff manner, "I lance boils. That is what I do. Now…what the hell is the potion people ask for?"

Tomo moved closer to the porch. He did not understand Italian, but was concerned by the man's loud and insistent voice.

"I will tell you," said Katya smugly, "for five dollars."

Dr. Costa's face turned red. "Are you crazy? Why would I pay you that much money? You told me you didn't go to school."

The angry doctor turned, stomped down the stairs, and swore in Italian as he disappeared.

Katya started to explain to the concerned Tomo what the doctor wanted. Before she finished talking, Dr. Costa once again appeared at the steps. "I will give you two dollars. Not a dollar more!"

Katya held out her hand onto which he placed two one-dollar bills, which she then tucked into the front of her blouse.

"You take a bar of lye soap," she said, "scrape it with a knife and add a few drops of warm water to make a paste. Then you add some salt a little bit of vinegar."

Dr. Costa's face was almost purple with rage. "Are you crazy?" He was yelling. "I paid you two dollars for that witches brew? You are a thief!"

Tomo, with shovel in hand, stepped in between the doctor and Katya. Dr. Costa moved back, fearing an attack, and changed his mind about demanding the return of the money.

"Ladra dannazione…damn thief." He shouted as he practically ran to the street.

Tomo went back to his digging, still a little unsure of what he had just witnessed.

Katya cleared the dishes, straightened up the kitchen, made the bed, and then combed her hair. She twisted the back into a bun. For the first time in her life, she tied a scarf over her hair, knotting it at the back of her neck. The white scarf only emphasized the beauty of her face.

She called out to Tomo. "Leave the digging for later. Come in and wash up. We are going to the store."

For a moment, Ivan didn't recognize Katya with her head covered as she entered the furniture store. He gave her a wide smile as he came closer. "What's this?" he asked, meaning the scarf.

Tomo had stopped at the door and was admiring some lamps with crystal prisms.

"I think I feel like a woman now and not so much a girl." she said with a smile.

Ivan took her hand in his, "You will always be that girl with the wild hair I met in Vladezemla."

She smiled at the remark. It pleased her.

"So," said Ivan, "What brings you here?"

"I came to show you the money I earned today." From her blouse she pulled the two paper dollars.

Seeing Ivan's surprised look made her laugh out loud. The laughter brought Tomo to Ivan's desk.

A stunned Ivan said, "Katya…where did you get that money?"

Ivan dragged her name out in a suspicious tone, "Katyaaaa."

Tomo blurted out, "She sold her boil potion."

"What?" Ivan was almost speechless. "No…you are making this up!"

Tomo went on, "A little angry man wouldn't pay five dollars but did pay two." Tomo added, "He was really mad when Katya told him how to make it."

"Is this true?" Ivan looked at Katya.

"Yes, it is. Dr. Costa heard about the mixture and asked me how it is made." she said.

Ivan shook his head in wonder saying, "You got paid nearly the amount I have to work a week to earn." He burst out laughing, "What other remedies can you sell?"

Ivan gave Katya a loving smile. "You never cease to amaze me."

"We will see you at home." said Katya, "We are going shopping." She waggled the two dollars in the air.

Katya and Tomo walked several blocks to 22nd and Jefferson to the Olympus store. This grocery store was Greek owned and had a large selection of foods. The store smelled wonderful. The mixed aromas of cheeses, sausages, and baked goods were intoxicating to Tomo. Here were foods he did not recognize.

Katya didn't speak Greek, so she would point to what she wanted or gesticulate with her hands when she wanted to taste something. She would hold up her two dollars to show Gus how much she had. He enjoyed watching the two excited Croatians while they tasted and shopped.

When her purchases reached the two-dollar amount, Gus shook his head, meaning they were all done. Then, smiling at the two crazy Croatians, he wrapped in newspaper a free hunk of feta cheese.

Having spent all of the two dollars, they had so much to carry, that Gus, the store owner, gave her some knotted mesh bags with which to carry all their purchases.

Ivan came home to the tantalizing aromas of kishka...blood sausage, spanikopita...spinach pie, stuffed grape leaves, assorted cheeses, olives, potatoes, and more. There was enough food for more than this one meal.

The table was set and the food laid out. Tomo and Katya were very pleased with the assortment on the table.

Ivan smiled, shaking his head at the display. He said, "This could be a wedding feast. The only thing missing is the roasted lamb."

Katya sat across from Ivan, while Tomo opened a bottle of wine.

Tomo, pouring the wine said, "I never saw such food, so many cheeses, and the olives, who knew how many kinds of olives there are."

Throughout the meal, Katya, Tomo, and Ivan laughed and talked about the day. Ivan mentioned that he did not see Ema and that Stevo had been unusually quiet. Tomo told Ivan how he and Katya carried home the purchases in mesh bags. He even jumped up to find one to show Ivan.

Ivan saw the glow in Katya's eyes. It was the excited look he remembered the first time he saw her, sitting across from him at his brother's wedding feast, five years ago.

Katya started to clear the plates, but Tomo motioned for her to stay seated. He put the dishes in the sink, and disappeared to the ice box behind them. When he returned, he had three plates of a delicious Greek dessert.

Ivan eyed the honey-soaked pastry. He picked up his plate, smelling the dessert.

"What is this? It doesn't look like strudel." he said, making a joke.

In unison, Tomo and Katya said, "It is baklava!"

They all agreed the honey dessert was something amazing.

At Olympus, Tomo did not see Katya pick up three rather plain demitasse cups. She would have preferred the ones with the fancy gold trim, but knew they would cost more. Also, she bought a small amount of Greek coffee.

Not since coffee on the terrace in Trieste had Ivan enjoyed an espresso. Now, proudly Katya placed her substitute for espresso before the three of them.

"Katya...oh, Katya," It was all that Ivan could say, he was almost speechless.

Tomo's eyes danced with excitement. He watched the way Ivan picked up the demitasse cup and did the same. Tomo said enthusiastically, "I LOVE America! Look at how we are eating. A king must eat like this!"

Katya and Ivan burst out laughing at Tomo's joy.

Katya said, "In another day or so, we will be back to beans and sauerkraut. This was just for today."

That night, a contented Ivan and Katya lay in bed, thinking over the events of the day, and the fabulous evening meal.

Crowding into Katya's thoughts were the words Ivan had spoken earlier in the day to her. *'Can't you love me?'*

For the first time since they were married in Trieste, on Lucia's terrace, Katya moved closer to Ivan. She asked softly, "Are you asleep?"

"No." he said, "Is something wrong?"

Katya pressed her body against his, her arm across his chest, her warm breath on his neck.

His heart pounding, Ivan asked, "Do you know what you are doing? Do you know what could happen?"

She didn't answer, only ran her hand across his body.

He thought his heart would burst, but then…that wasn't all that would burst this night.

CHAPTER 17

At the store, Ivan noticed that he had not seen Ema for the past three days. Stevo did not mention her and Ivan felt that, if and when, Stevo wanted to say something about her absence, he would.

It was August. The air was warm and stuffy in the store. The door to the kitchen was opened in the hopes that the air from the back door of the living quarters would bring in a breeze. Also, the double doors of the store were opened wide.

In his rolled up shirt sleeves, Ivan watched as a workman strung electrical wire against the wall. Another man, walking alongside, attached the wire to the wall with U-shaped tacks.

Ivan was so interested in the workmen that he didn't hear Stevo behind him.

Stevo explained, "I am having some electric wall fans installed, should have done it sooner." Looking at Ivan he said, "You look quite well, relaxed, and happier."

Ivan replied smiling, thinking of his renewed love life, "Yes, things are going well."

"Good," said Stevo.

Looking at the workmen, both slender and dark haired, possibly brothers, he said, "When they are done, send them back into the house. I need a fan in there."

Ivan pushed aside his books and walked out onto the floor of the store. He needed to stretch his legs a bit. Sitting any length of time made his bad leg stiff. With his cane in his hand, he stood before one of the large windows and looked at the activity on the street. Ivan moved to the open doors where he heard the sounds of a loud motor. He noticed people on the street had stopped walking and were looking at something which Ivan could not yet see.

Approaching and throwing up dust was a Ford 1912 Model T automobile. It looked like a fancy, motorized carriage. It had no cover and no doors. Some children, having never seen an auto, were running behind the tin lizzie cheering.

Also hearing the commotion, Stevo came from his living quarters to the open doors. Standing alongside Ivan, Stevo said, "I suppose I should get one of those. Henry Ford claims that soon everyone will be able to afford one of his automobiles."

Ivan said, "It may be awhile before I can even think of having one."

"By the way, how is Katya?" asked Stevo. "And Tomo…is he still with you?"

The warm expression on Ivan's face made Stevo envious. Ivan said, "We are a happy little family."

At the house, Tomo, working in the hot sun, wondered if he could make a wired section in the yard for chickens. He was bare to the waist, his lean strong body glistening from perspiration.

Katya was seated at the kitchen table, with a pile of mending before her, all of it needing attention.

She was so very satisfied. In the past three days, she felt a happiness and contentment she never before had. Katya chastised herself for wasting the past year blaming Ivan for what Destiny had done to her. She wondered why she had not felt this complete love for Ivan sooner. What she felt now was even better than what she had felt when they were young and first in love. Each evening, knowing Ivan would soon be home, filled her with excitement.

She and Ivan, lying in each other's arms at night, would talk about their plans for the future. They talked about Tomo, and how it was as if he were a younger brother, someone they could care for and help.

Katya would fall asleep, wrapped in the glow of love and the prospect of a wonderful future in America.

A commotion at the back door drew her attention. She rose from the chair seeing a white faced Tomo, holding open the door. She grabbed the table top for support when she saw Bobo carrying Ivan in his arms. Behind him was Stevo with Ivan's cane in his hand.

Tomo said, "Take him to the bedroom, this way."

Bobo knew where the bedroom was, having helped bring in most of the furniture.

They all followed Bobo and watched him put Ivan on the bed.

"Katya was beside herself with shock and worry. "What happened? Did you call a doctor…never mind let me look at him."

She bent over Ivan and took his hand, ready to assess his injuries. She touched his cheek then took his hand in hers…feeling his lifeless limb, she fainted.

Stevo caught Katya before she fell to the floor. He carefully picked her up in his arms taking her to the front room where he gently placed her on the parlor sofa.

Tomo ran to the kitchen for some water while Bobo kept repeating, "Poor Mrs. Katya…poor Mrs. Katya."

It was all Stevo could do to keep from wrapping his arms around her and hold her. He wanted so very much to hold her, to rock her in his arms…to comfort her.

Stevo tried to get Katya to take a sip of the water, but she did not respond. Tomo returned to the kitchen for a damp cloth.

Wiping her face with the cool cloth revived her. She stared at the three worried men looking down at her. Confusion gave way to realty and she struggled to get up.

Stevo gently pushed her shoulder to keep her on the sofa, but she struggled, finally standing. The three watched her as she, somewhat unsteadily, walked to the bedroom. There she took the only straight backed chair in the room and pushed it to the bedside. Sitting down, she took Ivan's cold hand.

Bobo was muttering, "Oh, Jesus." while Stevo and Tomo were disturbed that Katya was not crying. She sat calmly, staring at Ivan.

Stevo knelt beside Katya. "Katya," he said, "Katya, do you hear me? Say something."

Tomo knelt on the other side of her, "Draga, Dear Katya…please, Katya, look at me."

"Oh, Dear Jesus…" prayed Bobo.

Stevo touched Katya's shoulder getting no response. Still no tears, her gaze fixed on Ivan's face.

Stevo said to Bobo, "Stay with her for now. You and I will have to go to the store and make preparations." Because Katya could hear, he didn't say 'for the funeral', but that was what he meant. He said, "Tomo and I are going to talk in the kitchen."

In the kitchen, where Katya would not hear them, Stevo said, "You cannot leave her for a moment. Her behavior is not natural." Looking intently into Tomo's eyes, he asked, "Do you think she could harm herself?"

"My God," whispered Tomo, "We need to get a woman to help us. I don't know if I can watch her every hour." The young man glanced back towards the bedroom, "Why isn't she crying? She should be wailing, crying...something, anything, not this silence."

Stevo put a comforting arm on Tomo's shoulder, "I think she is in shock. Her mind hasn't grasped that he is gone." He let out a long loud sigh, "I am very worried."

At the locked store, with a closed sign on the door and the electricians sent away with plans to return another day, Stevo looked up a number and phoned Grace Adams.

"This is Steve Markovich," he said when she answered.

"Well, this is a surprise," was the pleasant reply. "Now, you know I don't tailor men's clothes."

"I know...I want a mourning dress for a friend." he said.

"Fine," she replied, "have her come in this afternoon and I will see what we can do."

"She can't come to you." Stevo was firm, "You need to see her in her home."

"Well, alright." said, Grace. "I can do that."

He gave Grace Adams Katya's address. After a long pause, Grace said, "Listen, Steve, you know I don't do business in the Patch. My clients are all on the north side of Gary."

Steve and the fashionable seamstress had been to dinner a few times and once went together to an event held in the Gary Hotel.

"You said you were free this afternoon." said Stevo. "I will send my man out to get you and I will pay whatever you want."

He waited for a reply...when there was none, he repeated, "Grace, I will pay you whatever you want. This is very important to me. In fact, you don't have to design anything special. Bring something you have that is black and make it fit her."

Grace said, "Alright Steve. I have the address and I can be there by one. Don't send your driver."

Milan was at the house when Stevo and Bobo arrived with the casket. Someone had come into the tavern with the sad news and word was spreading. Milan had never seen anyone in the state that Katya was in. It was as if she did not recognize him and it disturbed him.

When Grace Adams arrived at the house, Stevo and Bobo were already there re-arranging the furniture making room for the visitation, which could come possibly as soon as that evening.

Katya had watched with a dull look as Bobo and Stevo carried Ivan's body out of the bedroom and placed him in a wooden casket, lined with white tufted satin. The two men had changed his clothes and prepared him, while Katya looked on as if she did not see.

Grace was a young slender woman, light brown hair, hazel eyes, a pretty face, and sought after by several of the businessmen in Gary. She would be a valuable asset to any man, but she didn't appear to be interested in any of her suitors.

Grace entered the house her arms full of fabric and skirts, with more in her carriage. Her eyes grew wide when she saw a young man and a larger one, holding a beautiful woman under her arms, and practically carrying her. Milan and Tomo had a hard time getting Katya to let go of Ivan's hand. Still, Katya said nothing, nor seemed to understand what was going on.

"Let's go in the kitchen." said Grace, worried that Katya might react to the room where Ivan had been laying.

Katya was led into the kitchen. She stood looking straight ahead.

Grace went into the front room and asked Stevo, "Steve…is this woman alright in the head? Do I have to worry about her getting violent?"

"My God, no…" Stevo was taken aback by the question. "She is a lovely person. It is the shock of her husband's death. She hasn't shown any emotion from the moment we brought him in."

Grace gave Stevo a questioning look. "Don't leave me alone with her. Stay with me." she said. "Frankly, Steve," she added, "had I known of her condition, I would not have come."

Normally, Grace would have done some measuring, fitted the garments, adjusting here and there. Instead, she held the black blouse and skirt she brought up to Katya who stood still, showing no emotion. Satisfied that the two pieces she had would fit Katya, Grace said, "Well, how do I get these on her? She obviously can't or won't dress herself."

Stevo knew he couldn't help undress Katya. "Tomo, come in here." He called to the boy. "Please help Miss Grace get Katya in these clothes."

Tomo had a look of surprise at the request, "It isn't right that I undress her." he said.

Grace said to Tomo, "Well then, close your eyes and just help me. I will tell you what to do. I can't do this myself." She was running out of patience and she wanted to leave because she feared some unpleasant reaction from Katya.

When Grace was finished with dressing Katya, Milan, Bobo, and Stevo watched as Tomo led Katya, dressed in a long, plain black skirt with a black, lace-collared blouse, to a chair near the casket.

Katya sat and reached into the casket, resting her hand on Ivan's hand in which a rosary had been placed by Stevo.

Grace took Stevo by the sleeve and pulled him back to the kitchen where they could be alone. Hands on her hips, she gave him a stern look. "What are you doing with Gypsies?" she demanded. "You know they are trouble. Further more, how dare you get me involved?"

Taken aback, Stevo said, "Gypsies...what are you talking about?"

"Her bracelet," said Grace, "it is a valuable Gypsy bracelet."

Stevo stammered, "I have never seen such a bracelet."

Grace gathered up her box of supplies. "I will send you my bill. Oh, yes, the bracelet is on her left wrist under the sleeve."

With Grace Adams gone, Stevo and Milan sat in the kitchen. Seeing a bottle of wine, Stevo poured each of them a glass.

"Milan, can you stay a while longer?" asked Stevo. "Just long enough for me to call a priest and make arrangements for the burial. We need to bury him as soon as possible."

Milan drank his wine in one swallow. "Sure, I can stay. But, I am worried about Katya. He put his glass down, "Tomo told me that Ivan was hit by a car. Is that true?"

Stevo shook his head as if to make the memory disappear. "We were watching a Ford coming down the street. Children were running after it. Then," here he paused, "a child started to run into the street ahead of it. Ivan went to stop the boy, his cane touched a rock, and he lost his balance. My God...he fell right in front of the car. The child...made it safely across the street."

"Sveti Issus...Holy Jesus." said Milan softly.

Stevo never worked as diligently or quickly on a funeral as he did for Ivan's. A priest from the Slovene parish of St. George from Chicago happened to be visiting in Gary to help promote funds for priests coming from the Old Country. Stevo was able to get the priest to agree to come and say the rosary for the visitation and to perform the graveside funeral ceremony at the Tolleston Cemetery. The priest, not being from Gary, had never thought to ask if the burial would be in a Catholic cemetery.

The last call Stevo made was to the cemetery, getting promises that the funeral could take place the next day no sooner than two in the afternoon. Bobo was sent to 25th and Grant Street with money to guarantee the gravesite would be ready.

Stevo would deal with the death certificates later. Due to the warm August days and Katya's condition, he needed to bury Ivan as quickly as possible.

CHAPTER 18

Not many people came to the house to pay their respects. No notice was posted, so many did not know of Ivan's passing. The priest tried to comfort Katya, but it was as if she did not hear or see him. While he led the Rosary, Katya did not leave her vigil at the coffin. There were whispers among those in the house that she had lost her mind.

Usually at these visitations, people mingle, offer condolences to the widow, and say nice things about the deceased.

As soon as the praying of the rosary was completed, most of those attending were gone, even Father Badrich.

Roza had come, and seeing Katya in her state, bewildered her. She did not try to speak to Katya.

When she left, Milan and Mato stayed behind. Tomo sat in the front room, watching Katya, his heart close to breaking. Not only was Ivan gone, but Katya, for all purposes, was also gone.

Again in the kitchen, Milan, brother Mato and Stevo sat at the table, sharing the slivovica Milan had brought.

Milan said, "I didn't hear you announce when the burial will take place."

"It will be tomorrow at two o'clock in Tolleston." said Stevo. "I don't want a crowd." Looking through the doorway to where Katya sat, he said, "I am worried about her. People are already whispering that she is not normal...that she has lost her mind. I was hoping that only we who were the closest to Ivan would be at the burial."

Mato remembered the first time he met Ivan and Katya on the train from Lakawanna. They were his first friends in America.

Finishing the drink, he said, "I will go watch Katya so Tomo can come and talk with you. I don't think he has left her for a moment."

Entering the kitchen, looking very tired and bleary eyed, Tomo sat with the two men. Stevo poured him a slivovica. Both men noticed Tomo's hand trembled as he put the glass to his lips.

Seeing both men looking at him, Tomo said, "I am scared. How can I stay here and care for Katya? I want to stay with her, but I don't know what to do. How can I help her?" He broke down and cried.

Milan put his hand on Tomo's shoulder. "I know, I know, son...we are all wondering the same. Try and get some sleep. I will sit with Katya tonight."

Seated in one of the plush side chairs, Milan, during the night, occasionally nodded off. Whenever he opened his eyes, Katya was sitting in the chair beside the coffin, her hand on Ivan's.

Bobo drove the furniture truck/hearse with the sides covered in black fabric trimmed with gold tassels. Tomo rode with Bobo.

In the surrey sat Father Badrich, Stevo, Katya, Milan, and Mato.

It was a short ride to 25th and Grant from 18th and Washington. Approaching the cemetery, Stevo could see the workers standing near an open grave. Leather straps for lowering the casket were already in place.

The priest led the way, praying from his prayer book and swinging the brass incense burner as he walked toward the grave.

Milan, Mato, Bobo, and Tomo were the pall bearers, carrying the casket.

Katya balked when she saw the grave. She stopped walking, but Stevo gently guided her forward. He could feel her try to twist away. As he held her, he was hoping he wasn't hurting her arm.

The casket was placed on the straps. Katya kept trying to pull away from Stevo. Everyone but the priest was aware of the change in her. From being almost catatonic the day before, she was now struggling with Stevo, who was afraid to let her get free of his grasp.

With the graveside service completed, Father Badrich made the sign of the cross. Milan and Mato each picked up some loose earth, placing it on the casket. Tomo and Bobo did the same. The cemetery workmen started to unroll the leather straps, lowering the casket into the grave.

Katya screamed and flung herself toward the descending box where her beloved Ivan was encased. Milan and Stevo both grabbed Katya, pulling her to safety. She fell to her knees...sobbing...at last!

Stevo, with the priest in the front seat of the surrey, occasionally glanced back at Milan holding the sobbing Katya in his arms. The front of Milan's shirt was wet from her tears. Father Badrich was paid and deposited at the home where he was visiting.

Mato moved to the front seat next to Stevo. He asked, "Is it good that she is crying?"

"I think so," said Stevo, "at least it is normal. I have to tell you, I was worried about her, very worried."

Milan was not so much older than Katya, but whatever fatherly instincts were within him, were directed to this crying woman. He wanted to...he needed to protect her.

Tomo waited at the house, having been dropped off earlier by Bobo driving the hearse.

Milan carried the sobbing Katya in his arms, into the house to the bedroom. He gently placed her on the bed. Still crying, she turned her face to the wall. Milan looked down at her with great sadness. He slipped off her shoes and left the room.

The men agreed Katya no longer needed someone sitting with her constantly. Hearing her sobs relieved them of their fears. Now, in time, they felt she would be alright.

Tomo opened the ice box. "Not much in here." he announced. "We still have some olives. Look," he said. To their surprise, during the visitation, some cheese strudel and a bowl of boiled potatoes had been placed on top of the ice box.

The four men managed to make a meal of bread, cheese, and hard salami.

Tomo proceeded to tell them the story of Dr. Costa paying two dollars for Katya's boil medicine and how the money was spent. Relaxing, even smiling, they listened to Tomo describe the banquet of food bought at the Olympus.

Contented with drinks and food, the four men, Stevo, Milan, Tomo, and Mato, all caring for Katya in different degrees, discussed her future.

Tomo was the first to speak. "I don't know what we will do for money. If I go work in the mill, maybe someone will have to be paid to stay with Katya. And," he added, "I know there are bills to pay. I heard Ivan and Katya talk about the house and the furniture payments."

Stevo spoke up, "I'm not worried about the furniture." He looked at Milan, "We need to think about the house payments." As an after thought he said, "Unless she remarries or decides to move."

The looks of the three men made Stevo drop his eyes. Of course they knew what he meant by 'if she remarries.'

Milan said, "We have a month to worry about the house payment to Anka. I already sent her money for August. But," he added, "We also need to think about food."

"That's it then," said Tomo, "I need to find work. I'll go to the mill."

As if he had not heard Tomo's remark, Milan said, "Let's face it. We would each marry her if we could." He turned his gaze to Stevo, "You are the most likely. You can afford it."

Hearing this, Tomo was stunned. Leaping from his chair, he shouted, "What are you talking about? How can you discuss such a thing? We just buried Ivan two hours ago." He turned and ran out the back door to the privacy of the yard.

Milan let out a heavy sigh, "Well, Tomo is no longer a boy. He is a young man…a man in love with Katya…just as we all are."

CHAPTER 19

The next morning, Tomo heard a knock at the back door. It was Bobo, accompanied by a small black woman.

By way of introduction, Bobo said in his limited Croatian, "This is my cousin, Cleona. Boss wants her to help Mrs. Katya change clothes and whatever else she needs."

Cleona was a tiny woman. Her skin was not as dark as Bobo's. Her dark black hair was covered with a white scarf tied in back at the neck. Her clean blouse and long skirt were a faded blue, over which she wore a clean, crisp white apron. Her sharp black eyes studied Tomo, just as he studied her.

Bobo explained, "Boss wants me to come back in two hours. Cleona is his new housekeeper. She will split her time here and at the Boss' place."

Tomo eyed Cleona suspiciously, while she gave him a 'you ain't the boss' look.

"How am I going to talk to her? Does she speak Croatian?" Tomo asked.

Bobo laughed, "No, so you better learn English."

Tomo followed Bobo and Cleona as they went into Katya's room.

Taking one look at Katya, Cleona said, "Bobo, you didn't tell me I was caring for a sick woman." She pointed to Katya, "Look at her. She is white as a ghost and she done wet herself."

Bobo said, trying to soothe his aggravated cousin, "It ain't fittin for me to help you undress her. Besides, you cared for sick people before. Don't be goin uppity on me."

Hearing voices she did not recognize, Katya opened her eyes and looked up into the face of an annoyed Cleona. Katya blinked several times, thinking she may have been dreaming. Bobo moved Cleona aside and said, "Mrs. Katya, Boss sent Cleona here to help you. She will help you change clothes, clean up and eat a little something." He paused waiting to see if she understood. It was a few seconds before she attempted to prop herself up on her elbows.

Tomo watched from the doorway as Cleona put a supporting arm under Katya's back and with great care helped Katya to a sitting position, so that her legs dangled on the side of the bed.

Cleona kept up a conversation in a soothing tone, Katya understood almost none of the English. The little woman said, "Now, Missy, we is goin to change your clothes, wash you up and you is goin to go to the kitchen. You ain't stayin in this bed, besides I gotta change the sheets."

Going into the kitchen, Bobo said, "Don't you worry, Cleona acts tough, but she is gentle. She will take good care of Mrs. Katya. I will be back in two hours." Then he was gone, leaving Tomo with the little black woman who intimidated him.

Tomo stayed in the kitchen, drinking his morning coffee and staring at the sink against the wall, full of unwashed dishes from the evening before. He didn't want to leave the house or to leave Cleona alone with Katya. He would have liked to work in the yard. Digging and clearing the yard made him happy. He wanted to…needed to be useful.

He jumped to his feet at the sight of Katya, in a long, pale green cotton skirt and blouse buttoned up to the neck. Cleona held Katya around the waist, to steady her, as they walked into the kitchen.

Cleona chattered on as if Katya and Tomo could understand her, "Now, Missy, I will make some clover tea. It is good for you." She pulled a pouch of dried leaves from a bag Tomo hadn't noticed on a nearby chair. She continued with her dialog, "I brought some good bacon grease to put on your bread. It is gonna make you strong."

Katya, seated across from Tomo, with eyes puffy and red from crying, looked to him and asked in a barely audible voice, "Is she going to live with us?"

With relief that Katya was speaking, he said, "Oh, no. Stevo sent her here and she will help just a few hours everyday."

Again tears started to flow down Katya's cheeks at the realization that her world was again changed forever. Most of all, how could she go on without Ivan? Ivan…they had once again found one another. In her mind, she silently screamed the words, DAMN DESTINY.

Cleona moved about the kitchen as if it were hers. In no time at all, she had a cup of clover tea in front of Katya. "Now, be careful." she said, "It is hot."

Through her tears, Katya looked across the table to Tomo who looked back blankly. He didn't understand Cleona either. When the bread with bacon grease was presented, Katya turned her gaze to Cleona, who said, "Don't be givin me that uppity look. You need to eat that." Cleona tore off a piece of the bread with her fingers and put it up to Katya's mouth. Katya pushed Cleona's hand away.

"Fine, Missy." Cleona said, "You just wait, you are gonna get hungry."

Cleona turned to the sink and started to wash the dishes.

Katya drank the tea, which was good, but ignored the bread. She had no appetite.

At the tavern, Milan sat alone at a table. It was early in the day with not many customers. However, it was not unusual for the mill men working the night shift to come in for a drink. Sometimes Roza had a bowl of boiled potatoes and occasionally boiled eggs, offered for free to the customers.

It was always more quiet during the day, a good time for Milan to go over his accounts and to think. He watched his younger brother, Mato, behind the bar talking with a customer. It pleased him that young, slender Mato did not drink very much and was good with the men who came in often. When men came back, it meant they liked the service and the atmosphere. Most of all, Mato appeared comfortable here and he got along with his sister-in-law.

Milan caught Mato's eye motioning for his brother to join him. "Sit. Let's talk" he said.

Mato asked, "Something wrong?"

"Do I pay you enough?" Milan asked directly.

Mato shrugged his thin shoulders, "I suppose you do. You give me some money. I live here free. Eat here free and drink for free. Yes...I suppose you pay me enough."

Milan leaned his big frame back in his chair, tilting it. He studied his brother for awhile before saying, "How would you like to be my partner in the tavern?"

Mato's jaw dropped. "Are you serious?" All sorts of thoughts raced in his head. "Does Roza know?"

"The tavern is mine and it was long before I married Roza." said Milan, "I make the decisions concerning business."

"Thank you, Bratso...brother." said Mato, getting up to hug his brother. "I will be a good partner. You won't be sorry. I will make you proud."

Milan watched as his brother went back behind the bar. He saw Roza pass by Mato carrying a tray of clean glasses. Mato bent to say something in her ear.

"He did WHAT?" she yelled.

Leaving the tavern, Milan went directly to the Markovich Furniture Store.

Milan wandered around the store, while Stevo showed a woman the sewing machines he had to offer. One was a full cabinet machine which when closed looked like a desk cabinet, hiding any suggestion that it was a sewing machine. This one cost $16.75. The other machine was a standard drop head pedal machine, which cost $12.85.

Stevo wrote out a receipt for the down payment of the drop pedal machine, with the understanding that the lady's husband would come tomorrow with the balance due.

Completing the entry in the ledger, Stevo went to Milan. "What brings you here, anything wrong?" His first thought was of Katya.

"Can we sit at one of your fancy tables and talk?" asked Milan.

He motioned for Milan to take a chair at one of the large round dining tables, while he took the chair next to Milan, saying "I don't think you are here to buy furniture."

"No," Milan said, "I am here to ask for a job."

Stevo laughed, "You are joking."

"No, I am not." Milan said seriously, "I have given this a lot of thought."

"I'm listening," said, Stevo.

"With Ivan gone, you need someone you can trust. We have been good friends for years." He waited for a response from Stevo. When none came, he continued. "I am not the scholar I think Ivan was, but I can speak some decent English, read and write well enough to fill out a receipt, and I know how to add and subtract."

"What brought this on?" Stevo asked, "What about the tavern?"

Milan folded his hands on the table top. "Well, I am making Mato a full partner. That way I don't need to be there all day and all evening." He tapped his folded hands on the table and said, "As for what brought this on…it is because of Katya."

Stevo looked at his friend for a long moment. "What is it you know about Katya that I don't." he asked.

"It is something I gave Ivan my word I would never tell. And, I won't." said Milan, meaning the story of Zolton and the baby.

Stevo looked at Milan. He said, "Grace Adams told me that Katya wears a Gypsy bracelet. She saw it when she helped Katya into the mourning clothes." When Milan didn't reply, he let it go saying, "Explain to me why hiring you is good for Katya."

Milan hesitated before saying, "Katya doesn't belong in the Patch. We can't do anything about that, but we can look out for her. If I am here at the store, you can trust me to take care of business if you need to leave. I hope you won't have to leave for any serious matter concerning Katya, but…but,"

Stevo interrupted, "Let's give it a try. I don't want to interview strangers." Thinking of Ema, he said, "I want to surround myself with people I can trust."

Milan was familiar with the store, having been a friend and customer of Stevo's, so they dispensed with a tour of the layout. Agreeing to come in the morning at nine, Milan then went to see if Katya was better.

Arriving at the back yard, Milan saw Tomo digging. Tomo called to him, "She is in the house, alone. She told me to come out here."

Katya was still seated at the kitchen table, Cleona long gone. She would cry, sob, blow her nose, and the tears would start again.

Milan was alarmed when he saw her puffy face and swollen, teary eyes. He went to her, putting his arms around her shoulders. She turned, burying her face in his midsection. He wrapped his arms around her, holding her while she sobbed. He held her for what seemed like a very long time. She let go and looked up at him. "Oh, Milan…" was all she said.

He found a towel and placed it under the hand pump, wetting it. He wrung it out, and then placed the cool towel on her reddened face. She held the towel with her hands, feeling its coolness.

Milan pulled a chair closer to sit next to her. When she put the towel down, she wasn't crying. He waited patiently for her to speak.

"He is gone, Milan. At last we were living like husband and wife…and now he is gone." She picked up the damp towel again, pressing it to her eyes. She said, "You see, when we got married, it was because we had to come to America. We lived like brother and sister."

"I know, Katya." Milan said softly. "Ivan told me the story…back to when the Turk found you and later, why you had to escape to Trieste. I know."

She looked at Milan, her eyes appearing to plead for forgiveness, "Oh, Milan. We only had three days. I gave him my love for only three days." She reached for Milan's hands, "God has punished me, because I only gave him three days!" She started to cry again.

He patted her hand, not wanting to leave, but he needed to get back to the tavern.

"I can be back tomorrow." he said. "When I start working for Stevo."

Surprised, and through her tears, Katya looked at Milan saying, "But the tavern…why? Why are you working for Stevo?"

"Just until he can find someone as good as Ivan." he lied.

It was about four in the afternoon when Milan returned to the tavern. Roza, hands on hips, stared at him as he went into their living quarters to change clothes.

When he came out of their bedroom ready to work the bar, Roza was waiting for him. Hands folded across her chest, she demanded, "What do you mean making Mato a partner? He hasn't been here long enough to deserve being your partner." Angrily, she added, "I am your wife...I am your partner."

He walked past her, pushing her aside, "Yes, you are my wife. The business is mine."

She moved quickly in front of him. "You just want more time to be with that widow. I heard Ivan and Katya in the yard...I know she had another man's baby. Now, she is free, and you think you can get in line behind Stevo."

Roza blanched under the look he gave her. She stepped back from him. It was a dark look, one she had never seen before.

CHAPTER 20

Three days had passed since Ivan's burial. Katya wanted to be alone. Both Stevo and Milan stopped by to see how she was doing, but the visits were short because Katya didn't want to talk or she cried.

On this morning, long before Cleona arrived, Katya was already dressed and seated at the kitchen table. Her eyes were still puffy, but not as red and they no longer burned from the tears.

She had been sitting there before daybreak, wanting to be alone to think. Tomo, sleeping on the cot in the back porch, awakened when he heard her. He could see her form at the table by the moonlight.

He said softly, "Katya, are you alright? I'll sit with you. I'll make coffee."

Katya said, "No, Tomo. I just want to sit here alone. Go back to sleep. I am fine."

Katya thought about her life...what it had been, and...Dear God...where was it headed? She was twenty-two years old, but at this moment, she felt as if she were one of the wrinkled, gray-haired Baba's who could do nothing but eat and sit all day in the sun.

Staring out into the night, with the full moon brightly shining, Katya wondered why Destiny chose to deal so cruelly with her life. Katya's entire life was one of having something or someone which gave her great joy, suddenly snatched away from her. Some unexpected event appeared to remove from her life Sofia, her mother; Lucia, her grandmother; her passionate Zolton, her beloved; Queen Valina; and now her newest painful loss, Ivan.

At the thought of Ivan, she felt her chest tighten. No! She had to stop crying and had to think what to do next. These wonderful people, Milan, Stevo, and Tomo, all were wanting to help...to guide her. Thinking of Cleona, she wasn't sure she wanted someone she could not understand fussing over her.

She thought about her future without Ivan. Then, she remembered the debts. Oh, God...the money they owed! Instinctively, her hand touched her bracelet. The bracelet Queen Valina had given her for protection. Katya was sure it was valuable…but, it had proved its true value by saving her life not once, but twice. It saved her from the Turk and again when the Gypsy Roha tried to stab her. No, she decided, if ever she were to part with the bracelet, it had to be for a very special reason. Now, at this time, the debts were not the reason to take the bracelet from her wrist.

She noticed on her left hand the gold ring her Nona Lucia had taken from her own hand for Katya to have as a wedding ring. She remembered the young nervous priest, forced into performing the wedding ceremony. A smile played on Katya's lips. What a picture they made, Ivan, almost nude on the cot, with the priest visibly shaken and staring at the bracelet adorned with pagan symbols.

Katya slipped the ring from her finger placing it on the table. She looked at it a long time. She knew what she would do with it.

In the bedroom, Katya kneeled down looking under the bed. She moved the chamber pot aside and reached for the small wicker suitcase she had carried from Trieste.

Milan was at the store early so that Stevo could come to Katya with Cleona.

They found Tomo seated at the table in his undershirt. For breakfast, he dunked some dry bread in his coffee.

"How is Katya?" asked Stevo, who was neatly dressed, wearing a dark blue bow tie with his white shirt. Cleona went directly to the bedroom, where she found Katya seated among the contents of the wicker suitcase, which were scattered on the already-made bed.

"Well, look at you!" said Cleona, as if Katya could understand. "Here I thought you was in bed. Had your breakfast? I brought some sassafras bark. I'm going to make you some tea." Cleona bustled out of the room, past Stevo.

Stevo was leaning against the door jamb, his blue eyes watching Katya finger through the assortment of papers.

Softly he said, "Good morning, Katya."

She looked up, giving him a small smile. "Good morning, Stevo." She waved her hand over the scattered papers. "These are letters and

117

notes…all things Ivan put in here. He must have thought them important."

Still leaning in the doorway, handsome as ever, Stevo asked, "Would you like me to help you with the papers?"

She shook her head, "Not yet. Some of these look to be personal."

Stevo moved out of the way, when Katya rose from the bed, making her way to the kitchen.

Tomo was at the table staring blankly at Cleona, not understanding a word while she babbled in his direction saying, "Now, don't drop those crumbs on the floor. And it wouldn't hurt you to rinse out your cup when you are done."

Tomo looked relieved when he saw Katya and Stevo. They sat, while Cleona chattered on, pouring coffee for Stevo and sassafras tea for Katya.

Katya asked Stevo, "What is she saying?"

He smiled, "She is telling you that the tea will make you well."

"I'm not sick." she said. "But it is as if a horse has kicked me…in the stomach."

Stevo studied her face, the swelling had lessened, but her eyes were still red. "You look better, Katya." he said. "Whether you know it or not, you were sick, sick with shock and sadness."

She quickly turned her face away from his. She took a moment to compose herself. She was determined not to cry.

Tomo got up to get more coffee. He could have indicated to Cleona he wanted more, but then she would just start chattering again and he wouldn't understand.

Stevo noticed the gold band on the table. He picked it up, and with questioning eyes, he held it up for Katya to see.

Katya said, softly, "That was my Nona's ring. She gave it to me as my wedding ring."

He said, "You don't want to wear it anymore?"

She shook her head, no.

Katya, with some determination said, "Let's talk about Cleona."

Hearing her name, Cleona was at Katya's side. "Missy want more tea?" she asked.

As Tomo sat listening to the discussion between Stevo and Katya, he was relieved when Stevo reluctantly agreed that Cleona was not needed here. Tomo would do anything; even wash the clothes, if it would save him from Cleona's annoying talking.

That same day, about one in the afternoon, Katya and Tomo walked through the open doors at Stevo's store. A delighted Milan smiled when he saw Katya.

"Zdravo...how are you." he said, pleased that she was looking better. She was wearing the green cotton skirt and blouse, the same as the day before. A widow not wearing black for the first year was, in the Croatian culture, unacceptable.

Tomo acknowledged the greeting with a nod, as he started to put a cigarette to his lips. Milan stopped him saying, "Sorry, Tomo. We go outside when we smoke. The smell gets into the furniture."

Tomo, with a shrug to his shoulders, turned and went to the door onto the sidewalk.

Milan moved away from his desk, leading Katya to a table where they both sat down. "Is it hard for you to see me here, instead of Ivan?" he asked.

Her voice was low, "A little."

He touched her hand, "I am happy to see you. Is there a special reason you are here?"

"I found some money I didn't know we had." she said. From a cloth bag, she withdrew money...Italian lire and Austrian kronen. "I have no idea how much this is in American money."

Stevo, exiting his living quarters with advertising flyers in his hand, was surprised to see Katya. He had just seen her that morning, and she said nothing of coming to the store.

Concerned, he asked, "Is anything wrong?" He sat at the chair next to Katya.

Milan showed him the money. "She wants to convert these into American dollars."

"Where did you get these?" asked Stevo.

"Ivan had a money belt." she said.

"Let me call the bank." said Stevo, going to the wall phone. He called the First National Bank at 6th & Broadway.

Milan and Katya watched Stevo from where they sat. He was writing figures on a piece of paper. When Stevo hung up, returning to the table, he said, "Well, Katya, it looks as if you have enough to pay your bill and some left over."

Milan didn't turn his head, but looked sideways at Stevo, who ignored him. Milan knew Stevo was not telling the truth.

Putting his hand on Milan's shoulder, he said, "Don't get up. I can enter the payment in the book and get what is left for Katya."

When he returned, he counted out fifteen one-dollar silver certificates.

A very pleased Katya smiled at the two men. She said, "I have one more thing to sell." She lifted from the cloth bag, the gold wedding band.

Both Milan and Stevo were silent. When Stevo said nothing, she turned to Milan, asking, "Will you buy it?"

Before Milan could answer, Stevo said, "Here," pulling out two more one-dollar silver certificates. "I will hold the ring, if you ever want it."

Later, when Katya was gone, Milan said to Stevo, "I'd like to buy that ring from you."

Stevo replied, "I am planning some day to give it back to her...on her wedding finger."

"I was thinking the same." said Milan.

Putting the ring in his pocket, Stevo said, "You already have a wife."

CHAPTER 21

Katya said nothing to Tomo about the money or the bill at the furniture store being paid. Instead of the Olympus grocery store, they stopped at another store nearby. This time, they were very careful in their purchases, buying only the basics such as bread, eggs, sugar, flour, beans, and sauerkraut, splurging only for a couple thick ham hocks.

At supper, Tomo tried to make conversation, but Katya was deep in thought about the future, barely listening to him.

After rinsing off the dishes and leaving them to dry on the drain board, Katya went to the bedroom to continue going through the papers in the suitcase.

It was early evening and Tomo was restless. Katya was busy with the papers scattered on her bed, leaving Tomo alone. He didn't feel like working in the yard.

At the bedroom door, Tomo asked, "If I go out, will you be alright alone?"

She looked up at him, thought a moment and said, "I will be fine. I want to go through the rest of these papers that Ivan was saving."

"Well then," still not sure he should leave her alone, he said, "I am going to the tavern."

Katya undressed, changing into a long–sleeved, white cotton nightgown. Sitting on the bed, the wicker case in front of her, and surrounded by the assortment of papers, she started sorting them into appropriate stacks. She found the receipt for the ship fare to America and an accounting of the rent paid in Lakawanna. She found a listing of what Ivan received as pay when he worked at the National Bank in Lakawanna. She wondered why she had not found any U.S. money, only the European currency.

Tucked into the side of the case was a roll of papers tied with a string. Untying it, Katya smoothed the papers flat. These were outdated advertising flyers from the Markovich Furniture store, similar to what Stevo held in his hands earlier when Katya was at the store. Each of these sheets had writing on the reverse.

She turned a page over. To her surprise she saw her name KATYA printed in large letters on the page. Quickly scanning the page, she realized Ivan had written about her. She looked at another page, and another. The pages, written in pencil, were not numbered, only dated at the top. Katya decided he must have written these pages when he had nothing to do at the store.

The very first page began with, 'The most beautiful girl I have ever seen was on the day of my brother's wedding. She stood by a wagon in the field...'

This was about her! Katya read on. Here were the details of their meeting and most of all, his secret feelings for her. In awe, she read page after page, careful to place them in the order she found them. Tears rolled down her cheeks. No sobbing such as during and after the funeral, but heartfelt tears for the beautiful words written about her, and how much he loved her.

She left the bedroom with the unread papers going into the kitchen. Katya filled a glass of water from the hand pump and sat down to read more.

It was all here in his handwriting, the story of her life. Anything he had heard about her or witnessed, he chronicled. Written was what he knew of her escape from the Turk, and everything else he knew, up to and including their arrival in Gary. Throughout his writing, he poured out the feelings of his heart for her.

Katya pushed aside the papers. She dropped her head onto her folded arms, her tears finding their way to the table top. These were tears of shame, shame for not realizing what she could have had with Ivan. Most of all, the shame of knowing that deep inside of her, she blamed him for the course her life had taken, back to when his mother had sent her away. He had saved her life and yet, she had secretly punished him for their escape to America.

Emotionally exhausted, Katya returned the papers to the wicker case. She gathered the scattered papers from the bed, no longer interested in going through them. She did take out the small bundle of letters from home, letters she had already read many times. Now she needed to write to her family.

While having a drink at the tavern, Milan took Stevo aside saying, "Tomo has been here all evening, singing and drinking." He nodded towards the singer, "He says he needs money to help with the bills."

More than once, the musicians had invited Tomo to sing with them, offering to split whatever money they received. Instead of putting money in a hat or handing it directly to the tamburashi, money was slipped under the instrument stings for a special request or just for the good music.

"Katya has money." said Stevo, replying to Milan's remark.

Milan said, "You and I know she has, but Tomo doesn't."

Looking toward the musicians, Stevo rubbed his chin. "He isn't family to Katya." he said, adding, "Pour me another slivovica."

"I can't leave." said Milan, "Besides Roza would go crazy if she thought I was checking on Katya. So, you'd better go. See if she is alright."

Stevo glanced at Roza, at the end of the bar, wiping up some spilled beer with a bar cloth.

Stevo laughed saying, "Milan, Milan…more than one man has been hit in the head with a rolling pin for looking elsewhere."

Milan didn't find the remark humorous, he said, "Go to hell."

Laughing, Stevo gave Milan a salute and left to check on Katya.

It was about ten o'clock when Stevo was at Katya's back door. He could see the light in the kitchen. He knocked and soon she opened the door for him.

"Stevo," she said, "what brings you here? Come in."

Settled at the kitchen table, seeing the slivovica, Stevo asked, "May I?"

From the kitchen drain board, Katya found another glass. "Pour me one, too."

He raised his eyebrow at the request. Seeing her wet eyes, he said, "You've been crying again."

"I have been reading Ivan's papers." She took a sip of the slivovica, while Stevo took his in a healthy swallow. She said, "Did you know that he was writing about me, about my life?"

"No," said Stevo, "but, I think I would like to read it."

She shook her head, saying, "There are things about my life no one needs to know."

Stevo studied her. Even with reddened eyes and a red nose from crying, she was lovely. "Tell me," he said, "did he write about your Gypsy bracelet?"

Her hand instinctively went to her wrist where the sleeve of her night gown covered it. She asked, "How do you know about the bracelet? Did Ivan tell you?"

"No, it was Grace, the woman who brought you the clothes to wear for the funeral. When she helped you change clothes, she saw it and recognized it as a Gypsy bracelet." He took another sip of his drink, "How she knew it was Gypsy, I don't know."

Katya pulled up her sleeve, showing Stevo the bracelet, saying, "I don't think I want to tell you about it just yet, maybe someday I will."

"You've been crying, again." he repeated.

"The things that Ivan wrote about me and said about me, made me cry." She wiped her eyes, feeling the beginning of another tear. "He loved me far more than I realized."

"Of course, he did." said Stevo, "We all knew it...we could see it."

"Then, why didn't I?" she said, as if speaking to herself.

Stevo pointed to the letters on the table. "From your family?" he asked.

"These are old letters. We haven't received any here in Gary." Katya let out a sigh, "I need to write to them. Let them know about Ivan."

She finished her drink and announced, "I believe I want to go back to the Old Country."

What she said astounded Stevo. "You can't be serious." He said "The boats are full of people escaping Europe. Don't you know what is going on there? The Jews are escaping Romania in the hundreds. They can no longer own businesses. I read that a law was passed."

"Well," she said, dismissing his remarks, "I am not Romanian and I am not Jewish."

Stevo continued his argument. "Katya, this is spreading across Europe. In Budapest there is a National Anti-Semitic Party." When she made no reply, he went on, "Katya, I read as many newspapers as I can find. Not just the local Gary Daily Tribune or the Evening Post. Once a week, I get newspapers from other cities, saved for me by the train conductors coming through Gary. There is a feeling of unrest in Europe." He stood and paced the floor. Knowing she had some connection with Gypsies, he said, "In Munich right now the Gypsies are being fingerprinted."

Her head snapped up. She said, "What is fingerprinted? I never heard of such a thing."

He explained, "Each finger is pressed into ink and then onto paper. That is how they can keep track of each Gypsy."

"That is crazy," she said, "Gypsies move about, travel from place to place."

"Oh, Katya!" he was insistent "I am trying to make you understand that the Europe you left is changing. It has been changing for many years. In a matter of time, it may be dangerous to live there."

"Stop trying to frighten me," she said. "It is only a thought. I will write to my family and see what they think."

He sat across from her saying nothing, just looking at her.

Feeling his gaze, she reached across the table, taking his hand in hers. Her touch was warm. He resisted the urge to pull her across the table to him.

She said, "I hate it here. It is ugly and I can't go anywhere alone. It is dangerous and it smells." She took her hands away from his. "Oh, how I miss my Nona's hillside villa on the Adriatic. There the clean sea air smells so fresh."

CHAPTER 22

The next morning, a sheepish Milan said, "Good morning." to Stevo. They had been good friends for several years, so he did not apologize for the parting 'go to hell' remark he made to his friend and employer the evening before.

Stevo smiled at Milan's embarrassment saying, "And, good morning to you."

Milan went to his work desk at the back of the store. Noticing the open curtains in front of the caskets, Milan asked, "Another funeral?"

"No. I was checking the inventory. We need to order a replacement for the one we used for Ivan. I will be going to the Post Office in a little while." As an afterthought, he said, "If you need Bobo, just pull the cord on the wall behind you."

It was more convenient for Stevo to ride the streetcar to the Post Office, located at 7th and Broadway, than to take his buggy. At the Post Office, Stevo picked up his mail and paid for the stamps needed for his letters.

Frank Meyers, the assistant to the postmaster, seeing Stevo, said, "Mr. Markovich, you know a lot of people through your store. I have asked almost everyone and no one knows Ivan Balaban. I have two letters forwarded from Lakawanna. The former address was crossed out and only Gary, Indiana is printed on the envelope."

"Yes, in fact, Mr. Balaban has worked for me." Stevo said nothing about Ivan's death. He thanked Mr. Meyers, taking the letters. One was postmarked Italy and the other Yugoslavia.

Stevo went directly to Katya with the letters. He saw Tomo, bare to the waist, again working in the yard, clearing the brush. They waved a greeting to one another.

The door to the porch was opened to let in air. Not seeing Katya, Stevo knocked and called out, "Katya?"

Her voice came from the front of the house, "Come in, Stevo. I am in the bedroom."

Piled on the bed were Ivan's clothes, the remaining suit, two pairs of trousers, and three shirts. Katya had manhandled the chest from an opposite wall so that it was now under the wall crucifix left by Anka Klarich. When Stevo entered the room, Katya was trying to move the bed to another wall.

"What are you doing?" asked Stevo, coming alongside her, "Why isn't Tomo helping you?"

"Push," she said, "I want it over here." Perspiration glistened on her forehead. To his surprise, her sleeves were rolled up, allowing full view of the bracelet she had kept hidden for years.

"Why the change?" he asked, easily positioning the bed where she wanted it.

She looked at him, with those eyes...those damn mesmerizing eyes. "I just thought if I changed the room, it would not remind me so much of Ivan." She pushed her loose hair from her face, "Perhaps I can make it seem more like my own room."

Stevo said, "Let's go in the kitchen. I want to give you something."

Walking behind her, he noticed she was wearing a faded blue skirt and blouse. He wondered how many pieces of clothing she had. People would wonder why she wasn't dressed in black, or at least wearing a black arm band.

Before she sat down, she asked, "Would you like some coffee, wine, or water?"

Stevo sat across from Katya, who was seated so that the sink was at her back. He looked around the kitchen which didn't seem efficient. Katya had done nothing to organize the room. It had the kitchen table and chairs, the ice box, an iron wood stove, and the sink. No cabinets or storage for kitchen items. For the first time, he became aware that the room lacked the usual necessary kitchen items, such as bowls and various pots.

Katya interrupted his assessment of the kitchen, "Well, what do you have for me?"

"Oh, yes," he said, pulling the letters from his pocket. "These were at the Post Office for you." Then he added, "Well, for Ivan, but I suppose they are also meant for you."

Slowly Katya reached out her hand, taking the letters. She looked down at the return addresses, and saw that the one from Italy was from her mother, Sofie. The one from Yugoslavia was from Anton Vladeslav, Ivan's father.

Word from home! Katya's eyes began to water. At last…letters from home. With slightly trembling hands, Katya tore away the side of the envelope from Trieste, removing the very thin paper.

The tears in her eyes made reading impossible. She handed the page to Stevo, saying, "Please read it for me."

He said looking at the page, "It is dated July 2." When Katya made no comment, he began reading.

My Dearest daughter Katya, and beloved Ivan,

We send you love and hope you are well. The last letter we received from you was in June. I am not complaining, but the letters are full of details about the city where you live, where you work, but nothing about yourselves. You never mention if you are happy. We all pray that you are happy. We are all well. Alexie works at the Trading Company, as always. He hears news at the docks and is uneasy about the political situation in Europe. Germany is becoming stronger and there is talk of workers forming organizations. I don't understand any of this. Since you have been gone, no Gypsies have come through Trieste. Perhaps they have, but we have not seen them. And, Nona is very sad. Valina has not been to visit. Nona stands on the terrace often, watching the road for her old friend. Baby Aleksy is a joy to us all. He is the only bright spot in Nona's life now. I wish you could see your little brother. Aleksy is healthy, even though he was born a month early. He is now fifteen months old and we have to watch him because he tries to get into everything.

Katya reached across the table, pushing the letter in Stevo's hand down to the table. She said, "Don't read anymore." She was not crying, but the sadness in her face made Stevo wish he could do something, anything, to make her happy again. Happy the way she was that night when he danced with her at the tavern, that evening after they delivered the furniture to the house.

He picked up the letter from Yugoslavia. "Shall I read this one?"

"No." Her voice was low, "I already know it is bad news."

Stevo said, "Perhaps not. It might be good news."

"No…" she said again. "I feel it. It is bad news."

Stevo tried to engage Katya in conversation, but she seemed distant, lost in the thoughts.

Before leaving, he stood behind her. It was as if she didn't notice him, her eyes fixed on the unopened letter from Yugoslavia. Stevo rested his hands on her shoulders. Still she did not move. He bent kissing the top of her head. "Oh, Katya," he whispered then left.

Katya was still sitting at the table, with the two letters on the table when Tomo came in.

"News from home?" he asked, going to the hand pump to wash up.

When she didn't acknowledge him, Tomo became concerned. *Was she going back to that quiet world she had escaped to when Ivan died?*

She didn't notice when he sat across from her. "Dear God, Katya," he pleaded, "say something. Don't just sit there." He grabbed at her hand, shaking it.

Katya lifted her eyes from the letters to Tomo's face. Her voice was almost a whisper when she said, "I am alright. Really, I am."

She straightened up, leaning her back against the chair. "Too much is happening too fast." she said. "I don't know where I am going. I feel as if coming to Gary was a curse. I wake up each day, wondering what Destiny will throw my way."

Tomo noticed there was no food prepared. She must have been sitting there since Stevo left more than an hour ago. The cook stove was cold.

Tomo, getting up, said "Let me build a fire in the stove. I can cook some eggs and make tea or coffee, whatever you want."

"Don't bother making anything for me. I am going to my room." She gathered up the letters, saying to Tomo, "Don't worry about me. I need to think, to decide what to do with my life." She gave Tomo a small smile. "Go to Milan's, go sing. The people love to hear you sing."

Tomo slumped back into his chair. He wasn't smart enough to know what to do or say to make things better for Katya. She meant everything to him. Katya and Ivan were like family and now the family was broken. He would never leave her, but what if she left him? Would Stevo and Milan look out for him...still be his friends?

In the bedroom, Katya lit a lamp, opened the letter from Zagreb and read it. It was as she knew it would be...bad news. Anton Vladeslav, Ivan's father, wrote that Ivan's stepfather, Marko Balaban, the blacksmith, had died. No illness was named; just that he had become ill and never recovered. There was some news about Stefan and his German wife, Barbra, and that Barbra was worried about her father living alone in Germany.

Katya put the letter down without reading all of it. In the past, she hungered for letters from home from the family. Now, these letters didn't matter. It was as if they had nothing to do with her life as it now was. None of the family from the Old Country could put their arms around her and comfort her. Most of all, they couldn't tell her what to do. They had no idea what it was like in Gary, so how could they help?

She rummaged around in the cabinet desk and found several sheets of writing paper. She didn't need envelopes because it was common practice to fold the letter so that it could be addressed on the unwritten side.

Katya wrote two very short letters stating that she was now in Gary, Indiana. She said nothing about the house, the furniture, or how much she disliked the city. In detail, she wrote how Ivan had been killed attempting to save a child. She let them know a priest buried Ivan.

She was somewhat surprised at herself. Katya was very calm writing these letters. No crying.

The third and last letter she wrote was to Slavko Mravich, her very first friend on the ship, and later in Lakawanna. To Slavko, she first wrote about Ivan's death. Then, she wrote about her feelings about living in Gary. She unburdened herself to him in a way she had not to anyone else, the dangers of going out alone, and the unsanitary conditions of the Patch. The lack of women friends, every fear, every insecure feeling, she wrote in the letter.

CHAPTER 23

The Markovich Furniture store was closed on Sundays, even though most of the other businesses remained open, especially the taverns.

Close to noon, Stevo walked to the barn and found Bobo brushing the brown horse.

"Bobo," he said, "let's go for a ride today. Get the buggy ready."

The black man cocked his head saying, "Since when do we take buggy rides?"

Walking away from Bobo, Stevo said over his back, "I am walking to Mrs. Katya's house. Come there when you are ready."

With a big grin on his face, Bobo said, "Yes, sir, Mr. Boss."

Things Stevo had not thought about since leaving New Orleans now found their way into his mind. Katya mentioned the clean sea air and she was right. Now, for the first time, he thought about the New Orleans waterfront, where he and his father would board boats to fish. The air around the sea was clean and fresh.

All those years in New Orleans, the air had been filled with the overpowering perfume of flowers. The gardens were a kaleidoscope of colors and varieties.

At Katya's, instead of using the usual back door entrance, Stevo knocked at the front door. A very surprised Katya answered the door. "Stevo? Why are you using the front door?"

He was very formal asking, "May I come in?"

She stepped aside so he could enter.

He continued, "It is a beautiful day. Not too hot." He waved his hand toward the window indicating the weather. "Please get dressed, probably in the white skirt with the red appliqués and the white blouse."

Katya frowned, two tiny lines forming between her eyes. "Where are we going?"

Instead of going into the kitchen as he usually did, Stevo sat in one of the plush parlor chairs, as if his being there was a formal occasion. He said, "The buggy will be here soon."

Hearing the voices, Tomo came from the kitchen, surprised to see Stevo seated in a parlor chair. "What is going on?" asked Tomo.

Stevo said, "As soon as Katya gets dressed, we are going for a buggy ride."

"Where?" asked Tomo, a slice of cheese from lunch in his hand.

"It is a surprise." Turning to Katya, he said softly, but firmly, "Please get dressed."

She started to say something, but stopped. Curiosity had gotten the better of her. As she walked toward her bedroom, she heard Stevo say, "Please hurry."

Later, Tomo, with a smile on his face, watched as Stevo escorted Katya down the front steps to the waiting buggy. A somewhat bewildered Katya let herself be treated as if this were a formal event, instead of two old friends going for a buggy ride.

Bobo gave Katya a wide smile as she climbed the step into the buggy. She asked Bobo, "Where are we going?"

"Don't know." he said.

With Stevo and Katya both in the seat behind him, Bobo clicked his tongue and the horse moved.

Stevo said to Bobo, "We are going to the Lake Front Park."

Traveling east along the roads close to the Lake Michigan shoreline, Katya felt an excitement. As they left the city of Gary, the landscape was more natural, wooded, with an occasional homestead here and there.

Most of all, she noticed the air smelled cleaner. She could smell the forest of pine trees. Every once in a while, she would nudge Bobo's shoulder, pointing to a grouping of plants along the road, asking, "Bobo, do I need those?"

Stevo was pleased to see her so excited. He had not seen this side of her before. So far, he only knew the reserved Mrs. Balaban, or the grieving Katya. Now he thought he actually saw a sparkle in her eyes.

When Bobo neared the town of Miller, Stevo said, go to the lake, to Carr's Beach.

The huge sand dunes on each side of Lake Street were a marvel to Katya. She saw a shack on the top of a dune and wondered how a person would get to it. As they neared the lake, Katya could smell the water.

Bobo got the buggy as close to the beach as possible. Katya was in awe of Lake Michigan. The beautiful blue water and the sound of the curling white waves made Katya squeal with delight. She stood in the buggy and saw fishing boats in the water and men waist deep with fishing nets.

"Sit down, Katya." said Stevo. "We need to take off our shoes."

She was so excited, she obeyed without question. Stevo unbuttoned her shoes then slipped off his own.

Bobo was smiling at Katya's excitement. "Are you coming?" she asked him.

"I'd like to, but I'm staying with the buggy. The horse needs water." he said.

Katya had never seen sand. The beach at Trieste was strewn with rocks. The warm sand on her feet felt wonderful. Like a child, she kicked her feet throwing sand about.

Stevo rolled up his trouser legs. He took Katya's arm and together they walked in the warm sand. The beach, itself, was flat, but the mounds of sand forming the dunes with the various grasses were a thing of beauty.

Katya didn't bother to take off her stockings. She ran straight for the water's edge and let the waves lick at her feet. Holding up her skirt, she looked at the water filling up the footprints she left behind.

They walked together arm in arm, but only Katya was splashing her feet in the water. White birds circled overhead and every now and then, Katya saw a small, furry animal run in the grassy dunes. Stevo stood back when she splashed and laughed in her merriment. In the sunlight her red hair appeared brighter than ever. Her cheeks were rosy and her green eyes glistened with happiness.

They had been walking toward the east for some time. Every now and then, Katya would run to a dune and admire a wild flower.

"Let's turn back." said Stevo, "Time to go home."

Like a child, she pouted. "Oh, Stevo, I am having such a good time."

Playfully pulling her arm and turning in the direction to go back, he said, "Maybe we can come out another time."

Katya stopped to look into a boat pulled onto the sandy shore. In it was the fisherman's catch for that day.

"Stevo," said Katya, "my Nona and I would buy fresh fish from the fisherman in Trieste."

"Do you want fish? Then let's buy some fish." Stevo said.

A bit ashamed, Katya said, "I don't know how to cook fish. Mia, my Nona's housekeeper, did all the cooking."

"My dear Katya," said Stevo a bit smugly, "I was a fisherman before I came to Gary." To the short man in the boat, Stevo said, "Give me about six of the nice sized perch. Do you have something to wrap them in?"

Back in Gary, at Stevo's home, Katya sat at a table in the small, but efficient kitchen. Looking around, she realized her kitchen was not as nice as this one.

Katya watched as Stevo cleaned the fish, breaded and fried them.

"Is it true," she asked, "that you were a fisherman?"

"Yes, it is." he said. "We came by boat from Dalmacia, my Tata and I. We lived in New Orleans for fourteen years fishing and searching for oysters. Sometimes we would find some crabs, but mostly we fished."

Katya asked, "Why did you leave?"

"My father died." he said, placing a plate of fried fish for her and one for himself on the table. "After Tata was gone, I wanted a new life." Stevo did not want to tell her any more about him or his stepmother.

With the fish, Stevo served chopped red cabbage in vinegar and a cold potato salad, both left in the ice box by Cleona.

Katya looked at the food. "Stevo," she said, "I don't know how to cook." She looked embarrassed. "In Trieste we had Mia do the cooking, and in Vladezemla Klara took care of the kitchen."

Stevo watched as she took a bite of the fish. "I have not had fish this good since I was in Trieste." she said. Then she laughed, "I ate eel and didn't know it."

"Katya…" Stevo was thinking out loud, "Why don't you come here and have Cleona teach you how to cook?"

"Here?" she asked.

"Your kitchen isn't set up for real cooking." His tone was apologetic. "I hope I am not offending you. You need cabinets, a flour bin, jars and bowls."

Katya was considering the idea. She said, "I can't understand Cleona."

"You won't have to." said Stevo, "Just watch her."

CHAPTER 24

When Stevo walked Katya home, he took from her the three letters she wrote, promising to mail them in the morning.

Katya brought home some leftover fish for a very pleased Tomo.

It was now late evening and she was very tired. While Tomo ate the fish and potato salad, she told him about the beauty of the Lake Front Park in the town of Miller.

Later, alone in the bedroom, seeing Ivan's cane resting atop the dresser, she felt a pang of guilt. She should not have gone out and enjoyed herself so much. She knew that she should stay home and grieve. But Katya felt as though she had been grieving for a long time. She had been grieving for the love loss of Zolton, her home, and family in the Old Country, the baby, and now Ivan. Katya felt as if her heart had been broken forever.

Fingering Ivan's cane, she knew that if she were to succeed in this new country, she could not dwell on her losses, but had to make plans for the future. She wasn't sure what she wanted for the future, or what was available to her. But, she would think about it. If only she could sit in Anton's wonderful chapel at Vladezemla. She did so much thinking in that lovely little chapel.

That night, in a dream, Katya saw Ivan and Zolton walking together up a forest path. At first, she only saw their backs. When they turned, they were looking directly at her. In Zolton's arms was the baby. Both men smiled lovingly at her. They stood together for awhile, just looking at her. When they turned and walked away, Katya noticed that Ivan was not using a cane.

In the morning, Katya, still wearing her long cotton nightgown, found Tomo eating the last of the cold fried perch for breakfast.

"This is so good." he said. "Did Stevo really cook this?"

"Just the fish," she said, "Cleona made the potato salad." Pouring herself some coffee and milk, Katya said, "His kitchen is nicer than ours. Also, he told me that Cleona would teach me how to cook."

Tomo stopped eating, "She is coming back?" He was not happy.

"No," Katya laughed, "I am going to Stevo's kitchen. He said I can learn just by watching her. We will see." She said somewhat doubtfully.

In her room, Katya dressed and made the bed. She took the pile of Ivan's clothes from the only chair in the room and placed them on the bed. Sitting in the chair, she stared at the clothes. Her eyes drifted to his cane on the dresser. She remembered her dream...in the dream Ivan was not walking with his cane...and he was not limping.

Katya rose and stood in front of the dresser, looking intently at the crucifix above it. She stared at it so long, that it appeared to glow and change into the cross Katya remembered from the beloved chapel in Vladezemla. She had no idea how long she stood there, gazing at the crucifix.

Sitting again in the straight back chair, with closed eyes, Katya leaned her head against the wall. Had the dream been a sign, a message from Ivan? Why was Zolton in the dream with the baby? Did it mean that Zolton was with Ivan, dead?

She sat up straight. They had both smiled at her! Were they letting her go? Did they want her to make a new life for herself? Katya rose and paced the floor. The two men she loved and who had loved her were together in her dream. It had to mean something.

Tomo was almost done clearing out the yard, getting it ready for next spring's planting. He had even dragged out some junk from the shed. He kept a metal shovel and a rake made of twigs. There was a pump handle, and he wondered if there was a place in the yard for a pump. He would have to search for it.

In the kitchen, his head under the hand pump, he tried to cool off and clean up. He could see Katya and hear her drumming her fingers on the table. Drying his face and hair with a towel, he asked, "What are you thinking about?"

She turned to look up at him, "Us. I am thinking about us."

"Why? What is wrong with us?" he asked, a bit confused.

"Sit down." she said. "We need a plan, a plan for our lives."

Sitting across from Katya, with the towel draped around the back of his neck and his brown hair wet and mussed, he said, "You are saying 'we' and 'us'. I don't understand. We are not family."

"Yes we are." she said emphatically. "Destiny has made us a family. Of all the houses to run to and hide, you chose this one. You could have left after the first night, but you chose to stay. When Ivan died, you took care of me."

Katya went to him and put her hand on his shoulder, "So, you see...you have chosen to be my brother."

Tomo said nothing, and just put his hand over hers. He loved her. Yes, he loved her. Perhaps what he felt for her was a sisterly love. He didn't know. He did know that he would not leave her.

At the store, Stevo was disappointed that Katya had not come for a cooking lesson with Cleona. With some pleasure, he told an envious Milan about the day at the Lake Park Beach, and the intimate dinner for two of the fish he cooked. Perhaps he embellished a little, to tease his old friend.

When Stevo got off the street car from his trip to the Post Office, instead of going directly to the store, he hurried to see Katya. When he came through the open back door, he saw Tomo standing with his back to Katya, who was seated in a chair. Tomo was wearing a pair of Ivan's trousers inside out while Katya was taking in the back seam.

"What's this?" asked Stevo, a smile playing on his lips. "You are now a seamstress?"

Katya said, in a no-nonsense tone, "Help yourself to something to drink. I am making Ivan's trousers fit Tomo."

Stevo gave an ill-at-ease Tomo, a big grin. "No thank you," said Stevo, "I'll just watch and be ready to help if you stick him in the guza with the needle."

To both Stevo and Tomo's surprise, when Katya was finished with the sewing, she gave Tomo a swat on the butt, saying, "That's it. I'll do the other pants later."

Stevo got to the point of his visit, "I thought you were coming to learn to cook."

"I want to tell you and Milan of my decisions." she said. "I have made plans, but I need your help."

Stevo's eyes narrowed, "What sort of plans?"

She stood, gathering her sewing supplies. "Milan can't leave the tavern tonight, so I will come to the store later and talk with you both." Then, she paused, "is it alright if I come? If you have customers, I will wait or…" she paused, "you and I could go to the tavern and talk with Milan there."

"Going to the tavern so soon after Ivan's passing is not a good idea." said Stevo, thinking of Katya's reputation. "Come to the store. We will find time to talk there."

Katya waited patiently while both Milan and Stevo helped a woman decide on a wash machine. Katya only half listened as both men gave the nicely-dressed buyer the instructions, and showed her how to use the wooden barrel with gears. Katya had washed clothes in the river in Vladezemla, and thought the river washing was far less complicated than the machine. Stevo explained that it could wash five shirts at a time. It was important to spot wash with soap and pre-soak the evening before washday. Water needed to be heated and poured into the barrel. With the lid closed and the gear handle extended, one was to manually agitate the clothes using the handle for no less than ten minutes.

Milan stifled a smile when he caught Katya roll her eyes upward upon hearing all the instructions. Milan took the payment of $4.44, while Stevo made arrangements for the delivery of the wash machine.

With no other customers in the store, both men sat at a table with Katya.

Milan wanted to say something about Katya's outing with Stevo to the lake, but Stevo came right to the point saying, "Alright, Katya. What plans have you made…or are you thinking about?"

Milan's eyes widened, he hadn't heard about this. He said, "Yes, what plans?"

"First," she began, "I want to learn to speak American and to read and write."

Before either of the men could comment she said, "And, I am not going into mourning for a year. Ivan has released me."

The stunned looks on both Milan and Stevo's faces did not faze Katya. It was Milan who spoke first, "What do you mean, Ivan released you?"

Katya said, "Not just Ivan. Zolton was with him. They both let me go."

Stevo spoke slowly, "When did…you…see…them?"

"In my dream." she said. "They were together. Zolton had the baby in his arms."

Stevo didn't know about the baby, but Milan did. Milan asked, "Did they say anything…in the dream?"

"No," said Katya calmly, "but, I know what they meant. It means that Zolton is dead and that he and Ivan are together and they are letting me go."

Stevo took Katya's hand. "Katya, don't talk this way. It isn't right."

Milan looked at Stevo saying, "Many of the village women have powers. Perhaps you have been in America so long you have forgotten."

Being from New Orleans, Stevo knew more about magic and voodoo than Milan or Katya could ever fathom. He said, "Alright. Alright, I will believe that you strongly feel they have let you go." He spread his hands in a questioning gesture, "So, what does it mean?"

"I have been thinking about the old woman who took care of me and taught me about healing, Old Julia." When neither of the men said anything, she went on, "Julia told me that with all that she taught me, I would never be hungry or poor. I want to have a business of my own."

"And sell what?" asked Milan.

"I can sell different herbs and plants for various ailments." Katya said.

Milan looked doubtful, but Stevo said, "In New Orleans, we have shops like that. But I don't know if it would work here in Gary."

Katya ignored his remark and said, "I want Tomo to get an education. I don't want him working in the mills. Maybe he could be a doctor or a lawyer."

Milan and Stevo stared blankly at one another, then at Katya.

Milan said, "When was this decided?"

"I decided it." said Katya. "I want him to have respect." She looked away from the two men, "I have never had respect…ever. I have been called a witch and had rocks thrown at me." She looked at both men with determination, "I am in America now. It is going to be different here."

CHAPTER 25

Almost every day for two weeks, Katya came to Stevo's living quarters. There, Cleona told her the names of kitchen items such as pot, pan, spoon, and so forth. It wasn't long before Katya knew the American names for most of the cooking utensils.

Katya learned how to make flapjacks which, as far as she was concerned were thick palečinke with no filling. Cleona's corn bread reminded Katya of hard polenta.

While watching Cleona in the kitchen, Katya realized she did not have the necessary storage or supplies to prepare the meals she was being taught to cook. Katya admired the kitchen cabinet Cleona used. The wooden cabinet was a kitchen in itself. There was a bin for flour and one for sugar. The metal surface could be pulled out and used as a work table. This cleverly built piece of furniture had a place for everything a cook would use. Someday, Katya decided, she would have one of these cabinets. She wouldn't buy one just yet, it would take almost all the money she had put aside, and she didn't want to spend what she had saved.

As for Katya's language lessons, these were hit and miss, but effective. Stevo gave Katya a Sears Roebuck catalogue to look at. Within the pages were pictures of hundreds of items each with names and spellings. Milan or Stevo would help Katya with the pronunciation of the words and sometimes tell her the meaning of some of the descriptive ones, such as oak or smokeless or single. Her determination was so strong that it impressed both men.

Katya was also determined to have Tomo get a proper education. She insisted that Stevo help her find a tutor for Tomo.

"I can't do anything until he learns English." He would argue.

"I want him to learn American, not English." Katya would demand.

Exasperated, Stevo replied, "It is the same." Still, she did not understand and he was not about to explain the Revolutionary War. So Stevo said, "O.K, he will learn American."

Her lessons for the day over, she headed home. As Katya approached her house, she saw a man seated on her front steps.

He was facing the opposite direction, looking down the street. When he turned in her direction, Katya's heart skipped a beat. A friend! It was her first friend after leaving Trieste, Slavko Mravich from Lakawanna. He rose when he saw her running towards him. He didn't realize it was Katya, because she was not wearing the expected black clothing of a widow.

She nearly knocked him over, wrapping her arms around his thick body. His hair had been professionally trimmed, as was his mustache and beard. It was obvious he wanted to look his best. Over his arm, he carried the jacket to his brown tweed suit.

His eyes were bright at the sight of Katya. He wasn't sure she would appreciate an unannounced visit, but her joy at seeing him dissolved any doubts he may have had.

Katya unwrapped herself from him and they stood looking at one another. At last she said, "Oh, Slavko, my dear friend, Slavko."

He said, "I got your letter. I had to come."

She took his arm and led him to the back of the house where the door was seldom locked.

Slavko looked at the house and the unplanted yard. When he saw the cot in the porch, he wondered if Katya was renting or sharing the house with another family.

"Come in, come in." said Katya. "Why didn't you let me know you were coming?"

He walked into the kitchen, admiring the table and the ice box. He said, "I decided on the spur of the moment. Something just told me to come and see you."

Katya still held his hand, "Come let me show you the house. This is the parlor." Slavko was more than a little surprised at the grand parlor furniture.

Seated in the kitchen, a bottle of slivovica and a glass in front of Slavko, he asked, "Do you share this house?"

Katya said, "No, it is ours'...I mean mine."

Surprised, Slavko asked, "Katya, how is it you and Ivan have so much in such a short time? What has it been, three months?"

Filling his glass she said, "The house is not paid for. I make a payment each month."

"The furniture," he asked, "how is it you have such fine furniture?"

"Ivan worked at the Markovich Furniture store. He paid something each week." She didn't bother telling Slavko about what she found in Ivan's money belt.

Slavko didn't want to talk about the house or furniture anymore. He wanted to know about Katya. He expected a grief stricken widow, not this poised, confident woman.

"Katya," he wasn't sure how to begin, "Ivan told me that you and he were not living as husband and wife."

"Oh, but we were, insisted Katya. "Before the accident, we knew we loved one another. We fell in love all over again." Her face glowed as she spoke. "We found one another. We just didn't have enough time."

"Forgive me, Katya…" he hesitated, "how is it you are not in black and…and you seem almost happy."

"I am happy because I have a plan for my life. Finally, I think I can live in America." She poured herself a glass of water. "When Ivan and Zolton made me free, I knew I could live in America."

The bewildered look on Slavko's face let Katya know she had to explain. So, just as she had explained her dream to Milan and Stevo, she did to Slavko.

Slavko shook his head, saying, "Oh, Katya…Katya. I came here to help you and you don't need any help."

Katya stood. "I have not been to my friend Milan's tavern since the funeral. Let's go tonight." She didn't wait for a reply. "I want my Gary friends to meet my very first friend, the one who carried me up the stairs to the deck of the ship."

She emptied her water glass in the sink and said, "I am going to change my clothes. It won't take me long." And with that she was gone to her bedroom.

Slavko shook his head in wonder. This was not what he had expected. And yet, he had to admit this was more pleasant than a crying, grieving woman.

Looking around the room, he was pleased to see that Katya was living nicely. He wondered about the cot on the porch. Perhaps he could have stayed here, but he had already paid for a room at the Chicago Hotel on 20th and Broadway, only four blocks away.

Slavko lit a cigarette. A packaged cigarette, not one he had to roll himself. He was living a bit more elegantly than he was used to. A nice room in a hotel, a barbershop haircut and now packaged cigarettes. And, he was about to spend the evening with one of the most beautiful women he had ever seen.

Stevo, at the opened back door, stared at the nicely dressed man sitting at Katya's kitchen table, cigarette in hand, and a glass of slivovica in front of him.

Noticing Stevo, Slavko asked, "Hello. What can I do for you?"

It was all Stevo could do to keep from asking, "Who the hell are you?" Instead, he said, "I am here to see Katya Balaban. Why are you in her kitchen?"

Slavko was enjoying himself. Was this already a suitor for the widow? Slavko asked, "What is your business with Gospa Balaban?"

Annoyance showed on Stevo's face as he marched into the kitchen. He asked, "Just who are you? I don't know you."

Seeing the displeasure in Stevo's demeanor, Slavko said, "You don't have to know me. It is enough that Katya does."

Stevo started to go through the kitchen to look for Katya.

Slavko stood, showing his ample size. He said, "Please sit down. I would prefer it if you wait for Katya. She will be out shortly." It was all Slavko could do to keep from smiling. He knew he was goading this man's curiosity along with a bit of anger.

From the sink drain board, Stevo took a glass. With his annoyance evident, Stevo sat across from Slavko. He took the slivovica bottle and poured himself a drink. When Slavko said, "Please help yourself." Stevo was ready to grab this stranger, just as Katya walked in, dressed in her blue lace dress. One she had not worn since the first time Stevo saw her.

She smiled saying, "I see you two have met."

"No we have not." said Stevo, trying not to show his annoyance.

146

Grinning, Slavko put out his hand, "Slavko Mravich. Katya and Ivan lived in my brother's house in Lakawanna for about a year." He added, "We came over on the same boat, so we are old friends."

Taking Slavko's hand, Stevo looked into his mischievous dark eyes. Realizing that Slavko was playing a game with him, Stevo relaxed a little, smiled, and said, "It is a pleasure to meet and old friend of Katya's."

Stevo, now not so defensive, said to Katya, "I haven't seen you in that dress since the first day at Milan's."

"That is where we are going." said Katya.

Slavko interrupted, "First we are going to the Chicago Hotel for dinner. Then later we will go to your friend's tavern."

When at last, Katya and Slavko arrived at Milan's, both Milan and Stevo were envious that this stranger from Lakawanna was having an evening with Katya. She looked wonderful and she looked happy. Her first meal in an American hotel, being served by courteous waiters, along with enjoying a first slice of apple pie, made her feel very special.

At the tavern, two men gave up their table for the beautiful woman and well-dressed man. Roza was almost giddy with delight, seeing the scandalous Katya dressed in blue with a man none of them knew. It was as Roza had suspected all along, Katya was very possibly a fallen woman. Seeing Milan's scowl as he watched Katya and Slavko, she couldn't help but give him a smug smile.

Stevo was seated on a stool at the bar. His shirt sleeves were rolled up and his shirt collar was unbuttoned. The handsome Stevo was just as displeased as Milan. Looking past Stevo, Milan said, "So, that's Lakawanna. Not much to look at. We are both more handsome than he." This last remark was laced with sarcasm.

"At least I am." said Stevo, not turning to look at them. "What are they doing?" he asked.

Milan said, "Lakawanna just waved for Mato to come to the table. Katya is laughing. Shit! She just put her hand on his." Milan so disliked the nicely-dressed man, that he refused to use Slavko's name or, for that matter, to meet him.

Mato was in the back of the bar getting the bottle of kruškovac and two glasses which Slavko ordered. Milan gave his brother a look as if he had done something wrong.

"What?" asked a confused Mato, "What did I do?"

The musicians were taking a break, placing their instruments on chairs before heading for the bar. Tomo had been singing with the musicians, looking very nice in the shirt and pants Katya altered for him. Instead of going to the bar, he came directly to Katya and sat, not waiting for an invitation.

Slavko, not knowing about Tomo, was more than a little surprised at what he took to be a lack of manners.

Looking very pleased, Katya introduced the men to one another.

Tomo had already heard, in not such glowing terms, about the man from Lakawanna. He, too, didn't know what to think of this man who seemed so very comfortable with Katya. Tomo was as possessive of Katya as were Stevo and Milan.

To Katya, he said, "When I came home, you weren't there. I was worried."

Slavko showed only the slightest amount of surprise, but that explained the cot on the porch. Before Katya could answer, Mato brought the kruškovac...pear brandy and glasses to the table.

Slavko said, "Bring another glass for our friend."

Already anticipating this, Mato had a glass, which he placed on the table in front of Tomo.

Tomo didn't like the words, 'our friend'. It denoted a familiarity which Tomo didn't appreciate.

Slavko was aware that he was not a handsome man. But then, he wasn't ugly either. For the first time in his life, he had the attention of a beautiful woman and the jealousy of possibly three men. He was enjoying their visible annoyance.

As the host, Slavko poured the pear brandy into each glass. When finished, he raised his glass in the familiar toast, "Na Zdravlje." He touched glasses with Katya, but only raised his to Tomo.

Sitting straight in his chair, Tomo asked, "How long are staying in Gary." There was no warmth in the question.

"That all depends." answered Slavko, patting Katya's hand.

Watching from the bar, Milan said, "Lakawanna is touching her hand, again."

Throughout the evening, Milan never came to the table to greet Slavko, who brought murmurs from the customers when he placed a dollar bill under each of the musician's instrument strings, along with a folded bill into Tomo's shirt pocket.

Slavko motioned for Mato to settle up the bill. He paid for the drinks and gave a very pleased Mato a dollar bill for his service.

As Katya and Slavko were leaving, Milan made a point to disappear from the bar area. Katya said, "Oh, Slavko. I am so disappointed. I wanted you to meet my very good friend, Milan. He helped us so very much when we first came...and later, when I was alone."

"Another time." said Slavko, smiling. He had seen the looks Milan was giving him throughout the evening. He almost wanted to laugh out loud. What fun to be so envied!

CHAPTER 26

It was nearly eleven o'clock the following morning and Katya had not arrived for her usual cooking and language lessons.

Customers and business kept both Milan and Stevo occupied, but not enough to not be aware that Katya was absent.

With the most recent customer gone, Milan was re-arranging some furniture when he looked out the storefront window.

In a voice loud enough for Stevo to hear at the back of the store, Milan said, "Shit! Lakawanna is across the street." With disgust, Milan announced, "He has a huge bouquet of flowers."

This brought Stevo to the window. They watched as Slavko went into Strincich's Liquor House.

When Slavko exited the liquor store, he had a wrapped package in one hand and the flowers in the other. Slavko didn't look across the street, but was hoping that Stevo would see him with the flowers. Slavko didn't know that Milan would also be in the store. There was no denying that Slavko was enjoying himself, giving the needle to men obviously interested in Katya.

Slavko arrived at Katya's kitchen door to find Tomo at the table wearing old pants and a sleeveless undershirt. Not sure of the relationship between Tomo and Katya, he found this familiarity somewhat unacceptable.

Seeing the flowers in Slavko's hand, Tomo only said, "Oh, it's you."

At that moment, Katya hurried into the kitchen. Tomo saw the bright smile Katya gave Slavko. "I am ready." To Tomo, she said, "Slavko and I are going to the cemetery to visit Ivan's grave."

"Wait," said Tomo, "I will change and go with you."

Katya placed a hand on Tomo's shoulder. "Not this time, Tomo. Slavko and I want to go alone."

Katya, carrying the bouquet of flowers, wore her white skirt and blouse with the red appliqués along the hem. Slavko was in his suit, carrying his suit jacket and the bottle of kruškovac, Katya's favorite.

The early September day was pleasant, with gentle breezes caressing them as they walked to the cemetery. It would be a long walk, but the old friends didn't care.

The distance from Adams Street to Grant, to the Tolleston Cemetery was fourteen blocks. She held onto Slavko's arm as they walked. This was the first time Katya went for such a lengthy walk. The streets were unpaved in sections making walking a bit hazardous. Slavko got a good look at the slums of the Patch and was disappointed for Katya. He knew that in Lakawanna, his brother's home was not in the best section of town, but it was far better than what Slavko saw in this part of Gary.

Comfortable in each other's company, Slavko and Katya chatted. She asked him if he had married and he said that he had not. He asked about Tomo, and found the story interesting. She told him that she wanted to learn the language and hopefully have her own herbal medicinal business.

"Tell me about Milan." he asked, guiding her away from a hole in the street.

She smiled, thinking of her friend. "Milan is wonderful. From the day we met, he has been my friend. It was Milan who arranged for the house and for Ivan to work at Stevo's store." She shifted the flowers to her other arm. "It happened so quickly, getting the house and getting work for Ivan. I think it was all done within three days of our arrival."

At the cemetery, Katya said, "I wonder if I can find the grave. It was an awful day for me." She looked at Slavko apologetically saying, "Slavko, I don't remember that day."

He saw the pain in her eyes. Taking her by the elbow and guiding her into the cemetery, he said, "Let's walk through and see if we can find it." Walking and looking at the markers, Slavko asked, "Does he have a stone?"

Katya stopped walking. She looked at all the grave markers. She fell to her knees crying, "Oh, Slavko! I don't know. I never paid for one."

Slavko knelt at her side, holding her. "If there isn't one…we will get one."

He lifted her. With one arm around her shoulder, he guided her through the graves. Most of the names on the stones were German.

Katya's head was bent downward, not looking at anything when her foot hit a flat cement marker in the ground. It marked a newer grave which had no grass or flowers on it. The stone was only about two feet long and a foot wide. It was not standing upright, but was flat in the earth. The name on it was IVAN BALABAN, nothing else. No date of birth or date of death.

"Slavko...look." she said through her tears. "It is here." She knelt down, running her hand across the stone, brushing away some loose dirt. "I didn't do this." She looked at Slavko, who was now kneeing beside her.

Slavko took the bouquet of flowers from Katya's hand and laid it on the ground, beneath the stone marker. "Oh, Slavko." she said, leaning her head against his shoulder. He wrapped an arm around her and gently rocked her as she wept. Today, she only wept. She did not cry or sob, she only wept softly. The only sounds were of a dog barking in the distance and the sound of horse hooves on the pavement.

After a while, she straightened up, again running her hand across the stone with Ivan's name on it. She said softly, "I was not as good a wife as he deserved. Destiny cheated him when she put us together."

Both still kneeling at the grave side, Slavko took Katya's hand. He said, "Don't say that. He loved you so very much. He told me your story. I think I know it all." He settled himself into a seated position on the grass and watched as Katya did the same. "He understood you better than anyone else, and loved you in a way no one else has, or will."

Katya said nothing, but Slavko's words comforted her. She knew that the love she and Ivan had was meant to be. From the moment she first saw him, she loved him. People and events had kept Katya from realizing they were destined for one another.

They sat by the grave for a long while, no longer making conversation, watching birds flit about from stone to stone. Slavko tore the paper wrap from the bottle of kruškovac he had bought earlier. Twisting off the sealed cork, he said, "Let's have a drink to Ivan."

They had no glasses, so Katya took a swallow from the bottle. When it was Slavko's turn, he held the bottle up, making a toast. "To Ivan," he said, "A good friend, a good husband, and a man I admired very much." He took a long drink and then poured the rest of the bottle over the grave, placing the empty bottle alongside the flowers.

It was dusk when they returned to the house. They made a stop at a corner bar in Tolleston for a drink and a small meal of sausage and bread. The walk home arm in arm was a quiet one. Both of them lost in their own thoughts. Katya again feeling slight pangs of guilt about her life with Ivan, while Slavko wondered how to tell Katya what was on his mind.

Instead of going into the house, they sat on the front steps, enjoying the cool evening breeze. Tomo had already gone to the tavern to sing, but left a light in the kitchen, the glow visible to the front of the house.

Slavko screwed up his courage and asked, "Have any of your suitors asked for your hand?"

She dismissed his question with a wave of her hand, "There are no suitors." she said.

He wanted to laugh out loud, but didn't. Was she really not aware of Stevo's longing for her, or the tavern owner, Milan's, and even young Tomo's? He thought to himself that there were probably others. He knew how quickly widows were pursued in a mill town.

"Have you thought of leaving Gary?" he asked, lighting a cigarette.

"After Ivan died, I thought of going back home, back to the Old Country." she said, looking up at stars which were starting to come out. The moon gave off enough light so that they were not in total darkness. "I decided it would not be the same." She didn't explain about her letters from home.

Slavko took a puff of his cigarette, and clearing his throat again, asked, "Would you ever consider moving from Gary?"

In the moonlight he could see her eyes looking into his face. He continued, "I know you weren't happy in Lakawanna, but I have saved money. We could buy a house." He hesitated. Then he went on, "A house far enough away from Ivanka and that neighborhood." He waited for Katya to say something.

She wrapped her arms around him, holding him tightly. "Oh, Slavko, how wonderful you are." He felt her breath on his cheek. He wanted to turn his face so his lips would meet hers.

She took her arms away from him, instead taking his hands in her own. "I can't marry you." She hesitated, wanting to find the right words, "I am not ready to marry. Something is stopping me from thinking about marrying."

Katya saw the hurt in his eyes. "Dragi, Dear Slavko, what I feel for you...I don't feel for anyone else." She took his face in her hands saying, "You are my Dear Slavko." She softly kissed him on the lips.

Stevo, in a brooding mood, went to Milan's Tavern. He didn't say hello to anyone, going directly to an empty table far from the bar, against the wall.

Concerned, Milan wondered what was wrong. The two men always greeted one another with a friendly word or a friendly insult.

Carrying two beers in one hand, Milan put one in front of Stevo. With the other still in his hand he sat across from his friend.

Without acknowledging his friend, Stevo picked up the beer and took a hearty drink.

"Hey," said Milan, "are you going to empty the glass in one swallow?" He pushed his untouched glass of beer to Stevo asking "Are you going to tell me what is wrong?"

Stevo just shook his head. He didn't want to talk.

Milan said with conviction, "This is about that fancy dresser, Lakawanna, isn't it."

Stevo said nothing, just looked up at his friend.

Milan motioned to his brother at the bar for two more glasses of beer. Mato said a quick hello to Stevo, placing the two fresh beers on the table, and disappeared.

Sure that no one could hear them, Stevo said, his voice heavy with a combination of sadness and anger, "I was waiting for Katya to come home. She and Slavko have been gone all day."

"I know," said Milan. "Tomo told me they went to visit Ivan's grave."

"I was waiting across the street." said Stevo.

Milan raised his eyebrows, questioning.

Stevo took another drink of beer. "They didn't see me but I saw them. I saw them sitting on her front steps in the moonlight." He hit his fist on the table startling some of the patrons at the bar. "I saw them hug, and I saw Katya kiss him on the lips."

CHAPTER 27

The next morning, Stevo and Bobo were away making a furniture delivery, along with a stop at the Post Office on 7th and Broadway.

Bobo was aware of Stevo's dark mood. It was similar to his mood the night when Ema left. When Stevo was like this, Bobo made no attempt at conversation. Bobo did not know Stevo's history, or that he had lived among the mixed races of New Orleans for many years. He only knew that Stevo was comfortable around black people and treated them nicely. Bobo liked and respected Stevo.

Alone at the store, Milan was also in a dark mood. The picture described by Stevo of Katya kissing Slavko kept crowding his mind. He wondered what would happen now. Would Katya move to Lakawanna? No one knew what Slavko did. It never occurred to them that he was a mill worker. Was he a business man? He certainly dressed well and with all the tips he was passing out at the tavern, Milan thought of him as a man of means. What if Slavko moved to Gary? At that thought, Milan said out loud, "Oh, shit!"

A voice behind him said, "What's the matter?" Katya had heard his exclamation.

"Katya, you are here!" Milan was nearly speechless. He had not expected to see Katya back at the store. He thought she would be with Slavko, possibly packing to move away.

Still not willing to use Slavko's name, Milan said, "I expected you to be spending the day with your friend from Lakawanna." Looking around he asked, "Is he with you?"

She smiled thinking about Slavko, saying, "He left this morning. We said goodbye last night."

Milan was almost weak from hearing this news. He and Stevo had both thought Katya was gone to them forever. Not meaning to, he let out a small laugh of pleasure.

Frowning, Katya looked at Milan. She asked, "Are you alright?"

With a wide grin he said, "I am just fine. Nothing could be better."

Katya went to the back into the kitchen to see Cleona for a cooking lesson. She turned back once and saw Milan watching her. On his face was a happy grin.

Soon, Stevo came in the front entrance of the store, carrying an organ stool in need of a glass foot replacement on one of its three legs.

Milan approached Stevo, stopping him from going farther into the store.

With a sad look, and he hoped, a sad tone to his voice, he said, "Well...she is gone."

Stevo looked a little paler than when he had arrived.

Milan went on. "I have to sell the house. You have to sell the furniture."

Stevo nearly collapsed in a nearby chair. "It can't be true."

Milan said, "You saw it yourself last night. She kissed him. This morning she left for Lakawanna with him."

Stevo was sick to his stomach. Part of his problem may have been that he had too much to drink the night before.

He buried his face in his hands. He could not believe she left with that fat, bearded man without saying goodbye.

Milan couldn't contain himself any longer. He was laughing until tears ran down his cheeks.

Disgusted, Stevo asked, "What the hell is the matter with you?

From behind Milan came Katya with the Sears catalogue in her hand. She said, "He has been this foolish ever since I came in."

She looked at the two of them saying, "Slavko and I went to the cemetery yesterday. It took us a while to find Ivan's grave. Who arranged for the grave marker?"

Milan looked at Stevo because he knew nothing of the stone.

Stevo got up from the chair saying, "We do so many funerals and arrange for so many gravestones, the carver was happy to do this as a favor."

Katya said, "Are you sure I don't owe him any money? If I do, I want to pay."

Stevo held up his hand and said, "No, there is nothing to pay." Again he said, "It was done as a favor."

157

"All right, if you are sure." she said, adding "Do you mind if I take this catalogue home to work with Tomo on some of the words? I'll remember to bring it back in the morning."

"Of course," said Stevo. He gave her a wave, "See you in the morning."

Milan stood in front of his friend, with hands folded across his chest. Smiling he said, "Done as a favor, a free gravestone?"

Annoyed, Stevo said, "I pay you to work, find something to do."

Milan teased his friend, "With all the furniture, the funeral, the money exchange, and now a gravestone. You have a lot of money invested in her. You'd better marry her before I do."

As before, Stevo replied with, "You already have a wife."

At home, Katya helped Tomo with the alphabet. He had trouble writing the letters on the paper, but Katya was patient.

Tomo was so happy that Slavko was gone, that he would do anything to please Katya. He would learn to read and write for her. As for going to school…well, he would just have to wait and see what the future brought.

He was looking through some of the 1,162 pages of the thick Sears Roebuck catalogue when he started to laugh.

Katya was at the stove, frying some potatoes. She asked, "What is so funny?"

"Do women wear these?" He pointed to a page picturing corsets.

Katya leaned over his shoulder and looked at the corsets showing tiny, cinched-in waists. "I have never seen one." she admitted.

When Tomo left to sing at the tavern and the kitchen was tidy, Katya sat with the catalogue. Up until now, she only looked at the furniture and kitchen items. She had never gotten as far as the ladies' hats and clothes.

Looking at the pages of hats, she remembered her first trip to Zagreb with her godfather, seeing the beautiful woman in a yellow dress with a large, matching yellow hat. That was years ago, still Katya could picture it in her mind as if it were yesterday.

Katya kept turning the pages, looking at the different clothing for the American woman. The skirts depicted on the pages of the catalogue showed women in long, slender skirts, with a slight flair at the ankles. Not one picture showed a gathered peasant skirt and blouse. She saw capes and coats listed as mackintosh.

Tapping her fingers on the table, she stared out the open porch door thinking. She had five outfits, none of them in the American style, except perhaps the black skirt and blouse she wore for the funeral. It resembled the dresses depicted in the pages of the catalogue.

From the kitchen, Katya heard the knock on the front door. Seldom was the front door used, so it took Katya a few moments to answer the knock.

Roza, Milan's wife, was once again at Katya's home. It was five-thirty in the evening and Milan should have already been at the tavern from the furniture store, but he wasn't. Roza, certain he was with Katya, had come to confront them.

Seeing Roza, Katya asked, "What's wrong?"

"Where is Milan?" demanded Roza, stepping into the parlor. She tried to push past Katya to look about the house.

Katya put her hand on Roza's shoulder to stop her, saying "What makes you think Milan is here?"

When Roza was marching in the direction of Katya's house, Stevo was on the other side of the street. Unseen, he crossed the street and made his way along the side of the house to the back door. Slipping inside, he took off his suit jacket and rolled up his sleeves. He unbuttoned his shirt at the neck, before nonchalantly strolling into the parlor.

A very surprised Katya heard him say, "I didn't know we had company." He moved behind Katya, putting his arm on her shoulder. "Do you want some coffee?" he offered Roza.

Roza glared at Katya. She spat out her words, "I knew it. This explains the furniture. How many men do you need?"

Roza stomped out of the door back to the tavern.

Katya smiled at Stevo saying, "Well, now you have confirmed her suspicion that you and I are lovers. I am sure she thinks Milan is also my lover."

"Why would she think we are lovers?" asked Stevo as they walked to the kitchen.

"She came here the day after you delivered the furniture. She accused us of being lovers from the first day I saw you."

In the kitchen, Katya moved the catalogue aside to make room for cups. "Do you want some coffee? It is fresh."

Seated at the table, Stevo said, "Is that why you aren't friends with Roza?"

Pouring the coffee she said, "That and other things, private things she overheard between Ivan and me."

The smell of coffee wafted through the kitchen. Katya placed a dish of cakes in front of Stevo which Cleona had given her that morning, and sat down.

She watched Stevo pick up one of the fried cakes, breaking it in half before taking a bite. She said, "Back home in Vladezemla, I was called a witch. Here I am called a kurva...a whore."

She took a sip of the coffee. Before biting into the cake, she asked, "Why does Roza think Milan would be here? He has never been here alone."

Stevo said, "We don't talk about this, so it is private. Understand?" He looked at her, when she nodded that she understood, he said, "Not too far from here lives Loyza. Her husband had an accident in the mill and has only one leg. Loyza takes in washing and mending to earn money."

He let out a sigh, looking directly at Katya he said, "For twenty-five cents, she will do more than washing and mending."

CHAPTER 28

Stevo saw the Sears catalogue on the table. He pulled it towards him, noticing the page of ladies dresses. He asked, "Planning on ordering a dress?"

She shook her head. "No," she said. "I just realized I don't have any thing but Old Country dresses, except for the black outfit."

He took the other half of the fried cake from the plate. "These might not," he pointed to the page, "be suitable to wear here in the Patch."

"I've been thinking," Katya said, "what can I do to get out of the Patch? I'd like to be somewhere where there are nice clean roads and beautiful houses?" Before he could reply, she said, "That is why I am learning to speak American."

Only half joking, Stevo said, "You could marry a man with money."

Stevo nearly choked on the cake when Katya said, "Slavko asked me to marry him. He wanted me to go to Lakawanna with him."

Afraid to ask, Stevo said, "What did you say?"

She laughed, "Oh, I have such strong feelings for Slavko, but I said no." She munched on some cake waiting for Stevo to say something, when he didn't, Katya said, "I was sick on the ship and he carried me out onto the deck. In Lakawanna, he was like a brother to me."

"If you were married," said Stevo, "you would have someone to take care of you, to protect you."

"But I have you!" she cried out, as if he understood, "And I have Milan, and Tomo. I don't need a husband."

Without a pause, he said firmly, "Marry me, Katya."

He watched as she stared at him open mouthed. When she said nothing, he said, "You are going to marry me. Someday, you are going to be my wife."

He stood, picked up his suit jacket, threw it over his shoulder, and walked out the kitchen door without saying goodbye. Katya followed him out and down the steps. She watched him walk along the side of the house to the street. He never looked back.

Katya went back inside and sat dumbfounded at the kitchen table. Was she going to lose Stevo as a friend?

She didn't want to lose him, but she wanted to be in control of her own life. America was her opportunity to be an independent person. Could she be wrong?

For the first time in her life, she did not have to please anyone but herself. There was no family member to tell her she was doing something wrong. After all, in her dream, Ivan and Zolton showed her she was free.

She undressed, put on her cotton nightgown and went back to the kitchen. It was late when Tomo came home to find Katya pouring over the pages of the catalogue.

"You're still up." he said, seeing the catalogue in front of her. "What is so interesting?"

She pointed to a page. "There are all sorts of herbal medications for sale." she said. "I wonder if I could make up some medicines and sell them."

The next morning, Katya, with the catalogue in her hand, entered Stevo's kitchen. Cleona was already making fried day-old bread dipped in beaten egg. She called this French toast.

In the store, Katya put the catalogue on Milan's desk. He gave her a big smile and asked "How are you, today?"

She again wore her usual white dress with the red appliqués. Milan was all in grey, shirt and pants. He wore no tie.

"I am fine." she said, her eyes sparkling. "I think I have a plan for my life. I think I know what I want to do."

Curious Milan said, "What is it? Can I help you?"

"No," she replied, "not yet. I need to talk to Stevo about it and see if Bobo can help me." She walked towards Stevo.

Stevo was close to the store entrance, putting some cards on various tables showing reduced prices on sale items. He had already placed the straight-backed chair out on the sidewalk, indicating the store was open.

Smiling brightly, Katya said, "Good morning, Stevo."

To her surprise, he only politely said, "Good morning," not stopping the placing of the price cards to speak with her.

She followed him as he deposited the cards on each piece of furniture. A bit bewildered, she said, "I'd like to talk to you about my plan, of what I want to do."

"Perhaps later." he said, still moving and not stopping. "I have errands to run."

More than a little confused by Stevo's attitude towards her, she asked, "Will you stop at the Post Office to see if I have any mail?"

It was as if he had slapped her when he said, still not looking at her, "You can take the streetcar to 7th and Broadway to the Post Office. You know enough English to ask for your mail."

Katya swayed slightly, not sure what to say or do. She took a deep breath, walking out the open double doors to the street. She sat on the straight back chair in front of the store. *What had just happened? Did she do something to anger Stevo?*

After a few moments, Katya stood up. She reached in her pocket and pulled out some coins. The streetcar conductor would tell her if she had enough money to pay the fare.

Milan, at his desk at the back of the store, watched Stevo's strange behavior with great interest. When Stevo came to the desk, Milan said, "What is going on? Do I see a lover's quarrel?" He meant this remark to be humorous.

Standing in front of the desk, Stevo dropped the remaining price cards. Casually he said, "I asked her to marry me."

Milan's eyes grew wide. He said, "And...?"

Stevo looked Milan straight in the eyes and said, "She doesn't want to marry. She doesn't need a husband. She told me that she has you, me and Tomo."

Nervously, Stevo put a cigarette to his lips, which he would not light in the store. He said, "Also, Lakawanna asked her to marry him."

Milan reached for a cigarette from Stevo's Player cigarette package. "Let's go out for a smoke." he said. "We need to talk."

Outside, Milan standing with one knee bent, foot resting on the wall, said, "So how is this plan of yours supposed to work? There could be other men ready to help, and, what about Tomo?"

"Tomo doesn't know that much. Not enough to help her." said Stevo. "He is still a greenhorn."

Milan scratched the dark stubble on his chin. His dark eyes staring across the street, "She has a plan. What if that plan takes her away from us?"

Stevo, wanting to change the subject, said grinning, "I think I did you a favor yesterday. Roza came to Katya's house demanding to see you. My behavior suggested that Katya and I were intimate and Roza stomped out, convinced that Katya is a loose woman."

Milan confided to Stevo, "Roza is no longer the sweet girl I thought she was when she first came here. In fact, she is downright mean at times."

"She's jealous." said Stevo. "She can't help but be jealous. Roza sees the looks on the men when Katya comes to the tavern. Half the men in there would leave their wives for her…including you."

On the third day after Roza had been to Katya's looking for Milan, a messenger came to the furniture store, telling Milan he was needed at the tavern immediately.

He couldn't imagine what could be so urgent that it could not wait until evening.

When he arrived at the tavern, his brother Mato was in his usual place behind the bar serving the patrons. Milan looked around. Nothing seemed out of place, though he noticed some of the men at the bar looking sheepish or embarrassed, as if they knew something he didn't.

Mato nodded toward the living quarters near the end of the bar. Before Milan could get to the entrance, he saw a laughing Roza and a man he didn't know, come out of the kitchen. A nice looking man, probably younger than Milan, nice strong build, dark eyes and dark hair, his arm around her waist and she was looking up at him smiling.

Everyone in the bar looked from Milan to the couple, who had not yet noticed him. The mood was tense, the onlookers waiting for

164

Milan's reaction. Roza and the man did not see Milan approaching. She didn't expect him until evening.

Milan struck the man in the jaw so hard, that his head bounced off of Roza's face. The stranger was so stunned he didn't raise a hand to defend himself. Before the man knew what was happening, Milan had him by the back of the neck and the seat of his pants, flinging him out of the door. Then Milan turned to the ashen-faced Roza, her body trembling with fear. He grabbed her by an arm as she struggled, dragging her to the door. He kicked her with such force that she practically flew out the door, landing on the dirt in the street.

Before Roza could pick herself up and gather her wits or think of a defense, Milan was flinging what clothes of hers he had quickly gathered.

Despite a sore bruised knee, she limped to the open door. Afraid to enter, she called to Milan, "It doesn't mean anything." She was pleading, "I only wanted to make you jealous."

Milan kicked the door shut in her face. To his brother, he said, "I want all the locks changed."

That evening, Stevo came to the tavern to see what the emergency was that took Milan from the store.

Stevo sat at the bar waiting for Milan to have a free moment. Mato served Stevo a beer, whispering to him, "Milan is in a very bad mood."

Stevo could feel the tension in the room. There wasn't the usual joking and loud laugher. Instead, there were whispered conversations. The musicians were at the back of the room where Tomo sang with them.

Milan was busy tending the bar with Mato. Stevo looked around for Roza, wondering if perhaps she was ill.

Stevo had been sitting in the bar a long while, waiting to speak with Milan. While he waited, he made conversation with those he knew, listened to the music, and even sang along with one song.

It was getting late and the crowd was thinning. Stevo had just decided to leave when Milan tapped him on the shoulder and with a nod of his head, suggesting they go to a far table.

Settling in a chair opposite Milan, Stevo asked, "Where is Roza? Is she sick?"

"Maybe she is now." said Milan, the disgust apparent in his voice. "I threw her out. Actually, I kicked her in the ass and slammed the door in her face."

Stevo thought his friend was joking.

Seeing the doubt in Stevo's face, Milan said, "It is true. First I hit the guy in the face and threw him out. Grabbed her next and out she went." He let out a deep sigh, "They were coming out of the kitchen arm in arm. She didn't even have the decency to be discreet."

As if Mato could read their minds, he brought a bottle of slivovica and two shot glasses, placing them on the table. He left without saying anything.

Milan filled each glass, followed with the toast, "Na Zdravle."

Putting his empty glass on the table, he said, "I won't be working for you anymore."

Stevo asked, "Any chance of taking Roza back?"

"Absolutely not!" was his emphatic answer. "Mato told me that he suspected Roza was taking money. He said he thought he saw her more than once gather money as she wiped tables or the bar, money that never made its way into the till. Also, there were some men she gave free drinks to."

Milan said, "I'm sorry I can't work with you. I really enjoyed being with you and Katya. It was a nice change from the tavern. I hope you can find someone to work for you."

Stevo said, "I had worked alone for quite a while before Ivan came. I can do it again. It means closing the store when there is a funeral or making deliveries, but I'll get by."

Mato came to the table and nodded towards the door. He said, "Roza is here. She wants to talk to you."

Milan pulled some bills out of his bar apron pocket. "Tell her we have nothing to talk about. Give her this money. Her boyfriend probably dumped her and she needs a place to stay."

Stevo watched Mato go to the door and hand the money to a crying Roza. "What if she comes to me for help?" he asked.

"That is up to you." said Milan, "But you know it would put a strain on our friendship."

Mato was back saying, "She wants more of her clothes."

"Tell her I put her things in the yard." said Milan. "She'd better hurry before the goats eat them." To Stevo he said, I have already had the back door lock changed. Tomorrow, I will get a new lock for the tavern door."

On his way home, Stevo went a little out of his way, passing Katya's house. He saw the kitchen light. At the back door, he could see Katya at the table, with what looked like weeds scattered in front of her. He knocked softly.

She was surprised to see him. When she opened the door, Katya backed away, giving him room to enter. She was wearing her long, white cotton nightgown with a blue crocheted shawl around her shoulders.

"He asked, "May I come in and sit down?"

She didn't speak, only nodded. It was obvious she was still confused by his distant behavior earlier in the day.

Sitting across from him, she finally asked, "Would you like something to drink?"

He shook his head no, fingering the dried herbs on the table.

Katya wanted to ask him why he had been so cold to her, but she didn't. She just looked at his downcast face. At last, she said, "Why are you here?"

He sighed and looked up at her saying, "I came to tell you that Milan won't be at the store anymore."

Katya looked surprised and before she could ask why, Stevo said, "He and Roza have split, so now he needs to be at the tavern all the time."

"Why?" she asked.

He didn't want to go into the details, so he shrugged his shoulders. When he didn't say anymore, Katya said, "Is that all you have to say to me?"

He rose to leave, and she also got up. Neither spoke as he neared the door.

Stevo placed a hand on each of her shoulders, pulled her to him and kissed her. He wrapped his arms around her and kissed her as she had never been kissed before.

When he let her go, she stepped back, looking at him with wonder in her eyes.

Without a word, he was out the door and on his way home.

CHAPTER 29

The next morning was a rainy Saturday. The rain kept Katya home, unable to have a cooking lesson or to ask Stevo more American words. She found a newspaper someone left on the street car. Katya brought it home to see if she could read it. Words such as 'dissolve', 'hesitate', or, 'municipal', she didn't understand.

What she was missing most of all, was seeing Stevo. She didn't understand his behavior. He was barely speaking to her, almost ignoring her. And, yet, that kiss! It was all she could think about after he left, and pretty much what she was thinking about this morning.

Tomo was still asleep in his cot on the porch. Katya felt a cool breeze. She thought that Tomo might need another blanket. Then she realized he couldn't sleep on the porch in the winter. The only heat would be from the stove in the parlor and the cook stove in the kitchen. What would she do for firewood this coming winter?

She hurried into her room and from the trunk she hadn't looked into since arriving in Gary, she took a feather-filled comforter.

Tomo never stirred when she covered him with it.

Drinking tea, Katya stared at the assorted plants and herbs on the table. She knew what she wanted to do with them, but didn't know how to start. She was hesitant to ask Stevo, not sure if he wanted to help. And Milan...did she dare ask him, now that he had problems of his own? She looked at the open door to the porch where Tomo slept. He could not help her, actually, he needed her help, though he didn't think he did.

The rain stopped around noon.

Tomo ate his breakfast of bread and cheese standing over the ice box, because Katya's assorted plants were still scattered across the kitchen table. He wondered if all his meals would be eaten standing, while she worked with her plants.

Katya came into the kitchen dressed in her blue cotton skirt and blouse carrying her shoes.

Seeing Tomo dressed, she asked, "Will you walk with me to Stevo's? I need to ask him a few things."

"It's pretty muddy out there. Are you sure you want to go today?" he said.

"We can take our shoes off or watch where we step." She waited for a reaction from him. When there was none, she said, "This is important to me. And for you," she added. "We have to think how to arrange the house so you can sleep where it will be warm this winter."

"I hadn't thought of that." he said.

When Katya and Tomo arrived at the store, they saw Stevo working with customers, so they went around the back and entered the living quarters. Cleona was busy cleaning up from cooking breakfast.

Tomo looked longingly at the sausage and flapjacks on a side plate. This was a more appetizing breakfast than the bread and cheese he had eaten earlier.

Cleona, seeing him eyeing the food, put a plate on the table. She said, "You sit and eat." This much English he understood. Smiling at her, he did as she said and started to eat.

"Missy want some breakfast?" Cleona asked Katya. Katya, smiling, shook her head no. She sat next to Tomo, patiently waiting for Stevo to be free.

Cleona had pulled the curtain open on the window that looked out into the store. Stevo noticed the curtain was pulled aside and looked in, seeing Tomo and Katya. He stepped into the kitchen, greeting them both.

He was polite and businesslike, standing at the window where he could see if someone came into the store.

"I don't know if I have time to give you an English lesson today." he said, deliberately using the word 'English' instead of 'American'.

Katya asked, "Would you prefer we talk in the store so you don't have to watch through the window?"

"Let's stand here in the doorway." he suggested.

"I didn't come for a language lesson, I need some advice." said Katya. "I need to think about winter and where Tomo will sleep. The house is small and he can't stay on the porch."

"Let me think," he said, looking out into the store and not at her, as he spoke.

Katya couldn't understand his manner. She was remembering his kiss from the night before, and now he was behaving as if they hardly knew each other.

He looked past Katya and said to Tomo, "There is a loft above this kitchen. It would make an excellent bedroom for you. The heat from the kitchen would make it a warm place to sleep this winter."

Katya couldn't believe her ears. Stevo offered Tomo a far better place to sleep than she could. She looked at Stevo, disbelieving that he would take Tomo away from her. She would be alone. She thought she saw the slightest glint of merriment in his eyes. *He was doing this on purpose!* She stared at him. *He was doing this to show her that she could not get along without a man to care for her.*

Stevo left Katya when he saw a woman enter the store. She turned to look at Tomo who was devouring the last of the flapjacks. He dropped his eyes, and Katya knew he was considering Stevo's offer.

Stevo returned to the kitchen door, "Tomo, could you help me open up a cabinet. I want to show the lady how easily it can be done."

Katya sat at the table. Cleona came to her, putting a hand around her shoulder. She said, "I got some dried mint. I'll make you some tea."

Cleona sat across from Katya, each of them with a cup of mint tea. Cleona watched Katya with caring eyes. She had liked Katya when she took care of her after Ivan's funeral. She felt sorry for Katya, here, without family in a strange country.

Cleona asked, "What you planning to do, you, a pretty woman alone?" She nodded towards the store and Stevo. "I thought the Boss and his friend were looking after you."

Katya sighed, "So did I." She took a swallow of tea, "It seems I am supposed to be married and have a man take care of me." She looked at Cleona with determination, "I want my own money. I don't want to have to ask for anything."

"So, Missy," said Cleona, "how you gonna do that?"

"I was hoping Bobo would help me find plants I could dry and package up to sell as medicines." said Katya.

"Well," said Cleona, "you don't need Bobo for that. I know more than him about such things. I grew up in my Granny's kitchen."

Katya's face brightened. "I don't want to talk to Stevo about this. I want to talk with Milan. He knows about business, he will help me."

Katya looked out at Tomo, Stevo, and the lady deciding on the cabinet, and frowned. "How long is that going to take?" she wondered aloud. "I can't walk to Milan's alone."

Cleona gave the tea cups a quick rinse and announced, "I be goin' with you. You don't have to wait for that boy."

Katya noticed as they walked to Milan's, that Cleona would always step out of the way of a white person, sometimes even stepping into the street.

At Milan's, Cleona stopped at the door not wanting to go in. Milan, seeing Katya, came promptly to the door. He asked, "What's the matter?" Seeing Cleona, he asked, "Is something wrong at the store?"

"No, Mr. Milan, I just better not come in." He understood, but Katya didn't. To Cleona, he said, "Go around to the back, through the yard. Watch the goats don't get out."

To Katya he said, "I am so happy to see you." He was genuinely pleased with her visit. "Do you need something or did you miss me?" he said only half joking.

"Both." she said.

The tavern was almost empty with only a few men standing at the bar, from there, Mato waved a greeting to Katya.

Milan pulled out a chair for Katya. Seated beside her, he asked, "Something to drink?"

She shook her head no, saying, "I don't know where to start. I need help in starting a business and I don't know how."

Milan said, "All I know about business is this business, meaning selling alcohol." Stevo would know more than I. What kind of business do you want?"

Before Katya could answer, Milan saw the slender Cleona at the kitchen door behind the bar. She was motioning wildly to him. He and Katya both hurried to the open door of his living area.

Hands on hips thin, little Cleona admonished Milan, "You hear them goats? Hear them crying? How come no one has milked them? Should have been done this morning and here it is way past noon."

"Those were my wife's goats. She's gone and won't be back." said Milan.

"What you gonna do with them?" asked Cleona, bristling.

Milan shook his head, "I don't know. Sell them or give them away."

Cleona nearly jumped with joy, she said, "Then give them to me! My sister has two little ones and they need milk." She didn't wait for Milan to answer. She was taking the goats.

Preparing to go out the back door, Cleona said, "Missy, my sister lives real close to here. You wait for me, I be right back." To Milan, she said, "Don't you let her leave till I get back, you hear!"

Milan and Katya smiled at one another seeing how happy Cleona was. They almost laughed watching as she happily found a long piece of rope and tied the goats together, leading them out of the yard.

Returning to the table in the tavern, Milan said, "Where were we? Oh, yes, you were going to tell me about your business."

Katya folded her hands, then laced and unlaced her fingers. She said, "I know more than a little about healing." Milan only nodded, waiting to hear more. "When I was in Selna, Old Julia was the village healer. She taught me everything she knew. She told me that as long as I had the knowledge she gave me, I could take care of myself."

Milan had heard this before, but he let her speak.

She lightly tapped her hands on the table. "That's what I want to do. I saw in the catalogue they have boxes of medicines for sale. I want to do that."

Milan asked, "What does Stevo say?"

"Nothing," she said, "he barely speaks to me. He thinks I should marry a man with money and have someone to take care of me."

"And...and," she was searching for words, "he has even offered Tomo a place to live. I will be alone!"

This surprised Milan. He said, "Katya, I don't understand. I know he is fond of you. We both are. Perhaps you misunderstood."

A tiny tear trailed down her lovely face. She said, softly, "I don't know what to do. Everything was so wonderful. I had you, Stevo, and Tomo. Now I have no one."

It took every bit of Milan's willpower not to wipe the tear from her face...Not to pick her up in his arms and carry her to his rooms behind the bar.

Later in the day, when Cleona and Katya arrived at Katya's house, Tomo was there waiting for her. It was now past four in the afternoon. He was surprised to see Cleona with Katya.

Cleona saw the cloth bag with what she was sure were Tomo's clothes. On one of the kitchen chairs were Ivan's shirts and the pants Katya had altered to fit Tomo.

"What is this?" asked Katya. "Does this mean you are leaving...today?"

Feeling only a little guilty, Tomo said, "Stevo showed me the loft. It is very nice. We took a bed from the store and got it up there. Later I will get a chest for my things."

Seeing the clothes on the chair, Katya said, "Those are yours now. I want you to have them. Ivan would want you to have them."

Tomo gathered the clothes from the chair and pushed them into his sack. He stood around, not sure what to do or say. He didn't feel right about leaving.

When Katya didn't say anything, Tomo said, "Well, Katya, thank you for everything. I can still help you with the yard." He was embarrassed, "I'll be back whenever you need me."

Walking to the store and his new room, Tomo did feel guilty. Stevo had bribed him with the room, the bed, and the promise of Cleona's cooking, if he would leave Katya. Stevo admitted to Tomo that the plan was for Katya, without the help of Milan, Tomo, and himself, to realize she needed Stevo. She would, in time, agree to marry him.

In the kitchen, Cleona pulled out a chair and sat. She pushed aside some of the dried herbs still spread on the table, saying, "Sit down Missy. I have some ideas and you tell me what you think."

She looked at Katya, watching for a reaction as she spoke, "I live with my sister, giving her a little money each week to help feed the children. Well, now she can get by without money from me. She now has two healthy goats."

Katya did not understand where this was going.

Cleona continued, "I'm no dumb black woman, Missy. I just need help same as you." She was watching Katya's face. "This is a nice house, better than I have ever lived in." Now she saw a glimmer of something in Katya's eyes. She went on, "You let me live here and we will make a business of selling medicines. We can only do it if we are together."

Katya thought a moment. She said, "What about Stevo? How can you work for him and work here?"

"I can go there early and in two hours cook up everything he needs for the day. I put it in the ice box or on the warming shelf. The only reason I stayed longer was to help you with cooking and American words."

Katya leaned against the sink, wondering if this could work.

"Tell me what you thinkin' Missy." said Cleona.

"Where will you sleep?" asked Katya.

"Here in the kitchen. At the store, the boss' first housekeeper slept in the kitchen. We just need to move things around."

There was a knock at the back door. Bobo had his arms full of sacks and bags, all belonging to Cleona. He looked sternly at his cousin. He said, "Are you a crazy woman? Your sister said you are living here now."

He dumped all her belongings on the floor saying, "Skinny thing like you will freeze to death on that porch."

To Katya, he said, "I'm sorry, Mrs. Katya. I hope you know what you are doing, having her live here." As he turned to leave he said, "You will see, she is stubborn as a mule."

After Bobo left, neither woman said anything for awhile. Then, they looked at each other and burst out laughing. Both realized they were breaking unspoken rules and were starting an adventure together, one, a black woman, and the other, a greenhorn hunkie from the Old Country.

CHAPTER 30

A very annoyed Stevo confronted Cleona when she arrived the following morning to prepare meals for the day.

With his hands on his hips and his handsome face in a scowl, he said, "What made you move in with Katya?"

Cleona mimicked him by putting her hands on her hips. She answered him with, "Because that pretty woman can't be livin alone. I'll take care of her as long as she needs me."

She said nothing about their plans for a joint business. Cleona came very close to over-stepping herself when she said, "You just mad 'cause she don't fall all over you the way some of the women who come here lookin at, but not buyin, furniture do."

That remark was so true, Stevo had nothing to say. Finally, as he went through the door into the store, he said, "You just watch yourself, Cleona. Watch how you speak to me!"

Under her breath, with a smile on her face, she said, "Yes, Master Boss."

At the entrance to the store, Stevo opened the double doors and put the straight-backed chair out on the sidewalk.

Milan's horse drawn wagon pulled up in front of the store. Milan and Mato were on their way to the railroad station to pick up their usual order of beer barrels. Mato waved to Stevo, but stayed in the wagon, while Milan easily jumped down.

Seeing Milan, Stevo said, "Roza back home, yet?"

"No, and it won't do her any good to come back." said Milan. He followed Stevo into the store, "I hear Tomo is living here, now."

"There's a loft above the kitchen. We put a bed up there." said Stevo, as they walked to the back of the shop. "Want some coffee? It should be ready."

In the kitchen, Milan nodded a good morning to Cleona. "How are the goats?" he asked.

"I spect they are doin just fine at my sister's." she said, pouring him some strong chicory coffee.

Surprised, Stevo said, "You gave away Roza's goats?"

Stirring sugar into the coffee, Milan said, "I told you, she is not coming back."

Cleona went out the back door and into the yard. Each morning she took coffee to Bobo.

Thinking Cleona could no longer hear them, Milan said, "Katya and Cleona came to the tavern yesterday. That's when I gave Cleona the goats." He took a sip of the hot, delicious coffee before saying, "Katya came asking me to help her start a packaged medicine business. I don't know anything about that." Before Stevo could say anything, Milan said, "She was broken hearted. She claims she has no one, that we all have left her." He looked at Stevo, who remained silent. "She was crying, Stevo. It was all I could do to keep from wrapping my arms around her. Damn it, Stevo! I want to take care of her."

Later in the afternoon, Stevo took the chance of leaving a nervous Tomo to look after the store, while he went to see Katya. Tomo knew enough English to follow Stevo's instructions to be polite, show the furniture, and to explain that the owner had a very important meeting and would be returning shortly.

When Stevo arrived at Katya's home, he found Cleona and Katya re-arranging the kitchen. They could not move the iron stove because of the pipe that went into the wall, but did manage to push the ice box closer to the sink. This made room for the cot from the porch to be placed against an empty wall. It would have been better to have the cot nearer the cook stove, but they couldn't make that work. There was no room in the kitchen for Cleona's belongings, which were still in bags on the porch.

Stevo was touched with a pang of guilt when he saw the exhausted women push an empty crate under the sink to be used as storage.

Without a greeting, he asked in Croatian, "How can I help you?"

Neither woman saw him enter. Katya was flustered when she saw him. She still didn't understand his moods. Today, he was pleasant and wanting to be helpful.

Cleona nodded a greeting, leaving to go to the porch and sort through her belongings.

Katya said, "I'm sorry we can't offer you anything. You see we are re-arranging things."

"I see," he said, "anything I can do?"

Katya slumped in a chair at the table. "I don't know," she said. "Cleona needs a place to sleep." Katya indicated the cot. "But, we don't have anyplace for her things. What Tomo had, he kept in his bag, but I need a place for Cleona to hang up her clothes, a place for shoes, and more."

Stevo took the chair across from Katya. He said this time in English, "Let me send you a cabinet for Cleona. I can send one just the right size to fit against the back wall."

"How much will it cost?" Katya asked.

Irritated he said, "It doesn't matter what it costs. I want to give it to you."

Cleona, keeping her opinion to herself, heard the conversation but wanted to interject when Katya said, "No more gifts, Stevo. You made me understand that I am on my own now." She paused, looking toward the porch, realizing the need for the cabinet. She said, "Send the cabinet. I don't need to pick it out." She looked at his blue eyes and felt sad, "I want to pay for it."

Stevo wanted to say more. He wanted to let her know how he felt, how much he cared. When he had asked her to marry him a few evenings ago, he never expressed his feelings. Now, with Cleona in the house, he couldn't say the things he wanted to. He wanted to say it in Croatian, but he kept himself from saying what he should have said long ago.

And...he positively could not take her in his arms again and kiss her, which is what he wanted to do.

Tomo and Bobo were at the house in an hour with the oak chiffonier. It had five drawers and a flat dresser top. With it came keys for the locks on each drawer.

Seeing the dresser, Katya said, "We weren't expecting anything this grand. You probably should take it back."

Cleona was admiring the chest. "It sure is mighty pretty, Missy." she said, a big smile on her face, her dark eyes sparkling.

After Bobo and Tomo put the chest against the wall as directed by Cleona, Katya asked, "How much is it?"

From his pocket, Tomo pulled out the first official bill Stevo ever wrote out for Katya. The figure written on the Markovich Furniture bill was $2.25. The actual cost was $4.75.

Katya looked at it and said, "Wait here." She went into her bedroom for the money.

Cleona looked at the bill Katya dropped on the table. Digging in the pocket of her gray skirt, she pulled out coins, dropping them on the table top. There were three Liberty Head nickels, one Barber quarter, 2 Barber dimes and several Indian Head pennies.

When Katya returned, she had in her hand two of the dollar silver certificates from the money exchange she had made previously with Stevo. Katya looked at the change on the table. Cleona picked up the quarter and handed it to Katya, who caught the pleased look on Cleona's face.

Handing the money to Tomo, she said, "Here is the money. Please tell Stevo thank you and that we like the chest."

Bobo asked, "Mrs. Katya, if you need anything. You know I will help."

Tomo said, "I can stay and help with the yard if you want."

"Thank you, both." said Katya, with a smile. "Cleona and I can manage."

She watched the two men, both visibly embarrassed and confused, with what they didn't understand was going on between Stevo and Katya.

Cleona watched the men as they headed to the wagon. With a big grin she said, "You are right, Missy. We will manage."

The next morning at the furniture store, after Cleona was finished with her work in the kitchen, she walked out into the store. She went directly to the display of kitchen cabinets. She studied the low, two-drawer Acme table with a bin for flour and sugar underneath. It wasn't what she and Katya would need and it wasn't what she wanted. Next to the low, table top cabinet, she found the perfect one. It was the same table with a two door cabinet above it.

Stevo had been watching Cleona as she studied the cabinets. He didn't approach her, thinking she was just looking, and not buying.

Bold as a bee about to attack, Cleona marched up to Stevo saying, "I want that tall cabinet, but I don't want to pay the $7.45 price."

Stevo blinked and before he could reply, Cleona said, "I work for you and Bobo works for you, so I think you can give me a better price. And," she added smugly, "I see the better prices you give to some of those rich people comin here."

From her pocket, she pulled out a drawstring cloth tobacco pouch. She emptied the bag of all her change on the desktop.

Stevo kept from smiling. This little black lady was as feisty as could be. He saw a Morgan Silver Dollar, several quarters, dimes and nickels.

"How much is here?" he asked her.

"I don't know." she said, "You count it and tell me how much more you need."

Without counting the money, Stevo scooped up the change, returned the empty tobacco pouch to Cleona and said, "There is enough here."

She gave him a sly smile, knowing well he was practically giving the cabinet to her. She said, "Thank you, Mr. Boss. I be leavin now to make room in Missy's kitchen for the cabinet. This is gonna surprise Missy. She don't know I was buyin it."

Cleona went back into Stevo's kitchen. Done with her work, she gathered up her things.

Stevo almost laughed out loud when he saw Cleona, for the first time, instead of leaving out the back kitchen exit, she walked proudly through the store and out the double doors. After all, she was a customer.

CHAPTER 31

The first of October was pleasant, with leaves turning into shades of yellows and reds. For the first time, Katya felt as if she saw some beauty in the Patch. Perhaps she was becoming used to living there.

She and Cleona, with large potato sacks, roamed the countryside for plants.

Cleona's knowledge of the healing properties of plants astounded Katya. Most of the plants in this area, Katya did not recognize. They gathered nettles, ginger root, along with some sassafras tree bark.

Cleona said, while foraging through the ground near the Little Calumet River, "We will be doing much better in the spring finding healin flowers and plants."

Seeing Katya's disappointed look, Cleona said, "Don't you worry, we gonna do just fine. I got us some milkweed plants to put in the yard. Next spring you just wait and see what we can do with them."

The back porch of Katya's house was now the storage and sorting room for the collection of plants they had accumulated. Where Cleona found the screens to make drying boxes, Katya never knew. Newspapers scrunched up in the shape of baskets held some of the plants. A wire was strung across the length of the porch for plants and stems with leaves.

The junk man was ordered by Cleona to make regular stops in front of the house to show what he had accumulated. Always looking for glass jars, bottles, or even some crock jars, the two women behaved like children at Christmas digging through his wagon.

Milan made occasional visits to Katya, always bringing a little something. Cleona and Katya were especially delighted to receive the occasional pieces of roast pig or lamb from some wedding or christening party Milan had been invited to.

As far as Milan was concerned, he was no longer married. He had not heard from Roza, which surprised him. He expected her to beg to come back, or for money. The last he heard about Roza, was that she worked in a boarding house. He also heard she left with one of the men who had a job in Whiting at the Standard Oil Refinery.

181

Divorce was not common, but remarrying while still married was done. It was not uncommon for men who left wives and children in the Old Country, to marry in America and start new lives.

This late afternoon, Milan was bringing the two women some cheese strudel which he bought at the Serbian Brothers' Market at 1724 Massachusetts.

Coming through the back door into the porch bewildered him. To him, what he saw was just a collection of weeds. He hoped Katya knew what she was doing. Like Stevo, and everyone else, he assumed this was all Katya's doing and that Cleona was only her live-in housekeeper.

This is how Cleona wanted it. In time, it would be evident the women were business partners, but for now, no one needed to know.

Milan was impressed with how efficiently the kitchen had been arranged, even with the sleeping cot against the wall. He saw a few empty glass jars on the shelf of the kitchen cabinet Cleona purchased. Despite all the plants, which seemed to be everywhere, Milan liked the order of the kitchen.

At the kitchen table, Katya sat across from Milan. Cleona placed a plate before each of them, but not one for herself. She always behaved as a servant, except when alone with Katya. This was not at Katya's request, but something Cleona herself wanted.

Finishing the strudel and their coffees, Milan said, "Katya, I would like to take you to a theatre."

"When?" she asked, then adding, "I don't know what a theatre is."

"A theatre is where people dance and sing on a stage. You will like it." he said.

"Come," he said, "put on your blue dress. We can take the streetcar downtown."

"Go on, Missy," urged Cleona, "you get dressed and go."

Katya stood a bit undecided, then abruptly turned and went to her bedroom.

"I'll go help her." said Cleona.

Stretching his legs out and leaning back in the chair, Milan lit a cigarette.

"Well, you look comfortable." said a voice behind Milan, startling him.

Sitting upright in the chair, Milan turned to see Stevo, smiling sheepishly.

Dressed nicely in a brown suit with a tan necktie, and as handsome as ever, took the chair opposite Milan.

"Taking the night off?" asked Stevo.

Unhappy at Stevo's intrusion, Milan said, "Yes, I needed a night off."

Stevo, always needling Milan, especially when it had to do with Katya, asked, "What do you hear from Roza?"

"Go to hell." said Milan, using his standard answer to any of Stevo's annoying questions.

Katya came into the kitchen looking wonderful in her blue lace dress. Stevo, more than a little surprised, stood to look at her.

"You look beautiful," he said. "I haven't seen you for awhile."

Katya was visibly flustered by Stevo's appearance. She hadn't seen him in more than a week, and now here he was at the same time as Milan.

"Hello, Stevo," she said, "it is nice to see you"

Milan, wanting to get away from Stevo said, "Come Katya, we must go."

Stevo, his voice dripping with charm said, "Am I keeping you? I am so sorry."

"Yes, you are." said Milan, "We have to catch the streetcar." Taking Katya by the arm, he said, "Come Katya."

Katya was becoming uncomfortable. Something in the exceedingly polite tone of each man's voice didn't sound normal.

Stevo asked, "Where are you going?"

To Milan's regret, Katya answered, "To the theatre."

With slits for eyes, Milan glared at the exuberant Stevo, who said, "Oh, I would love to see the Petticoat Minstrels. I hear it is a wonderful show." Stevo took Katya's other arm saying, "Let's go together. I will pay for the tickets."

At the Orpheum Theatre near 8th and Broadway, Katya was in awe of the burlesque show. The only performances she had seen in the past were the Gypsy street dancers in Trieste or the Tamburitzan performers in the Market Square in Zagreb.

Nothing shocked her tonight, not the low-cut blouses or the tights worn by the dancers, which showed every line of their legs. Throughout the performance, she sat leaning forward in her seat, watching the people on the stage and looking at all the nicely-dressed people in the audience. Her eyes danced with excitement. She loved it!

Leaving the theatre with the crowd, Katya noticed many men were going down a different street. "Where are they going?" asked Katya. "Is there another show somewhere?"

Both Milan and Stevo, on each side of Katya, kept on walking in their chosen direction. The direction which many of the other men from the theatre were headed was towards the street with the nickelodeons, the saloons, and the numerous brothels.

Like a spoiled child, Katya stopped walking. She announced, "I don't want tonight to end so soon." With a look from Stevo then to Milan, she said, "I don't want to go home."

The men looked at one another. Stevo said, "Back there is the West Hotel. We can stop for a drink or a sandwich."

Katya spun the men around and headed in the direction of the West Hotel.

Two glasses of wine later, on the streetcar ride back to the house, Katya praised the evening. She couldn't thank Milan and Stevo enough for the wonderful time she had.

The men had to laugh at her childlike enthusiasm about the singing, the costumes, and the dancing. She had never seen such dancing. The ladies kicked their legs up so high!

The walk from the Broadway streetcar to Katya's house was a little more subdued. It was obvious Katya was wearing down. Oh, but it had been a great evening!

At her house, the kitchen light, as always, was burning. Neither Milan nor Stevo wanted to be the first to leave, so they both walked her to the kitchen door.

Katya stepped up on the first step. Facing the men, a little tipsy, she put a hand on Stevo's shoulder, and the other hand on Milan's shoulder. She leaned forward giving Stevo a light kiss on the lips and next, she kissed Milan on the lips.

Without a word, she turned and walked into the house.

When she was inside and the door was closed, Milan said, "That does it. I am going to marry her."

CHAPTER 32

At the bottom of the wooden trunk, Katya found some of the winter clothes she had worn in Lakawanna. Today, she wore a plain, brown tweed woolen skirt with a matching cape with slits for her arms. Her collarless blouse was thick cotton, long sleeved, and buttoned up the front.

Mississippi Slim, the black junkman, rang his hand bell while waiting on the street in front of Katya's house. Hearing the bell, Katya and Cleona ran out to see what they could buy. Cleona was wrapped in a wide-knitted scarf, enough to keep off the autumn chill. She jumped up to the seat alongside Slim and immediately spotted a large cooking pot. She reached over and grabbed the four-gallon pot, handing it to Katya.

"Got any more pots?" she asked, digging through some papers and rags, looking for empty bottles.

"Sit still," said the bearded man, "I know there is another smaller pot, got them from a restaurant." He got down, walking to the back of the wagon. Nodding a greeting to Katya, he started to push his wares around until he found the pot.

Seeing the smaller pot, Cleona told Katya, "Take that pot, Missy. We gonna need it, too."

Finding nothing else they could use, Cleona paid twenty-two cents for the two galvanized pots.

Later that morning, done with her work in Stevo's kitchen, Cleona got permission to have Bobo use the delivery wagon to take her and Katya back to the area around the Little Calumet River. Witch hazel bushes were in bloom this time of year, and Bobo grumbled while Cleona delivered orders as to which bushes she wanted.

At the house, Bobo wasn't pleased as he dragged the branches along the side of the house to the back. There were so many branches, not all would fit on the porch. Bobo muttered, "Crazy women," as he tried to leave a path on the porch into the kitchen.

Grudgingly, he left the hatchet and hammer with promises that Cleona would return them promptly the next morning.

Katya and Cleona were almost always together, so Katya was amazed when an item, such as the large, straw basket as big as a bushel, appeared in which to put the witch hazel flowers.

"Why did we take the whole bush," asked Katya, "if we only need the flowers?"

Working methodically and quickly pulling the yellow, spidery flowers off the branches, Cleona said, "We gonna use it all, even the branches."

At the store, when Bobo told Stevo what the two women had done, Stevo went to Katya's house to see what was going on. He shook his head in disgust when he saw the mess of flower petals and leaves strewn throughout the porch and on the kitchen floor.

"For God's sake," he exclaimed, "what is all this about?"

Before Katya could admit she didn't know what it was all about, Cleona said, "Missy is making a powerful lotion from this bush. She gonna bottle it and sell it."

Stevo took Katya by the arm and pushed her into the kitchen, leaving Cleona on the porch.

Not stopping in the kitchen, he led Katya into the parlor, where Cleona could not hear them. Stevo pushed Katya onto the sofa, sitting beside her.

For a moment, he just looked at her, shaking his head. When he spoke, he said, "What am I going to do with you?"

When she only stared at him and didn't reply, he said, "Where are you going to sell this lotion? Where are you going to get the bottles or labels?" He stood up, the frustration building within him. "What do you know about business? Nothing!" Stevo paced the floor still ranting, "You need to stop this foolishness. It won't be long and you won't have any money left."

He looked at her upturned, tear-stained face saying, "Oh, shit, Katya…"

Tears were trailing down her cheeks. She looked so helpless, almost childlike. He sat next to her putting his arms around her. She nestled her face in his neck and he felt her warm tears on his skin.

"Damn you, damn you, Katya," he said, "why won't you let me take care of you?"

Katya would not admit to Stevo, or anyone else, but she was becoming unsure of her plan to sell medicinals. Stevo was right, she knew nothing about business. It was one thing to have a neighbor in the village in need of a poultice or a special tea, but packaging and selling to stores were beyond her.

Stevo held onto Katya for a long time. Her arms were around him and he liked the feel of them. When she finally pulled away, like a child, she wiped the tears from her face with the sleeve of her blouse.

His voice was not as harsh as before. "Why do you insist on doing this? I can't see you succeeding."

Katya looked at him, her eyes almost pleading for understanding, she said, "I need to do something with my life, because I need to be somebody."

He took her by the shoulders, looking into her sweet, beautiful face, he said, "Then, be Mrs. Stevo Markovich."

He would have kissed her, but Cleona was at the door. "Missy," she said, "I need help filling that big pot with water."

Instead of going back to the store, Stevo inwardly cursed himself for staying to help the women. He chopped the branches, hacking at them until they were slivers which Cleona put in the large pot of boiling water. He knew of witch hazel lotion and thought it was easier to buy a half-pint bottle for twelve cents than it was to make it.

He had to get back to the store. He knew that leaving Tomo there for more than a short while was not a good idea. Stevo had already been gone far longer than he had intended. Leaving, he noticed the wood pile at the base of the steps was low. He had planned to leave Katya to fend for herself, but he couldn't. He couldn't bear the thought of her being cold or not having wood to cook with. Bobo would deliver some firewood in the morning.

The following morning, after delivering firewood to Katya, Bobo informed Stevo that an injured Milan was at Katya's house, and had spent the night there.

Stevo practically ran to Katya's house. He found her on the back porch, sorting through the remaining witch hazel cuttings.

Looking up she said, "Oh, Stevo, thank you for the firewood. Cleona and I were going to go to the woods to gather kindling."

Stevo only nodded at Katya and went directly into the house. Cleona was in the kitchen stirring the huge pot filled with broken-up bark.

Seeing the look on Stevo's face, Cleona said, "He be in the bedroom."

Milan looked very comfortable in Katya's bed, leaning against two large pillows. Seeing Stevo, his surprised look changed to a sheepish grin.

"Good morning, Stevo." he said, with a 'cat ate the bird' look on his face.

Standing next to the bed scowling, Stevo demanded, "What happened? What happened that you couldn't leave last night?"

Milan pulled himself to a sitting position dangling his legs on the side of the bed. He showed the bruise on his knee to Stevo, saying, "I fell over those branches in the porch. I hurt my knee so badly that I couldn't walk home." He still wore that grin which was infuriating Stevo. Milan said, "Katya was so upset, she insisted I stay the night. She insisted I sleep in her bed so she could take care of me."

"And...did she?" demanded Stevo.

Still with that sheepish grin, Milan said, "Oh, YES, she did."

Stevo, swayed for just a moment. Then he kicked Milan in the bruised knee as hard as he could.

"Yeba!" swore Milan, grabbing at his knee.

Even with his pained knee, Milan was laughing as he saw Stevo marching out of the room. Stevo continued in his fury, through the kitchen, and down the stairs, without a word to Katya, who stared in bewilderment.

Cleona came to the bedroom door, her arms folded over her chest. She said, "Mr. Milan, the devil is gonna get you for that lie!"

CHAPTER 33

Several days had passed since Stevo saw Milan in Katya's bed. Hurt, angry, and upset, he had not been to see Katya, nor had he gone to the tavern. Tomo noticed how quiet Stevo had been at the store and his absence from the tavern.

One afternoon when Katya came to the store, Stevo pretty much ignored her, and when he did speak to her, he appeared cool and disinterested. She left the store in tears.

Cleona had an idea she knew what was gnawing at Stevo. She and Katya were going downtown to a pharmacy in the hopes of buying some bottles and corks. She decided that before Katya came back, she should explain to Stevo the joke Milan had played on him.

Seeing no customers in the store, Cleona slipped through the kitchen door going to the desk where Stevo sat brooding.

Seeing her, he said, "Something wrong?"

"You still mad at Mr. Milan?" she asked.

He was a bit taken aback by the question he thought impertinent. He said, "Why would that interest you?"

"Because, ain't none of it true." she said. "Missy slept on the sofa all night, Mr. Milan playin with your mind."

Relief flooded Stevo's face. "Is this true? Are you telling me the truth?"

She grinned, pleased to see him smile. She said, "I told Mr. Milan that the devil would get him for telling such a lie."

Stevo jumped up. "Where is Tomo? I need to see Katya right away."

"She is comin here. We goin to buy some bottles downtown." said Cleona.

Stevo ran into the kitchen and shouted up to the loft, "Tomo, Tomo. Get down here, hurry."

Just then, Stevo saw Katya through the open door talking with Bobo in the yard.

He ran into the yard, grabbing Katya's arm, pulling her away from Bobo. As he nearly dragged her to the kitchen, he said, "Katya, I am so sorry, so very sorry. I misunderstood something Milan told me."

"I know," she said, "he thinks it is very funny. He told me he was teasing you."

"Oh, Katya…" he took her hand and kissed it.

She looked at him sideways taking her hand back. She said, "Is this how it is going to be? This game the two of you are playing? If this goes on, I will not be friends with either one of you. I will do without you both."

He grinned, looking at her lovingly, he said, "Oh, Katya. You will have us both always. Even after you and I are married, Milan will still be a pain in the ass."

Stevo insisted on going with Cleona and Katya to the pharmacy on 7th and Broadway. It was a short ride on the streetcar. With Stevo accompanying them, there was no problem buying two dozen eight-ounce glass bottles and the right size corks. Stevo insisted on paying for these.

A quick stop at the Post Office produced a letter for Katya from Trieste.

On the streetcar back, Cleona sat in the seat behind Stevo and Katya, happily clutching the bag of bottles and corks. She couldn't wait to get home and start filling the bottles.

Stevo asked Katya, "Do you want to read your letter now?"

"No," she said softly, "I know it is more bad news."

"Would you like to go to the tavern? We haven't been there for awhile." asked Stevo.

"Not tonight," she said, "Cleona and I have to bottle up the extract. Our kitchen is a mess."

When they got to their stop, Stevo said, "Come by the store tomorrow. I've missed you."

"I'll try." she said, as she and Cleona headed for their home.

There was only one funnel to use, so filling the bottles took awhile. Both Cleona and Katya were very pleased. When the bottles were filled and corked, Katya lined them up on the kitchen cabinet shelf, to be admired.

Pleased with what they had accomplished, Katya said, "Now we have to figure how to get labels for the bottles. And we need a good name.

"It is your idea and your recipe," said Katya, "Let's call it Cleona's Extract."

Cleona picked up a bottle carrying it to the table where she sat down, studying it.

"No, it has to be special. My black name ain't gonna make it special." she said. "What are some of the names from the catalogue?" she asked.

Sitting across from her, Katya tried to remember the names. "There is *Princess Cream* and *Famous Parisian*, and oh, yes, *Oriental*." She remembered more, "There was *Venus* and *Peerless*."

"Cleona turned the bottle in her hand, saying, "How about Queen? I want to think it is good enough for a queen."

Katya brightened, "Instead of Queen, how about Royal? It would mean the same thing. Don't you think?" she asked.

Cleona said, "*Royal Witch Hazel.*" She thought about it. "I like the name. It sounds elegant."

Seeing Stevo with customers, they didn't want to intrude by going directly into the store, so Katya and Cleona entered Stevo's kitchen door.

While they waited, Cleona made some red clover tea. Katya reached for two magazines on the table. These appeared to be old and well-worn issues, both had dates of 1910. One was the Woman's Home Companion and the other was the Ladies' Home Journal. Katya liked these better than the Sears Roebuck catalogue. The pictures all pertained to women's clothes, hair styles, and outrageously huge hats. Katya didn't care for the hats, but the dresses interested her.

Entering the kitchen, Stevo said, "I see you found the magazines. What do you think?"

Flipping through the pages, Katya said, "Where did you get these?"

"Watch the store." he said to Cleona, as he sat next to Katya.

Stevo said, "I get these along with the newspapers from the train porter. I give him a little something for his trouble."

"I'd like to take these home." said Katya.

"Of course, they are yours." said Stevo.

Katya closed the magazines and put them aside. She said, "Cleona and I need your advice. We need labels for our witch hazel extract and we don't know how to get them."

Stevo let out a long sigh saying, "You two are determined, aren't you?"

Standing at the door, still watching for customers, Cleona made a face at the back of Stevo's head.

Katya ignored Cleona. She said, "We need help in putting the information on the label."

"First," he said, "you need a name."

Katya beamed. "We have a name. *Royal Witch Hazel*." Just then an idea popped into her head, "With a crown over the name."

Hearing this for the first time and liking it, Cleona smiled.

Stevo had to leave the table several times to help customers. Each time when he returned, Cleona kept watch at the door, while he helped Katya work on the label design.

Seeing Katya's excitement as the label took form, delighted Stevo. When the design was completed to both Katya's and Cleona's satisfaction, Katya wrapped her arms around Stevo's shoulders, kissing him on each cheek, saying, "Oh, Stevo! I am so excited."

Stevo said, "I will work with the man who does the printing for the store. He will know what size is good for the bottle you are using."

While Cleona was out visiting with her cousin Bobo, Stevo said to Katya, "There is a meeting of the Hrvatksa Bratska Zajednica this evening. I would like you to go with me."

"What is this and why should I go?" she asked.

"It is a good place to meet other Croatians. This Gary group is only a part of several other groups in the United States. It is like one big family."

"First there is a meeting, then later, we have a little zabava...get together. You will meet more of our people."

Back home, Katya asked Cleona if she minded being alone when Katya went out for the evening.

Cleona laughed, "Missy, I like it here. Growin up I slept five in a bed. The house was always full of family. Livin with my sister, I slept with the children." She waved her hand in a circle taking in the kitchen, "It is so nice to be where it is quiet and I can be alone. Don't you worry about me, go out and have a good time."

Having looked through the two magazines Stevo gave her, Katya decided the closest to the American style of dress she had were the black vestments from the funeral.

When Stevo came for Katya, he couldn't help but be pleased how lovely she looked. Her red hair, beautiful creamy complexion, and emerald green eyes seemed to be enhanced by the black clothing. Her black, crocheted shawl was just enough to ward off the coolness of the evening.

Katya and Stevo followed the small crowd into what appeared to be a closed restaurant. Chairs were lined in rows for a meeting. More men than women were seated in the chairs.

There were four chairs facing the seated people.

Stevo waved or nodded to several people, who openly stared at his companion.

The language spoken was Croatian, but Katya didn't understand the meaning of the minutes that were read of the previous meeting, or the number of paid memberships, or the announcements of some births and deaths.

When the meeting was completed, the chairs were moved to line the walls and people gathered in groups for conversation. A table with refreshments was laden with cakes, strudels, and coffee. Beer and wine could be purchased at another table.

A few people came to meet Katya and greet Stevo. To Stevo's disappointment, only a few married women came with their husbands to meet Katya. He had expected many of the women to come and make her feel welcome.

No one joined them, which Stevo found unusual. As a rule, new people were very popular and the center of much interest.

Milan came towards them. "I'm late." he said. "Hello Katya." To Stevo, he gave a sheepish grin, saying, "Still mad at me for my joke?"

He pulled a chair closer to Stevo and Katya, noticing that they were being stared at. To Stevo he said, "What's going on? Why aren't people coming to meet Katya?"

The words were barely out of his mouth, when across the room, he saw Roza whispering to a group of men and women, who had disapproving looks on their faces.

Milan said, "What the hell is Roza doing here? I thought she was in Whiting." He stood up, walking towards her. The moment she saw Milan, her face became pale, and Roza hurried through the crowd into the back room. Milan followed her out the door, but she had disappeared.

Not wanting to socialize, Stevo and Milan walked Katya home. They tried to make conversation with her, but she was very quiet.

When they came to Katya's house, going in through the kitchen, Cleona was already resting on her cot. The three of them tiptoed to the parlor and sat down. It was obvious Milan and Stevo wanted to talk to Katya, to explain why she was not greeted as Stevo had hoped, but Katya wanted to be alone.

Milan said, "It was Roza. She was spreading lies about you. I am sure of it. I will break her neck the next time I see her."

Katya's eyes glistened with tears. Milan and Stevo each wanted to wrap their arms around her, instead, each held one of her hands.

In a very low voice, she said, "Back in the Old Country, I never cried. When I ran away from my brother-in-law to Old Julia's house, I didn't cry. When I escaped from the Turk, I didn't cry. When the people on the road and in the fields called me a witch, I didn't cry. I didn't cry when Ivan didn't come after me to Trieste, or when Roha tried to kill me, or when the gypsy women threw stones at me. Instead of crying, I was angry!

She stood up, pulling her hands away from Milan and Stevo. "What is wrong with me?" Katya started to pace the floor. It was as if she spoke to herself and not to them. "What do I care what these people think of me? They are nothing to me. Why have I let myself be so sad in Gary? You two, Tomo, and Cleona are all that matter to me."

Not knowing what to say, Milan and Stevo looked at one another, then at Katya, still pacing the room.

Silently, Stevo and Milan watched Katya. They were witnessing a transformation in her. Neither was sure they liked what they were observing. Her manner, and even the tone of her voice, were hardening.

She stopped pacing. Standing in front of the men, hands on her hips, she said, "I am going to make money in America. That is what Cleona and I are going to do. We are going to make money, plenty of it."

The figure of Bobo appeared behind Katya, startling everyone in the room. He looked upset. "Boss, you gotta come to the store. I got Tomo up in his room. He is hurt bad, real bad."

CHAPTER 34

They all climbed in Bobo's wagon, even Cleona, wearing her nightgown and shawl.

Up in the loft, Milan and Stevo were sickened when they saw the young man's bloodied face. His hands were bruised and swollen, indicating he tried to defend himself.

Upset at the sight of Tomo, Stevo asked, "What happened? Who did this?"

Tomo, through swollen lips, barely whispered, "Fight at the tavern."

Without a word to anyone, Milan was down the stairs and out the door, practically running to his tavern.

Cleona was warming water on the stove, while Katya dug through a cabinet for towels.

Bobo stood in the kitchen feeling helpless, saying, "I found him lying on the ground by the door. Thank you, Jesus...I thought he was dead."

Stevo came down to the kitchen, "I think we need a doctor."

Katya rushed past him going to the loft. Her heart sank when she saw Tomo's face. She swayed for a moment. It was as if she were reliving the night in Vladezemla. That awful night when the Gypsies brought Ivan's bruised and battered body to his home after the Turk's attack.

She knelt beside the bed, studying Tomo's face, not daring to touch it for fear of hurting him. Still on her knees, she called out, "Cleona, bring the towels."

Katya stood when Cleona came carrying the warm towels in a pan.

Stevo, fascinated, watched as the two women studied Tomo's face. They were discussing what they should do. It was as if Stevo watched two doctors in consultation.

Katya said, "Do we dare touch his face? I am afraid we will hurt him."

197

"We should give him some whiskey." said Cleona. To Stevo, she said, "Mr. Boss, you go get some whiskey."

When Stevo returned with the whiskey, Cleona very carefully and slowly, in small amounts, administered the liquor between Tomo's lips.

"Missy, what you think about making a witch hazel poultice for his face, instead of trying to clean him up?" asked Cleona.

Katya said, "I wanted to put something on his face, but I don't know about the plants here." She turned to Stevo, "Please send Bobo to the house for some of the leaves off the branches on the porch."

Trying to stay out of the way, Stevo, with shirt unbuttoned and sleeves rolled up, watched as Katya and Cleona worked. Cleona went to the kitchen bringing up raw honey and more towels.

When Bobo returned with the leaves, Cleona dipped them in hot water, cleaning and softening them. She laid them on towels to cool.

When the leaves were no longer hot, Katya spread a thin layer of honey on each leaf. Cleona gently laid the honeyed leaves on Tomo's face. There was no reaction from Tomo when the leaves were applied.

When his face was entirely covered with the leaves, Cleona gently placed a warm towel over his face, careful not to hinder his breathing. She then cleaned his hands. Tomo never stirred. The whiskey must have done its work, for he slept.

Cleona said to Katya and Stevo, "I be sittin with him for awhile. You both go down. I will call when I needs you." She found a stool and settled herself at the bedside.

When Milan arrived at his tavern there was a CLOSED sign on the door. Inside, he was shocked with what he saw. The place was a shamble of broken chairs, bottles, and tables.

The place was empty. Fear clutched his heart as his called for his brother, "Mato, Mato, where are you?" Milan ran behind the bar to the living quarters where he found Mato lying on a cot, holding a wet towel to his face. Mato had a bump on his forehead along with some bruises.

"Sveti Issus!...Holy Jesus!" exclaimed Milan, rushing to his brother's side. "Are you in pain? Is anything broken? Who did this?" The questions shot out of his mouth like bullets.

Mato pulled himself up on an elbow. Milan helped his brother to a sitting position. Mato said, "Get me something to drink."

Returning with a glass of slivovica, Milan's hand trembled as he handed it to Mato. Milan said, "Tell me what happened."

Mato slowly shook his head from side to side, as if not believing what had happened.

He said, "Some men, maybe four or five of them...strangers, came in. They looked around and asked for you. I said you weren't here. Then one of them said he is probably with the red-haired widow."

Milan's head snapped up at this, he said, "Are you sure he said that?"

"Yes," said Mato. "When Tomo heard this, he told the man that he should mind his own business." Mato wiped his face with a towel. "Then one of the men asked if he was the one who lived with Katya. Tomo told him it was none of his business and that's when Tomo got hit in the face."

Mato stood up shakily going to the doorway he said, "Let's go in the bar. I need another drink."

The brothers found two intact chairs and an unbroken table. With glasses and a bottle between them, Mato continued the narration of the fight. "Our regular customers slowly started to leave. I can't blame them. Whatever was happening wasn't their fight. Tomo hit back and someone said that Tomo was one of Katya's men."

Milan was almost in shock. In the four years of having the tavern, nothing like this had ever happened.

Milan filled both glasses as Mato continued to talk. "When one of our regulars was leaving he said that the men were not from around here. He was right. I didn't recognize any of them." Mato took another swallow from his glass. "Milan," he paused, "one of the men said to Tomo, 'You are going to get what we came to give Milan'."

Milan's eyes grew wide, his mouth dropped open. He was stupefied. He couldn't think of anyone he had offended or wronged that would want to do this to him.

Mato said, "I heard someone say that these men were from Whiting."

Milan locked the doors and spent a sleepless night watching over his brother and thinking.

This was all Roza's doing. Roza now lived in Whiting and the men were supposedly from Whiting. Roza had no way of knowing that Milan would not be at the tavern. He seldom went to the Croatian Fraternal meetings, but Milan knew that Stevo was a dedicated member and would be there. Of all the nights to be away, in all the months of not going to the meetings, this was the night he was gone.

Milan was sick to his stomach with worry and guilt. The beating Tomo and his brother got were because he threw out Roza. This was her revenge. At this moment, he thought he could kill her.

The CLOSED sign remained on the door the next morning. Milan told Mato to rest, not to worry about cleaning up the place. He would take care of it when he returned from Stevo's. Right now, Milan had to know about Tomo.

There was also a CLOSED sign on the Markovich Furniture store door. Stevo was not only tired, but too worried about Tomo, to conduct any business.

It was a Sunday, and many of the businesses were still open. Taverns usually were open 24 hours seven days a week. Some specialty stores were closed on Sundays, but Stevo often would remain open for business.

Milan found Stevo and Katya, both looking tired, drinking coffee.

"Got some coffee left?" asked Milan. "I didn't bother to make any. My place is a wreck."

Katya poured the coffee, offering more to Stevo, who declined.

"How's Tomo?" asked Milan. "This is my fault. Those men came looking for me." He bounced his fist on the table in frustration. "These men came to get even with me for throwing out Roza."

Stevo said, "Cleona is upstairs with him. He slept through the night. I did hear him moan once or twice."

Full of guilt, Milan asked, "What about his face? Will he...will he look alright?"

Katya said, "We will know in a day or so."

"This is my fault." Milan said again. "I should have been at the tavern. They were looking for me. When they found out the Tomo lived with Katya, they said they would give him what they came to give me."

Katya gasped, her hand flew to her mouth.

Both Milan and Stevo saw the pained look on Katya's face. In unison, they both asked, "What is it?"

Katya almost collapsed in a chair. "This wasn't your fault." She said to Milan, "It's my fault for making Roza angry, for not being her friend." She was pleading with her eyes when she looked at them, "I let her be jealous of me when I could have made her see she was wrong."

Milan closed his eyes, shrugging his shoulders said, "Well, she wasn't wrong."

Katya dismissed Milan's remark. She said, "Yes, I am to blame. Because of me, Ivan became crippled. Because of me, we had to come to America."

She looked at them with a realization in her eyes, "Don't you see?" she said, "What has happened to you, Milan, and to Tomo is because of me. If I had never come to Gary, none of this would have happened."

Stevo grabbed Katya by the shoulders, raising her out of the chair. He said angrily, "Stop it. Stop blaming yourself. I don't want to hear this kind of talk."

Katya smiled somewhat sadly while looking at Stevo, and said, "Oh, Stevo. You don't know. Don't you see that I have a Strange Destiny?"

CHAPTER 35

For several days both Cleona and Katya spent most of each day, and part of the nights, taking care of Tomo. When Tomo showed signs of healing with no infection, Cleona bathed his face with a stronger solution of witch hazel than was in the bottled extract.

Stevo was disturbed by the visible change in Katya's personality. She was quiet, as if in deep thought, or perhaps planning something. With Stevo she was friendly, polite, and almost businesslike. Any of the childlike traits he found so endearing were gone. He expected the same sort of excitement when the printed bottle labels were delivered as when they had purchased the bottles. Katya only looked at the labels saying, "These are very nice, just what I wanted."

Another reason for Katya's quiet mood was because of the letter from Trieste. In all the excitement, she put off reading the letter, feeling it was bad news. When she finally read the letter from her mother, Sofia, it carried the news that Katya's beloved Nona Lucia had died. She mentioned this to no one, for she couldn't bring herself to talk of it.

Cleona and Katya, to Stevo's delight, spent more time working in his kitchen. They worked on their witch hazel bottles while still looking after Tomo.

Stevo enjoyed having them in the kitchen. Cleona not only took care of Tomo, but she prepared the meals. Sharing meals with Katya at his table gave him a sense of what it would be like to be together always.

Katya carefully spread mucilage on the back of the labels and just as carefully positioned the labels on the bottles. This was more complicated than she had expected. Too much glue meant leakage along the edges and smears across the printed words.

Stevo, coming back from the Post Office, smiled while watching Katya work on the labels with great precision. When she placed a finished bottle on the table, Stevo said, "Here is package for you."

"For me?" Katya said, seeing it was from Trieste.

She stared at the small packet. Stevo said, "Well, open it. Someone has sent you a gift."

Seeing Katya pulling at the string wrapped around the packet with no success, Stevo cut the string with a knife. Katya pulled away the wrapping from the box. When she lifted the protective layer of cotton, she whispered, "Oh, my Nona, my beloved Nona!"

In the box was the beautiful large red coral cameo brooch which Lucia had received as a wedding gift from her beloved husband Aleksy. She wore it at the throat of her blouse every day from the day of her marriage to the day she left the Earth to join him. Now it belonged to Katya. Katya put the brooch to her lips and kissed it. She was flooded with loving memories of the villa by the Adriatic and the wonderful people there.

"I need a mirror." said Katya, looking around the kitchen and not seeing one.

"Come here," said Stevo, "there is a mirror in my room."

He watched as she stood before the long mirror and pinned the brooch at the neck of her black outfit. She looked at her reflection and smiled, warmed by the memory of how Lucia had worn this brooch in the same way.

She looked at her reflection, the first time seeing it in a full length mirror. Katya turned from side to side observing the movement of the skirt.

"Stevo," she said, still studying her reflection, "I need some new clothes. I don't want to order them from the catalogue. I want to see the fabric and how the dress will fit."

Remembering the seamstress Grace's unhappy encounter with Katya before the funeral, he said, "Let me look into it."

With each passing day, the resentment grew greater in Milan. He wanted to go to Whiting and look for the men he did not know. It would have been just as fruitless to look for Roza. He just couldn't get his mind around the fact that the woman he thought so sweet when he married her, had become so hateful.

Just like most of the men who came to America, choosing a wife was not so much about love as it was about convenience. Men needed wives and women needed someone to take care of them. There were no careers for an uneducated woman. If a woman did not have relatives to live with, many of them were forced to turn to prostitution.

That is how it was with Milan and Roza. Roza had been sent for by her fiancé, but he had been killed in a mill accident by the time she arrived. Milan looked after Roza and finally, they married. No great romantic love, just two people taking care of one another.

Milan didn't realize how little he cared for Roza until Katya had come into his life. He fell for Katya in a way he didn't think was possible. He wanted to be near her, to do things for her. While Ivan was alive, it was a love from afar. But after the funeral, the need in him to be near her was so great, that he neglected his business, leaving most of the work to Mato.

On this early morning, with just a few men at the bar, Milan sat brooding at a table. He nodded greetings at the men, who said, "Good Morning." No one asked about the fight, even if curious. It was none of their business, so they kept their thoughts to themselves.

Mato slipped away from the bar and joined Milan at the table. Keeping an eye on his customers he said, "I know you are my older brother, but I need to tell you what I have been thinking." When Milan said nothing, Mato continued, "If what I say angers you, then I will leave and find somewhere else to stay."

Hearing these words, Milan looked at his slender-faced brother, saying, "What could you say so terrible to me that I would send you away?"

Mato, needing a shave, put the palms of his hands to his face, forming the words he wanted to say in his mind. Dropping his hands to the table he said, "Bratso, Brother, Roza was very hurt." Seeing the annoyed look in Milan's face, Mato almost stopped, but continued, "You see, she knew she wasn't very pretty. But, I thought she looked fine, and thought she was a good woman."

At this comment, Milan's eyes narrowed. Mato didn't stop, he said, "She was good until you went to work for Stevo." Mato waited for a reaction from his brother, not seeing one, he went on, "I think it made Roza feel pretty when the men flirted with her. I warned her, but the more you were away, the more she paid attention to the men."

Mato looked away from his brother's gaze, saying, "Milan, I would have given anything to have a woman like Roza. She was your wife and I said nothing. It was killing me to see her with the men. When she took them in back, I couldn't take it anymore. That is why I sent for you."

After a long while of silence, Milan said, "So, little brother, you are saying that this was my fault?"

Mato said nothing, fearing he had angered his brother. Just then, a customer tapped his beer mug on the bar, meaning he wanted another.

When Mato returned, he didn't sit down. He was unsure how his brother felt hearing what he had said, so he stood at the table.

"Sit, sit," said Milan, "I really hated Roza after the fight. I wanted to hurt her."

Seeing the concern in Mato's eyes, Milan said, "I won't do anything to her. I didn't realize how much I hurt her. I wish I had known how much you cared for her...maybe, just maybe, if she wanted, you could have been together." Milan sighed and looked away. He said, "Oh, shit! Is anyone happy in this world?"

Cleona was happy! She was pleased with the healing of Tomo's face. It had only been a week and most of the swelling and redness were gone. Tomo insisted on coming down to the kitchen. He was tired of ice packs and honey masks on his face. Stevo helped Tomo down from the loft.

Sitting at the kitchen table, Katya admired Tomo's face.

To Tomo, Stevo said, "Come, I have a mirror. Come see how well your face looks."

Cleona sat next to Katya. Handling one of the finished bottles, she said, "Missy, I got another idea."

Seeing the questioning look on Katya's face, she said, "We gonna make a beauty cream using honey." She grinned at Katya, "What you think? How does Royal Beauty Cream sound?"

Katya was speechless. She stared at Cleona. What was she thinking? As Stevo and Tomo were returning, Katya finally said,

"Cleona. We haven't even sold one bottle of the witch hazel, and you want to make something else?"

Stevo and Tomo sat at the table looking from Cleona to Katya. Stevo said, "What's going on?" To Cleona, he said, annoyed, "Now what do you want to make?"

She pointed to Tomo's face, saying "Look at his face. Look at his skin. He be prettier now than before the fight."

Katya moved closer to Tomo, studying his face. She said, "I can see under the redness, his skin is beautiful."

Embarrassed, Tomo said, pushing Katya's hand away from his face, "Stop it. A man is not supposed to be pretty or have beautiful skin."

Being ignored by the women still discussing Cleona's idea, Stevo got the coffee pot and poured Tomo some coffee, also placing a piece of apple cake in front of him.

Stevo and Tomo exchanged a 'now what?' look.

CHAPTER 36

There were subtle personality changes in almost all of those within the close circle of Katya's friends, even in herself. Many of the insecurities of her younger days haunted her. She wasn't called a witch, but the fact that she had not made any women friends made many believe she was a loose woman. Katya wasn't interested in socializing. She was now fully dedicated to the business she and Cleona had started.

Stevo also was aware of the changes within himself. For one thing, he grew a mustache, adding to his good looks. He stepped back from pursuing Katya. His feelings for her did not change, but now he had more competition for her attention. He wasn't pleased when a drummer, a term used for salesmen, took notice of Katya.

Jim Slade worked for the Thompson & Bros. Lamp Company. Jim had a great personality, which helped him make sales easily. He was not quite six feet tall, good looking, with wavy black hair, a trim black mustache, and friendly brown eyes. His suits were fashionable with vests. To keep warm, he wore a long woolen coat with a fur collar.

He was not only a very successful salesman with accounts in Indiana and Illinois, but also part owner in the company. He had photographs and sketches of the lamps he sold, but also had actual lamps to show and sell from his blue 1911 Chevrolet Classic Six automobile. His image as a successful salesman was confirmed by the clothing and car.

Stevo's heart sank when in mid-November, Jim Slade, showing Stevo pictures of his lamps, saw Katya come out of the kitchen into the store. She was only steps away from the men. Jim dropped the photos on Stevo's desk and went directly to Katya, who wore a brown skirt and tan, high-necked blouse, the coral cameo at her throat.

Seeing Katya, her hair elegantly pulled back into a bun, her green eyes hypnotizing him, he said, "Steve, tell me this is your sister."

Trying to keep his annoyance from showing, Stevo said in a level tone, "No, Katya is not my sister."

Not taking his eyes from Katya, Jim took her hand in his saying, "Well, Katya, tell me who you are and what you are doing here. Do you work for Steve?"

Katya slipped her hand from Jim's. Her manner was cool and polite. She said, not using 'Stevo' because only the people in the Patch used it, "Steve is my dear friend. He allows me to work here."

Jim was full of charm. He had to know more about this beautiful woman and how 'dear a friend' she was to Steve. He took Katya's elbow, leading her to a nearby table where they sat. He called out to Stevo, "While I talk with Katya, look at the pictures of the lamps."

Stevo left the pictures where they were dropped and joined Katya and Jim at the table. There was the slightest change in the salesman's look, as if he may have over-stepped himself.

Trying to keep the conversation light, Jim said, "Well then, Katya, if you aren't a sister, you must be a cousin." He was trying to get some indication of Katya's relationship to Steve.

"If you must know," she said, "Steve is helping me with my business."

Jim brightened. He could talk business without stepping on Steve's toes. "What sort of business are you in?" he asked.

As if summoned, Cleona listening at the door came quickly to the table. She put down their two products saying, "Here, Missy, show the man." She disappeared as quickly as she came.

Seeing the questioning look on Jim's face, Katya did not disclose that Cleona was a partner, she said, "Cleona works for me." She handed the extract bottle and the honey cream jar to Jim. "This is what we make. Both are excellent."

Jim looked at Katya's beautiful face and skin, asking, "Do you use these?"

Stevo's eyes blinked, unnoticed by Jim, when Katya said, "Of course. I have used these for years. My family made these formulas in Europe."

Jim liked the packaging. A very slender pink ribbon tied in a bow was added to the neck of each bottle and jar. He was impressed with the elegant presentation of both items. The cork on both the bottle and jar were sealed with wax.

Most of all, he was impressed with Katya. Stevo and Katya looked at one another, while Jim Slade fingered the two beauty items.

Being a salesman and very friendly with people, he said with conviction, "Katya, I think I can sell these for you."

He saw the quick look Katya gave Stevo. Not sure what the business arrangement was between Steve and Katya, Jim turned to Stevo. "Steve, I go to a lot of fancy lady's shops. I think these would fit nicely in some of them." He glanced at Katya, but she let Stevo be in charge because she didn't know what to say.

Stevo said, "We don't do consignments. You buy outright at our wholesale price."

Another new American word: 'consignment'. So much more for Katya to learn.

Cleona, with her ear to the kitchen door, was tingling with excitement, while Katya was almost faint, not understanding what was going on in front of her. Her mind was whirling and she wasn't hearing the conversation.

The next thing Katya knew, they were standing and Stevo shook hands with Jim.

Stevo said, "Give us a little time to pack up the boxes and I will write up an invoice."

Jim smiled broadly, "While you are doing that, I am going to take this pretty lady to lunch." He looked at Katya, "Would you like lunch in the Gary Hotel dining room?"

Katya looked at Stevo. He wasn't pleased, but he gave a very slight nod.

Katya said, "I've never been there."

Beaming, Jim said, "Get your coat. We'll drive there in my car."

Perhaps the most noticeable change was with Tomo. The beating left him a bit quiet and withdrawn. His face was completely healed, showing no scars, yet he seldom went to the tavern. Instead, he studied English with the enthusiasm Katya had hoped for. Her English, or American as she liked to call it, was very good. She constantly asked Stevo the correct usage of words.

To Stevo's delight, Tomo showed a growing interest in the store. Not only did he help with furniture sales, but he was excellent working funerals with Stevo. It was working funerals that pleased Stevo the most. Tomo showed a caring gentleness that the families of the deceased appreciated.

Tomo's reading and writing were improving. It would take more practice before he could write out an order or the proper burial papers.

Still, Stevo was pleased with Tomo's work, so much so, that Tomo now received a weekly salary.

At the tavern, customers noticed the change in Milan. They had never seen him so reserved. He had always been ready with a bawdy remark or a joke. Milan no longer drank hard or laughed as hard. Just as Katya carried the guilt that she had indirectly been the cause of the fight, so did Milan, but with more conviction.

It took several days to repair the furniture damage from the fight. Milan and Mato worked to repair what broken chairs and tables they could salvage.

In the past, Milan discouraged gambling, but now he had two slot machines and a table in back for card players. Once, he had hoped to make the tavern a gathering place for families, now, he considered it a place to make money. The other bars had 24-hour card games and some even had women in back. He wasn't going to get involved with women in the back. That was a sure way to invite fighting amongst the men.

The weather was cold and business was not as brisk as it had been. He had electricity, which was not dependable, so if needed, he had two wood burning parlor stoves.

He missed Katya and Stevo greatly, while it was Tomo the customers and musicians missed. Stevo stopped by once or twice, but didn't stay long. The friendly insults and jokes between them were just not there as they once were.

Stevo invited Milan to come to the store and visit with him and Katya, but Milan was reluctant to leave the tavern. There was always the thought in the back of his mind that the men from Whiting would come back to finish what they started.

CHAPTER 37

Sunday, December 31, 1911.

Katya was at her house. The rooms resembled a warehouse instead of a home. She and Cleona had moved all the parlor furniture to a corner of the front room. There were bottles, jars, and boxes filled with natural excelsior used to pack and protect the bottles and jars when transporting.

Practically no meals were prepared in the kitchen, which now was where they made the witch hazel extract and the honey face cream. Cleona still slept in the kitchen, and if Jim Slade continued selling their products, it wouldn't be long before Katya's bedroom would be used for storage.

When Tomo was convalescing, it became a habit for Cleona to cook meals in Stevo's kitchen where they ate together. That is where they two women were headed this evening, as soon as Katya finished dressing.

This was New Year's Eve. Katya wasn't sure what that would mean in America. She only remembered New Year's in Vladezemla, where there was a nice meal, toasts at midnight, and occasionally, a gift of money to signify prosperity for the coming year.

No longer caring what people thought of her for not wearing widow's black, she was slipping into a blue silvery dress. Now, all her new dresses had a high collar where she pinned the beloved coral cameo brooch. Her hair was twisted and piled high on her head, held in place with an ornate tortoise shell comb. It was her Christmas gift from Stevo.

The night was cold, only nine degrees. The temperature had dropped thirty-seven degrees during the day. Katya, along with Tomo and Stevo, was going to the New Year's Eve celebration at Milan's. She missed Milan and was looking forward to what the celebration would be like.

Because of the temperature, Bobo drove them to the tavern, with instructions to come for them at 12:30. Even with fur lap robes covering their legs, they felt the cold.

They arrived at the bar at about nine o'clock to find it crowded and loud. Seeing Tomo, several people shouted greetings, hoping he would sing.

When Milan saw Katya, he almost stopped breathing. She looked like a jewel in the silvery dress with her hair up. He smiled and nodded almost shyly to her, while giving Stevo a friendly wave.

It was so crowded that Mato had thought to store a table behind the bar, anticipating Stevo and Katya's arrival. Moving it out into the tavern, a table cloth appeared, as did glasses and a bottle of Italian wine. The Chianti was a pleasant surprise for Katya. She looked to the bar and gave Milan a smile, he only nodded.

Most of the people were quite happy and many already were drunk. The tables were placed around the walls to leave a dance area in the center of the room.

Katya and Stevo danced a kolo, which meant Katya had to hold the hem of her skirt off the floor for fear of tripping. They danced to a couple slow tunes, but mostly they watched the people and enjoyed hearing Tomo sing.

Mato kept an eye on Stevo and Katya's table, bringing small dishes of cheese, some fried dough sprinkled with sugar, and a plate of roasted lamb. During the day, the lamb was prepared in a spit in the yard behind the tavern. It wasn't a party, a zabava, without roasted lamb.

Many people came to greet Stevo and Katya. Even some women came to wish them a Sretna Nova Godina...Happy New Year. Milan remained behind the bar. Katya glanced his way every now and then, seeing him looking her way. He never came to greet Stevo or Katya, which was unusual. Stevo dismissed it thinking Milan was busy.

The closer it got to midnight, the noisier the room became. Mato passed out noisemakers to each table. Katya had never seen such things. One was a metal disk on a handle with a wire holding a wooden ball. When it was shaken, the ball hit the metal disk, making quite a racket. There were also horns and whistles.

As the close of 1911 approached, men had their pocket watches in their hands, watching the time, preparing to greet 1912.

When someone shouted "Happy New Year", Katya had never seen such chaos. The noise, the shouting, the whistling, and the blowing of horns were things Katya never saw or expected.

Another thing she never expected was all the wild kissing. Men kissing each other on the cheeks while giving the women a quick kiss on the lips. Tomo came running to Katya and gave her a quick kiss on the lips, and wished her a Sretna Nova Godina. Stevo reached across the table, pulling her to him, also giving her a New Year's kiss. It appeared acceptable for men she didn't know to kiss her on the cheek or on her hand. Everyone was kissing everyone.

Milan came to the table. Without a word, he lifted Katya under her arms so she stood in front of him. He pressed his lips to hers, holding her in his arms. Onlookers nearby became quiet and stared at the length of the kiss. Stevo waited for Katya to push Milan away.

When Milan finally let go of Katya, her cheeks were pink. He leaned forward and whispered in her ear, "Ljubim Te"...I Love You. He did not acknowledge Stevo. Milan returned to his place behind the bar.

Katya dropped into her chair, aware of the stares in her direction.

Solemn faced, Stevo asked, "What did he whisper to you?"

"I couldn't hear." she lied.

On the ride home, Tomo was especially aware of the tension in the air. He didn't even try to make casual conversation. He sat up front with Bobo, who gave him a look indicating he also felt the tension.

The kiss was not the only thing that upset Stevo. The fact that Milan did not give Stevo a sarcastic wink or some parting goading remark indicated to Stevo the kiss was not meant to make him jealous. That kiss was meant for Katya.

When the buggy stopped at Katya's house, Stevo made no motion to help her get down. Tomo took Katya's hand to help her step out of the buggy.

She said, "Good night and thank you, Stevo."

He only nodded.

Tomo walked Katya to the back of the house, and waited until she was inside before going back to the buggy.

From her cot, Cleona heard Katya come in. She asked, "Have a good time, Missy?"

Katya said, "Cleona...Cleona, I was kissed tonight as I have never been kissed before." She looked at her friend, "I felt the kiss all the way to my stomach."

"Mr. Boss kiss you like that?" she asked

"No," said Katya, "It was Mr. Milan."

"Oh, Oh!" said Cleona.

CHAPTER 38

This time, Katya knew why Stevo behaved in a cool manner towards her. Just as before, he was very polite and all businesslike. There was no talking away what happened at midnight. She didn't dare mention the kiss...nor did she want to talk about it. Most of all, she could not forget that Milan had said, "Ljubim Te."

Not quite a week had passed since that night. Cleona and Katya still came to the store to work in Stevo's kitchen, gluing labels and going over their accounts.

The days passed rather nicely, with Cleona and Katya in the kitchen, seldom going out into the store. Meals were a bit strained...polite, but strained. Katya couldn't find a topic of conversation to which Stevo responded with interest.

For some reason, none of this bothered Tomo. He chatted with them at the table and they answered him without hesitation.

Tonight, after the evening meal, Katya said to Stevo, "Will you help me with the bookwork. I need to know what profit we have. It is time I gave Cleona what is hers."

"Of course I will help." he said politely, lighting a cigarette. He reached for a bottle of wine and poured some in a glass. "Wine?" he asked Katya.

She shook her head no. From an empty chair, she took a box of receipts and the checks from Jim Slade for his sales.

Katya moved her chair closer to Stevo and watched as he went through the various receipts. He had a paid out column and cash received column. It wasn't long before Katya understood what he was doing and how he figured their net profit.

When he was finished, he handed her the paper with the result.

Katya looked at Stevo with wonder, "Did we really make that much?" Motioning to Cleona, she said, "Come look at this. Cleona, we have some money."

He had meant for Katya to struggle, to know how much she needed him, but he couldn't do it. Even with the hurt he felt, he had to help her and Cleona.

"We need to decide how much money you will need for more bottles and labels." he said. "Tomorrow, we will go the Gary State Bank and open an account." He pointed to the checks, "With an account you can deposit or cash checks."

"How much money do we owe you?" asked Katya.

Stevo took a sip of wine. He thought a moment, putting down his glass, saying, "You don't owe me anything. Most of what I helped you with was a gift."

Katya laid her hand on his. He wanted to pull away, but couldn't. He enjoyed her touch. She said, "Stevo, I want to give you back the parlor furniture."

Seeing his look of surprise, she said, "I can count the times it has been used. The set is as good as new. We have sheets spread over the pieces now."

"Where will you sit?" he asked. "I see you barely have room in the kitchen."

"All we need is a place to sleep," said Katya. "We spend most of the day here with you and almost always have evening meals with you. Besides, we need the room for boxes and bottles."

Her hand was still on his. He hated himself for not having the will power to pull his hand from hers. "Are you sure you want to do this?" he asked.

She nodded yes and so did Cleona, but Stevo couldn't see Cleona at the far end of the room.

"Alright, after the bank in the morning, Bobo and Tomo will come and get the parlor set."

Katya gave him a grateful smile and he felt himself weaken. Why couldn't he stay angry? He thought to himself, '*If she knew the power she has over me, she would have it all*'.

With the sales of their products, Cleona and Katya were feeling pleased.

Katya had her money in a bank account, but Cleona didn't want any part of banks. She didn't want anyone to know what she had or where it was.

With the new clothes, money in the bank, and her ever-increasing grasp of English, Katya was becoming a stronger woman. She was at a place in her life where she was pleased with herself. Since her tight circle was made up of Stevo, Tomo, Milan, Cleona, and Bobo, no one else mattered to her.

Busy with their growing sales, packaging medicinals was put on hold. Instead, Katya and Cleona were toying with an idea to make a soap using their honey cream base.

This afternoon, Katya, dressed in a fashionable green dress with lace at her throat to offset the coral cameo, wandered about Stevo's shop. She was remembering the first day she came there to look at furniture for the house. The house which now was the laboratory for Royal Beauty Products and no longer in need of nice furniture.

Returning to Stevo's desk, she asked, "What are you studying?"

He was holding a paper announcing a meeting for plans for a Croatian Catholic church. He felt a certain amount of guilt saying, "There is going to be a meeting to raise money for the Croatian church. I feel terrible. Ivan and I started a pledge drive, but with Ivan's...Ivan's accident and everything happening since, I haven't continued with it."

Katya took the paper from his hand, looking it over. She asked, "Were you planning to go to the meeting?"

"I should," he said, "If only to turn over the book of pledges we already have. I don't know if after all this time the people will honor their pledges."

"When you go, I would like to go with you." she said. "I miss going to a church. Someone told me there is a big church, Holy Angels, but it isn't near and it isn't Croatian."

She leaned against his desk, half sitting and half standing. Stevo was aware that she smelled of honey and flowers. She said, "Ivan's father had the most beautiful little chapel in the back of his house." She had a faraway look while she spoke. "It was beautiful with a large cross with Jesus looking down at us. It was my favorite place. When I felt alone or frightened, that was where I sat, in the back." She smiled wistfully at Stevo. "Oh, I would love such a private chapel, all my own."

It took all of Stevo's willpower not to say, "Marry me. I will build you a chapel all your own." Instead he said, "The meeting is tomorrow night."

The fundraising meeting for the Croatian church was held in a store. The crowd was not very large. Scattered chairs, boxes, and barrels were used for seating. Most of those in attendance were men. Only a few women were there. Almost everyone knew Stevo, and most of them knew of Katya, who looked very beautiful in a sinful, maroon dress. One never wore any shade of red when a widow. The women were shocked, but the men couldn't stop admiring her, and wishing they were Stevo.

Stevo turned over his pledge records. Everyone listened to the unnecessary reasons presented for the need of a Croatian church. A few people asked how much money needed to be raised, who would be the treasurer, and where would the church be built.

When the presentation was complete, the man in charge asked if anyone was willing to make a pledge that evening. Katya stunned the crowd by being the first one to stand. She confidently walked to the front of the gathering and placed the ten-dollar gold piece she had held in her hand throughout the meeting on the table.

There was a gasp from the crowd and Stevo thought to himself, *'Oh, shit. I have to make a matching or bigger pledge.'*

Stevo got up and stood behind Katya while she waited for the receipt she requested.

Waiting for Katya, he felt in his breast pocket for his wallet, hoping he had enough not to shame himself. There were times he could shake her, and this was one of them.

Walking out of the meeting, Katya gave Stevo a mischievous smile. He took her arm as they walked, "You could have told me what you were going to do."

"Don't you see what I did?" she asked. "Now the men have to do their best to match what we gave. If not match it, then work to raise the money in other ways."

"Yes," he said, "I see what you did and you did it to me."

After leaving Katya at her back door, Stevo walked to his store.

In the Patch, there were saloons everywhere and bloody battles were commonplace. This is why Katya and Cleona never ventured to the area between Broadway and Madison Avenue, from 10th to 15th Streets.

When Stevo reached his kitchen door, he saw Tomo waiting for him. Tomo said anxiously, "People have been by. There were some killings outside Jack Johnson's gambling joint." He handed Stevo a piece of paper, "Here are the names." With a worried look, he said, "I don't know if we have enough caskets."

Stevo smoothed his mustache, thinking. He said, "We only have two adult caskets. Having caskets delivered from the casket company downstate in Batesville will take too long. It's too late to call other stores now." He scratched his head, "First thing in the morning, I'll start making calls."

"Will they deliver them to us?" asked Tomo.

"I have to think about this." said Stevo. "We need to make sure all the names on this list will use us."

Once inside, Stevo sat tapping his fingers on the kitchen table, thinking. He got up and went to his desk in the store where he found a personal phone directory. He dialed some numbers and waited. It was eight o'clock in the evening. It took the person on the other end quite some time to answer.

When the phone was answered, Stevo said, "Hello George. This is Steve Markovich from Gary. I need a favor."

Stevo listened to the person on the other end of the connection and then replied, "I am going to need at least four adult caskets. I don't care what kind you have, but I would prefer pine." Stevo listened further and said, "Alright, I'll take what you have. No, you don't have to deliver, we're coming out tonight. We will probably make it to your store about eleven thirty or midnight." Stevo then said, "Thanks George, I appreciate it."

He turned to Tomo, saying, "Find Bobo and tell him to get the delivery wagon ready. We're going to Michigan City tonight. Then go to Katya. Tell her that she and Cleona need to spend the night here while we are gone."

Stevo did some fast calculating to decide how much cash he would need for four or five wooden caskets. The trip to Michigan City with the horse and wagon would probably take three hours, another hour or so to load and settle accounts. Stevo was certain they would be back before daylight.

Being almost nine o'clock, Katya and Cleona were both in their nightgowns. Upon departing, they wrapped themselves in blankets to keep warm and hurried the block and a half to the store, not bothering to change clothes.

"Thank you for coming." Stevo said when they were in the kitchen. "The three of us will be gone most of the night and I can't leave the store unattended. Someone needs to answer the phone."

Katya said, "Tomo told us what happened."

"We take care of things, Mr. Boss." said Cleona.

While the men were taking care of last-minute details, Cleona made some chamomile tea with honey for Katya.

As Stevo was leaving, he said, "I've checked the store doors. They are locked and barred. You know to leave a low light in the kitchen."

Cleona went up to the loft to sleep in Tomo's bed.

Sipping her tea, Katya was wide awake from the short walk. She found the newspapers Stevo liked to read on a side table. She spread the papers out on the kitchen table and scanned the pages, seeing how much she could understand.

How long she looked through the papers, she wasn't sure. Her tea was gone and she got up to see if there was more, when she heard a gentle knock at the door.

She wondered if Stevo had forgotten something. Pushing aside the curtain, she was surprised to see Milan.

Opening the door, she said, "Milan, what is wrong? Has something happened?"

Stepping into the kitchen, he closed the door behind him, turning the lock.

He said, "Tomo told a friend of mine, who was passing by, that they were going to Michigan City."

Katya didn't speak. She looked at this big, rough man and the memory of his kiss must have shown on her face, because he took her in his arms and kissed her again. He felt her go weak. He lifted her slim body in his arms and carried her to Stevo's bed, where he made love to her as he had never made love to any woman before.

He was gentle, loving, and considerate. Milan was amazed that he was capable of so many feelings for a woman. He had been with many women in his life, but had never before felt the emotions flooding him tonight.

Her touch set him on fire and her soft moans inflamed him more.

Katya had never known that such exquisite emotions could be within her. She thought she had loved Zolton, but when they made love on the hill in Vladezema, she felt none of what coursed through her now. Loving Ivan had been sweet, and yet, never did she experience the sensations that engulfed her tonight.

They lay with their arms around each other for a very long time. Her skin felt warm and moist. Milan pulled the sheet up to cover her.

Throughout their lovemaking, neither spoke. It was as if they didn't need words.

When he let go of Katya and rose from the bed, he was silent.

She didn't know what to say.

She watched him gather his clothes. When Milan was dressed, he approached the bed, kneeling beside where she lay. He took her face in his hands and kissed her, ever so gently. "Ljubim te...I love you." he said. When he stood to leave, he looked down at her, saying, "You know what I feel for you. If you want me, you will have to come to me now."

Then he was gone.

CHAPTER 39

When Katya slept, her dreams were crowded with people. Zolton and Ivan still appeared side by side. None of the people in her dreams spoke to her. Queen Valina, now along with Nona Lucia, smiled at her. To Katya, this meant that Queen Valina had died. These visitors in her dreams only looked at her, leaving her to wonder what their nightly appearances meant.

Traveling through the cold and the darkness, the men returned from Michigan City at around four o'clock in the morning. They unloaded their cargo, and adjourned to the kitchen for some coffee. They knew there was no time to sleep before the busy day ahead.

Later, having gone home to dress, Katya and Cleona were back at the store. Tomo and Stevo worked with the family members of the men who had been killed. Katya watched throughout the morning as grieving people came to make arrangements with Tomo and Stevo. The viewing, if there was time for it, was done in the family's home.

Stevo usually tried to make the arrangements with thoughtfulness and without any urgency. Today was different, as there were so many arrangements to make. He and Tomo were very tired, having traveled all night.

Stevo approached Katya, saying, "You may be uncomfortable helping us, but we need you."

She looked at Stevo replying, "Of course, I can stay here all day."

"No," he said, "I really need you to go with Tomo to a home, while Bobo and I go to another. We can't get this done today unless we split up."

Katya didn't hesitate. She knew it had to be done and she could never refuse Stevo a favor.

There were five deceased to care for. Katya and Tomo, as did Stevo and Bobo, did one family in the morning and one in the afternoon.

The fifth deceased was someone new to Gary with no family, living in a boarding house for only two weeks. The landlady had no room for the casket, nor any money to pay for one. This last body was put in a pine box and stored in the barn until the burials of the others took place. The weather was still cold enough that Stevo didn't have to worry about the body decomposing anytime soon.

For several days, with all the activity of the funerals, Katya and Cleona took care of the store. Katya even managed to make a couple sales. She sold a lamp and a small side chair.

Katya was grateful for all the activity, hoping it kept Stevo so occupied that he didn't notice the change in her. Whenever she was alone, she relived that night with Milan over and over again in her mind. The memory stirred her.

Cleona saw the change in Katya, and knew why, but said nothing.

Katya was so confused. She didn't know what to do. Was it possible to love two men at the same time? If she chose one, she could lose the other.

Oh, but the memory of that night with Milan was deep within her.

Five days later, Stevo, Tomo, and Bobo were exhausted. Four burials were done with one more waiting in the barn. That one could wait another day or so without risk.

It was Sunday and the CLOSED sign was on the store door. At home, Katya and Cleona made room on their kitchen table to drink one of Cleona's many herbal teas. They, too, needed some quiet time away from the store. More witch hazel extract needed to be cooked and more face cream needed to be put in jars.

Cleona said, "Do you think we will ever have Jim Slade here?"

The question surprised Katya. "Why do you ask? I see no reason to have him here."

"Because," said Cleona, "what if we don't be at the store, like now? What if something happens and Mr. Boss don't want us anymore? Then how we gonna sell to Mr. Jim?"

Katya's shoulders sagged. She let out a long sigh, knowing what Cleona was getting at. She said, "I won't let that happen."

"O.K., Missy." said Cleona, "As long as you know what you is doin.'"

Late that Sunday afternoon, Stevo stopped by the house.

Cleona moved some boxes and bottles to make room for Stevo to sit at the kitchen table while he waited for Katya to come from her bedroom.

He shook his head looking at the disarray which was now their workroom. Stevo looked at Cleona asking, "How can you two live this way?"

Standing by the stove, stirring the extract in the large pot, Cleona said, "We do what we have to do."

When Katya came into the kitchen, she was wearing a blue cotton robe tied at the waist. Seeing him in her kitchen, she felt uncomfortable. She said, "Stevo, hello. Is something wrong?"

He stood when she came in. "Nothing is wrong. It has been a very busy week. We are all tired." Stevo sat when Katya took a chair at the table. "I can tell this week has been hard on you, too. So I came to take you out to dinner."

Katya looked to Cleona then back to Stevo. Cleona said, "Go on, Missy. You need to get out." She didn't wait for Katya to reply, "Come on, I help you get dressed."

On the streetcar ride downtown, Stevo made several attempts at conversation with little success.

He said, "Your friend from Lakawanna took you to dinner, and Jim Slade took you to the Gary Hotel. I thought it would be nice if we went to the Gary Hotel dining room."

Katya gave him a small smile, but said nothing.

Seated in the center of the streetcar, Stevo turned to Katya saying, "Have I done something? You have been avoiding me, you hardly speak to me."

Katya looked at Stevo then dropped her eyes. She said, "Oh, no. You haven't done anything, nothing at all." She hesitated, "I just have something on my mind."

"Can I help you with it?" he asked, taking her hand in his, "If it is business you know I will do whatever you need." His blue eyes were troubled.

The streetcar stopped at 6th and Broadway, across the street from the hotel.

The dining room was as Katya remembered it. Tables tastefully set with crystal and silver-plated serving pieces on white table cloths. Palm plants were stationed in various places throughout the room.

When they were seated, Katya looked around the room. Each guest was nicely dressed. Many looked elegant. Katya never wore a hat, so she particularly noticed that all the women dining had large, decorated hats with feathers, flowers, and netting. Tonight, she had her hair in a coil, wearing only the tortoise shell comb from Stevo and the silvery dress she wore on New Year's Eve. She felt confident about her attire.

Still she had to ask Stevo, "Do I look alright? I notice all the women are wearing hats."

He smiled that someone so beautiful could still have to ask about her appearance. Stevo said, "You are the most beautiful woman in the room."

Stevo rose to greet Grace Adams, who came to their table. Grace shook hands with Stevo and smiled at Katya, saying, "You look wonderful. So much better than the last time we met."

Katya did not remember this attractive woman wearing a shiny, blue satin dress. Up-to-the-minute in fashion, thought Katya, remembering the pictures from the ladies' magazines she saw.

Stevo held a chair for Grace. Seated, she looked at Katya, "You don't remember me do you?" When Katya looked bewildered, Grace said, "I brought the black dress for you to wear when your husband died." Seeing Katya blink her eyes, Grace apologized, "I'm sorry, I did say that rather bluntly." Grace did notice that Katya was not dressed in mourning, and that she looked stunning in the silver dress with a gorgeous cameo at her neck.

Katya said, "Forgive me for not remembering you." Katya's eyes ran over Grace, studying her hat and clothes. She especially liked the beaded purse she placed on the table.

Katya watched as Grace placed her hand over Stevo's saying, "I won't keep you. I just came to point out the woman at the far table in the lilac dress and Bird of Paradise hat." She nodded in the direction of the attractive woman. "She is recently a widow, bought a lovely house on the north side." She will be in need of furnishing the house with the finest." She smiled at Stevo, "I am sure what lovely pieces you don't have, you will be able to order." Now she patted his hand, "And Steve, I know you won't forget who brought this wealthy customer to your store. By the way," she added, "you know a customer like this expects personal attention. She won't ask for any reduction in prices, but she will expect your…full attention."

Stevo nodded, knowing what she meant. "Do you want me to meet her tonight?" asked Stevo.

Not knowing Katya's name, Grace said, "If your lovely companion doesn't mind sitting alone for a few moments."

Stevo looked at Katya and she nodded that he should go.

Katya watched how Grace put her arm through Stevo's as they made their way through the tables to the lady with the Bird of Paradise hat. Beneath the hat, Katya saw blonde hair and a very pretty face. Dangling pearl earrings matched the waist-long strand of pearls she wore.

Katya felt a twinge of something when she saw Stevo take the woman's hand and kiss it. She wasn't sure what it was.

With a graceful gesture, the woman motioned for Stevo to sit. Katya watched as the two women practically sparkled when talking with Stevo. Not in Trieste or Zagreb had she seen such women. To Katya, every nod of the head, every gesture or smile, was done with elegance.

Katya noticed that once, when Stevo started to rise, Grace took his hand so he sat down again. For a moment, just a moment, Katya thought Grace gave her a triumphant smile. Katya hoped she had imagined it.

On the streetcar ride back from dinner, Stevo was very apologetic for having left Katya alone at the table for as long as he had. Adele Manning, he explained, was new to Gary. She was recently widowed. Her husband had been part of a banking family and from what Stevo understood, a good deal older than Adele.

Katya was quiet. So much was going on in her head. Every now and then, she remembered Milan and what she felt for him. Then the memory of Grace Adams pushed away her thoughts of Milan. She broke the silence by asking, "Have you known Grace Adams long?"

"Yes," said Stevo, "ever since I came to Gary. She introduced me to several of the important people in town."

On the walk from Broadway to Katya's house, Stevo again tried to apologize for being at Adele and Grace's table for as long as he had been.

Katya said, unconvincingly, "That's alright."

When Katya went in through the kitchen door, Stevo waited for awhile, before gently knocking.

Cleona heard the soft knock, and came to the door. "Something wrong, Mr. Boss?" she asked.

He said, "Katya has been different all week. Do you know what is on her mind?"

Cleona shook her head, "No, I don't."

Stevo asked, "Has Mr. Milan been here to the house lately?"

"No," said Cleona truthfully, "He ain't been here since you and him took Missy to the theatre."

CHAPTER 40

The next morning was a Monday so Cleona and Katya were back at the store. Cleona started making breakfast while Katya walked about the store. As she looked at Stevo's inventory, she couldn't help but think that Adele Manning might, just as Katya had, find the furniture too ordinary. If Adele came from wealth, then she surely would prefer the European furnishings Katya lived with at Lucia's in Trieste.

Stevo was nowhere to be seen, so Katya greeted two women who came in the store. She asked if they were looking for something in particular, but they just wanted to look around. So Katya went to Stevo's desk, letting the women know she was available to answer any questions.

The women left, promising to come back. Stevo had been in the barn giving Bobo instructions to take the coffin to a certain cemetery for burial. There would be no ceremony, just a burial, for the man with no family or friends.

Later in the day, when Bobo returned, Katya said to Stevo, "I'd like Bobo to go to Milan's and drop off the house payment for me."

Stevo gave Katya a long look. She dropped her eyes, not able to look him in the face. He said, "When I close the store, you and I will go to Milan's." Stevo watched for her reaction. He said, "It is a sunny day, the walk will be nice."

Katya turned away from him, walking towards Stevo's kitchen. She said over her shoulder, "Alright. We will go."

Just as the day before, there was very little conversation during the walk. Stevo was sure there was a reason for Katya's reluctance to see Milan. Also, Stevo had missed his old friend with the jokes and insults.

At the tavern, Stevo thought he felt Katya hesitate when he held the door for her to enter. Instead of going to the bar and speaking with Milan when she saw him, she only nodded a greeting and went directly to a table.

Stevo went to the bar and shook hands with Milan, who returned his smile. "Give us two wines." said Stevo. Milan only nodded, offering no conversation.

Stevo carried the two glasses of wine back to the table himself. He was aware that Katya looked everywhere but at Milan. Stevo caught Milan looking at Katya, but Milan never came to the table.

When Katya and Stevo finished their wines, Stevo asked, "Do you want another?" Katya shook her head no. "Well, then give him the house payment and let's leave."

She didn't move. Exasperated, Stevo said, "Give me the money." He took the money from her hand and went to where Milan was standing. "Here, damn it. This is the house payment." He looked hard at Milan as the man gathered up the money. "What the hell is going on between you two?" asked Stevo, keeping his voice low so they would not be overheard. Still Milan said nothing, just shrugged his shoulders.

Stevo stood waiting for Milan to say something…anything. When Milan remained silent, Stevo went to the table took Katya by the arm, and pulled her toward the door.

The walk back was not a casual saunter, but a brisk walk. At one point, Stevo stopped walking and took Katya by the shoulders. He said firmly, his blue eyes boring holes into her, "This is enough! The two of you can't behave so stupidly over that New Year's kiss."

Katya's eyes grew wide. *He thought their odd behavior was due to the kiss!* Stevo continued, still holding her shoulders, "I know he embarrassed you, but everyone was drunk that night." He let go of her shoulders, "It's time you forgot about it."

Somewhat relieved, Katya walked beside Stevo, wondering if she could forget the night of lovemaking.

Tuesday was the day Grace Adams and Adele Manning were to come to Stevo's store. As usual, Katya and Cleona were in the kitchen. Breakfast was over and Katya was tying ribbons on her honey cream jars.

Stevo was taking more time than usual getting dressed. When he opened his bedroom door, Katya stood up to look at him. She leaned against the table, her hands folded across her chest. He looked splendid! Every hair was in place. He was clean shaven with his mustache neatly trimmed. The blue tie he wore brought out the color of his blue eyes. Katya didn't recall seeing the grey charcoal striped suit he wore before today.

Katya was disappointed to see him looking so handsome.

She followed him out into the store. He made himself busy going through papers, but Katya saw him look up every now and then at the store windows.

It was shortly after ten when Katya saw the Chalmers Touring Car with the top up, stop in front of the store. Adele Manning was driving this stunning car. With her was the annoying Grace Adams, and both women were beautifully dressed.

Katya quickly disappeared into Stevo's kitchen.

It displeased Katya immensely to see the apricot-colored dress on Adele bring out the beauty of her light skin and blonde hair.

Stevo bowed graciously to both women, kissing both their hands. Without hearing the conversations, Katya knew the women were being charming.

Just as Ema Harper, Stevo's then housekeeper, had watched Stevo show Katya the furniture, Katya now watched from behind the kitchen curtain. She was not pleased to see Stevo holding Adele's hand as he guided her through the store.

Cleona came to the curtain to see what was holding Katya's interest for such a long time. Seeing the beautiful women, Cleona only said, "My, my."

Stevo pulled out chairs at a nearby table for the ladies. He hurried to the kitchen door, nearly knocking Katya over. To Cleona he said, "Bring two glasses of wine...on a tray."

Katya gave him a look that should have turned him to stone. He dropped his head to hide the smile her annoyed look caused.

Still hiding behind the curtain, Katya watched as Stevo brought out an order form to write out which pieces were chosen. Stevo moved about pointing to items. When Adele nodded, he would write the item on the sheet. To Katya's surprise, Adele picked out the most gaudy and highly-carved pieces. Furniture with lion's heads and paws adorned the base of tables, and cherubs clung to the sides of bookcases.

Smoking was never allowed in the store. So when Adele pulled out a package of Murad Turkish Cigarettes, Katya couldn't believe Stevo gave her a saucer to collect the ashes.

Katya could not hear what was being said, but she could see all the flirting and laughter. Stevo again nearly knocked over Katya when he opened the door. Now overtly grinning at her, he asked for Tomo.

Tomo, coming down from the loft, also looked especially nice. He must have had a haircut the day before. Wearing a suit and a tie, he looked like a man. Katya wondered when he had stopped looking like a boy.

To her surprise, Tomo kissed Katya on the cheek as he went into the store.

Stevo popped his head into the kitchen, saying, "We will be gone for a little while." Instead of calling him Tomo, he said, "Tom and I are going with the ladies to have some lunch."

Grace did not recognize Tomo as the young man who was in Katya's kitchen before the funeral. He had become so mature and handsome. As they walked towards the store doors, Grace took Tomo's arm.

Stevo was sure Katya was seething and he loved it. She now might know how many times she had made him feel this way.

The Chalmers Touring Car returned in about two hours with only Adele and Stevo. Katya watched through the windows from a hidden spot as Stevo and Adele appeared very cheerful while saying their goodbyes. Katya didn't like that he kissed Adele's hand when they parted.

Cleona and Katya were still pasting labels when Stevo returned. He didn't bother to come into the kitchen, but went directly to his desk and started making phone calls to find a four-poster bed which could accommodate sheer privacy curtains.

Near closing time, Katya heard Tomo return. She watched from the kitchen door as Tomo and Stevo talked and laughed. Katya watched as Tomo moved close to Stevo, saying something in private. Stevo laughed again, giving Tomo a friendly hit on the arm.

Coming through the kitchen door, Tomo once again gave Katya a kiss, as if she were his mother. She grabbed his arm and smelled his neck. He smelled of Grace Adams' lilac perfume.

"You smell of perfume." she said.

Tomo laughed and continued up to the loft. Stevo overheard this and asked Katya, "Do you want to smell my neck?"

CHAPTER 41

For two weeks, Adele Manning, sometimes with Grace Adams, would come to the store. Not everyday, but enough to annoy Katya.

There were two funerals during this time. Stevo must have called Grace because the women never came to the store when he was not there.

Katya didn't ask any questions, but on a couple occasions, to her dismay, Tomo came in smelling of lilac perfume after having been out all night. His habit was now to give Katya a mother's kiss on the cheek whenever he left or returned to the house.

Stevo had occasional lunches with Adele Manning, but to Katya's knowledge, there were no all-night disappearances. But then, how would she know?

She still thought of Milan, however, but not as much. Her mind was now filled with Stevo and his interaction with Adele. Until now, Stevo had only shown her attention, and she found herself very displeased at the time he spent with the very beautiful Adele.

Another possible annoyance with Adele Manning was that she never wore the same dress or hat twice. Katya envied the beautiful fabrics and dresses every time she saw her. The jewelry was also interesting. Katya only wore the coral cameo brooch. Adele Manning wore long, waist-length single-strand necklaces. Each time the necklace was different, a strand of pearls, crystals, garnets, jade, or even large amber beads.

Jim Slade kept Katya and Cleona very busy. He now not only sold their two products himself, but sold them at a smaller profit to other jobbers, which kept Cleona and Katya cooking and bottling far into the night.

Stevo had to admit that the two women had hit on a good way to make money. He would have loved having Cleona and Katya as full-time help at the store, but he was secretly pleased at their success.

Sometime after all of Adele Manning's purchases had been delivered to her lovely north side home, and the accounts were settled, a builder came to the store.

Katya and Cleona, curious as ever, watched as Stevo led the man around the interior and exterior of the flat roof building. From behind the kitchen curtain, both women watched as the man spread out a large piece of paper on a table. With a pencil, he showed something to Stevo.

When the man rolled up the paper and left, Stevo came into the kitchen for some coffee. He said nothing about the man Cleona and Katya found mysterious. Both women waited for Stevo to tell them who the man was and what he was doing. Stevo just sipped his coffee, watching the store from where he stood. He knew their curiosity was killing them, still, he said nothing.

Instead of asking outright who the man was, Katya tried a different tact. "Are you going to repaint the store?" Taking another sip of coffee, he just shook his head no.

Katya cocked her head to the side, studying Stevo. She asked, "Are you selling the store?"

"No." he said, putting the empty cup on the table while going into the store to help a customer.

For the rest of the day, Stevo did not discuss the reason for the man's visit.

When Cleona and Katya arrived early the next morning, there were ladders leaning against the side of the building in several places. Men were on the roof, while others were hauling lumber up the ladders.

On the front door of the store was a sign: REMODELING ~ PLEASE EXCUSE THE INCONVENIENCE. He also had a similar sign with smaller letters written in Croatian.

A smiling Stevo, wearing a collarless tan shirt, had his sleeves rolled up. He looked delighted and grinned at Katya when he saw her.

"What is all this?" she asked.

"Living quarters," he said. "There isn't enough room in the back of the store."

With no more explanations from Stevo, Katya and Cleona tried to manage their daily routine of pasting labels and sealing the corks with wax amid all the noise and distractions of men coming and going in the outer yard.

Katya couldn't stand not knowing what was going on. She hitched up her skirt, pulling it up in between her legs, shocking onlookers, and climbed one of the ladders.

One of the workmen got Stevo's attention, pointing to Katya who was slowly ascending the ladder. He had to smile. *That was his Katya!* He quickly got on the ladder a few rungs beneath her to protect her, if she lost her footing.

She shocked the carpenters when she got to the top, climbing over the foot high wall of the roof. Katya didn't bother to undo her tucked up skirt, bringing surprised smiles from the workmen. As if she knew what was going on, she surveyed the rooftop.

Stevo, right behind her, asked, "Well, are they doing the job right?"

With all seriousness she said, "Is the roof strong or is it going to fall in?"

Stevo shook his head at the wonder of her. What other woman would think of these things? He said, "The roof is going to be re-enforced, strengthened. That way it won't cave in."

She walked among the men, who no longer were working, but smiling at her, some even openly laughing.

Stevo took her arm, guiding her to the ladder. He said, "Now, Missy"…using Cleona's name for her, "How are you going to get down? You came up here in that hitched-up skirt…By the way, a lady doesn't do that." He frowned, "Your skirt won't make it easy for you to climb down."

Now Katya had an audience of carpenters gathered as she tried to get on the ladder. Stevo was already on the ladder waiting for her to climb on. The fullness of her skirt, even while hitched up, hindered her getting on the ladder.

Stevo climbed back onto the roof to assess the situation. "Wonderful," he said, "now what am I going to do with you?"

One of the men said, "Give her a hammer. She can work while she is up here." Even Katya laughed when she heard that.

Two of the workers made a board with a long rope tied to each side, as if it were a child's swing. One of the men said, "We can lower our new foreman down with this."

Concerned, Stevo hurried down the ladder to the sidewalk below. Nervously, he watched as the men held the ropes tightly as they slowly lowered Katya. A small crowd watched from across the street, having no idea why a beautiful woman was being lowered from the roof in such a manner. When Katya reached ground level, Stevo helped her off the board and the onlookers across the street clapped their approval.

A little later, Milan stopped by the store, speaking only to Stevo. He didn't see Katya and he didn't ask for her. Rumors had reached the tavern that Katya had been stranded on the roof of the store and had to be rescued by the workers.

Stevo told Milan the correct story of how Katya got to the roof on her own. A relieved Milan left, barely staying ten minutes.

In the days that followed, the workmen found Katya's curiosity entertaining. She no longer went on the roof, but did walk through the yard to see what was being delivered, along with its purpose.

Stevo was impressed with her curiosity and her intelligence. She constantly asked questions about the construction work going on above them.

Once the outer part of the structure had been framed and closed in, a stairway was put in from the store showroom to the upper level.

Katya wanted to go up to see what the workmen were accomplishing, but Stevo made her promise not to enter while work was being done. So, each evening when the workers left, Katya would go up to see how much had been completed. She was full of questions. How many rooms? How many bedrooms? Will there be an office?

Tomo was taking over more of the funeral duties, which Stevo found beneficial. Families of the deceased would let Stevo know how pleased they were with the kind and thoughtful handling of all the details.

At dinner, which Katya shared with Tomo and Stevo, Tomo said, "Did you see the building two doors down is for sale? Well," Tomo paused, "I was thinking it could be a good place for a Funeral Home."

Stevo thought about this. He said, "But our people have visitations in their homes. Such a building would be a waste of space."

Tomo put down his fork saying, "It will be necessary in the future. Think about it. It would be more convenient for the families."

Katya said nothing, listening with interest.

"I have done some investigating," said Tomo. "Everything I need to know, you have already taught me. We don't do embalming and we don't have to. It isn't a law."

"Then we have twice as many bills." said Stevo. "The building, the electricity, the advertising…"

That night, when Katya and Cleona went to the house where they now mainly worked and slept, Katya found the valuable bracelet Queen Valina had given her many years ago, which she hadn't worn lately. It had been her amulet, meant to keep her from harm. She felt she didn't need it any longer. Nothing in America would harm her.

The next day, Stevo was a bit confused when he saw Katya lead the salesman, Jim Slade, outside. He saw them talking. Stevo couldn't see what she showed Jim, who appeared to agree to what she was saying.

When they came in, Stevo was curious. He asked, "Making private business deals behind my back?"

Still, after all this time, Jim was not sure what the arrangement was between Steve and Katya. Jim said, "Katya was showing me something she wants to sell."

"Really?" said Stevo looking at Katya. "Something I can't see?"

Using his American name, Katya said, "It is mine, Steve. I can do whatever I want with it."

Jim didn't want to get in the middle of an argument, so he handed the Gypsy bracelet to Stevo, saying, "Katya wanted me to try and sell this for her."

Stevo took the bracelet from Jim. "Thanks, Jim. I can help Katya with this matter." He put the bracelet in his desk drawer. Katya just walked away. She wandered around the store for a few seconds then went into the kitchen.

Stevo said, "I'm sorry you got in the middle of this, Jim. It is a private matter. In fact, I don't think you know how valuable this bracelet is or why she has it." Stevo said, "Tell me what your order is this time." Jim told him how much he wanted and Stevo went to the kitchen door. He told Cleona how many bottles and jars to pack up, then said, "Jim and I are going across the street for a drink."

At Strincich's liquor store, Jim and Stevo sat on metal chairs at a small, round table. Each was sipping a glass of wine. Stevo said, "Jim, I don't know why Katya wants to sell the bracelet, but she shouldn't."

He saw Jim's questioning look and explained, "That is an ancient Gypsy bracelet with real gems in it. It was given to Katya by a Gypsy Queen."

Seeing Jim's doubting look, Stevo said, "It is true. Katya's life could be a written story." Stevo took a sip of wine while Jim stared at him, "You see, she was sold to a Turk near Zagreb, when she escaped she met up with the Gypsies."

"Wait a minute, Steve." said Jim suspiciously. "She told me her family was from Trieste."

"Yes," said Stevo, "Her grandmother owned the Vincenti Trading Company, which now belongs to Katya's mother and stepfather. Their ship sails throughout the Adriatic."

Jim, shaking his head, not sure if he should, said, "I have to tell you, Steve, I really like Katya." He finished his drink and motioned for another. "What is your relationship with her? I would like to make my friendship with her a bit stronger."

Jim saw the slight flicker in Stevo's eyes. Stevo waited a bit before replying, "I am not sure what our relationship is. You see, I am not the only man who would marry her tomorrow if she said yes." Remembering Slavko from Lakawanna, Stevo said, "Actually, there are two others."

Jim's eyes got wide. "Are you serious?"

"Absolutely," said Stevo. "We all admired her while her husband was alive. Once he died, we each let our feelings be known."

"She is a widow?" Jim was surprised. "Why doesn't she wear black?" he asked.

Stevo shook his head and slapped the table with his palm saying, "Because she has a mind of her own and she doesn't care what people think of her."

"I have to tell you Steve, she is one hell of a woman." said Jim.

Stevo said, "You have no idea, Jim…you have no idea."

Back at the store, Jim's order of the Royal products was on the table. Katya had learned how to write an invoice and it was tucked into the box.

Stevo, at this desk, heard Jim say to Katya, "I am running out of time today. The next time I come, let's have lunch at the Gary Hotel again."

Katya smiled at Jim Slade, saying, "That would be nice."

Jim put the boxes in the back of his Chevrolet Classic Six. As he drove away, he thought to himself…*She is one hell of a woman.*

CHAPTER 42

That evening, after dinner when Cleona and Katya had gone for the night, Stevo sat alone at the kitchen table. He was lonely. Tomo had friends of his own and was often gone in the evenings. Stevo smoked his cigarette and tried to read a newspaper, but had no interest. He finished his wine and stubbed out the cigarette. Damn it! He needed company.

Stevo rolled down his sleeves, fastened his neck button, and the shirt cuff buttons. In his room, he looked into the long mirror, picking up a brush and giving his light brown hair a smoothing.

Wearing a wool coat, he was ready to leave. He paused at the door. On a side table were jars of the Royal Extract and Honey Cream. Picking up one of each, he slipped them in his pockets and walked out the door to head to Milan's.

When Stevo opened the door of the tavern, he was assailed by the noise. It was obvious the patrons were having a good time.

Milan showed some surprise when he saw Stevo. His eyes made a quick search for Katya when he waved a greeting. Stevo went directly to Milan, who tried to hide his nervousness at Stevo's appearance.

By way of greeting, Stevo said, "I miss you, you pain in the ass. Find time to sit and talk with me." Stevo went to a side table along the wall, away from the crowd. He slipped off his coat, hanging it on the back of his chair.

In a matter of minutes, Milan came to the table with two glass mugs of beer. He felt somewhat uncomfortable, not sure how the conversation would go.

Stevo and Milan clinked glasses and each took a swallow. Stevo was the first to speak. "Ever since that New Year's kiss you and Katya have been acting strangely." Stevo waited for Milan to say something, when he didn't, Stevo said, "I told Katya she had to get over the kiss, to let it go."

Milan felt a huge wave of relief. Stevo had no idea that Katya and Milan had made love or that it was the reason for their behavior.

Needing to say something, Milan asked, "How is Katya?"

Stevo took another swallow of beer. He said, "She and Cleona are living like Gypsies in Katya's house." Looking at Milan he said, "Do you know they have almost no furniture?"

At Milan's look of surprise, Stevo said, "She gave me back all the parlor furniture. Her house is a warehouse, a factory." Stevo reached back into the pockets of his jacket hanging on the chair. He pulled out the two Royal products. "Look," he said, "they have turned the house into a factory. There is nowhere to sit. They only sleep there, having their meals with me at the store."

Milan picked up one of the bottles. He asked, "Is this made from all those branches they had on the porch?

Stevo nodded "They make so much of this stuff that they have a salesman coming by twice a month for boxes of it." Half complaining and half laughing, Stevo said, "See the wax covering? My kitchen smells of melting wax. They seal the corks in my kitchen during the day, when I need them to answer the phone, or help a customer."

Now Milan had the bottle in one hand and the jar in the other. "Are you saying they make money with these?"

Stevo nodded, "Katya has an account at the Gary State Bank. I don't know what Cleona does with her money."

With the talk about Katya and Cleona's Royal products done, there was a gap in the conversation.

Stevo reached across the table. He tapped Milan's hand saying, "Damn it! Can't we make things between us the way they were, the three of us, you, me, and Katya together, teasing one another, laughing?"

Milan let out a sigh, leaning back in his chair. He was not going to tell Stevo about his night of lovemaking with Katya. It had been so special, something so different for him...he could never talk about it. Instead he said, "I declared myself to Katya."

"You what?" Stevo's eyes were wide.

Now, with elbows on the table, Milan said, "I told her how much I love her. If you must know, it was rather intense." He watched Stevo's face for a reaction, seeing none, he went on, "I went so far as to tell her that if she wanted me, she would have to come to me."

Stevo looked at Milan, his voice was low and thoughtful when he said "The fact that she can't face you means she cares. She cares more than I guessed."

"The problem is," said Milan, "she cares about us both. Very possibly she doesn't know how you feel."

Stevo laughed almost embarrassed, "I have asked her to marry me more than once."

"And…" Milan waited for a reply.

Stevo's reply was a shrug of the shoulders.

Again, Stevo said, "I want us to be the way we were, the three of us, together."

"I still love you." laughed Milan embarrassed. "But what passed between Katya and me was so strong, we can't go back."

At these words, Stevo felt a slight twinge somewhere deep in his body. He wanted his friend back. Trying to lighten the mood, he said, "We may have some competition. The salesman I was telling you about announced his intention today to court our girl."

The conversation had become thin. These two old friends had nothing more to talk about. Baring their souls the way they had left them both, in a matter of speaking, naked.

With no more to say, Milan looked around the busy bar. He said, "I should get back to work. Mato has been running his ass off taking care of the crowd."

Milan rose looking with sadness at his old friend. Seeing the two Royal products on the table, he picked them up. Staring at them for some time, he said, "I'd like to keep these."

Stevo nodded for Milan to keep them. His visit to the tavern was meant to reaffirm their friendship, to return their relationship to what it had been in the past. Instead, Stevo felt a loss he hadn't felt since his father's death in New Orleans.

Before going out the door, Stevo stopped at the bar and shook Milan's hand. The eyes of both men reflected sadness. Only Stevo knew that Milan's parting words were meant as a tribute to their years of friendship.

For the last time, Milan said affectionately, "Go to hell."

On his way home, Stevo walked past Katya's house. As always he saw the low light from the kitchen reflecting through the window.

After his visit with Milan, Stevo was so very sad. Tonight, more than ever, he would like to be wrapped in the comfort of Katya's arms. He wished he could knock at her door and be invited in.

Instead, this handsome man of means, admired by many, walked home to the loneliness of his bed.

Stevo was awake early, long before Katya and Cleona were to arrive. He sat at the table, drinking the coffee he made himself and smoking a Murad Turkish cigarette instead of his regular Player brand. He bought the Murad cigarettes because Adele Manning smoked them.

In his mind, he played over his evening with Milan. Did Stevo dare ask Katya to make a choice between them? Was he willing to risk the closeness, the friendship they now had, on the chance she would leave his life forever? What if she didn't choose either one of them, but left for Lakawanna?

Tomo, his eyes sleepy and his hair tussled, nodded to Stevo. He poured himself a cup of coffee then sat across from Stevo.

Stevo snorted a laugh. When Tomo looked at him, he said, "Katya is right. You do smell of lilac perfume."

Tomo dropped his eyes, smiling. "Grace does not remember me from Katya's kitchen. She thinks I am a relative of yours." He looked at Stevo, "I hope you don't mind that I didn't deny it."

As if he were Tomo's father, Stevo said, "You realize this can't go anywhere."

"I know...I know," said Tomo with a sheepish grin, "you wouldn't deny my having a good time would you?"

Stevo dropped the subject, but with a smile on his face.

The two men drank their coffee and smoked cigarettes. Breaking the silence, Stevo said, "I have been thinking about the funeral home you want to open."

Tomo's eyes brightened.

Stevo continued, "Right now it is a matter of money. Well," he paused, "not only money. I want you with me. I don't have a son, though someday I may." He put down his coffee cup and said, "I think of you as a younger brother, someone to help and take care of." Tomo said nothing, so Stevo continued, "In time, we could become partners."

"Oh, Stevo..." was all the stunned young man could say.

Stevo stubbed out his cigarette, leaving a small line of smoke trailing from the ashtray. "I would like to get married." he said. "I have not taken any time away from the store since I came here more than four years ago." Stevo stood up and went to the door, looking out into the yard, "I've been thinking about New Orleans." He looked at Tomo, "That's where I came from."

He turned, seeing the bewildered look on Tomo's face, "New Orleans is at the bottom of the United States. There is no other city like it. Instead of a train, I think I would like to take a boat on the Mississippi all the way to New Orleans."

Tomo didn't understand any of this. He knew Stevo was born in Dalmacia. Tomo knew nothing of New Orleans, or where the Mississippi was.

He asked brightly, "Are you and Katya going to get married?"

Stevo didn't answer. He just walked slowly to his room, closing the door behind him.

Tomo was still at the table when Katya and Cleona came in carrying bottles and jars to label, seal, and tie with ribbons.

It was now Katya and Tomo's habit to kiss when they met. "You smell like lilacs." She said, frowning.

"I know." He replied, smiling broadly.

As the women were depositing their bags, Tomo said, "Are you going with Stevo to New Orleans?"

Both Katya and Cleona stared at Tomo.

Katya asked, "What is New Orleans?"

Cleona's eyes sparkled with excitement. She said, "I heard about New Orleans. It be a beautiful place full of flowers and the most beautiful Creole women." She laughed out loud, "Those white men down there wants the Creole women."

Katya turned to Tomo, asking, "When did he tell you he was leaving?"

Tomo shrugged, "He just said he wanted to get married and wanted to take a boat to New Orleans."

Cleona said excited, "It be the Mississippi."

"Yes." said Tomo. "That is the word he said.

Katya collapsed in a chair. Thoughts raced through her mind. *So that is why he is building living space upstairs. Is he bringing home a bride from this New Orleans place?*

Tomo took Katya's hand asking, "Are you and Stevo getting married?" He kissed Katya on the cheek, "Well, it is about time."

The three of them looked at Stevo, nicely dressed and handsome as always, come out of his room.

Seeing them stare at him, he asked, "What's the matter?"

Weakly, Katya asked, "When are you going to New Orleans?"

Stevo burst out laughing. "Oh, that. I hope to when I get married."

In a very small voice, Katya asked, "Who are Creole women? Are they beautiful?"

Still laughing, Stevo said, "I see Cleona has been talking. Yes, Creole women are considered very beautiful."

CHAPTER 43

Throughout the morning, Katya was troubled with thoughts of Stevo building living quarters above the store and talking of going to New Orleans. Is there someone in New Orleans he would marry? For the first time, Katya felt adrift. What would happen to her if she no longer was part of Stevo's life? She and Cleona practically lived at the store. In her mind, it was an extension of her house.

Stevo also had things on his mind. What would his days be like without Katya and Cleona cluttering up his life everyday? Yes, he decided, there were times they drove him crazy, but he loved having them both around. He discovered last evening that he didn't like being alone. Most of all, Stevo wondered if Milan was the one Katya preferred.

Later in the day, standing at the kitchen door, Stevo motioned for Katya to join him in the store. He sat at his desk and pointed to the side chair for Katya to sit.

From the desk drawer Stevo removed the ancient bracelet he took from Jim the day before.

Handing it to Katya, he said, "Please wear it. Promise me you won't try to sell it."

Katya took the bracelet and studied it. She said, "For years I have worn it hidden under my sleeve. Hiding it has become a chore and so does explaining why I have it."

Stevo came around the desk, sitting on its edge, facing her. He said, "You don't have to hide it. In the time I have known you, you seem not to care what people think, so why worry about what they might think of the bracelet now?"

With the bracelet on her wrist, Katya fingered it, saying, "The bracelet was just one more thing to make people believe I was a witch. That, and maybe my red hair."

Stevo took Katya's hand studying the bracelet. He said, "Katya...in New Orleans we have many witches. But, we call them voodoo priestesses. People come to them for magic spells, potions, and even magic dolls."

Still holding her hand, Stevo said, "I can't say why, but when I saw the bracelet in Jim's hand, I knew you had to wear it. Events come in threes...the bracelet has saved you twice. Please wear it always."

"Stevo," Katya was alarmed, "What do you mean? Do you think something is going to happen to me?"

He let go of her hand, saying, "I can't see in the future. I only know the moment I saw that bracelet, I knew it needed to be on your wrist." He added, "Don't hide it. It needs to be seen."

Going back to his desk chair, Stevo asked, "Why did you want to sell it?"

"To help Tomo buy the building for a funeral home." she said.

Stevo smiled, saying, "Tomo and I have talked about this. Someday he will be part owner of this store and perhaps we can do the expansion then."

Katya wanted to ask Stevo more about his future plans. She was curious about the living quarters upstairs, about Tomo and the business, but most of all, about going to New Orleans. Before she could ask anything, Jim Slade came through the door.

Since Jim had been there just the day before, Stevo asked, "What brings you back so soon? It hasn't been two weeks."

Grinning at Katya, Jim said, "I had to come back to take this gorgeous girl to lunch."

Just before closing time, a worried Stevo watched the street for Katya and Jim's return. If they were gone any longer, the lunch could turn into supper.

At last, the Chevy pulled up in front of the store. Her face shining, wearing a big smile, Katya did not wait for Jim to open the car door for her. She jumped out, running into the store.

"What a wonderful afternoon." she announced. "I have to tell Cleona." And she was gone into the kitchen.

What the hell...thought Stevo, What kind of a lunch did Jim treat Katya to?

Jim was not at all as exuberant and cheerful as Katya when he entered the store.

Jim offered no greeting. He just said to Stevo, "Come with me. I need a drink, and wine won't do."

Bewildered, Stevo called for Tomo to lock up. The two men walked across the street to the liquor store and again sat at the same table they occupied the day before.

Seated, and not waiting for service, Jim called out, "Whiskey...bring the bottle."

The server looked at their table. Stevo pointed to himself, saying, "Vino."

Stevo waited for Jim to say something...anything.

After Jim downed the first shot of whiskey, he said, "Damn, Steve. That Katya is the most fascinating woman I have ever met." He poured himself another glass of Fig Rye. "If she would go with me, I would drive out of your life tomorrow." He downed his drink. "But, I tell you, today she scared the shit out of me."

Stevo's jaw dropped. What could Katya do to scare this man? He said, "What are you talking about?" To Stevo this made no sense. He demanded, "What did she do to you?"

"I thought she was going to get me killed!" Jim said, agitated.

Exasperated, Stevo pressed on, "What did little Katya do to you? How could that woman harm you? Damn it, Jim...talk. Start at the beginning."

With the aid of the whiskey, color was returning to Jim's face. He said, "In the car, I noticed Katya was wearing the Gypsy bracelet. To make conversation, I told her that I passed what I thought to be a Gypsy camp near Whiting." Jim paused, shaking his head before going on. "She lit up like a candle when she heard that. She insisted I take her to see the camp."

He looked at Steve, solemnly saying, "As a businessman, you know how we watch out for Gypsies. I can't believe I agreed to take her there." This time he only sipped at his drink, "I thought we would just drive by the camp for her to see it." Raising his voice, he said, "How the hell did I know she would jump out of the car and go into the camp?"

"Oh, shit." said Stevo, remembering how fearlessly she climbed to the roof of the store.

"I didn't want to get out of the car, but I couldn't let her go there alone. What kind of a man would I be?" Jim was almost pleading as he explained. "Then the crowd of serious looking men surrounded us. I tried to take her arm and go back to the car, but she pulled away."

Jim nervously tapped his fingers on the table as he spoke. "She started to speak to them in some foreign language. A rough looking guy came out of a brightly-colored house on wheels. I could tell she was asking questions. You should have seen the gold earrings the Gypsies wore…men and women."

"Go on…" Stevo prodded.

"I am telling you, Steve, I was getting nervous. The crowd was pressing around us. I was even thinking if we got out alive, my car would be gone." Seeing Stevo's anxious face, he continued.

"Probably the oldest, most wrinkled woman on Earth was helped by two men from the same brightly-colored wagon-house the man came from. That's when Katya gave me a surprise." He gave Stevo a look of wonder, "Can you believe she bowed to this old lady? She reached out her hand to the woman. I thought the old woman was blind, but she saw Katya's bracelet and said something to the people around us. There was a murmur and I thought…this is it. They are going to murder us and take whatever we have. Instead, the crowd started to back away."

Breaking away from his story, Jim asked, "My God, Steve…who is this woman?"

Stevo took a sip of his wine, saying, "Someone I still want to marry. Go on, Jim. What else happened? I see you are alive and you still have your car."

"The old woman wanted to know who I was. Katya said something and I could tell the crowd was dismissing me as an uninteresting person…which was just fine with me. The only words I remember Katya saying were Valina and Zolton. The woman and her son shook their heads, so I know they didn't recognize the names. We were there quite a while. I kept looking around, worried, not sure what would happen next. I was hoping we could leave, but a woman brought Katya and me cups of something to drink I didn't recognize. I didn't touch mine, but Katya drank hers."

Jim motioned for another wine for Stevo. He went on with his story, "A strange thing happened. Two women came to Katya. They pulled aside their hair and each one had a missing ear. I never said a word while we were there.

When we got up to leave, I swear it was unreal. Katya kissed the old woman. Then as we walked to the car, hands reached out to touch Katya, and some even bowed. As we were getting into the car, a little girl ran up to Katya, giving her a piece of ribbon.

On the drive back, Katya was so elated she kept thanking me for taking her to the camp. I have to tell you, Steve, I don't know when I have been as uncomfortable as I was this afternoon."

CHAPTER 44

Katya could barely wait to tell Stevo about the trip to the Gypsy camp. As usual, he was having his morning coffee and this time, the not-so-strong Player cigarette. Spread before him was the Hearst Chicago paper The Herald-Examiner.

Seeing Katya fairly bursting through the door, along with Cleona, whose arms were loaded with bags, Stevo said, "Good morning, my little Gypsy."

Katya's eyes lit up. She exclaimed, "Did Jim tell you about the Gypsy camp?" She threw off her shawl and plopped onto a chair across from Stevo.

Not wanting to tell her Jim's version of the afternoon, he asked, "Why don't you tell me. After all, he couldn't understand the conversation."

"Oh, Stevo, you were so right!" Seeing his quizzical look, she said, "About the treatment of Gypsies. Remember when I thought of going back home? You told me how badly the Gypsies were being treated?"

She smiled a thank you to Cleona, accepting a cup of coffee. "In Bohemia, the government is cutting off one ear of each Gypsy woman. I was told the same is being done in Poland. My God! I hope it is not going on in Croatia."

Katya had a disgusted look when she said, "It is their way of identifying Gypsies. She stirred sugar into her coffee, saying, "You only told me about the fingerprinting."

Stevo said, "I didn't know about the ear cutting. It sounds very cruel."

Changing to a lighter subject, Stevo said, "Jim was surprised at the treatment you were given by the Gypsies."

Katya put down her cup. She looked at the wall past Stevo, as if reliving the event. She said, "As crazy as it may sound, I think the bracelet is magical. This Roma tribe came from Poland and didn't know of Valina or Zolton, but they did recognize the symbols on the bracelet." Now she looked directly at Stevo, saying, "They really thought I was a Roma Gypsy Queen. I told them I wasn't. Stevo…the respect they had for the bracelet…I can't explain it.

That afternoon Stevo was very busy with customers and sales. At one point, he asked Cleona to find Tomo.

"He went someplace. I don't know where," was her answer.

"Katya? Where is Katya, I could use her in the store." said Stevo.

"She is gone." said Cleona. She could feel Stevo's annoyance through the kitchen door.

"Where is she?" Stevo's voice had an edge to it.

"Don't know." lied Cleona.

Stevo came to the kitchen door and looked hard at Cleona, saying, "You know everything that goes on around here."

"Not everything." she said, going quickly out into the yard.

At Milan's Tavern, Tomo sat alone at a table waiting for Katya. She made Tomo promise not to tell Stevo of this visit. The promise Tomo gave her made him feel as if he were betraying Stevo, yet Katya meant as much to him as Stevo.

Milan and Katya went behind the bar to the living quarters where Milan and Mato shared the small living space. In the kitchen was a cot used for napping. This is where Katya and Milan sat.

She declined an offer of refreshments. Milan didn't like the worried look on her pretty face, or the glistening of her eyes. He was aware that Tomo was out front waiting for her. They sat in silence for a long time. It was obvious she couldn't say what she wanted to.

Milan said, "Alright, Katya…why are you here?"

With that the tears flowed, spilling over her cheeks and alarming Milan. He took her in his arms saying, "My God, Katya…what has happened? What is wrong?"

She held onto him, not speaking. He gently pushed her away asking, "Why are you here?"

Katya reached for the kitchen towel. She dried her eyes and wiped her nose. In a voice Milan could barely hear, she said, "I want you to say I can marry Stevo."

"What the hell?" he shouted so loudly it could be heard in the bar. Realizing this, he lowered his voice, "You come here to ask my permission? When did I go from being your lover to being your father?"

With a broken heart she said, "It is because I love you that I ask you."

Milan was angry, saying "I didn't think you were that kind of a woman, Katya. A good woman doesn't play two men against each other."

"Oh, Milan," she said with passion, 'I love you…I love you…but, I think I love Stevo more."

She was breaking Milan's heart. He could see the sincerity in her eyes. He pulled her to her feet, wrapping his large arms around her, almost sobbing, he kept repeating, "Damn you, Katya…Damn you."

Then he said in her ear, "When I said you had to come to me, I wasn't expecting this."

He asked, "If I say no, will you marry me instead?"

She pulled away from him to look into his eyes. She could see the hurt and a little anger in them. She said, "If you say, no…then I will never marry."

He wrapped his arms around her, rocking her, and whispering in her ear, "Damn you…damn you."

There was no conversation between Tomo and Katya on the walk from the tavern. Tomo saw the swollen, tear-stained eyes, but asked nothing. Instead of going back to the store, Tomo delivered Katya to her own house. He didn't go in with her, stopping at the back steps, the very steps where she found him hiding those many months ago.

She gave him a sweet kiss of thanks on the lips and went inside without a word.

Returning to the store, Tomo was greeted by an angry Stevo. "Where have you been?" he demanded, "And where is Katya?"

"Stevo…please don't ask me."

In the two days that followed Tomo and Katya's disappearance, the mood at the store was very quiet and reserved. Each did their work, but he now missed the chatter and conversations that Stevo once thought as unnecessary.

Stevo approached Tomo once again at their morning coffee before Katya and Cleona's arrival, but all Tomo said was, "Stevo, it is not my place to say anything."

Stevo's annoyance became concern. He didn't have a clue as to where they had gone or what was going on to keep them all so private.

Katya appeared no longer interested in the progress of the work being done upstairs, which troubled Stevo. In fact, one of the workmen jokingly asked where their new foreman was, for she no longer went in the yard checking on the new deliveries.

After another quiet evening meal, when Katya and Cleona prepared to leave, Stevo asked Bobo to see his cousin home.

Stevo took Katya by the arm, leading her into the privacy of the store.

He said, "You and I are going for a walk." When she tried to decline, he was firm. "I said, we are going for a walk...and a long talk."

Taking Katya's arm while walking towards Broadway, Stevo asked, "What is going on? I am used to you and Cleona having secrets, but now you have Tomo in on something."

She shook her head, with her eyes down. Katya didn't want to talk.

Stevo was determined, but in a calm voice, he said, "You know, Katya. I don't care if this takes all night. You won't go home until I know what is going on."

Katya remained quiet during the walk to Broadway and on the street car to 9th Avenue. Stevo helped her off the car and across the street to the Café Budapest. Stephan Kertesz, the owner, recognized Stevo and found them a private table.

There were some people eating a light supper. The café was not a full restaurant providing large meals.

With a bottle of wine on the table and their glasses full, Stevo said once again, "Are you going to tell me what is wrong?" He took her hand, "Katya, I have been here for you since the first day I saw you at the tavern. Can't you trust me enough to tell me what is troubling you?"

Stevo saw her hand tremble slightly as she picked up her wine glass. She avoided his eyes as she took a sip.

"I am waiting…" he said.

Hesitantly, she started, "There are a few things. Things I am wondering about." Her eyes were everywhere but on him.

He grabbed her chin, making her look at him. "Alright," he said, "let's start with the first thing you are wondering about."

She pulled her chin away from his hold, but did keep her eyes on him.

"Well," she began, "how much do you like Adele Manning? I see you smoke her brand of cigarettes."

Stevo would have laughed out loud, had he not seen how seriously Katya asked the question.

Stevo chose his words carefully, he blue eyes dancing with delight. "Adele is a beautiful woman. She was only a customer and I may never see her again. As for the cigarettes…I haven't had Turkish cigarettes in years. I bought them just to try them."

There was the slightest flicker of relief in Katya's green eyes. She asked, "Why are you talking about leaving for New Orleans?"

He smiled at the memory of New Orleans, saying, "Because it is beautiful there. The smell of flowers could make you dizzy. The ocean breeze, the musical sounds of people speaking and singing…I miss it."

Her eyes were fixed on him as she asked, "Is there someone in New Orleans you want to marry?"

Now he burst out laughing, so much so, that a few heads turned in their direction. "Why would you think that?" he asked, still laughing.

She was not pleased with his laugher when she said, "Because you are building a place to live above the store and because, you talk of going to New Orleans when you marry."

He took Katya's hands in his, "Oh, my Katya. I am building a place so you don't have to go to that warehouse you call a home each night."

Her eyes grew wide. "Really…you are telling me the truth?"

He refilled their wine glasses. "Yes," he said, "I am telling you the truth."

Stevo held his glass up in a toast to her. She smiled and touched his glass with hers. They each took a drink.

"Now, my little Gypsy," he said in a very serious tone, "What is it that Tomo or you will not tell me."

Katya took a deep breath, letting it out slowly. She said, "I went to see Milan."

Stevo's eyes narrowed ever so slightly, but he said nothing. Seeing he was waiting for her to speak, she said, "I went there to tell him that I couldn't marry him."

"Because....?" Stevo asked.

Nervously she said, "Because, I really want to marry you."

Stevo and Katya were married in a civil ceremony at the Gary City Hall on 7th and Massachusetts Street. To the officiating judge's surprise, Cleona was one of the witnesses along with Tomo.

At the ceremony, Stevo slipped Katya's old wedding ring on her finger. It was the same wedding ring Lucia had slipped off her own hand when Ivan and Katya married on the terrace in Trieste. The sight of the ring, and the fact that Stevo had saved it for her, made her love him even more.

The plan was to be re-married when the Croatian Catholic church, Holy Trinity, was competed at 23rd and Adams Street.

Two weeks into their marriage, Katya was still not allowed upstairs. In the past, she could go upstairs when the workmen were gone. Now, she was forbidden to go up ever. She stared longingly at the stairway on the side of the store's showroom which led to the level above. A cord was strung across with a placard stating PRIVATE affixed to it.

At supper, Stevo announced in a very firm tone to Cleona, "If I find out you allowed Katya to go upstairs...I swear...I swear, Cleona, I just may have to beat you."

Cleona looked hard at Stevo, her hands on her hips saying, "Now, you is foolin me."

Ignoring the stares of Tomo and Katya, Stevo warned, "You'll see. Just let me find out she went upstairs...and you'll see."

The next day, Stevo took Cleona upstairs to show her the secret. When she saw what Stevo had planned, she agreed to keep Katya from going there.

Finally, the job of the upstairs living space was completed. Katya stood quietly at the kitchen door watching Stevo pay the man in charge. She saw them shake hands, bid one another a good day and then Stevo was alone.

Katya slipped into the store and quietly moved alongside Stevo at his desk. He knew she was there, but pretended not to notice. She moved closer, bumping his chair with her hip...still he did not acknowledge her presence.

Realizing he was teasing her, she playfully slapped the back of his head announcing, "I am going upstairs." When he still didn't move, she said, "I am going upstairs and don't you lay a hand on Cleona!"

She ran across the store to the stairs, pulled away the cord and hurried up the stairs. Laughing at her, Stevo hurried after her.

The first room she entered was a parlor or sitting room. A narrow hallway led to a bedroom on one side and on the other an office or reading room. At the end of the hallway was a closed door. When Katya opened the door, her jaw dropped in awe. Stevo was right behind her. She turned to him, "Oh, my Dearest Stevo," she said, "how did you ever do this?"

This was not an outdoor chapel such as she loved in Vladezemla. Instead, he had constructed an indoor chapel for her.

On the wall was a large four-foot crucifix with the body of Jesus above a long, narrow linen-covered table. A blue crystal rosary and a large candle holder covered with a glass chimney rested on the table. Next to the table was a pedestal on which stood a hand-painted chalk figure of the Madonna. In front of the table was a kneeler. To the back of the small room stood an actual pew cut to fit the space.

Katya wrapped her arms around Stevo, resting her face on his shoulder at his neck. Though her words were muffled, Stevo heard her say, "Oh my, Dearest...you will never give me a gift better than this." She kissed his neck, "I love it...I love it so much."

Stevo let go of Katya and slipped out the door. Before going downstairs, he peeked at her through the slightly opened door. She sat on the pew and looked around, studying everything. When Stevo saw her go to the kneeler, he quietly closed the door to let her pray.

Monday was traditionally a laundry day. Doing the laundry by hand took the better part of the day, followed with ironing all day on Tuesday. As a rule, business in the store on Mondays was light. Stevo chose this particular Monday to take Katya to Chicago for the day.

Stevo and Katya took a streetcar to 4th and Broadway to board the Chicago Lake Shore and South Bend train to downtown Chicago.

When she first came from Lakawanna, the train ride from Chicago was not exciting for Katya, because she was not happy with America. But today she was like a child insisting on sitting by the window to watch the passing scenery.

Stevo suggested she wear her blue lace dress. It was one of his favorites. At her throat, she wore Lucia's coral cameo each and every day. The Gypsy bracelet was on her wrist and she no longer gave it a thought, for Stevo wanted her to wear it, so she did.

Leaving the crowded train station, Katya was in awe of how many people were all around them. Stevo guided Katya through the throngs of people onto Wabash Street. Automobiles and streetcars were everywhere, making Katya stare in wonder. She held firmly onto Stevo's arm for fear of getting lost in the crowd and never finding him.

Walking one block or so, they were on the corner of State and Washington. Katya stared open-mouthed at an enormously large building. Gary had some large buildings, but not even the Gary Hotel was anything like the Marshall Field department store where Stevo was taking his Katya.

Stevo steered Katya through the large glass doors trimmed in brass.

"What kind of a store is this?" whispered Katya to Stevo, "What do they sell here?"

Stevo was very pleased. This is what he wanted. He wanted Katya to be amazed, to find the day an adventure.

Her eyes could not take in all of the merchandise. There were such beautiful things on every counter and in every showcase. The saleswomen wore black dresses with white collars and white cuffs. Each wore her hair neat and close to the head. Katya saw they wore no jewelry, except a watch on a neck chain.

The display cases were on the side of the room, artfully placed near gigantic pillars. Looking at the room, Katya thought this must be what a palace looks like. She looked up asking, "Is this one store or several in this building."

Stevo explained, "There are 12 floors and they are all one store."

"How will we ever see it all?" she asked, dazzled by the enormity.

"We can't see it all." said Stevo, leading her to an elevator.

Reading the store directory near the elevators, Stevo took Katya to the International and Art Department.

As soon as they stepped out of the elevator, Katya cried out, "Stevo, these are like the things my Nona Lucia had in her home." Katya practically ran from item to item. "Look," she said, stopping to admire a round brass, engraved table from India. "My Lucia had a smaller one in her large room. And look there," she pointed to a Nubian figure holding a tray. "One like this stood at the foot of the staircase."

Katya was as happy as a child seeing all the beautiful things she remembered from the Trieste hilltop villa. The paintings, the wall tapestries, the oriental rugs, all made Katya's eyes dance.

Stevo was getting tired and wanted to sit somewhere. Seeing on the directory there was a tea room, he and Katya found their way there. The round tables were covered with white linen cloths topped with floral centerpieces.

Katya and Stevo were shown a small table for two. Stevo ordered some tea and an assortment of cakes, while Katya's eyes surveyed almost everything and everyone in the room. She noticed there didn't seem to be any ordinary looking people here. The women all looked so elegant, while their male companions all appeared prosperous.

When leaving the tea room, Stevo wanted to see the Walnut Room. He said to Katya, "The next time we come, we will have lunch here."

At that time, women were not allowed without a male escort in the Walnut Room. Stevo motioned to Katya "Look, there is a fountain in the center of the room." He pointed for her to look up. She saw the beautiful ceiling. Katya had no way of knowing it was made by Tiffany, or its value.

When the elevator opened on the second floor to let some passengers out, something caught Stevo's eye. He took Katya by the arm, leading her to a shiny glass display case. He said, "Pick which one you like."

She looked at the countertop displaying several beaded and tasseled ladies purses, very similar to the one Katya saw on Grace Adams' wrist.

"Stevo...you don't have to buy me anything. Today has been enough of a gift." she said.

"Please." he said, fingering one with an ornate picture made up of tiny beads. The beads depicted a woman seated under a trailing rose bush. "Pick one out."

She looked at the purses, each one lovelier than the last. She said, "I want you to pick it out. That will make it all the more special."

On the train ride back to Gary, a very contented Katya took Stevo's hand in hers. She lifted his hand to her face and brushed her lips against the back of his hand. When she let go of his hand, he touched her cheek with his fingers.

She held up the purse with the trailing rose bush, saying, "This was the most beautiful one." Katya smiled lovingly at Stevo, saying, "I think you are a more wonderful husband than I expected you to be." Tired, she leaned her head back, closed her eyes, and whispered so only Stevo could hear, "I love you."

CHAPTER 45

With the upstairs livable, sleeping arrangements needed to be changed. Before giving over his room to Tomo, Stevo lifted the loose floor board removing the Cheroots cigar box which held his secret savings. Its new hiding place was in the hollow base of the pedestal holding the figure of the Madonna in Katya's private chapel.

Cleona was pleased that the loft was now her space. It was small and private. The dresser she and Katya purchased was brought to the loft. She was fond of that dresser with the locks and keys on each drawer.

Katya left her dresser at the house. She only wanted the trunk, Ivan's cane, and the wicker suitcase full of Ivan's papers, which now included some of Katya's own writings.

Tomo and Cleona were pleased, noticing the happy mood of Stevo since he married Katya. She made him laugh. Stevo was never sure what she would do next.

He told her to put a piece of paper on the furniture she wanted taken upstairs. When he looked out into the store, every piece of furniture had a piece of paper on it. Katya hid alongside a cabinet waiting to see his reaction.

Cleona giggled when she saw Stevo playfully chase Katya through the store. It pleased Cleona to see the hugging, kissing, and to hear the laughter.

Until now, Stevo had been a serious businessman, appearing only to be interested in making a profit. That is, until he met Ivan and Katya. He was generous with them, but not sure why he felt the need to help them. In time, he realized it was because of Katya.

Sitting as his desk in the back of the store, Stevo was going over the bills. Hearing someone come in, he looked up to see Milan. Their friendly rivalry for Katya's affections had become more serious after Ivan died.

Still fond of one another, but feeling the strain and embarrassment of their love for Katya, their greeting was only cordial. Stevo stood to shake Milan's hand.

"I won't keep you long." said Milan, "I have a wedding gift. It is really more for Katya than for you both."

"Sit down, let's have a drink." offered Stevo. "Katya is in the kitchen. Let me call her."

"No…no…" said Milan, dropping a piece of paper on the desk. He said, "I have to go." He left without a goodbye.

Stevo picked up the paper unfolding it. It was the deed to the house which Katya now made monthly payments for.

Stevo hurried into the kitchen, "Katya, look at this." he said, startling both Katya and Cleona who were gluing labels on their bottles. "Look what Milan gave you."

Confused, Katya asked, "Where is Milan? What is it?"

"He has given you the house as a wedding gift." Stevo held the paper for Katya to see. She pushed the paper away, "Where is he?" she asked again.

"He is gone." said Stevo, watching her run through the kitchen door into the yard then through the gate to the sidewalk. About half a block away, she saw Milan walking.

"Milan! Milan!" she shouted running after him.

Hearing his name, he turned and stopped. Katya came running to him. She paused for only a second looking into his sad face. She wrapped her arms around him saying, "Oh, Milan. You don't have to give me the house." She stepped away from him. Again looking into his face, she said, "Please let me keep paying you each month."

He cupped her chin with his large hand. Sweetly and lovingly he said, "Damn you." Dropping his hand he walked away leaving Katya standing alone.

Stevo followed Katya out the door to the sidewalk where he watched Katya and Milan. Tomo, hearing the commotion when Katya ran out the door, followed Stevo and now stood beside him.

Witnessing Katya and Milan holding each other, a very concerned Tomo asked, "What does that mean?"

Stevo said, watching Katya walk slowly back to him, "It means they have love for one another."

The worried look on Tomo's face made Stevo smile. "Look…" Stevo explained, "She left him and is walking back to me."

He patted Tomo on the shoulder, saying, "You are still too young to know there are many kinds of love."

Back in the store, Katya pulled a straight back chair alongside Stevo at his desk.

She put her elbows on the desktop, resting her chin in her hands. Doing so, she was crowding Stevo, who was trying to write. She let out an exaggerated sigh. He ignored her, trying to complete his work. She inched a bit closer, letting out another audible sigh.

Putting down his pencil, pretending annoyance, he said, "Alright...what do you want?"

Feigning the look of a child to her father, she said, "I think we should have a dog."

Now Stevo let out a long sigh. "Alright...you can have a dog and Bobo will take care of it in the barn."

She pouted. "But, then it will be Bobo's dog and not mine." She moved her chair away in a show of defiance, saying, "A dog would protect me when you are away."

"When would I be away?" he said, not sure what brought on this conversation. "Besides, you have Cleona, Bobo and Tomo. And...I am not planning on going anywhere."

Just then, the hinge on the kitchen door sounded. Stevo looked up at the door. He saw no one. Moments later, he saw sitting at Katya's knee, a brown and white short-haired dog with the scarred face of a street fighter and half an ear missing.

Stevo jumped from his chair saying, "Are you crazy? Where did he come from?"

Stevo's loud voice and jump from the chair alerted the dog's protective instincts. The dog, with his head on Katya's knee, warily watched Stevo.

Still standing, Stevo demanded, "Where did you find him?" Then, Stevo said, "Don't pet him...he smells."

With no further discussion, as if a decision had been made, Katya rose. The street dog stood, backing away, waiting to see what Katya would do. When Katya walked through the kitchen door, the dog followed, as did a disgruntled Stevo.

Stevo said firmly, "We are not keeping that mongrel."

Ignoring him, Katya and the dog walked through the kitchen and into the yard.

"Where do you think you are going?" Stevo demanded, trying to sound as if he were in authority.

Katya turned, giving Stevo an adoring smile. She said, "To give him a bath."

She knew, and so did Stevo, that she had won this round. They both knew that he loved her too much to refuse her anything.

As he went back into the kitchen, he was smiling because Katya knew he would give in. Even disagreeing with Katya was fun.

Cleona, hands on her hips, gave Stevo a narrow-eyed look. She said, "And you think you is Mr. Boss."

After a nice bath, the scruffy, medium-sized dog didn't look quite so awful. There was no way of identifying this dog's ancestry, as he was a mix of various breeds. He was spotted brown over white with a slender build.

The dog did not leave Katya's side. As long as she stayed in the kitchen, he seemed content to lie under the table. If it appeared she would go out or into the store, he stood ready to follow.

Cleona fussed over him, feeding him, and putting healing salves and ointments on his wounds. If a dog could smile, he did. There were times it appeared that he grinned at Cleona when she spoke to him and dabbed at his sores.

During dinner, Mahlee, the name Katya gave him, meaning "little one", stayed under the table.

Cleona told Katya to go with Stevo. She would clean up the kitchen herself.

The moment Katya and Stevo started through the kitchen door to go upstairs, Mahlee wanted to follow.

Stevo looked sternly at Katya, saying, "If you expect to keep him, he stays in the kitchen!"

Katya nodded obediently. She walked alongside Stevo up the stairs, all the while hearing Mahlee's sad whimpering.

Upstairs, Stevo slipped off his shoes, unbuttoned his shirt, and settled in a comfortable, overstuffed chair. Reading the newspaper, he tried to ignore what had become barking.

Katya poured Stevo a glass of wine and placed it on the table next to his chair. He gave Katya a look which let her know the wine was not going to make up for the new sound heard from below. Barking turned to howling, which had now become a high–pitched, mournful sound as if the dog were in great agony. This annoying sound went on for several minutes.

At once, the howling stopped! Stevo put down the newspaper, looking toward the silence. Katya looked at the door. She heard footsteps on the stairs and a loud knock at the door. When she opened the door, the dog scampered in, his tail wagging happily.

Stevo got up, "Oh, no!" he shouted to Tomo who was at the door. "You take him right back with you."

Very calmly, Tomo announced, "He stays up here with you. If you send him back down, Cleona and I have decided we will kill him."

Katya leaped into Stevo's arms, knocking him back into the chair. She covered his face with kisses, all the while promising, "The dog will be no trouble. You won't even know he is here."

Tomo went down to his room, knowing that Stevo had lost this battle.

In the days that followed, Stevo tried his best to dislike the dog. He felt a man's dog, like his horse, should be something other men admired.

Mahlee's face was healing nicely, but he still was in no way a handsome animal. With one ear standing straight up and the other half gone along with a small bald spot on the side of his face, probably from a battle, Mahlee looked pitiful.

Today, when the kitchen door was opened, Mahlee walked into the store going to Stevo's desk.

Annoyed at the dog's presence, Stevo shouted to Katya, "I think the dog wants to go out."

"He has been out." called back Katya.

"Come and get your dog!" shouted Stevo.

Katya came through the door saying, "Really Stevo, must you be so mean?"

They both looked around and did not see Mahlee. Worried, Katya ran to the open double doors leading to the sidewalk. She did not see the dog. She hurried farther out looking both ways.

Her look of worry changed to one of disappointment. She asked sadly, "What did you do to him? Did you hit him? Why would he run away?"

Just then a woman came in. Stevo gave Katya an exasperated look as he went to greet the customer.

On her way into the kitchen, had Katya looked down, she would have seen a skinny, wagging tail from beneath Stevo's desk.

In the weeks that followed, Mahlee had decided that it was Stevo, and not Katya that he preferred. The dog's eyes followed Stevo everywhere. During the day, secretly pleased, Stevo allowed Mahlee to sleep beneath his desk. In the evening, the scruffy dog lay curled beside the chair as Stevo read the paper. At night, on a worn wool blanket, Mahlee was on the floor at Stevo's side of the bed.

With Katya and Mahlee in his life, Stevo's tough businessman veneer was being chipped away.

CHAPTER 46

Even with the new renovations upstairs, Stevo had thoughts of leaving this store location and moving to the north part of town, away from the Patch. He was making a decent income, but the immigrants were not as interested in furnishings as they were in the accumulation of money. Money was sent to the Old Country to help the family left behind or to pay for the passage of loved ones to America. A few buyers from the north part of Gary came to his store, only because he had good merchandise at a better price.

1913 was not such a good year. There was a recession in the country and it affected the workers in the steel mills. At one time the American Sheet and Tin plant was down for ten days, leaving 1,500 men without work. Orders for steel at the Illinois Steel Co. and American Bridge Co. were not as good as in previous years.

Stevo heard rumors that immigrant children were going into the north part of Gary to search in the garbage cans of the wealthy.

From the New York and Chicago newspapers, Stevo read about the creation of the Federal Reserve Banks and the income tax. There were predictions of price increases and the Fed doubled the money supply, paving the way for inflation.

Only the very wealthy made it through this time. Instead of starting or helping new businesses, they found tax shelters.

This hit the low-paid immigrants hard. They were now paying income tax on what little they earned. Grocers gave credit until some of them had to close their stores for lack of money.

Stevo and Tomo supplied caskets for funerals, often with only the promise of future payments. Many of the promises could not be kept.

Jim Slade continued to buy the Royal products made by Cleona and Katya. They now added their Honey Cinnamon Bar Soap to the Royal product line. Because most of Jim's stores were in high-end communities, he was still able promote the product successfully.

Katya and Cleona continued the production of their items at Katya's old house. The house smelled of herbs, drying branches, honey, and more recently of lye, for the making of the soap.

For several weeks, each night in her dreams, Katya was visited by Ivan and Zolton, side by side. Also, Valina and Lucia together, would come and just smile. None of them spoke to her in her dreams. Katya felt comforted by these dream visits.

With Mahlee under the supper table, Tomo, Stevo, and Katya were being served the evening meal by Cleona. Cleona seldom ate with them, preferring to share the meal with her cousin, Bobo.

Sitting across from Katya, Stevo studied her face, which appeared flushed.

"Are you alright?" Stevo's voice showed his concern. "You look different."

Cleona hurried to the table. "I thought she looked awful pale today when we were workin at the house." Cleona put a hand to Katya's forehead. "Oh, Jesus!" she cried out, "She be burnin up!"

Tomo, sitting next to Katya, was shocked to find her body had gone limp. Stevo ran ahead, flinging open the door and running up the stairs leading to their apartment, as Tomo carried the limp Katya in his arms. Once inside, Tomo placed Katya on the bed.

Right behind them hurried Cleona with a pitcher of water and some towels.

"Take them clothes off her." said Cleona, as she soaked a towel in the water.

Tomo undid Katya's shoes while Stevo removed her Cameo brooch and unbuttoned her blouse. Tomo and Stevo worked quickly removing her clothes. His love and concern for Katya transcended any embarrassment on Tomo's part at seeing her almost naked.

"Git another towel wet." said Cleona, bathing Katya's face as she lay on the bed in her underclothes. Tomo started to pull a sheet over Katya to cover her when Cleona said, "Don't cover her. We got to cool her down."

Stevo leaned against the wall, all the color gone from his face. Looking down at Katya, so still, so helpless, made his blood go cold. Noticing the Gypsy bracelet on her wrist, Stevo whispered, "Do your magic."

Throughout the night, Stevo stayed at Katya's side. Cleona spooned water between Katya's lips, fearing the fever would dehydrate her.

With the daylight, there was no improvement in Katya. Stevo, wearing the clothes from the day before, sat on a stool next to the bed, holding Katya's small hand.

Tomo came dressed in fresh clothes. To Stevo, he said, "I'll be in the store. You don't have to come down." Looking at Katya, he asked, "Is she any better?"

Stevo said, "I think we need to send for a doctor. She is still fevered." Stevo raised her hand to his lips, "It's as if she is asleep."

In about an hour, Tomo returned with a doctor, an older man, unhappy to be called to the south side of Gary. He took Katya's pulse, listened with his stethoscope, and announced she should be in a hospital.

"What is the matter" asked Stevo, now standing on the other side of the bed, watching the doctor.

Putting the stethoscope in his bag, the doctor admitted, "I don't know. But she should be at the hospital where she will get constant care." He said this as he looked about disapprovingly.

Stevo was annoyed with the doctor's superior attitude. He said, "If you can't tell me what she has or what you think she has, I am not confident that she will get more superior care than we can give her here."

Feeling insulted, the doctor closed his bag with a loud snap. "You need to pay me for the treatment." he said.

"Yes," said a weary and disappointed Stevo. "For the treatment...go to the desk downstairs. You will be paid there."

Mahlee spent most of the night under the bed. This morning, he stood on his hind legs, his forepaws on the side of the bed. The dog looked from the sleeping Katya to Stevo, as if expecting an explanation. Stevo scratched the dogs head, saying, "She is sick. She is very sick."

Cleona didn't make breakfast this morning. She ordered Stevo to go downstairs and have coffee while she bathed and changed Katya.

Stevo descended the stairs with a heavy heart. Mahlee at his side could sense Stevo's unhappiness.

Bobo asked about Katya, and then disappeared back into the barn.

With all the expertise of a nurse, Cleona bathed Katya, who occasionally fluttered her eyes, but never fully awoke. She put a cotton gown on Katya and even accomplished to change the bed sheets. Keeping clean sheets might be a problem. There were only so many changes available.

When Stevo returned, Cleona informed him she was going to make some broth for Katya.

Keeping vigil on the stool next to the bed, Stevo kept talking to Katya, hoping she would hear him. His heart skipped a beat when she opened her eyes, looking directly at him.

He was so joyous he had tears in his eyes. "Oh, my Katya!" he said kissing her warm cheek, "You are awake...Katya...Katya?"

It was as if a stone landed on his heart. She didn't respond. She appeared not to know him.

Cleona entered carrying a dish of beef broth with bone marrow floating in the liquid. Seeing Katya with her eyes open, Cleona said, "Praise Jesus! You is awake."

"I don't think so." said Stevo, "She doesn't know me."

Ignoring Stevo's remark, Cleona said, "You help me get her settin up, so she can eat."

Pillows were plumped behind Katya's back to support her. Stevo lifted her gently so she leaned against the pillows while sitting up. Now, her eyes traveled over his face. She looked steadily into his eyes, as if trying to remember something."

"Katya...Katya..." Leaning close he whispered, "Oh, my little Gypsy, it's me Stevo."

Her green eyes flickered for a moment as her memory returned. Very slowly, she turned to look at Cleona. She smiled at them both.

Stevo dropped his head on the bed next to Katya's resting hand and felt the tears roll down his cheeks.

Cleona, as usual, took charge saying, "Now, Missy. You gonna sip this broth. I made it special for you. I sent Bobo to the market for a thick bone with lots of marrow, just for you."

After a few sips of the broth, Katya looked around the bedroom. Her voice sounded soft and almost far away as she asked, "Where is Ivan? Is he gone?"

Both Stevo and Cleona stared wide eyed at Katya.

Katya said, "He was here last night. There..." she pointed to the foot of the bed.

With a slight tremor in her voice, Cleona asked, "Did he say anything?"

"No." answered Katya, calmly. "He just stood there looking at me."

After the broth was consumed, along with Cleona's tea of an unknown herbal concoction, Katya and Stevo were alone.

Katya's hand lightly patted Mahlee's head, who was now allowed to lie at her side on the bed.

Looking at Stevo, Katya asked, "What happened to me?"

"You had a terribly high fever. We spent the night watching over you and bathing you to cool you down." He took her hand and kissed it again, saying, "You seemed so far away. We couldn't wake you."

Bewildered, Katya said, "But I was here in the room. I saw you."

She pointed to the ceiling, "I was up there the whole time, watching everything. I even saw the doctor."

Stevo felt faint. He remembered this sort of talk from the voodoo women in New Orleans. He felt a shiver go through his body.

Both Tomo and Cleona offered to watch over Katya so Stevo could rest, but he refused to leave. He needed to stay with her as long as she would stay with him.

Stevo did doze at times during the night. On one occasion, he saw Katya lift her head from the pillow and look at the foot of the bed. Stevo followed her eyes to where she looked and he saw nothing. He saw recognition on her face and knew that she saw something...or someone. Stevo's heart nearly stopped beating when he saw the dog, lying alongside Katya, raise his head and look to the foot of the bed.

The next morning, Stevo and Cleona could see that Katya, with food and rest, was looking paler, thinner.

Again, Cleona cleaned Katya and changed the bedding. Yesterday, she had Bobo take the soiled sheets to be washed. Today would be the same.

For breakfast, Cleona soaked raw oatmeal in goat's milk overnight to make gruel. To this, she added honey and freshly ground cinnamon.

While Cleona fed Katya, Stevo washed and shaved. His reflection in the mirror confirmed how worried and tired he was. In fresh clothes, while Cleona was still with Katya, Stevo took Mahlee out in the backyard. Stevo lit a cigarette, inhaling deeply.

He looked at the clouds slowly drifting in the sky and wondered how Destiny could be so cruel. How could Destiny give him so much happiness for such a short time?

He could feel his time with Katya slipping away.

Tomo met Stevo in the kitchen, telling him that Jim Slade was in the store.

"I can't see him." said Stevo.

Tomo said, "He is here for more Royal stock. Should I tell him that Katya is ill?"

"No...I'll speak with him. I have to pass him to go upstairs." said Stevo.

Seeing the tired and troubled look on his face, Jim said, "Steve, have I come at a bad time?"

Stevo tried to smile saying, "Tom will take care of you. Tell him what you need and I'll have Cleona pack it for you." He hesitated, feeling he should say more, "I'll make sure we have a good visit the next time you come."

Upstairs, with Cleona gone, Stevo was again at Katya's side. He held the hand with the Gypsy bracelet and silently cursed it for failing to do its magic.

In a low whisper, Katya said, "Stevo..."

"Yes, Katya...I am here." he said. "What do you need?"

Mahlee, lying at her side, raised his head at the sound of her voice.

Katya said, "Stevo, please light the candle in the chapel. Leave the door open."

Returning from the chapel, he saw her closed eyes, and panicked. He said, "Katya...Katya?"

Relief swept over him when she opened her eyes saying, "I was just resting my eyes. That bright light hurts my eyes."

Stevo could feel his heart beating faster. WHAT bright light? The shade on the only window was drawn to keep the room dim.

"I can smell the candle burning in the chapel." She said, pleased. "Stevo..."

"Yes...Katya." He looked at her in the bed. It was as she had shrunk, she looked so tiny. "What do you want?"

"Do you think Milan would come to see me?" she asked.

Stevo took a calming breath. Her wanting to see Milan frightened him even more.

Bobo was sent to tell Milan of Katya's condition, and that she wanted to see him.

Milan was there within twenty minutes. He ran through the kitchen, past Cleona packing witch hazel bottles, through the store startling Jim Slade, who was now, more than ever, convinced something was terribly wrong.

Milan ran past the sitting room, finding the bedroom next to it.

Seeing Katya, so small and frail, he fell to his knees alongside the bed. He looked over at Stevo, his eyes pleading for an explanation. Stevo could only shrug his shoulders.

Milan took Katya's hand. "I'm here Katya." He said, trying not to let his voice betray his fear at seeing her so pale.

"I'm so glad you are here." She said in a small voice. "I need you to tell me that you forgive me for marrying Stevo."

Alarm registered in Milan's eyes. He looked to Stevo. With no emotion, Stevo left the room. He went to the chapel. He knew and understood why Katya needed Milan's forgiveness...forgiveness for her loving him more than Milan.

Not since childhood had Stevo knelt and prayed so fervently before the Lord on the Crucifix. The large candle within the glass chimney flickered, sending Stevo's prayers up within its smoke.

Stevo didn't know how long he had been in the chapel. Making the sign of the cross, he rose to join Milan and Katya.

Milan was still on his knees, his head resting on the bed alongside Katya. Her hand rested on his head, her eyes closed.

Hearing Stevo return, Milan rose, wiping his eyes.

Katya opened her eyes. Smiling, she said to Stevo, "Milan forgives me."

Sometime during that night, Zolton, Ivan, Queen Valina, and Lucia came to guide Katya through the bright light.

CHAPTER 47

A month after Katya died, Stevo went to the Cemetery where Katya had been interred alongside Ivan. This time, instead of a flat stone lying in the ground, a two-foot tall red granite headstone marked where Katya and Ivan lie. Stevo didn't have birth dates for either of them, only the dates of their passings. He had the stone marked in halves, one side for Ivan Balaban and the other for Katya Markovich. There was no other information, such as husband or beloved wife.

From the road, Stevo could see someone sitting near Katya's and Ivan's graves. He recognized Milan.

Stevo crept up quietly behind Milan, gently nudging him in the back with his knee.

Startled, Milan let out a yell and jumped. Seeing Stevo, he said, annoyed, "Can't a man have any privacy?"

Stevo sat on the ground next to his old friend. He said, "I thought you might be the one bringing flowers. I see them here whenever I come."

"So...what are you going to do about it?" said Milan in a tough voice.

"Nothing." said Stevo, "As long as you keep the weeds around the stone pulled."

At that, Milan punched Stevo in the arm.

They both sat for a long time, not speaking. Finally, Milan said with a slight crack in his voice, "Damn, she was special." He wiped a stray tear from the corner of his eye.

"She had to be..." said Stevo, "For both of us to fall in love with her."

Milan looked at Stevo, saying, "Are you going to let Lakawanna know?"

"I hadn't thought about it." He said, "I probably should. I did send letters to her family back home."

So they sat together, again not speaking, each smoking a cigarette.

They each felt her loss so keenly that neither could come up with the friendly insults they shared in the past. It would be a very long time before they could do that again.

Milan swatted at an annoying fly while Stevo watched a red cardinal alight on the headstone. The male bird kept an eye on the brown female nearby.

Milan got up. He looked at Stevo, who planned to stay a little longer. Milan said, "Come to the tavern." With affection, he said, "I think it is time we got drunk together."

Stevo looked up at his friend. He smiled, saying, "Yes. I suppose it is time we did that."

Cleona continued to work for Stevo. He told her that Katya would want her to have all that was part of the Royal business. When Cleona objected, he gave her more to object to by giving her the deed to the house Katya and Ivan once owned. In the years to come, Cleona would think about her little Missy. Because of her Missy, Cleona had money and a house. "Praise Jesus!"

In the back of Milan's Tavern, where Milan slept, was a shelf next to the bed. On the shelf were a small standing crucifix, a candle, some matches, and a sealed bottle of Royal Witch Hazel Lotion. Next to it was a sealed jar of Royal Honey Cream. Each night before going to sleep, he would hold one of the Royal bottles, remembering the red-haired beauty that walked into his tavern one morning and changed his life forever.

Stevo visited Katya's chapel often. He sat in it more than he kneeled, but it gave him comfort, just as Mahlee's companionship reminded him of Katya. On Stevo's bedside table were Katya's coral cameo brooch and alongside it lay the Gypsy bracelet. On his little finger, he wore the wedding ring he bought from Katya. The ring he gave her when they married. He would never take it off.

Tomo had Katya's wicker suitcase. Stevo couldn't bear the pain of going through Katya's private papers. Tomo felt someone should see if there were any important papers that might need attention. He found the sheets written by Ivan on the back of expired sales flyers. With fascination, Tomo read the story of Katya's earlier life, as Ivan wrote it. The stories of being stolen at birth, sold to a Turk, escaping, falling in love with a Gypsy, and at last, finding her family in Trieste, amazed Tomo.

Then he came across more sheets, this time written by Katya. She bared her soul on the pages. Tomo read about himself and the feelings that Katya had for him when she found him under her steps. Her love of Milan and Stevo were recorded along with her struggle for which one to choose.

Tomo spent the better part of the night going through the pages. When he finished reading, it was late into the night. He marveled at what a special person and woman Katya had been. His heart was heavy as he gathered the sheets, putting them back in the order he had found them.

Pushing the wicker suitcase under his bed, he said aloud, "Someday…someday, I will find someone to write Katya's story."

THE END

AUTHOR'S NOTE:

Katya had been feeling under the weather for some time. There were bouts of vomiting and fever, followed by some chills. She kept these symptoms to herself in the hopes that she might have been pregnant.

The cause of her death was not fully known. The grippe, or flu, may have contributed to her demise. Little is known of the illness before the 1918 flu pandemic, which took the lives of 25 percent of the U.S. population.

It could have been food poisoning from unclean foods, or even the water used in drinks. Some of the Gypsies in Whiting died after having similar symptoms.

Other Books in the *Destiny* series:

DESTINY'S DOWRY

DESTINY DENIED

Available from BookLocker.com, or wherever fine books are sold.

CPSIA information can be obtained at www.ICGtesting.com
Printed in the USA
BVOW04*0352310714

361109BV00008B/30/P